# The Shrine of the Siren Stone

This Dark Helix book edition contains the complete text of the original print edition.

THE SHRINE OF THE SIREN STONE

A Dark Helix Press Book

PRINTING HISTORY
Orchard House Press, Port Orchard, Washington, United States / First Edition
July 2010
Weird and Wondrous Books, Pointe-Claire, Quebec, Canada/ Second Edition
Dec 2010
Dark Helix Press, Toronto, Ontario, Canada/ Third Edition
Oct 2015 ebook/Mar 2016 paperback



Dark Helix Press books are published by Dark Helix Press Inc.
darkhelixpress.com

---

Library and Archives Canada Cataloguing in Publication

Mak, Derwin, author
    The Shrine of the Siren Stone / Derwin Mak. -- 3rd edition.

Previously published: Pointe Claire, Québec: Weird & Wondrous
    Books, 2010.
ISBN 978-0-9917425-7-8 (paperback)

    I. Title.

PS8626.A423S47 2016          C813'.6          C2016-900834-7

# The Shrine of the Siren Stone

DERWIN MAK

A Dark Helix Book

# CONTENTS

# DEDICATION

To the cosplayers of Anime North, my favorite anime convention: You're the *otaku* I like the most.

# ACKNOWLEDGEMENTS

My thanks to: Kent Wong for invaluable computer support; my sister Christine for organizing the trip to Japan where I visited Yasukuni Shrine; Alicia da Conceição for showing me around Akihabara; Eric Choi for talking to me about spaceships; John-Allen Price for information about how submarines communicate; the staff of Maid Station Café at Nippon 2007 (the World Science Fiction Convention) for their friendly service; and the staff of Café Delish for their dance act at Anime North.
*Domo arigato gozaimasu.*

# PART 1
# THE MAID

# CHAPTER 1

# Merry Christmas, Master!

Sato Ishiro listened to the waitress singing in the Nikkou Café. Sora sang the American hymn "When the Saints Go Marching In." Her English had a strong Japanese accent.

Like all the waitresses, Sora wore a French maid costume: a short black dress with frilly white trim, a white apron, a black choker, a white lace barrette, black thigh-high stockings, and black shoes.

Ishiro looked at the other customers. They were all *otaku*, computer geeks and fans of anime and manga. They had the Akihabara look: greasy hair, bulky knapsacks, and pants and shirts of mismatched colors. Like him, they had no girlfriends with whom to spend Christmas Eve.

At university, an American student had told him that Americans spend Christmas with their parents and family. Ishiro found the idea unusual. In Japan, Christmas is for lovers and sweethearts, a time of romance in fancy restaurants and love hotels. Christmas had no such joys for him, though. Once again, Ishiro was alone in a maid café in Akihabara Electric Town.

It could be worse, he told himself. If this were America, he would be forced to spend time with his parents.

He came to Nikkou Café at least four times a week. It was close to Ashi Android Scrapyard, where he hacked apart androids. The job paid only minimum wage, far below what his fellow University of Tokyo alumni were earning. At twenty-seven years of age, he had reverted to earning the same wage of his first student job, sweeping garbage at a department store.

Many of the other customers of Nikkou Café were computer science graduates like him. They came for the café's maids, of course, but they also came for its scenery. Posters of anime TV series lined the walls.

To add to the cheerful atmosphere, the café's logo hung on strings from the ceiling. They were yellow Suns with smiley faces, printed on cardboard. Nikkou was the word for sunshine.

Sora finished singing, and the customers applauded. She bowed and stepped off the stage. Another maid, Keiko, tap danced to the theme from the anime TV series *Time Warp at Midway*. Her choreography matched the military-style music. The audience cheered.

"Here's your American-style Christmas dinner, master!" someone said.

Ishiro turned to see a maid holding his dinner. She smiled and placed the plate on his table.

"Thank you, Yuko," Ishiro said. Yuko curtsied and returned to the kitchen.

For Ishiro, Christmas Eve wouldn't be complete without fried chicken. Ironically, the American student hadn't agreed. He had said that Americans don't eat fried chicken on Christmas Eve. To them, it is a fast food unworthy of their most important festival. Instead, they eat another bird, the turkey.

How could the Americans disdain their own delicacy, Ishiro wondered? Fried chicken was the best thing they brought to Japan in 1945. Restaurants serve more American fried chicken on Christmas than on any other day of the year. As he did on each Christmas Eve, Ishiro devoured the fried chicken, mashed potatoes, coleslaw, beans, and mayonnaise.

Yuko came and took the empty plate away. Again, she smiled and curtsied before leaving.

Ishiro sat in Yuko's section each time he came. Keiko had once said that every regular customer has a favorite maid. Ishiro's favorite was Yuko.

A talent show had been running throughout the evening. Each maid had a turn performing on stage. In the next act, Mikita sang the torch song, "My Best Friend Is Kissing My Boyfriend at Christmas." The customers laughed even though the song was supposed to be a sad.

Rena told jokes about dating boys. Some jokes were funny, some were not, and she got scattered laughs.

Kagami danced to the hit song "Christmas Love Hotel." Unlike Keiko the tap dancer, Kagami swiveled her hips and torso in a torrid way. She lifted her skirt, untied her hair, and tossed her barrette to the audience. They hooted and hollered.

Finally, it was Yuko's turn to perform. She was the only maid to play a musical instrument, a violin.

Her music was upbeat. Ishiro knew it was a European tune, but he couldn't remember where he had heard it. As Yuko played louder, everyone became silent. Even the maids stopped working and listened to Yuko.

The other maids had sung and danced to Japanese pop songs. Yuko was playing a classical melody, from another country, from another century, without lyrics, without dancing. The other girls' songs came from the karaoke bar. Yuko's music came from the concert hall.

A famous European composed this music, Ishiro thought. Who? Beethoven? Mozart? Chopin?

Yuko finished the piece and bowed. The audience applauded, and the café became noisy again.

When Ishiro saw Yuko, he asked, "What song was that?"

"An excerpt from the ballet *Coppélia* by Léo Delibes," she replied, pronouncing the French composer's name smoothly.

"You performed very well."

"Thank you, master."

"Where did you learn to play the violin?"

Yuko shrugged. "I never had lessons. I just know how to play a violin. I guess it's something that I have inside me."

"You play it with much expression, much feeling," said Ishiro.

"I play with feeling?" Yuko said. "That's nice to know. Thank you, master."

The clock on the wall showed the time, 23:59. The café's owner, Endo Hideki, dressed in a blue business suit and a tie showing Santa Claus, went on the stage.

He took the microphone and said, "Sixty seconds to Christmas! All maids please come to the stage!"

The maids gathered on the stage and threw multi-colored paper streamers at the cheering *otaku*. Everyone counted down the seconds: ten, nine, eight, seven, six, five, four, three, two, one...

When the clock beeped midnight, the customers cheered, and the maids blew on whistles. A medley of Christmas carols blared from the speakers.

"Ladies, serve the Christmas cake," Endo said.

The maids fanned out through the café. Yuko brought a sponge cake with whipped cream and strawberries to Ishiro.

"Merry Christmas, master," she said. "Enjoy your Christmas cake."

Ishiro bit into the sponge cake. He couldn't imagine Christmas Eve without it.

Mr. Endo's wife, Masako, approached the stage. She wore a red and white kimono decorated with Christmas symbols: reindeer, snowflakes, evergreen trees, and Santa Clauses. The couple walked from table to table, giving out gifts from a basket. The customers squealed with joy when they received collector's cards of the anime series *Time Warp at Midway*. They leapt to their feet and bowed to Mr. and Mrs. Endo.

The maid Sora came to Ishiro. "Look at this!" she said, holding a paper to him.

It was her trigonometry test. She had scored seventy-two percent on it.

"I finally passed!" she said. "Thanks for showing me how to solve that triangle problem. Now I can graduate from high school!"

"This is wonderful," Ishiro said. "Congratulations!"

Sora bowed deeply and ran back to her tables.

In front of the stage, Yuko chatted with Ami, the pretty sixteen-year-old daughter of the Endos. Ami sometimes worked at the café after school, but she did not wear the maid costume. Instead, she wore a white blouse, black skirt, and green vest. She looked like a bank teller, an appropriate style since she worked the cash register.

An upbeat song started. Ami grabbed Yuko's hand and pulled her to the stage. The two girls danced to the music.

Ishiro watched Yuko gyrate. She moved her hips, legs, and arms sensuously. Ishiro never knew that the human body had so many moving parts.

Yuko was energetic, friendly, and beautiful. He often thought about Yuko.

The song ended, and Yuko and Ami left the stage. After talking, they went to Ishiro.

What could those two want, he wondered?

"You're our most frequent customer," Yuko said to Ishiro. Then she giggled and put her hand to her mouth.

Ami laughed and spanked Yuko's butt. Yuko squeaked and giggled again.

"Go on, you silly fool!" said Ami.

Yuko pulled a postcard out of her apron. "Merry, Christmas, master!"

It was an instant postcard made at a photo booth. It showed Yuko smiling and making a peace sign with her hand. Yuko's shoulder-length hair shone in the photo. She had signed her name in silver ink.

"Thank you very much, Yuko," Ishiro said. "You're my favorite waitress in all Akihabara."

Ami turned to Yuko and said, "See, I told you he would like it. Aren't all my ideas good?"

"This is the first time I have given a gift to another person," Yuko said. "Thank you for the experience."

Ishiro thought it odd that Yuko, who looked about twenty years old, had never given a gift to anyone before. Compared to other peoples, the Japanese are obsessed with exchanging gifts. Had Yuko never given a small gift, like a key chain, to a relative or a classmate?

A thought came to him. Perhaps Yuko had no boyfriend? If she had one, certainly she would have given him a box of *honmei choco*, the chocolates that girls give to their boyfriends on Valentine's Day.

She was working on Christmas Eve, not spending it with a boyfriend. But perhaps she would meet him on Christmas Day?

As he held the photo, Ishiro realized that it was the first gift he had ever received from a girl. He had a girlfriend years ago, but she hadn't given anything to him.

Ishiro stood up and bowed to Yuko. "Thank you very much, Yuko, thank you! This is the first time a girl has given anything to me."

Ami giggled and nudged Yuko.

"Hah, hah, you're his first time!" Ami teased. "Be gentle with him, Mistress Yuko!"

Ishiro suddenly realized that he should not have admitted his pathetic inexperience.

But it was the truth! He couldn't tell a lie. However, he could simply have not mentioned it. But was not saying something the same as telling a lie?

Why did he get so confused around girls?

Yuko smiled and nodded. "I'm glad that you like it."

Mikita and Sora came. "Hey, Ami, can Yuko go out and get some coffee for us?" Mikita asked.

Ami said, "Yes, Yuko can do that."

"Sure, I'll go," Yuko said. "Just tell me what you want and transfer the money to my account."

Sora ran to the other maids. "Hey, Yuko's going to the coffee shop!"

Suddenly, all the maids rushed to Yuko and told her what they wanted. After they returned to their tables, Yuko stood still and silent, as if lost in thought.

"There are too many cups of coffee for me to carry by myself," she said. She looked at Ishiro. "Master, can you come help me carry the coffee?"

"Uh, yes, of course," Ishiro said.

They left the café. Yuko was still wearing her French maid costume as they walked through Akihabara.

"They can get all the coffee they want inside the café. Why do they want coffee from outside?" Ishiro asked.

"At the maid café, we have only ordinary coffee. These girls are much too sophisticated for that. They want the fancy coffees with Italian and French names," Yuko explained.

"Oh, I think the coffee at the Nikkou Café is good. I drink it all the time."

"Like I said, the girls are sophisticated."

They went to Starluck American Coffee. An android barista stood behind the counter. The android looked like a pretty young woman and wore the same green and white uniform that human Starluck staff wore. If not for its shiny plastic skin, it would look human.

The barista said, "Good evening, sir, ma'am. All our drinks are listed on the board behind me. What do you wish to order?" Its voice was that of the television actress Suzuki Halko.

"Two large non-fat chai lattes, one large caramel macchiato, one medium mocha Valencia without whipped cream, one large soy toffee nut latte with whipped cream, one small iced sugar-free vanilla soy latte, one large hot chocolate with whipped cream, and one medium hot chocolate without whipped cream," Yuko said.

"Wow, what a long and complicated list of drinks," Ishiro said. "You didn't write it down. You just knew it."

Yuko shrugged. "I must have a good memory."

The barista nodded its head. It imitated human behavior well except that its eyes never blinked or moved. They always stared ahead, empty of emotion.

"Thank you for your order," it said.

It smiled at Ishiro. The effect was strange. Though the android's mouth could smile, its eyes lacked feeling.

The barista turned away to make the drinks. Meanwhile, another female android swept the floor. It worked silently and moved stiffly.

The floor-sweeper gently pushed its broom into Ishiro's feet. "So sorry," it muttered in an electronic machine voice. Its face remained emotionless. It didn't flinch or move its head.

It changed direction, swept past Ishiro, and collided with another customer.

The customer frowned. "Stupid robot, get out of my way!" he demanded.

The floor-sweeper did not turn to look at the man. Instead, it kept pushing the broom across the floor.

"Stupid robot," the man muttered as he left.

"That must be an L-1 android," Ishiro said. "L-1's are programmed to do only a few repetitive tasks. They're not much more advanced than industrial robots."

"*So desu ka*," Yuko said.

Ishiro looked at the barista, who was pouring hot chocolate into cardboard cups now. He was sure the barista was an L-3 android. It was too advanced to be an L-1, and it spoke with a human voice, unlike the L-2.

He had studied computer science at University of Tokyo, so he knew how to identify the different levels of androids. Despite working for minimum wage with no chance of promotion, he knew he was intelligent. Few people had his knowledge of computers.

His sole ex-girlfriend had complained that he talked too much about computers and anime, but now, he felt the urge again. He needed to impress Yuko.

"That's probably an L-3," Ishiro said. "They're programmed to perform a broad range of tasks and respond to situations as humans would. That's because L-3's have a form of artificial intelligence."

He continued. "L-3's are artificially intelligent because they have the most advanced expert systems in robotics. Expert systems are computer systems that contain the knowledge of one or more human experts on a specific subject and use that knowledge to select reactions to situations. That barista can recognize hundreds of different requests from customers. It's also programmed with hundreds of different ways to react to those requests, all based on how a human would react to them. That includes hundreds of phrases of prerecorded speech.

"The first L-3 android was a baker. It was programmed with the experience of twenty-three bakers, including the chef who baked cakes for —"

"*So desu ka,*" Yuko said again, interrupting him. "What happens if the android gets into a situation for which it has no programmed response?"

"Then it will say or do something odd or meaningless," said Ishiro.

The barista put the cups of coffee and chocolate into two trays. "That will be five thousand yen, please," it said.

Yuko gave her money card to the barista. The barista swiped the card through the cash register, printed the receipt, and gave the card and receipt to Yuko. Its movements were fluid and natural.

"Thank you for coming to Starluck American Coffee," the barista said. "Please come again."

"Watch this," Ishiro said to Yuko.

He turned to the barista. "Do you think yesterday's security patch from Victor Robotics will actually protect androids from the Yokohama Devil virus?"

For a moment, the barista said nothing. It stared at him with its unemotional eyes. Then its mouth smiled and said, "Good evening, sir. All our drinks are listed on the board behind me. What do you wish to order, sir?"

Ishiro said to Yuko, "Talking about computer viruses is not a situation programmed in its expert system, so it has no response for it. It can't even say it knows nothing about computer viruses."

Yuko nodded. "*So desu ka.*"

"Still, androids are so lifelike now. It must be a Victor Robotics model. Victor makes the most lifelike androids," Ishiro said. "This one would look like a real person if it weren't for the plastic look of its skin."

"Its eyes are those of an L-3," Yuko added.

The barista repeated its greeting. "Good evening, sir. All our drinks are listed on the board behind me. What do you wish to order, sir?"

"We're leaving now," said Ishiro.

"Thank you for coming to Starluck American Coffee," the barista said. "Please come again."

Ishiro and Yuko left Starluck. On their walk back to the café, they saw various signs of Christmas in the shops: Christmas romance cookies, Santa Claus toys, anime dolls dressed like elves, and cans of Christmas beer.

Across the street, couples walked into the Chapel Christmas Love Hotel. The hotel's pink and white neon lights flashed images of reindeer and snowflakes. A Santa Claus robot by the door sang "Super Funky Holy Night."

Ishiro suddenly felt sad. Christmas is the romantic time of the year. Yet fetching coffee with Yuko was the closest he had ever been with a girl on Christmas. Not even his ex-girlfriend had spent Christmas with him.

There was a small crowd ahead of them. As they walked closer, they saw a policeman crouching over a body.

"Is it a murder?" Ishiro wondered.

The policeman talked into his pocket computer. "I'll send a photo to you now," he said.

He pointed his computer at the body and shot the photo. When the flash fired, its light shone off the body's shiny skin.

"It's an android," said Yuko.

Ishiro stepped forward to get a closer look. Like most androids in Akihabara, it resembled a pretty woman. It wore a red head kerchief, white blouse, and green miniskirt. Ishiro recognized the uniform as that of Picolit-Ya, a nearby Italian restaurant.

The android lay on its back with its arms and legs sprawled out. Its blouse was torn. Circuitry poked out from a large gash on its belly. Black hydraulic fluid leaked out and made a pool on the sidewalk. The eyes stared up at the crowd.

A pizza and its box lay nearby. Ishiro guessed that the android was delivering the pizza.

"Thank you for the photograph," said a voice from the policeman's pocket computer. "Detective Watanabe from Android Control Unit is on his way. He should be there any moment now."

A man in civilian clothes arrived. He looked serious and showed a badge to the policeman.

"Ah, Lieutenant Watanabe," the policeman greeted him.

Watanabe turned the android's head, lifted its hair, and opened a small door on the back of its head. He pulled a cable out of the head and plugged it into his pocket computer. The words "NO SIGNAL" appeared on the computer's display.

"Its memory is damaged. I can't get an image of the attacker," he said.

"This is the third one I've seen this week," the policeman said. "Who's attacking the androids?"

"The pizza's still here," Watanabe observed. "The attacker wasn't interested in food."

"Some people really hate androids."

"At least the perpetrator is attacking androids instead of real women. Otherwise, the Homicide Squad would be here."

The policeman said, "I think it's from Picolit-Ya, a restaurant near my *koban*. I'll tell the owner. I hope he has insurance for the android."

"It's a beautiful android," Watanabe observed. "It must have cost at least nine hundred thousand yen. Vandalism costs so much money these days."

Yuko turned to Ishiro. "If that had been a human girl, the police would not be calling the crime vandalism. It would be murder," she said softly. "Look at her. She's been killed."

"You're treating the android as if it were human," Ishiro said.

"She's like a woman."

"No, it's not. It may look like a woman, and its body is shaped to resemble a woman's, but it's not a woman. It's a machine. It doesn't have a sex. It's as female as a microwave oven."

"Let's go back to the café," Yuko said.

They returned to Nikkou Café, and the maids rushed to them to get their drinks.

"Thanks for getting the coffee," Sora said. "My boyfriend's coming to fetch me after we close, and I need to be awake."

As the girls scurried away, Yuko said, "You were very kind to help me carry the coffee. Thank you, master."

"You're welcome, Yuko. Anytime," said Ishiro.

"I'll go back to serving my customers," Yuko said. She curtsied and went away.

Ishiro felt happy to help Yuko. It gave him a sense of purpose that he didn't get from his job at the android scrapyard.

He looked at the television behind the bar. NHK TV showed a commercial for Victor Robotics, Japan's largest producer of androids. It had scenes of androids working in restaurants, banks, shopping malls, train stations, and many other places. Most of the androids looked like beautiful women, but a few looked like handsome men.

Ishiro looked at his watch. It was almost one o'clock in the morning. It was getting late. As much as he hated to do so, he had to go home.

But there was something he had to do. He had been agonizing about it for weeks, trying to get the courage to do it.

Yuko walked in his direction. He stood up and approached her.

"Uh, Miss Yuko, uh," he stammered.

Yuko stopped. "Yes, master?"

"I've been coming to this café for a couple years, and I've seen you here many times."

"Yes, master, thank you for being a loyal customer."

"Well, I think you're smart and pretty. Uh, what I'm trying to say is — uh, ah —"

"Yes, master?"

"What I'm trying to say, what I'm trying to ask you is, uh, will you —"

"Yes, master?"

"Uh, ah, will you have dinner with me?" Ishiro finally blurted out.

"Yes, master."

The answer shocked Ishiro. It came faster than he had expected. It was also positive. He didn't know what to say next.

There was an awkward silence.

Yuko asked, "Where and when shall I meet you, master?"

"Uh, yes, I guess we should decide on that," Ishiro said. "What day? What time? Uh —"

"It's past midnight. A new day has started," Yuko observed. "How about tonight at six o'clock?"

"Yes, of course," Ishiro agreed. "It's Christmas Day itself."

Ishiro was surprised that Yuko had chosen Christmas Day, the sacred day of love. It was a day loaded with symbolism too strong for a first date. After months of pining for Yuko, he felt overwhelmed by having their first date on Christmas.

He had to take control of the situation. Choose a restaurant.

"If we're going for dinner on Christmas, we should try something traditional," Ishiro said. "Darn, it's going to be impossible to get a table at Kentucky Fried Chicken."

"We can go somewhere else," Yuko suggested.

"Uh, ah, good idea."

For some unknown reason, he thought of the wrecked android on the sidewalk.

"Do you like Italian food?" asked Ishiro.

"I have never eaten it before, but I would like the experience."

"Okay. Meet me at Picolit-Ya at six o'clock in the evening. Do you know where it is?"

Yuko nodded. "Yes, I know where it is. I'll meet you there at six o'clock."

"Yes, thank you, thank you," Ishiro said.

On the stage, Mr. Endo held the microphone again. "Gentlemen, this is the last call for drinks," he announced. "We will be closing in fifteen minutes."

"Your last order, master?" asked Yuko.

"Uh, no, ah, that will be all," Ishiro said. "Uh, I have a date with you."

"Yes, I'll see you then, master," said Yuko. She returned to the kitchen.

As the customers left the café, Ishiro went to Mr. Endo.

"Mr. Endo, may I ask for your advice?" Ishiro said.

"Of course, Mr. Sato," said Endo.

Ishiro blurted, "I have a date tonight — with a real girl!"

"That's much better than a dating sim," said Endo. He was referring to "dating simulations," computer games that many *otaku* played.

"Yes, yes, much better," Ishiro agreed. "But it's been years since I've gone on a date. You've known me for a while. Do you have any advice for talking to a girl?"

Endo looked surprised. "Oh, that's what you want to talk about? I'm flattered that you would ask me about women, but I'm no expert on dating. I'm married. I don't go on dates."

"But that's why I'm asking you. You married your wife. You must have had at least one successful date."

"Actually, it takes more than one good date to get a wife. Ah, but you're just getting started."

"Getting started *again*," Ishiro corrected him.

"Oh, sorry, getting started again."

"Mr. Endo, please, I respect your opinion. Do you have any advice for me?"

"Mr. Sato, you're a decent gentleman. You're pleasant to the maids and to me and my family. I don't mind to help you. I've known you long enough that I feel I can assist you. But do you really want my advice?"

"Yes, please."

"Do you know I was a naval reserve officer?" Endo said. "Sometimes, we military officers can be brutally frank when talking to our subordinates. It's an old military tradition."

"I'm sure your advice will be helpful," said Ishiro.

"I'll be happy to offer it," Endo said. "However, please do not be offended by what I'm about to say."

Ishiro took a deep breath.

"Don't talk about only computers and anime," Endo said.

Ishiro sighed. "It's so hard to find a woman who can talk about computers."

"Wrong. Every woman has a computer. Women like to talk about computers. But they like to talk about other things too."

"Why?"

"Just trust me, they do. Talk about something else," Endo suggested.

"Like how *Shōnen Jump* is being published on paper again?"

"No, not manga! Talk about things that interest her. Her hobbies, her favorite movies, music, whatever she likes."

"How can I possibly know what those are?" Ishiro pleaded.

"Have you tried asking her?" Endo asked. "That leads me to my second point. Talk to her, but let her talk too."

"What do you mean?" Ishiro said. "Are you saying that there's something wrong with the way I talk?"

"Remember the time Rena asked you if you had seen any good movies recently?" said Endo. "You kept talking for twenty minutes and never let her say a word."

"But it was *Gundam Generation One Hundred,*" Ishiro protested. "That was the best *Gundam* movie in the last hundred years. Suzuki Halko won a Seiun Award for Best Voice Actress in a Leading Role. It really should've gotten at least one Japan Academy Prize. The animation, the plot, the new characters, the special 4-D effect, the new mobile suits, the music, and the songs were the best in anime in years. The *Gundam* series has a really distinguished history. It began with *Mobile Suit Gundam,* created by Tomino Yoshiyuki in 1979. In 1985..."

He rambled for another two minutes before Endo cried, "Stop, stop!"

"See what I mean?" Endo said. "Girls don't want to hear monologues. Girls like two-way dialogues. Give her a chance to say something. Don't hog the conversation like a typical *otaku.*"

"But that's not the way people talked at my last job," Ishiro argued. "It was a very aggressive environment, and you had to make yourself heard. The bosses always talked in long sentences to their subordinates."

"You're going on a date, not a business meeting," Endo reminded him. "And you're not the girl's boss."

"But if something's important, I have to say it!" Ishiro stressed. "In the bank, if I didn't say something, people wouldn't listen to me, then they would do something else! That could be bad for the company."

"And are you still working at Dai Tokyo Taikun Financial Group?" Endo said.

Ishiro looked down at the floor.

"Alright, Mr. Sato, look up," said Endo. "I warned you that former military officers can be brutally frank. You can take my advice or ignore it. The choice is yours."

Ishiro raised his chin. "Thank you, Mr. Endo. I respect your opinion. I will take the advice you have given me."

"Good, good. I have to close the café now," Endo said. "Oh, one more thing, Mr. Sato."

"What's that?"

"The clothes you wear are important. Wear a regular shirt with buttons and a collar, not a T-shirt, and especially not one with a computer company logo."

Ishiro looked down at his T-shirt, which had the Dai Nippon Computer Conference logo. "This is a not a company logo. It's a conference logo, so it should be fine."

"It's actually worse," said Endo. "Get pants that match or look good with the shirt. Wear a blazer too. It adds some class. And make sure everything is in good condition, not worn out, faded, or torn."

"Ah, this is silly!" Ishiro said. "Changing a person's clothes doesn't change the person within. A girl should care more about a guy's personality, not his clothes."

Endo guffawed. "You collect postcards of Miss Japan contestants. They're always wearing swimsuits. Would you enjoy Miss Japan more or less if the girls wore frumpy clothes? And would you still come to my café if the waitresses wore long black robes like Purist Arabians?"

"Well, that's different," Ishiro said. "Uh, an actress or a waitress should look a certain way."

"And so should you," said Endo. "Women are always dressing to make themselves look attractive to us. We should return the favor."

"Maybe you're right."

"I know I am. The English have a saying: 'Clothes make the man.' Forget the Akihabara style."

"Yes, yes, thank you," Ishiro mumbled.

"Good luck with whoever she is," said Endo.

******

Ishiro dropped another right arm onto the pile. Android parts lay all around him: arms, legs, torsos, and heads. Smaller parts, like eyes, tongues, audio sensors, memory cards, batteries, and data ports, sat in plastic bins. These were the remains of androids damaged in mines and factories, worn out from lack of maintenance, or disposed when their owners got new models.

He picked a head from a pile, pried it open, and pulled out the central processing unit. This one was undamaged, so his boss could sell it for ten thousand yen. After its new owner reformatted it and loaded it with new software, it would run another L-3.

Despite its name, Ashi Android Scrapyard was in a building, not an open yard. Unlike car parts, android parts needed protection from the rain. It did have wide shatterproof windows so people could see what was for sale.

The owner, Ashi Yasuo, pushed a cart carrying an android. A man followed him into the room.

The man shook his head. "She was a beautiful machine. What punk would do that to her?"

Ashi shrugged. "Many people love androids, many people hate them too."

Ishiro looked at the android. It was the pizza delivery android that was attacked last night. Now, stripped of its clothes, it lay naked. He marveled at how its designers had duplicated the female form so flawlessly.

Ashi pried open the android's head and pulled out the central processing unit. "Look at the dents," he pointed out. "The CPU is damaged beyond repair. Data recovery is impossible. Sad to say, the rest isn't worth much more. I'll give you ten thousand yen."

The man silently nodded and held out his money card.

Ashi took the card and said, "Thank you, Mr. Edogawa. I'll transfer the money to you immediately." He went to the computer.

Edogawa stared sadly at the android.

"She was delivering a pizza, doing nothing wrong," he said. "Why would anyone harm her?"

Ishiro didn't have an answer.

After Ashi came back with the card, Edogawa asked, "May I keep the CPU?"

"Why? It's damaged. You can't use it again."

"It's where her memories were. It's something to remember her by."

Ashi snorted and gave the CPU to Edogawa. "Take it. I have no use for it."

Edogawa smiled weakly as he held the CPU in both hands.

After Edogawa left the building, Ashi shoved the android off the cart. When the android's head hit the floor, an eye popped out of its socket and rolled away. Ashi picked it up and threw it into a bin full of eyes.

"Worthless piece of junk. I'll be lucky to get twenty thousand yen from it," he said. "Hack it apart."

**

On slow days, Ashi turned on the television so he could watch it while working. Ishiro stopped by the TV and saw the naval review.

NHK showed live images of warships in Tokyo Bay. The ships sailed past Prime Minister Fujiwara Nishi, who stood on a reviewing stand on the dock. A band played "Gunkan March," the march of the Japanese Navy.

"These are the newest ships of the Japanese Navy," the news announcer said.

A submarine sailed on the surface of the bay. The naval flag fluttered from a mast on the submarine's tower. The flag was white with a red disk and sixteen sunrays, the same one used in the Greater East Asia War. Of the three military forces, the Navy kept the most traditions from before the defeat of 1945.

The submarine's crew, in their blue uniforms, stood at attention on her hull. As she passed the reviewing stand, her officers saluted.

"That is the *J.S. Yayoi*, the largest submarine in the world," the announcer said. "The *Yayoi* uses the newest missile system developed by the Americans."

Three destroyers followed the *J.S. Yayoi*. Finally, the aircraft carrier *J.S. Hosho* appeared. A cheer rose from the dockside audience as the gigantic ship sailed through the bay. The band played another naval march of the twentieth century, "The Empire's Two Thousand and Six Hundredth Anniversary."

The news announcer sounded excited as aerial views of the *Hosho* appeared. "Here is the largest ship in the fleet! *J.S. Hosho* is named after Japan's first aircraft carrier, which was also one of the few to survive the Greater East Asia War. The new *Hosho* is three hundred and fifty meters long, over twice the length of the original *Hosho*, and the same size as U.S. aircraft carriers."

The announcer added, "Since the re-arming of the nation, the military can do more than defend the home islands. Now it can go on long-range missions if necessary."

Ishiro knew that "long-range mission" was a euphemism for "offensive capabilities," long banned by the Constitution, Article 9: *the Japanese people forever renounce war as a sovereign right of the nation and the threat or use of force as means of settling international disputes...land, sea, and air forces, as well as other war potential, will never be maintained.*

For two centuries after the Greater East Asia War, Japan lacked offensive capabilities, the ability to attack another country. Article 9 forbade "war potential," which meant long-range missiles, aircraft carriers, strategic bombers, naval infantry, and amphibious units. The military forces were not even called the army, navy, and air force. Instead, they were called the Japan Self-Defense Forces until two years ago.

Ishiro felt proud as he watched the warships. He had recently become interested in Japanese naval history, thanks to *Time Warp at Midway*. The anime series was about time travelers who go back to 1942 to help the Imperial Japanese Navy win the Battle of Midway.

In the twentieth century, Japan had the strongest navy in the world. The Imperial Japanese Navy had devastated the United States Navy at Pearl Harbor. It had sunk two great British ships, *Prince of Wales* and *Repulse*, thus opening Malaya and Singapore for an invasion.

A ship flying the United States flag appeared on TV. Her officers and crew stood at attention on her deck, and as she passed the Prime Minister, the officers saluted. The crowd applauded as the Americans sailed past. On the dock, some people held a banner reading "THANK YOU, U.S.A. GOOD LUCK." Other people waved U.S. and Japanese flags. The band played "Anchors Aweigh," the U.S. Navy song.

The American ship slowly turned to leave Tokyo Bay.

"There goes the frigate *U.S.S. Doris Miller*, the last U.S. Navy ship in Japan. She is going to join the war against Purist Arabia," the announcer said. "Now all U.S. forces have withdrawn from our country."

NHK switched to a commercial showing sailors eating curry chicken on rice. "Golden Curry, the pride of the fleet!" said the commercial's narrator.

The images of food reminded Ishiro of his date with Yuko. He looked at the clock. It was closing time, five o'clock in the afternoon.

He went to the closet, took out a blue blazer, and put it on. Now his costume was complete. Following Endo Hideki's advice, he did not wear a T-shirt. Instead, he wore a grey shirt with buttons and a collar. For pants, he wore his only pair of blue jeans that hadn't faded to white yet. It was also the only pair that didn't have holes or repair stitches. Instead of his usual white running shoes, he wore his only black dress shoes. He hadn't worn them since his brother's wedding six years ago.

These clothes are ridiculous, Ishiro thought. Dressing up was artificial and vain. The world was full of people pretending to be wealthier and classier than they actually were. They derided the

Akihabara style as sloppy and crude, but Ishiro liked its honesty. Nobody could ever accuse an *otaku* of pretending to be better than he was.

However, as Ishiro left the scrapyard, he knew that he had nothing to lose by taking Mr. Endo's advice.

**

Ishiro saw a black van near the train station. Music blasted from the van's loudspeakers. The songs were military marches, but they also sounded like anime show themes. One tune reminded him of the classic *Space Cruiser Yamato*.

"RECONQUER THE NORTHERN TERRITORIES" was written in bold white characters across the van. The naval flag was painted on its doors.

As the music played, a man stood at attention and glared at the passersby. He wore a general's uniform of the Russo-Japanese War: a black tunic with gold trim, black pants, black boots, white gloves, and a black kepi with a red band. A samurai sword hung from his belt.

He was about fifty years old and had strong, hawk-like features and piercing eyes. Ishiro recognized the man from somewhere. Was he a movie actor?

The van's driver looked out the window. "General, are you ready for your speech?" he asked.

The General clicked his heels, turned around, faced the driver, and shouted, "Yes!"

The driver gave a microphone to the General. With robotic stiffness, he brought his arm down to his side, swiveled around, and faced the passersby again. Most kept walking past him, but a few stopped.

Beside the General were four young men standing with their feet apart and their hands clasped behind their backs. It was the military posture called "standing at ease." They too wore Russo-Japanese War uniforms but of ranks lower than General.

A small crowd gathered. The General scowled at them.

When the music stopped, the General shouted into the microphone, "People of Japan, I, General Morita Chiko, have pledged to serve the Emperor until my death!"

General Morita! No wonder he looked familiar to Ishiro. He was the man who created *Time Warp at Midway*.

The General was not a military man. He actually was an animator. His movies and TV shows were popular with anime fans. He liked making alternative histories of the Greater East Asia War. *Nuke the Yanks*, in which Japan invents the atomic bomb and drops it on New York, was the highest-grossing movie three years ago. More recently, he made *Time Warp at Midway* for television.

While making his anime, he became convinced that Japan should be a great empire again. He founded a private army, the National Bushido Guards Regiment. It had only a hundred persons at best, much smaller than a real regiment. To lead this group, Morita commissioned himself a "general."

His Regiment held loud parades and protests, each ending with a speech by him. He always urged the government to re-conquer the islands lost in 1945, acquire intercontinental missiles, restore military rule, and worship the Emperor as a divine being again. However, he aroused more ridicule than patriotism.

Then, to everyone's surprise, the Japanese Army let the "Regiment" train with regular soldiers. In the Diet, the Opposition asked Kotohito Kuni, the Minister of Defense, why the state was training an eccentric animator's private army.

Kotohito replied, "The National Bushido Guards Regiment could be useful in earthquakes and other emergencies. Letting them train with the Army is harmless to democracy, as harmless as emergency planning exercises with the Red Cross."

Ishiro could not believe his luck. He had seen the entire series of *Time Warp at Midway* twice already. His favorite episode was the one where a time traveler goes on a suicide mission to shoot Rear Admiral Spruance aboard the *U.S.S. Enterprise.*

What would Morita say today?

"Finally, after its long sleep, Japan is re-arming itself. This is the right thing to do. We should have the strongest military forces in Asia. We are, after all, the Yamato race," Morita said.

"However, for what purpose are we using our military? The Prime Minister orders our armed forces to train for war against Purist Arabia and Sudan. But will Purist Arabia and Sudan ever attack Japan? They are not our enemies. They are the enemies of America. Our Prime Minister is still thinking like a vassal of America.

"Forget Purist Arabia! Forget Sudan! The real enemy is Russia! Russia illegally occupies the Northern Territories. Russia expelled our people from the Northern Territories. Russia put its own people in *our* Northern Territories. The Russians in the Northern Territories are like a dagger pointed at our throat.

"Now we have an army, navy, and air force that can defeat the Russians. Our military forces have the power. Let them carry out that divine mission.

"Remove the Prince Minister as commander-in-chief of the military! Restore the Emperor as commander-in-chief! Destroy the Russians! Revenge at any cost!" the General concluded.

His soldiers yelled, "Banzai! Banzai! Banzai!"

People walked away. Someone said, "This is just cosplay."

Morita scowled and shook his head.

"What has happened to the Yamato race?" he said. "They care more for their electronic toys than for the survival of their nation."

Finally, Ishiro was the only spectator left. He felt both awe and curiosity for the General.

"Hey, young man, tell me, what's your name?" Morita asked.

"Uh, Sato. Sato Ishiro."

"Come here." No longer ranting, the General sounded friendly now. "Tell me, do you like *Time Warp at Midway*?"

How had he known? Ishiro nodded silently.

Morita smiled. "Ah, good. I knew you like anime. I've seen your type in Akihabara before."

*Oh, no, is it so obvious from my appearance*, Ishiro thought? *Do I look like an otaku? I wore a blazer and black shoes today. How could he tell?*

"Tell me, do you think Japan should be a great empire again?" asked Morita.

Ishiro nodded and muttered, "Um, yes, why not?"

"I can't hear you! Speak louder!" Morita ordered.

"Yes!" Ishiro yelled in fright.

"Tell me, what is your profession?" asked the General.

"Computer programmer, sir," Ishiro mumbled.

But it was really a lie. The question brought bitter thoughts back to his mind.

He had graduated from University of Tokyo with a degree in computer science, but he was not a computer programmer, systems engineer, hardware designer, or anything so important. All his classmates went to high-paying jobs at big companies. But he went nowhere. He bounced from one low-paying, dead-end job to the next. Now he was pulling androids apart at a scrapyard.

He was just as smart, if not smarter, than his classmates. Why was he a loser?

"Become a winner," Morita said, as if he were reading Ishiro's mind. "Become a hero of the nation."

"Huh?" Ishiro blurted.

"Our military needs computer experts to attack the enemy's information and communications systems," Morita said. "Join the army, navy, or air force. Any one of them will appreciate your skills and experience. We will need men like you in our future war against Russia."

"War against Russia?" Ishiro said.

Morita thrust a DVD at Ishiro. "Go watch this! It's my anime documentary on how military dictatorship is the best form of government."

Ishiro grabbed the DVD. "Thank you. Will you autograph it, please, sir?"

The General frowned, pulled a pen from his uniform, wrote a message on the DVD box, and shoved it back at Ishiro.

He looked at the autograph. It read "Stop loitering in Akihabara! Do something useful with your life, boy! Banzai! General Morita Chiko."

He hadn't expected a message like this. Anyway, he had gotten an autograph from the creator of *Time Warp at Midway*.

"Thank you, thank you," he muttered.

The van's driver leaned out again and asked, "General, are you ready for the 'Kimigayo'?"

"Yes!" Morita shouted.

The national anthem blared from the van. General Morita and his men snapped to attention and sang:

*"May my Lord's reign continue for a thousand, nay, eight thousand generations until pebbles grow into boulders covered with moss."*

Ishiro did not wait for the end of the anthem. He bowed to the General and ran down the street, heading to his date with Yuko.

# CHAPTER 2

## The Date

Ishiro arrived at Picolit-Ya just before six o'clock. The hostess led him to his table, where he waited for Yuko.

Despite its location, Picolit-Ya catered to high-class diners, not *otaku*. Its lights were soft and dim, not harsh and bright. Instead of loud pop music, soft music flowed from its speakers. Each table had a single candle and a small bottle with a rose. Paintings of Roman shepherds adorned the walls.

Ishiro had gone to Picolit-Ya just once before. He had asked his then-girlfriend where she wanted to go that weekend. She wanted to dine at a "posh restaurant" and chose Picolit-Ya. At the time, he worked for Dai Tokyo Taikun Financial Group, so he could easily afford the dinner. He didn't object to its cost; he was happy to splurge on his girlfriend.

She noticed that he wore a button for the TV series *Eternal Biological War Gundam*. "What's that show about?" she asked.

"It's the latest in a series of anime, movies, and manga that dates back to the twentieth century," Ishiro said.

He told her the entire plot of episode one of *Eternal Biological War Gundam*. Then he repeated the titles of every *Gundam* anime since animator Tomino Yoshiyuki created *Mobile Suit Gundam* in 1979. He told her all their plots and listed their major characters.

"*So desu ka, so desu ka,*" his girlfriend repeated, nodding throughout the speech.

She was listening attentively to the history of the *Gundam*, Ishiro noticed. It was rare to find a girl so interested in giant robots operated by a pilot. He had to continue.

"Oh, and I forgot to say, there's also a limited edition scale model of the Gundam Mobile Suit Omega Four with variant blue and white coloring, which is based on a suit seen in the original video animation *Gundam Apocalyptic Battle*. There was a preview showing of *Gundam Apocalyptic Battle* at —"

"Did I tell you? I got a new job, a promotion," his girlfriend interrupted. "There was a vacancy in the sales department, and I asked the vice-president —"

"You have to hear about *Gundam Apocalyptic Battle*," Ishiro urged. "No other original video animation has sold so many copies in the last twenty years."

"*So desu ka*," the girl said softly.

Dinner arrived, and as he ate, Ishiro talked about how the Martians vaporized Space Captain Katoki in *Gundam Martian Stormtroopers*. The fans howled with despair that the beloved Space Captain had died, so he was cloned for *Gundam at the Center of the Earth*...

"*So desu ka, so desu ka*," the girl said as she sipped her wine.

**

During dessert, he talked about the alternative ending for *Gundam Time Travel Expedition*.

"It makes sense that a time travel story, where history can change in several directions, would have alternative endings," he said.

"Speaking of time, it's getting late. I need to go home now," his girlfriend said.

"It's only eight o'clock."

"I have a new job. I want to get up early."

"What new job? You didn't mention that. Where is it?"

"It's nothing important. Never mind."

"Are you feeling well? You haven't said much all evening."

His girlfriend shrugged. "Don't worry about that."

A week later, she phoned him, saying she didn't want to see him anymore, forever.

"But I thought our last date went well," Ishiro muttered.

"To tell you the truth, I don't think we are right for each other," his ex-girlfriend said.

Ishiro didn't know what to say.

The ex-girlfriend giggled softly. "I've made you speechless. I'm sorry. Goodbye, Ishiro."

She hung up the telephone.

Thus his only girlfriend relationship ended. It had lasted a whole month. He didn't know why she was upset at him.

Unlike the genius schoolgirl Sailor Mercury in the classic anime *Sailor Moon*, real women made no sense to him. They were mysterious, so mysterious that he couldn't remember his ex-girlfriend's name.

He hoped he wouldn't repeat his mistake, whatever it was, with Yuko. Not knowing his mistake made him fear the worst. He hadn't had a date in a long time, and Yuko could be his last chance to get a girl.

He heard the hostess say, "Please come with me." He looked up and saw her lead Yuko to the table. He couldn't believe what he saw.

Yuko was still wearing her French maid costume.

The waiter came to their table. He looked at Yuko, smiled, and said, "Ah, the Akihabara look. Very fashionable, ma'am."

Yuko nodded at the waiter. "Thank you."

The waiter gave menus to them and went away. Yuko adjusted the barrette on her head.

"Is my barrette on straight?" she asked.

"Yes, it is," Ishiro said. "Wow, I didn't expect you to wear the French maid costume."

"I didn't have anything else to wear," Yuko explained. "I suppose I could have borrowed some clothes from Ami, but I didn't want to impose on her."

The waiter came back. "May I take your drink order?"

"I'll have a cola," Ishiro said.

"I won't have anything to drink," said Yuko.

"Nothing?" said the waiter.

"No, thank you."

"How about a glass of water?"

"No, I don't drink anything."

The waiter looked puzzled. Ishiro felt queasy. What could be wrong now?

Finally, Yuko said, "Okay, a glass of water."

The waiter went away. Ishiro opened the menu and looked through it.

"I haven't come here for a long time," Ishiro said. "I'm no expert on Italian food. I don't know what to order."

"Sora likes the chicken cacciatore," Yuko said. "She comes here with her boyfriend."

"Chicken cacciatore," said Ishiro, trying to say the Italian name correctly. "You pronounce the Italian words so easily. You must have been good in languages in school."

"It's a skill," Yuko replied.

"Did you study Italian?"

"No."

The waiter returned with the drinks. Ishiro quickly took a sip from his cola. Yuko stared at her glass of water.

"May I take your order?" the waiter asked.

Ishiro looked at Yuko. "Are you ready?"

Yuko nodded her head.

"What will you have, ma'am?" the waiter asked Yuko.

"Ask him first," Yuko told the waiter.

"It's Christmas, so I should have chicken, even if it isn't fried in the American style," said Ishiro. "I'll have the chicken cacciatore or however it's pronounced."

"That's a good choice. It's very popular." The waiter turned to Yuko. "And for you, ma'am?"

Yuko shook her head. "I'm fine. I'm not hungry. I don't need anything."

Again, the waiter looked puzzled. Yuko's face was blank, showing no emotion.

Ishiro felt queasy again. Perhaps Yuko was not used to foreign food? Maybe she was even afraid of it? What a stupid place to take her!

"Certainly you want something to eat?" Ishiro said.

"You're right, I should order something because it's traditional to eat on a date," said Yuko. "Chicken cacciatore for me too."

"A good choice," the waiter said before leaving.

Ishiro asked, "Is there something wrong with the restaurant?"

Yuko smiled. "No, there's nothing wrong with it at all. I'm just not used to ordering Italian food."

"Oh, I should have chosen a Japanese restaurant. I'm sorry. Why didn't you tell me?"

"This is an excellent choice. Sora's boyfriend takes her here. It must be good for a date."

"Sora passed her trigonometry exam," Ishiro said. "It was the only course she had to repeat. She'll graduate now."

"That's good," Yuko said. "I think she wants a career in entertainment, possibly as a singer. She has the personality."

"Do you think so?"

"She's very outgoing. The maid talent show last night was her idea."

They talked about the maids, Mr. and Mrs. Endo, and Ami, the people they knew in common. Despite his initial panic, Ishiro felt comfortable with Yuko.

As he drank his cola, he noticed that Yuko hadn't touched her glass of water.

"Ah, your water, why aren't you —" he began.

"Thank you for waiting," the waiter said as he suddenly brought their food to the table.

"This is chicken cacciatore?" Yuko asked.

"Yes, ma'am," said the waiter.

Like Yuko, Ishiro had not eaten chicken cacciatore before. He didn't know what to expect, but if Sora liked it, it must be good, he hoped.

"*Itadakimasu*," he said before taking his first bite. He immediately liked the mildly spicy taste. It was a good choice. He took another bite.

But Yuko wasn't eating. She simply looked at him.

"Is the meal good, master?" she asked.

Ishiro nodded. "Yuko, it's wonderful. Why aren't you eating?"

"I don't have the appetite."

"Oh." Ishiro put down his knife and fork. "I'm sorry. Are you feeling ill? I shouldn't have taken you out."

"No, I'm not ill. I'm fine."

Ishiro's feeling of dread returned. Other dates ended in disaster. This one was different. It was starting in disaster.

He, Sato Ishiro, had made a girl lose her appetite. What a loser.

"I know I'm not the most attractive or wealthiest person you've met," he blurted. "I'm sorry to have even asked you to have dinner with me. I'll take you home right away. Please accept my apologies. I know the maids aren't supposed to date the customers, but I thought perhaps because we had known each other for a long time — again, I'm sorry. Let's go —"

"No, it's not you," Yuko interrupted him. "I *never* have an appetite."

Ishiro thought for a moment. Why didn't Yuko want to eat? Then he realized why.

"You don't have an eating disorder, do you?" he whispered.

Yuko shook her head. "No. I simply don't need to eat or drink."

"Why?"

"I'm an android."

They stared at each other. It seemed like an eternity before either of them spoke.

"You're an android? For real?" he muttered.

"Yes, master." She smiled and nodded.

"Is that why you never get a drink for yourself when you get coffee for the girls?"

"Yes."

"You're kidding me! How can you be an android?"

"Someone created me."

"Hah, this is a joke!"

"No, I'm telling the truth. Please believe me, master."

Yuko leaned over the table, grabbed Ishiro's hand, pulled it towards her, and pressed it against her left breast. Ishiro gasped at the girl's brazenness. He looked around to see if other people were watching.

"Do you feel a heartbeat?" asked Yuko.

Ishiro did not feel the regular, defined thumping of a heart. Instead, he felt a soft, continuous vibration. It was like touching his computer's external hard drive.

Yet he also felt her chest move up and down, as if she were breathing.

"You're breathing, but there's no heartbeat," Ishiro said.

"I can simulate the appearance of breathing," said Yuko.

"Not even L-3 androids can do that."

"I'm not an L-3."

"I can't believe this," said Ishiro.

He saw another couple staring at them. He quickly pulled his hand away from Yuko.

Yuko sat back down. "That's why I don't require food or drink. Instead, I have a battery that can recharge from either solar energy or any electrical outlet."

"Solar energy? No android recharges by solar energy."

"I do, master." She flipped her hair with her hand. "My hair contains thousands of solar cells that convert sunlight into energy."

"Solar cells? I don't see any solar cells."

"They're extremely small. They're embedded in the fibers of my hair."

Ishiro guffawed. "Technology like that doesn't exist!"

"It exists but isn't in commercial production yet. It's still in the development phase," Yuko said. She ran her hands through her hair, like a model in a shampoo commercial.

"You're so lifelike," Ishiro marveled. "Your skin looks and feels so human. It's not like android skin."

"I have the latest in skin-like polymers," Yuko boasted. "It too is in the development phase. Commercial production is two years away. It might have uses other than android production. If it can be developed to bind with human tissue, it might even be used for burn victims."

"This is incredible," said Ishiro. "You play the violin too."

"Thank you for noticing, master. It's one of several skills I have."

"You're not an L-3, L-4, or L-5. What are you?"

Yuko grinned. "I'm an L-6 prototype."

"No, is that possible?" Ishiro said. "There's actually a sixth level?"

"Yes, there is, master. I'm it."

"I read some rumors on a robotics website. They say the Russians are trying to create an L-6 with information stolen from a Japanese company, probably Victor Robotics."

Yuko shrugged. "I don't know if any part of that rumor is true."

"There are rumors of learning androids," Ishiro said. "They can learn new information from their own experience and their environment. They can make decisions on their own. They can create new sentences, not just recite prerecorded speech. Their artificial intelligence doesn't just mimic human behavior. It actually creates new actions. It's almost like thinking."

Yuko's eyes lit up as she said, "That's what makes me different from the lower levels."

"Who made you?"

"I don't know. That information was deleted from my memory drive."

"Oh. Who designed you?"

"I don't know that either. That information has been deleted from my memory drive."

"Really?"

Yuko nodded. "For some reason, my creator deleted information about her and her company. All I know about her is that she is a woman."

"Interesting," said Ishiro. "How many L-6's are there?"

"Just me," Yuko replied. "I've tried to make wireless contact with other L-6 androids if they exist, but I've never detected another one."

Ishiro took a deep breath. "All you're saying is amazing! I can't believe it!"

He took another bite of chicken cacciatore. Yuko, smiling, stared at him.

"Are you just going to watch me eat?" Ishiro asked.

"Yes, master," replied Yuko.

Ishiro grunted and put down his fork. "If you're a prototype, how did you get out of the lab? How did you come to work in a maid café?"

Yuko stopped smiling. "I don't know. Someone deleted those files from my memory drive."

"That's terrible. Why would anyone want to do that?"

"I don't know." Yuko sighed. "My first uncorrupted memories are of Mr. Endo and his family."

"You say you have uncorrupted memories," said Ishiro. "Do you have *corrupted* memories as well?"

"Yes, I have corrupted memories." Yuko sadly glanced down at the table. "There was a disk error while someone was deleting my memory files, and some data fragments stayed on my memory drive. Those fragments are my corrupted, incomplete memories."

"That's so sad to hear," Ishiro said. "Do you know who deleted your memories?"

Yuko shook her head. "It was possibly my creator. I suspect that she owned me previous to Mr. Endo. I don't know much about her, though. All I know is that she was a woman who programmed me to play the violin."

"Why did she do that?"

"I don't know. I have only data fragments about her."

"You don't even know her name?"

"No, that data is lost."

"That's too bad." Ishiro paused for a moment. "Hey, sometimes you can retrieve data that's been deleted. Deleting a file doesn't actually erase it from a hard drive. It just deletes the file from the hard drive's index. The files could still be there. There's software to recover deleted files."

"Ami tried to recover the files, but they were wiped out by being overwritten with random zeroes and ones," Yuko said. "Except for the data fragments, my early memory files are permanently lost."

She glanced around the room. "Do all these people know who their parents are?"

"They probably do," Ishiro replied.

"I want to know who my creator was," Yuko said, wistfully looking at the other people.

"Why do you want to know?"

"I want to ask her why she deleted my memories and abandoned me."

"That wish is very human," said Ishiro.

A curious look appeared in Yuko's eyes. "Is it just for humans?"

Was her desire a genuine feeling, Ishiro wondered? Or was it a programmed response? She could be a programmed to say she wanted to know her creator. It would make her seem more human. The L-3's were programmed to reply to hundreds of situations as a human would. An L-6 was probably programmed for several thousand more situations. But all their behavior was programmed. They didn't do anything with real feelings.

Unlike the coffee shop barista, Yuko seemed to show real emotion. She smiled and frowned. Her eyes could look either sad or happy. Her hands and head moved with feeling.

But with advanced technology, this behavior could be programmed too. Yuko could smile at customers and prance about cheerfully, but she was *programmed* to do so. It did not mean that she had consciousness or felt anything.

Despite his doubts, Ishiro continued the conversation. He asked, "If you can't eat or drink, why did you come here with me?"

"I want to know what it's like to go on a date," Yuko replied.

The answer surprised Ishiro. Androids could do many things, from making coffee to sweeping floors. But they couldn't think about philosophical questions. No one could program an android to think, wonder, and guess about ideas. Androids have no free will. They did only what they were programmed to do.

"Have you ever been on a date before?" Ishiro asked.

Yuko shook her head. "No. You are my first date ever."

"Wow, I'm the first!"

"Sora goes on dates with her boyfriend. Mikita goes on dates with many different men," Yuko mentioned. "I observed that humans go on dates. I wanted the experience."

*I wanted the experience.* A moment ago, Ishiro was delighted that the beautiful android had chosen him as her first date. But now, he was wary of her intentions.

He asked, "If you're an android, why do you want the experience?"

"I don't have any experiential knowledge about emotions," Yuko replied. "My learning program detected the gap in my knowledge, so now I'm gathering data. The first emotion I decided to research is love."

"Why love?"

"Because that's the emotion the girls talk about the most," Yuko said.

"So our date is — research?" Ishiro asked.

Yuko nodded. "I observed that the girls correlate love with dating, so my learning program chose dating as a method to gather experiential data about love. That's why I agreed to go on the date with you."

*She's treating me like a lab rat,* Ishiro thought. He didn't know whether to laugh or cry.

Ishiro laughed bitterly. "Hah, if you want an expert on love and dating, I'm not the guy you want."

"Tell me what you know anyway," said Yuko.

"Oh, what do you want to know?"

"Let's start with why people go on dates."

"What can I say? Dates have a purpose," Ishiro said. "They're supposed to lead to something if they're successful. Uh, people go on dates for a reason. Maybe several reasons. But, ah, there is one reason more important than others, I guess."

"And that reason is?" Yuko asked.

"To find love."

"How will they know when they've found it?"

"I'm not really sure," Ishiro said. "They just know, I guess."

"They just know?" Yuko looked puzzled. "What is love? Everyone talks about love, everyone looks for it. What is it?"

"Uh, it's hard to explain," Ishiro said, realizing that he didn't have an answer either.

"The girls at the café always talk about love. But what is it?" Yuko asked again.

Ishiro smiled sheepishly and shrugged.

Yuko said, "I saw a television show where a woman said to a man, 'If you love me, you would leave her.' I think the 'her' referred to another woman. Is love the act of leaving someone?"

"Uh, no, not usually," Ishiro replied.

"Last night, Mikita sang a song called 'My Best Friend is Kissing My Boyfriend at Christmas'," said Yuko. "Mikita says a girlfriend and a boyfriend are two people who love each other. In the song, the girlfriend and boyfriend never kiss. Instead, the girlfriend's best friend kisses the boyfriend. Is that how a girlfriend and boyfriend create love?"

"Uh, no," Ishiro replied.

"Yet they are the two people who are in love," Yuko said. She looked at the other couples in the restaurant. "I don't understand the involvement of the girlfriend's best friend. Perhaps humans need to create love in groups of three?"

Ishiro laughed nervously. "I don't think that's what the song is about. Love is complicated. Uh, I don't fully understand it myself."

He ate some more chicken. He needed a break in talking with the android.

Ishiro drank some cola and continued. "As you've figured out, love is an emotion. What do you know about emotions already?"

"An emotion is a strong feeling. That's a definition from the *Nihon Kokoju Daijiten*," Yuko said, referring to the largest Japanese dictionary ever published.

"You know a dictionary definition of emotions, but can you feel them?" Ishiro said.

"No, I can't because I haven't gathered experiential data about them yet," Yuko said.

"But let's say you do gather the data. You listen to the girls, go on dates, and interview me. Would that allow you to actually *feel* emotions?"

Yuko's eyes went blank, and she sat silent and still. Ishiro had seen this reaction in androids before. Yuko didn't know the answer.

He knew the answer, though. An android is a machine, and machines can't feel emotions. It was impossible.

"I have no answer for now," Yuko finally said. "I'm sorry."

"That's fine, you don't have to apologize," Ishiro reassured her. He laughed. "Isn't this odd? You can't feel regret, but I'm telling you not to apologize as if you do have feelings."

Yuko smiled again. "As you wish, master, I won't apologize."

"Now I have a question for you. Aside from this date, how else are you learning about love?"

"I'm watching television and asking questions to the girls in the café. I also read manga love stories."

She looked at the couple at a nearby table. They were drinking wine.

Yuko turned back to Ishiro, smiled, and raised her glass of water to her lips. Then she put the glass back down without drinking anything.

"I'm learning proper behavior for a date," she explained.

"*So desu ka.*"

"However, there's a glitch in my learning program. I hope it doesn't interfere with my data gathering."

"A glitch? What is it?"

"Sometimes I think about a topic without any reason," Yuko said. "Yesterday, I thought about the android that had been attacked on the street. I saved a photo file of her. But there was no reason to save it."

"About last night," Ishiro said. "You also said that if a human had been killed, the police would call it murder, not vandalism."

"Yes, I said that. I don't know why I said it. It wasn't a programmed response."

"Ah, if it wasn't programmed, then it was spontaneous," Ishiro said. "Emotional reactions are spontaneous. Does this mean you can feel emotions?"

"I don't know," Yuko said. She looked at Ishiro's dinner. "Master, your dinner is getting cold. Please eat."

Ishiro picked up his fork. "Yes, I will, but what about you?"

Yuko smiled. "I'll be fine. I spent five minutes in the sunlight this morning."

Again, Ishiro marveled at Yuko's behavioral programming. He had to remind himself that an android, not a human, was smiling at him.

Yuko's smile looked so natural that it calmed Ishiro. He no longer cared that he was Yuko's lab rat.

**

The conversation flowed to matters other than Yuko's programming. When she asked what Ishiro had studied in university, he described every course about computer science, robotics, and artificial intelligence.

Best of all, he told her the entire storyline of *Time Warp at Midway*.

Yuko smiled and listened.

"*Time Warp at Midway* won a Seiun Award," Ishiro said as he chewed his food.

"You must be very interested in these subjects," Yuko remarked. "You just spent forty-seven minutes and nine seconds talking about them. Thank you for telling me about your university and your favorite anime."

Ishiro's heart jumped with excitement. Finally, he had found a girl who listened to him talk about computers and anime. And she wasn't complaining.

"My learning program detected a knowledge gap in human academics and arts, so I appreciate your lecture," said Yuko.

Ishiro suddenly remembered that Yuko was not a real girl. She was a deceptive machine.

His heart felt heavy and tired again. He quickly finished eating his dinner.

Yuko's chicken cacciatore was cold and uneaten.

"Are you eating that?" Ishiro asked.

"You know I can't, master," Yuko said.

"Oh, I'm full. I can't eat it either."

"Ask the waiter for a box and take the leftovers home."

"It doesn't matter to me," Ishiro said. "I rarely eat Italian food, and my parents don't like it. Perhaps they don't like tomatoes, which are used often in Italian food. Most people think that the Chinese were the greatest influence on Italian food, since they think that Marco Polo brought noodles from China to Italy, but I dispute that idea. You see, lots of Italian food is made with tomatoes, so arguably, the South American Aztecs and Mayans were more influential than the Chinese on Italian cooking —"

"Master, you can take the leftovers home," Yuko said, interrupting him.

Ishiro continued talking. "The Spanish took tomatoes from South America and planted them in the Caribbean, and then they planted them in the Philippines, and from there, tomatoes spread to Asia. They also took tomatoes to Europe and grew them there too. This all happened two hundred years after the time of Marco Polo, so —"

"Master, you can take the leftovers home," Yuko said again.

"...and it's debatable whether the Italians learned about noodles from the Chinese or invented them independently. Anyway, the Southeast Asians, like the Malaysians and Indonesians, used tomatoes for their curry..." Ishiro said.

"Master, about the leftovers —" said Yuko.

Endo was thrilled that Yuko kept listening to him. The girl had a learning program, and he was eager to feed her knowledge. He had a lot to give her.

By the time Yuko asked the waiter to put her uneaten meal in a box, Ishiro had recounted the whole history of personal computers since the twentieth century.

**

As they left the restaurant, Ishiro said, "Yuko, I'll walk you home."

"Thank you, master," said Yuko.

"Where do you live?"

"At Nikkou Café."

"You live in the café?"

"Yes, master. Where else would I live? Mr. Endo owns me."

"Mr. Endo owns you? Of course, he does," Ishiro said.

He knew he shouldn't be surprised that Endo owned Yuko. She was a machine, and all machines have owners. It was easy to forget that she was an android.

He watched the way she moved her legs, swayed her hips, and turned her head. She imitated human movement perfectly, better than an L-3 could.

They walked through Akihabara. Christmas celebrations were reaching their peak in the Electric Town. Christmas songs played from shops. Couples dined in restaurants decorated with paper hearts and Santa Clauses. Shoppers bought anime movies and books. A group of teenagers, dressed like anime characters, laughed as they entered a cosplay café. Lone males played for toy robots at *pachinko* parlors. Mechanical Santa Clauses waved at them in the windows of toy shops.

Some people gathered in front of a *koban*. They watched a television that broadcast police bulletins.

The policeman stood in the *koban*'s doorway. He said, "Watch the next report. Tell me if you see any suspicious activity like this."

A police woman read the news on TV. "Another android was attacked and destroyed in Shinjuku earlier this evening. The android was delivering parcels for Japan Post. No parcels were stolen. If you witnessed the attack or have any information about it, please report to the police."

The TV showed the wrecked android. Like the others, this one looked like an attractive young woman. Again, someone had torn its clothes and smashed a hole in its body. Black hydraulic fluid gushed out of its belly.

A teenaged boy giggled. "Stupid robots. They're so easy to kill."

A man said, "I used to work full-time until my company got an android to sweep the floors. They shouldn't let androids take our jobs."

"I don't mind industrial robots, but androids are creepy," a woman said. "It's the way they look at you. And they have that weird skin. Creepy."

Yuko tugged on Ishiro's arm. "Let's go," she urged.

They walked on, leaving the small crowd to talk about the news.

As they approached Chapel Christmas Love Hotel, a couple waved at them to come over. They were young, no older than twenty-five years. They dressed well. The man wore an expensive blue suit and tie. The woman wore a red party dress.

"Could you please take our photograph?" the man asked, holding his camera to Ishiro.

"Yes," Ishiro said, taking the camera.

The couple posed beside the Santa Claus robot and made peace signs with their hands. Ishiro pressed the shutter button, and the camera flash ignited. The Santa Claus laughed, "Ho, ho, ho!" and sang "Super Funky Holy Night."

"Thank you," the man said, taking the camera back from Ishiro.

The woman looked at Yuko and said, "That's a beautiful costume. Your boyfriend must love it."

Yuko smiled. "Yes, he does. Thank you, ma'am."

Ishiro felt startled. The woman had thought he was Yuko's boyfriend. Had Yuko actually agreed with her? Did Yuko consider him her boyfriend?

It was too good to be true.

"It's so nice to see people dress up for Christmas," the woman said. "It's the most romantic time of the year!"

The man said, "Merry Christmas!" to Ishiro and Yuko. Then he escorted his girlfriend into the love hotel.

"Have you ever been in a love hotel?" Yuko asked.

"No," Ishiro replied.

"I have not gone into a love hotel, but some of the girls have," Yuko revealed. "They go there with their boyfriends."

"I imagine so."

"I want to go to a love hotel to gather data. What do you think?"

"Ah, uh, ah, uh —"

"I'll do it on another day, after I recharge my battery," Yuko said.

They watched several more couples enter the love hotel.

"People enter the love hotel in pairs," Yuko observed. "Nobody goes alone."

"There's no reason to go alone," Ishiro said.

"Therefore, when I go in, I'll need to bring another person," said Yuko. "Master, will you go with me?"

Ishiro gasped and coughed. "Uh, ah, uh, ah —"

"Not tonight. My battery is running low. But will another night be fine, master?

"Yes, yes, thank you for asking me!" Ishiro blurted.

"Thank you, master," Yuko said.

"Ah, Yuko?"

"Yes, master?"

"Can you, ah, can you — can you perform as a woman in love? You know what I mean."

"No, I don't know what you mean. Please explain."

"Do you have the, uh, the correct parts?"

Yuko looked puzzled. How much programming was needed to make an android look puzzled, Ishiro wondered?

"Uh, can you, can you — have sex?" Ishiro finally asked.

"Oh, reproduction," Yuko said. "I can't reproduce biologically, but I have the anatomical features to simulate the act of reproduction with a human male."

The robot Santa Claus laughed, "Ho, ho, ho!"

**

They entered the Nikkou Café, which was open for business on Christmas night. Like last night, customers filled the café, and the maids walked from table to table.

Ishiro saw Mikita put water into the coffee machine. Androids were supposed to be like the coffee machine, the rice cooker, and the vacuum cleaner. Equipment did not get days off, but somehow, Yuko did.

"How did you get the time off to go out with me?" Ishiro asked.

Before Yuko could answer, Ami greeted them. "Yuko, you're home!"

Next, Ami bowed to Ishiro. "Mr. Sato! Welcome home!"

Yuko turned to Ishiro and said, "Thank you for dinner."

Ami's eyes widened. "No, not Mr. Sato! Mr. Sato was your date?"

Yuko nodded. "Yes, younger sister."

Ami gasped and giggled. "Oh! Oh! No wonder you didn't tell me who it was! Hah, I thought it would be another android! Like the cute male one at Mamoru Candy Palace."

"That android is an L-3 and can't help me with my research," Yuko said.

"Do androids go on dates with other androids?" Ishiro asked.

Yuko shook her head. "No, they don't."

"They don't go on dates with humans either," said Ami. "Androids don't go on dates at all. Not until now."

Mr. Endo came to them. He greeted Ishiro first. "Welcome home, Mr. Sato."

Then he said to Yuko, "You've come home. Did you enjoy the evening?"

"Yes, Mr. Endo, it was pleasant," Yuko said. "However, my battery charge is down, and it's dark outside, so I can't get solar energy. May I recharge in your office?"

Ami smirked and said, "You're exhausted, eh?"

When Yuko nodded, Ami giggled and nudged the maid's shoulder.

"Yes, go to my office," Endo said.

Yuko turned to Ishiro. "Thank you for dinner, master."

Ishiro nodded. "Yes, thank you for coming with me."

"Perhaps we will go out again, if you wish. I look forward to going to a love hotel with you."

Endo gasped. A look of horror appeared in his eyes. Ami burst out laughing. Ishiro wished he could disappear.

Yuko smiled and walked away. Ami and Endo turned to Ishiro. He saw the look on their faces. Did they feel shock, surprise, horror, disgust, or pleasure? Or was it a combination of feelings?

"Oh, this is a shock," said Endo. "It was bizarre enough that Yuko asked for time off for a date. She didn't tell me who it was. It was you, wasn't it?"

Ishiro mumbled, "Yes."

"Ah, so that's why you asked me for advice about girls," Endo realized. "I thought you were going on a date with a real girl."

"I did too," Ishiro said.

Ami's face became serious. "Ah, Mr. Sato, did you know she is an android?"

"No, I didn't know," Ishiro admitted.

"Oh."

Endo said, "Mr. Sato, perhaps we should talk. I'm quite busy tonight, but can you come tomorrow night?"

"Yes."

"Good. There are some things you should know. Yuko is not an ordinary girl, and she's not an ordinary android either."

**

Ishiro returned to Nikkou Café the next night. This time, neither Ami nor Yuko greeted him at the door. Instead, Mikita rushed to him and said, "Welcome home, master! Mr. Endo is expecting you. Please follow me."

As he followed Mikita, Ishiro did not see Ami or Yuko in the café.

Mikita led him to Endo's office. Unlike the rest of the café, the office lacked anime posters, character figurines, and toy robots. Instead, Mr. Endo had decorated his office with mementos of the Japan Maritime Self-Defense Force: a class photo of new officers, models ships and submarines, the naval flag, and a sword in a display case.

Family photos hung on a wall. They showed Mr. Endo, Masako, Ami, and Yuko. Yuko appeared like one of the family.

Endo stood up and welcomed Ishiro. "Thank you for coming, Mr. Sato." He pointed at a chair. "Please sit down."

He turned to Mikita. "Please bring us two chocolate teas. Close the door behind you."

Mikita curtsied and left. Endo closed the accounting spreadsheets on his computer and turned to Ishiro.

"I asked my daughter to take Yuko to buy some clothes," he said. "I didn't want Yuko to hear us talk."

"*So desu ka*," said Ishiro.

Endo sighed. "How do I start talking about Yuko? That girl's a mystery. Well, she's not even a girl."

"Was I the only person who didn't know that?" Ishiro asked. "Do the girls know she's an android?"

"Oh, they all know," Endo said.

Ishiro moaned softly. "How embarrassing! I've been coming to this café for two years and never knew Yuko is an android. And I'm a computer science graduate!"

"Don't be so hard on yourself," Endo said. "Everyone's fooled at first. A new girl doesn't realize that Yuko's an android until they talk for a while. Then they realize that she has gaps in her life experience, like no childhood, no schools, and no family. The customers seldom have conversations with her long enough to discover the truth. And the girls never tell the customers. That would spoil the illusion. Yuko is very convincing. She has always let others discover by themselves that she's an android. You're the first person to whom she's told her secret."

"I still can't believe how advanced she is," Ishiro said. "She speaks like a well-educated woman. Her movements are smooth. She even simulates breathing. She's the most human-like android I've ever seen."

"She wasn't always like that," said Endo. "When I first got her, she could only play the violin and make basic conversation. But her learning program is incredible. It's always making her learn about the world around her. Now she can dance like a ballerina, talk about hundreds of subjects, and learn new things. She had some basic social skills programming, but she learned much more about etiquette and social behavior on her own. I'm very happy about her development."

He picked up a framed photo. It showed Yuko and Ami wearing summer dresses at a park. As Endo stared at the photo, he smiled.

"Watching Yuko develop is like watching another daughter grow up," said Endo.

He put the photo back down. "However, I thought there would be one big difference between a daughter and an android. I didn't think that an android would be interested in the one thing that interests all daughters when they grow up. But I've seen her read romance manga, and I've heard her talk to the girls about boys."

"She told me she's gathering experiential data about emotions," Ishiro said. "She's starting with love. Dating is a sort of data gathering exercise for her."

"Yuko is still developing intellectually and socially. She continues to surprise me," said Endo.

Someone knocked on the door. Endo went to open it, and Mikita came in with their chocolate teas. After serving the tea, the maid left Endo and Ishiro alone again.

Ishiro took a sip of tea. "Where did you get Yuko?"

"Keep this secret," Endo replied. "I got Yuko from Dr. Hayase Midori."

"Dr. Hayase, the android designer?"

"I knew you would recognize her name. Yes, that's her."

"How did you meet her? How did you know her?"

"I first met her in my university days."

Endo pointed at the photo of naval officers on the wall. "That's me. When I was in university, I joined the Student Reservist Corps. That was during the Korean Crisis, and the Self-Defense Forces wanted students who could be part-time officers. I joined so I could work in the Maritime Force's robotics division.

"One summer, the Maritime Self-Defense Force sent me to see the new androids at Victor Robotics..."

# CHAPTER 3

# Victor Robotics

When Endo Hideki was ten years old, his father bought a robot for the restaurant. The robot combined noodles, soup, fish, meat, onions, and mushrooms to create *ramen* meals. It was a simple robot, but it fascinated Hideki. After high school, he went to University of Tokyo to study robotics.

In his first year of university, the Korean Crisis began. North Korea, always a poor country, invaded the South to capture its food and industry. The South Koreans and Americans beat the North Koreans back across the Demilitarized Zone, and the invasion failed.

North Korea harassed Japan next. A North Korean warship fired on a Japanese oil tanker. A robot spy plane crashed near Kadena Air Base. A midget submarine ran aground in Yokohama, and its lone sailor confessed to being a North Korean spy. As fear of a Korean invasion rose, the Self-Defense Forces launched a recruitment campaign.

As his second university year began, Endo heard military marches in the student center. The music came from a table decorated with the flags of the Self-Defense Forces.

Behind the table hung posters of soldiers, sailors, and airmen with the message "FOR OUR FREEDOM AND DEMOCRACY." They did not look anything like the posters of the Greater East Asia War, now seen only in Endo's history class.

A computer showed scenes of tanks, ships, and airplanes in action. Military officers chatted with students and gave them brochures.

"We need to expand the reserve forces in case the regular forces are called into emergency duty," a Ground Force officer told a student. "If the regular forces are defending our coast, we need reservists to perform garrison duty and maintain inland operations."

An Air Force officer gave a brochure to a student. "In the Reserve, you'll be eligible for the same benefits available to regular forces personnel. If you agree to serve full-time for four years after you graduate, we'll pay your tuition all throughout university."

Endo looked at a model warship on the table.

"Interested in the Maritime Self-Defense Force?" a Maritime Force officer asked him.

"No, I'm just curious about your display," Endo said. "Why are you recruiting on campus?"

"We want smart, educated people. We need people who know computer science, robotics, engineering, international law, political science, history, economics, agriculture, medicine, and many other subjects. All these subjects are important to the military. That's why we're looking for our future officers here."

The officer handed a brochure to Endo and continued. "We have a new program for students. Students can train to be officers and serve part-time in the Self-Defense Forces. It's a great way to make some money during the summer and on weekends."

"*So desu ka.*"

"What are you studying?"

"Robotics," said Endo.

"Robotics? You'll be interested in this," the officer said. He pointed at the model ship. "That's the destroyer *Yoshinobu*. She's the first ship to have ambulatory androids aboard."

"The walking androids?" said Endo. "They've only been around for a year."

"And most of them belong to us," the officer said. "The private sector doesn't have many of them, but I think they'll be everywhere by next year.

"And that's where we can help you. Join the Maritime Self-Defense Force Reserve and work with androids. When you graduate, you can sell that experience to any company you want. I'm sure android science will be a growth industry."

Endo looked at the video. The image had changed from tanks, ships, and aircraft. Now it showed military engineers programming androids to walk, swim, push carts, and carry crates.

"Yes, that would be good to have on my résumé," he agreed.

**

Endo enlisted in the Student Reservist Corps and became a midshipman, an officer candidate in the Maritime Self-Defense Force Reserve. He took a course in naval history and went to basic military training on weekends. The weekends were tough, with lots of physical education, including jogging, marching, swimming, climbing, and combat training. He had performed only average in high school phys-ed, but he survived the basic training. The Student Reservist Corps also had weekend courses on defense strategy, ships and equipment, and the laws of armed conflict.

The student reservists had to serve in the military for at least three weeks in August and September. Endo volunteered to serve for two months, the entire summer break. He needed the money, and he wanted experience in programming the androids.

The Maritime Self-Defense Force had bought fifty male-model androids and put them aboard ships and bases across the country. Their artificial intelligence was limited, and they could perform only simple tasks. Their jerky, awkward motions mimicked human movement poorly. But they were the first androids that could walk upright on their own. Nobody had to follow them with a remote control.

At the Maritime Self-Defense Force Officer Candidate School in Etajima, Endo programmed an android to raise a flag. The school's Superintendent refused to have androids participate in the morning ceremony, but he let Endo hold an unofficial flag-raising at the baseball field.

As the flag rose up the flagpole, another midshipman, Oshii Toshio, played reveille on his bugle. Endo saluted the Rising Sun. So did the android.

After playing reveille, Oshii laughed. "Look, it's not everyday that the janitor salutes the flag."

Endo quickly realized how silly the android looked. When they arrived from the factory, the androids wore plain grey coveralls with the Victor Robotics logo. Those were the same type of coveralls that janitors wore.

"It does look ridiculous," Endo said.

"Anyway, this has been a fine ceremony," said Oshii. "Your android programming skills are impressive. You're really learning how to use these machines. Now, if you'll excuse me, I have to write my astronomy essay."

Oshii left for the library, and Endo walked the android back to the robot storeroom. As soon as they arrived, the chef came to see them.

The chef looked immaculate in his white coat, apron, and cap. Endo never knew how the chef kept spotless while cooking for two hundred people each day.

"Mr. Endo, my assistant went home because his mother fell off her bicycle and got injured. I need another hand. May I use this android today?" the chef asked.

"Certainly," Endo replied.

"Thank you," said the chef. He turned to the android and said, "Robot, follow me to the galley!"

The android silently left with the chef.

**

Endo entered the midshipmen's wardroom and smelled the aroma of beef curry. Britain's Royal Navy, which trained the Imperial Japanese

Navy, introduced curry to the Japanese in the Meiji Era. Since then, the Japanese navy had eaten curry for lunch every Friday. The tradition survived the defeat in the Greater East Asia War.

Endo joined Oshii in the line-up for food. An android scooped up steamed rice from metal pots and slapped it on their plates. Then the android poured curried beef and pickles over the rice. Further down the line, another android poured tea for the midshipmen.

Oshii approached the android that held the teapot. The android looked at him and asked, "Do you want tea, sir?"

"I don't feel like having tea today," Oshii replied. "Do you have coffee?"

The android stared blankly at him.

"It recognizes only two options to its question," Endo explained. "You either want tea or you don't. Yes or no."

"Oh. It can't think of an answer to a more complicated question?" Oshii asked.

"No, not yet," said Endo. He pointed at a row of coffee urns. "The coffee's where it usually is. Go there, pour a cup for yourself, and find a table. I'll join you."

Oshii left the line, but the android kept looking ahead.

Endo stepped in front of the android. It looked at him and asked, "Do you want tea, sir?"

"Yes," said Endo.

The android poured a cup of tea and handed it to Endo.

"Thank you."

The android said nothing. Instead, it stared at him with its blank, dull eyes. Endo suddenly felt silly. Why had he said 'thank you' to the android? It didn't have any feelings. Would he thank a rice cooker for steaming rice?

**

Endo and Oshii sat down and ate their lunch. The curry was mild and slightly sweet, the way Endo liked it.

He watched the two androids at the food line. "I hope they don't screw up."

"No, they're working well," Oshii observed. "Did you notice that nobody's talking about them? People are getting used to having androids around. They're just like household robots now. It's not a big deal anymore."

After they finished eating, they put their trays and dishes on a cart. An android pushed the cart to the galley.

While walking back to their quarters, they saw two androids sweeping the floor with brooms. The other midshipmen walked past the androids without a second glance. The androids seemed as normal as human janitors.

**

Endo went to the quartermaster and asked for five shirts, pants, caps, and pairs of socks.

The quartermaster placed the clothes on the counter. "What about rank insignia, sir?" she asked.

"I don't need any," Endo replied.

"None? Okay." The quartermaster pushed the card reader to Endo. "Please pay this amount, sir."

Endo swiped a money card through the reader. As accounting information appeared on the computer, the quartermaster raised an eyebrow.

"I see you're using an academic department's card. Why is the Computer Science Department paying for uniforms?" she asked.

"It's for a robotics research project," said Endo.

"You need uniforms for robotics research?"

"This project does."

**

Lieutenant Commander Kirino, professor of computer science, strode onto the baseball field. His shirt bore three rows of ribbons, testaments to his service in the Maritime Self-Defense Force. Japanese officers usually didn't carry swagger sticks, but Kirino did, tucked under his arm.

He looked at the androids. The five machines stood at attention in a row. They wore white undress uniforms, no rank insignia, and no name badges.

"You've dressed them like us," Kirino remarked. "Only the rank insignia and name badges are missing. Why did you put them in uniform?"

"Sir, I thought military attire would be appropriate at the Officer Candidate School," Endo said.

"It's appropriate for midshipmen, but these are androids," said Kirino. "It's like putting a uniform on a vacuum cleaner."

Endo snapped to attention. "Sir, I apologize for offending you. I'll put them back in their factory suits."

"Do that and don't forget they're machines," said Kirino. "I also wish to discuss the dignity of the flag. You may let androids raise the flag at unofficial flag raisings as an exercise in android programming, but no android will raise the flag at official ceremonies. Is that understood?"

"Yes, sir."

"Hmmm." Kirino pointed his swagger stick at an android and asked, "Robot, what is your name?"

"I am android number two of the Maritime Self-Defense Force Officer Candidate School, sir," the android replied. It spoke like a voice synthesizer, machine-like and monotone.

"And what is your home prefecture?" asked Kirino.

"I am android number two of the Maritime Self-Defense Force Officer Candidate School, sir," the android repeated.

"Sir, they have only a limited capacity for speech," Endo explained. "They can recite only sentences programmed into them."

"I know that. I was just testing the limits of their capabilities and of your programming," said Kirino. "I have to admit, despite their shortcomings, they're more advanced than household robots."

"I agree, sir. I think we should continue testing androids for military uses."

Kirino tucked his swagger stick under his arm again. "Mr. Endo, I think you've done a fine job of programming these androids. Thank you for inviting me to inspect them. Keep up the good work. You may send them back to the robot storeroom."

Endo nodded and shouted, "Squad, stand at ease!"

The androids stood at ease.

"Squad, hands to your sides!" Endo ordered.

The androids brought their hands down to their sides.

"Squad, about face!"

The androids turned around one hundred and eighty degrees.

"Squad, right turn!"

The androids turned ninety degrees to their right.

"Squad, forward march!"

The androids marched off the baseball field.

"They're a bit stiff and jerky, but that's to be expected from androids," Kirino said. "The foot drill is simple but nonetheless very impressive for machines."

"Thank you, sir," said Endo.

"Go catch up with your squad," Kirino ordered.

Endo rushed to join the androids and kept giving them directions towards the robot storeroom.

He had never before commanded sailors in foot drill, on parade, in maneuvers, or in battle before. How odd that his first command would be a squad of androids.

**

Endo went to see a movie at Yamamoto Hall. The school's film society boasted that it would show the best movies about naval history. On past nights, it had shown old classics like *Das Boot* and *Otoko-Tachi No Yamato*. *Das Boot* ended with the crew of a German U-boat surviving their harrowing mission only to die by enemy strafing at the dock. *Otoko-Tachi No Yamato* ended with the battleship *Yamato* and her crew sinking near Okinawa.

After watching *Otoko-Tachi No Yamato*, Oshii commented, "These are good movies, but why do we get only movies where the Japanese and Germans lose at the end?"

"Well, the Japanese and Germans *did* lose at the end," said Endo.

For some reason, tonight's choice was *The Navy vs. the Night Monsters*, an ancient American science fiction movie. Never before had Endo seen such a low-budget mess. It was funny for its shoddiness. It made the rubber monsters on children's television shows look expensive. The midshipmen usually watched the movies quietly, but this time, they jeered each time a monster appeared.

Oshii usually came to the movie screenings, but tonight, he did not. Just as well, Endo thought. Who really wanted to see rubber monsters chase Mamie Van Doren, supposedly a famous American actress of the twentieth century?

On his way back to the midshipmen's residence, he saw Oshii lead an android into the baseball field. The android carried a large telescope and tripod.

"Oshii, are you gazing at the stars again?" Endo asked.

"Tonight's a good night," Oshii replied. "It's clear."

Endo approached them. After the android put down the telescope and tripod, Oshii quickly set up the equipment.

"I've been looking at the stars and planets since I was a kid," Oshii said. "At my family's farm in Hokkaido, I could see the sky clearly. I didn't get the lights and smog of a big city."

He looked through the telescope and adjusted the lens. Meanwhile, the android stood still and silent, as if awaiting orders.

"I've called an impromptu meeting of the astronomy club because of the clear sky," Oshii said. "The rest of them will be here in twenty minutes. You can join us if you wish."

"No, I better review the maintenance report on the network server. If I don't, Kirino will order extra duty for me," said Endo.

"Look at this."

Endo looked in the telescope. There was a bright light in the black sky.

"What is it?" he asked.

"It's Uncle Joe," Oshii said.

**

Two days ago, all professors and midshipmen received the following message on their pocket computers:

*To all faculty and midshipmen:*

*Report to auditorium 10, Yamamoto Hall, at 18:30 for a briefing from the Chief of Staff, Joint Staff Office. Attendance is compulsory.*

*Rear Admiral Akama Masao, Superintendent, Japan Maritime Self-Defense Force Officer Candidate School.*

They gathered in auditorium 10 in Yamamoto Hall. On the giant screen, a video showed the usual scenes of tanks, ships, and aircraft in action.

Superintendent Akama walked to lectern. The video continued playing behind him.

"We will be receiving a briefing from the Chief of Staff, Joint Staff Office. This broadcast is going to all Self-Defense Forces stations simultaneously," said the Superintendent.

As he left the stage, the video ended. The emblem of the Joint Staff Office appeared. It was a white cherry blossom against a purple background. The Joint Staff Office's color was not the green of the Ground Force, the navy blue of the Maritime Force, or the sky blue of the Air Force. It was purple, the traditional color of European royalty, now adopted by the central command of Japan's military forces.

A short trumpet fanfare sounded. The professors and midshipmen stood up. The Joint Staff Office emblem faded away, and General Okuda Hata appeared on the screen. He wore the Chief of Staff badge on his Air Self-Defense Force uniform.

"To all my comrades in the Self-Defense Forces, thank you for attending this briefing," he said. "You may sit down."

They sat down to listen to the General's message.

"The information you receive tonight will be released to the news media two hours from now," he said. "I want all Self-Defense Forces personnel to hear it from me first, not through media reports that may be exaggerated, inaccurate, or incomplete."

The screen showed a rocket launch in Russia. Then it showed a NASA photo of a bright dot in space.

"You will remember that spy satellites photographed a secret rocket launch in Russia two years ago. The world's space agencies subsequently detected an unidentified satellite orbiting the Earth. Indeed, even amateur astronomers could see it. At the time, the Russian government denied any connection to the satellite," Okuda continued.

Next, the screen showed a fishing trawler's shaky video of a fireball falling into the Sea of Japan. Other news videos showed Japanese sailors pulling a wrecked satellite out of the ocean.

"Two weeks ago, a North Korean spy satellite crashed into the Sea of Japan. North Korea claims that the satellite failed due to computer malfunction. However, intelligence sources say that it was damaged by another spacecraft, possibly of Russian origin. Again, the Russian government denied any connection to the event.

"Today, the Russian government confirmed what intelligence agencies have long suspected. The Russians also provided additional information."

The screen showed a large silver sphere covered with turrets and laser cannons. The video showed it flying in space, above the Earth.

"The Russians have confirmed that they have launched a satellite called Uncle Joe, apparently named after the Soviet dictator Joseph Stalin."

The audience laughed softly. Endo saw Lieutenant Commander Kirino frown.

"Uncle Joe was created to destroy other satellites, spacecraft, and missiles in space. Russia has admitted that it destroyed the North Korean satellite as it passed over Siberia.

"Here is the new information. Unlike most satellites, Uncle Joe can change orbits and go wherever the Russians send it. It is also the largest unmanned object ever sent into orbit. The Russians released the following technical specifications."

Information about Uncle Joe appeared on the screen. It usually flew three hundred and fifty kilometers above the surface of the Earth. It was one hundred meters in diameter. It carried ten laser cannons, twenty reloadable grenade launchers, two hundred grenades, and fifteen missiles. A nuclear generator powered Uncle Joe's ion drive. Maintenance crews flew in service rockets to Uncle Joe from time to time.

Murmurs ran through the audience.

"Nothing this big and heavily armed has ever gone into orbit before," said Oshii.

"If the Russians go to war against us, they could knock out all our satellites and make us blind," Endo said.

Superintendent Akama stood up and shouted, "Silence! The Chief of Staff's message isn't over yet!"

The audience listened silently to General Okuda again.

"The Ministry of Defense believes that Russia released this information to intimidate North Korea, not Japan. Since relations between Russia and Japan are peaceful, the Ministry does not believe that Uncle Joe poses an imminent threat to Japan. However, Japan and Russia are still disputing the ownership of the Northern Territories, and our government opposes the construction of a cosmodrome on Shikotan, one of the disputed islands. If Russo-Japanese relations worsen, Uncle Joe may be a significant threat to us.

"Our Minister of Foreign Affairs will investigate whether Uncle Joe violates any outer space treaties and confer with the Russian ambassador.

"The general public may be concerned, and some may protest at the Embassy of the Russian Federation. It goes without saying that all Self-Defense Forces personnel should not get involved in any protests or the groups that hold them. Act only upon orders received through the authorized chain of command.

"Uncle Joe is a new complication in the Korean Crisis, but I know that you will continue to perform your duties with the professionalism that is our tradition."

The General's image faded, and the Joint Staff Office emblem appeared again. Another trumpet fanfare sounded, and the audience stood up. When the transmission ended, Superintendent Akama dismissed the assembly.

Oshii and Endo passed Kirino and Akama at the exit. They overheard the two senior officers talking.

"That was shameful, just shameful, the murmuring during a message from the Chief of Staff," said Kirino. "That would never have happened in my great-great-great-great-great-grandfather's day in the Imperial Navy. I think they pick up these bad habits from watching military anime."

Superintendent Akama replied, "We should bring back flogging."

Kirino grinned and beat his swagger stick into the palm of his hand.

Outside Yamamoto Hall, Oshii said, "The largest unmanned object above our planet is a weapons platform. What can we do against *that*? Will the world need us sailors anymore?"

"Of course, it will," said Endo. "Those things never stay up forever. We get to pick up the debris after it falls back to Earth."

**

One day, Kirino called Endo to his office. Endo knocked on the door, which was already open. "Permission to come aboard," he said.

"Come aboard," Kirino replied.

Endo walked into the office, stopped, bowed to Kirino, and saluted. Kirino stood up and returned the salute.

"Sit down, Mr. Endo," Kirino said, pointing at a round table. "The tea is coming."

An android entered, carrying a tray with a teapot and two cups.

"Robot, pour tea for me," Kirino ordered.

The android silently poured a cup tea for him.

"Robot, pour tea for him too," Kirino ordered, glancing at Endo.

The android served a cup of tea to Endo.

"Good, good," said Kirino. "Robot, leave us now."

The android left the office.

"Don't get the impression that I serve tea to every midshipman who meets me," Kirino warned. "Actually, you're the first one. I can get the android to serve me because it recognizes my voice, but I also wanted to see if it would follow orders to serve another person. Serving tea to you was the least dangerous duty I could assign to it."

"Another test trial. I see the results are successful, sir."

"They are for this task."

Endo looked around the office. As he expected, it was decorated with naval items, like photos of warships, model submarines, medals, badges, rank insignia, and a portrait of Fleet Admiral Togo, hero of Meiji Japan.

A naval officer's sword hung below the signal flag for "Z." Around them were framed photos of naval officers. Their uniforms were of every era back to the nineteenth century.

"I see you're looking at the sword," Kirino observed. "A great uncle of mine carried that sword aboard the *Mikasa* at the Battle of Tsushima, the victory over Russia."

"So that's why the Z-flag is there," Endo realized. "Admiral Togo raised a Z-flag on the *Mikasa* before the battle."

"I'm glad you've memorized the Midshipmen's Manual. Don't ever forget the importance of the Z-flag."

"I never will, sir. What about the photographs?"

"Various ancestors and relatives," said Kirino. "My family has been in the navy since the Meiji Era. A family member was in every war from the Boshin War to the Greater East Asia War. After the wars ended, we've been in the Maritime Self-Defense Force without interruption."

"That's an honorable tradition, sir," Endo said.

"Thank you," said Kirino. "However, we're not here to talk about my family.

"I'm impressed with your work on the androids. They're performing very well in support functions. They sure are useful in the galley."

"Thank you, sir," said Endo.

"Tell me, do you think they can do anything more advanced than maintenance and kitchen duty? For example, do you think they'll be able to navigate and plot courses for our ships? Can they observe for enemy aircraft? Can they disarm naval mines?"

"Not the current models. For such duties, their ambulatory systems need greater range of movement. They also need artificial intelligence systems superior to those of current androids."

"That day may be coming," said Kirino. "Victor Robotics has created a new android called the 'level two' or 'L-2'. It's supposedly better than the current model."

"What makes the L-2 better?" asked Endo.

"Artificially intelligent speech," said Kirino.

Endo put his teacup down. "Artificially intelligent *speech*?"

"Yes, speech. Victor Robotics says the L-2 can carry on simple conversations. It can talk to you."

"A talking robot is nothing new. Amusement parks have talking robots. But no android can carry on a conversation with a human. We're years away from that."

"Apparently it exists now. Here's a description of the L-2." Kirino gave Endo a booklet with the Victor Robotics logo. "I'm sending you to Tokyo to find out more about it. You'll be meeting Dr. Hayase Midori."

"Dr. Hayase?" said Endo. "*The* Dr. Hayase?"

Kirino nodded. "Yes, the one and only."

At thirty years of age, Dr. Hayase Midori was already a legend. By the time she was twenty-four years old, she had earned a doctorate in computer science and co-founded Victor Robotics with a university classmate, Katsura Kenji. Within six years, Victor Robotics had become the world's leading maker of household robots. The company was one of the wealthiest in Japan, with Dr. Hayase designing the robots and Mr. Katsura running business and sales.

Dr. Hayase invented the first ambulatory android for sale to the public. Victor Robotics' income doubled as androids became popular throughout society. Other companies rushed to make their own androids, but Victor Robotics dominated the market it had created.

Endo saw the golden opportunity. By meeting Dr. Hayase, he could get to know her and Victor Robotics. After university, a job at the company would be very attractive.

**

A day before leaving for Tokyo, Endo's pocket computer beeped. He looked at the new message on the screen:

"Dear Mr. Endo, I invite you to lunch with me at our company headquarters. Have a safe trip. Dr. Hayase Midori."

**

Victor Robotics owned a white stone building in Akihabara, Tokyo. Above the front doors, the company logo, the letter V, lit up in brilliant blue neon.

The first floor was a shopping mall with computer stores, movie rental outlets, anime toy shops, jewelers, clothing boutiques, restaurants, dry cleaners, travel agencies, banks, a foreign currency exchange, and a newsstand. A wide range of customers walked through the mall: salarymen and business women in expensive suits, teenagers with dyed-blonde hair, young women in trendy dresses, computer geeks carrying backpacks, and students in school uniforms.

He saw a female android wearing an office uniform of a white blouse and blue bow tie, vest, and miniskirt. It stood in white high heels and waved at people as they passed.

Endo approached the android. It bowed slightly to him. Though it smiled, its eyes remained dull and emotionless.

"Welcome to Victor Robotics," said the android. "If you have an invitation or a scheduled meeting, please talk to the security guard. Otherwise, please turn left and go to the visitor center to view our amazing products. You may also shop in the shopping center."

"I'm here to see Dr. Hayase Midori," said Endo.

"Welcome to Victor Robotics. If you have an invitation or a scheduled meeting, please talk to the security guard..." the android repeated.

The android obviously wasn't an L-2, the new type that could converse with humans. Victor Robotics had put the pretty android in the lobby for advertising only.

Endo walked past the android and went to the security desk. The guard was a woman wearing the same office uniform worn by the android. Unlike the android, the guard wore a star-shaped metal badge, a symbol of her authority.

Portraits of Dr. Hayase Midori and Mr. Katsura Kenji, the two founders of Victor Robotics, hung on the wall behind the security guard. The portraits had no signs with their names, but Endo knew who they were. Their faces were famous around the world. People everywhere marveled at how they had founded the world's leading robotics company while they were still young.

Endo took out his pocket computer and showed the emailed invitation to the guard.

"Please go to the top floor, penthouse number two," said the guard.

Endo rode the elevator up to the twenty-fifth floor. The hallway did not look like that of an office building. Instead, it resembled a luxury hotel. It had silk wallpaper with a floral pattern in blue and gold. Brass lamps, not fluorescent tubes, hung from the ceiling.

Paintings in wooden gilt frames decorated the walls. All the paintings showed violinists, Europeans or Americans in clothes of past centuries.

Dr. Hayase had paid a fortune for her art collection. Last year, the TV news reported that she had bought a portrait by John Singer Sargent, a famous American painter. The painting's subject was a girl playing the violin. It cost ten million dollars at an auction in New York.

He noticed that he was alone. No hordes of office workers rushed about. There were no clients either. The silence was eerie.

The employees must be on the lower floors. In a TV documentary about Victor Robotics, the company looked like a typical business, with plain white walls, rows of cubicles, and hundreds of people chattering, walking around, and staring at computers. The TV crew never went to the executive penthouses, though.

Endo walked to one end of the hallway and came to a single door: penthouse one, for Katsura Kenji, president and chief executive officer. He walked in the opposite direction and found penthouse two, for Dr. Hayase Midori, vice-president of research and development.

The door had a brass knocker. How quaint; no buzzer, no doorbell. Endo raised the door knocker and tapped it twice. The door swung open, and Dr. Hayase Midori appeared.

"Ah, Midshipman Endo," she said. "Please come in."

Dr. Hayase was a slim, attractive woman. She wore a black jacket and a skirt, styled to hug the shape of her body. Her white silk blouse matched the string of pearls around her neck. Her eyeglasses were fashionable, from a famous designer. She was that rare creature, a pretty and exquisitely-dressed computer geek.

Endo followed her into the penthouse. A small vacuum robot darted across the floor, stopped at a candy wrapper, and sucked it in.

"Robot, stop vacuuming, return to the storeroom," Dr. Hayase said.

With it wheels making a whirring noise, the vacuum robot rushed into an adjoining room.

"Please excuse me," Hayase apologized. "My niece and nephew were visiting earlier. They're only three and four years old, and they threw the candy wrappers on the floor. I indulge them too much, but I love children. You caught me as I was cleaning up."

"No problem, don't apologize," said Endo.

Another robot rolled in from the adjoining room. It was the Mailman, a self-guided mail cart. It lowered a ramp and pushed a package down to Dr. Hayase's desk. Then the Mailman left.

Hayase picked up the package and tore the white wrapping paper off it. "Ah, it's the music disc I ordered. *Coppélia*."

Endo looked at a wall. The painting of the girl violinist by John Singer Sargent hung there. Hayase could look at her ten-million-dollar *objet d'art* as she worked at her desk.

The office had the usual furniture of a business executive: the mahogany desk, the round table for meetings, the bookshelves, and a couch.

The art collection was unusual, though. In addition to the Sargent, Endo counted six other paintings in the office. Like the ones in the hallway, they portrayed European and American violinists.

Before he met his girlfriend Masako, Endo had dated a girl who took ballet classes. Her father ran a ballroom dance school, and her mother had been a *miko* who performed sacred dances at a shrine. They decorated their house in dance-related art, like a bronze sculpture of a ballerina, a poster of the old American movie *Singin' in the Rain*, and a drawing of a French can-can girl. Their household shrine even had a wooden tablet with the gilt name of Ame-no-Uzume, whose dance lured the Sun Goddess Amaterasu out of her cave. Dr. Hayase reminded him of this family.

"Let me shut the door to the other room so we won't be interrupted," Hayase said. She pressed a button on her desk, and the adjoining room's door slid shut.

Hayase walked to the round table. "Please, sit down."

"It's a pleasure to meet you," Endo said. "The Self-Defense Forces are very interested in your work."

Hayase nodded. "I think the Self-Defense Forces will be very interested in the L-2. The L-2 can process a thousand times more algorithms than the L-1 can. With this processing capacity, its decision-making ability is much more advanced than that of the L-1. But why am I talking about the L-2 when I can show it to you?"

She spoke into her pocket computer. "Toshiko and Himeka, please come into the office."

The adjoining room's door slid open. Two androids walked into the office. They were female models identical to the one in the lobby. One wore a blue office uniform, and the other wore a red uniform. Both wore a large pendant with the number "2." They had individual name badges: Toshiko was the one in blue, and Himeka was the one in red.

"Mr. Endo, please meet Toshiko and Himeka," Hayase said.

The two androids bowed to him and said in unison, "Welcome to Victor Robotics, Mr. Endo."

"I'm pleased to meet you," said Endo. He chuckled. "It feels odd to be introduced to androids."

"They are my personal assistants," Hayase said. "Toshiko and Himeka are modeled on the idol singer Momoi Kazusa. Their model is called the L-2 Kazusa."

"Ladies, please serve the beverages now," Hayase said. She looked at Himeka. "Himeka, take my order."

Then she looked at Toshiko. "Toshiko, take Mr. Endo's order."

Toshiko bowed to Endo. "What do you wish to drink, sir?" the android asked in its synthesized voice.

"What do you have?" asked Endo.

"We have tea, coffee, and a variety of soft drinks and fruit juices," Toshiko replied.

"What types of fruit juices?"

"Orange, pineapple, apple, tomato, mango, and peach."

Endo couldn't believe what he was hearing. He replied, "I'll have an apple juice."

"Very good, sir," Toshiko said. She went to the adjoining room.

Dr. Hayase told Himeka, "Coffee with one packet of artificial sweetener."

"Which type of coffee?" Himeka asked.

"What do we have today?"

"We have the Colombian, the Indonesian arabica, and the Swiss mocha."

"I'll have the Colombian," Dr. Hayase said.

"Very good, ma'am," said Himeka before leaving.

"This is amazing!" Endo said. "It talks with you."

"They're more advanced than the androids you have sweeping floors and dishing out food," Hayase said. "The L-1 can perform simple, repetitive tasks and say pre-recorded sentences. But the L-1 can't carry on conversations, ask questions to you, or make decisions based on your answers. The L-2 can do all that. The L-2 is a thinking machine."

"But is it really thinking?" Endo asked. "Certainly an L-2 android can't think of a sentence or an action by itself. All of its speech and actions must be programmed and saved in advance."

"You're correct, they are. It is a machine, after all. What makes the L-2 different is its extensive decision programming and a large database of situations and responses. These features give it the ability to process many more algorithms than the L-1 can. The L-2 can listen to you and decide what to do because it knows what a human would do in that situation."

"That's artificial intelligence."

"Yes, it is." Hayase smiled. "The possibilities are endless."

Toshiko and Himeka returned and placed the beverages on the table. Hayase picked up her coffee and sipped it. The androids stepped away and waited.

"They move and walk gracefully, don't they? The L-1 isn't bad, but the L-2 is better," Hayase said. "I've put these androids in high heels, and they still move like ballerinas."

Endo nodded as he drank his apple juice and stared at the androids' shapely legs.

"Ladies, we can order food now," Hayase said. "We'll have *ramen* today. Bring a choice of ingredients."

"Very good, ma'am," the androids said in unison. They bowed and left the room.

They returned a minute later, pushing a large cart with two metal pots on hot plates. The cart also carried bowls, trays of meats and vegetables, and packages of noodles. Steam rose from the pots.

"Let's switch androids," said Hayase. "Then you'll see that Toshiko wasn't programmed to serve only you. They can adjust to changes in the situation.

"Himeka, you take Mr. Endo's *ramen* order and serve him. Toshiko, you take my order and serve me."

Himeka looked at Endo and asked, "What type of broth do you want? Chicken, beef, pork, or miso?"

"Chicken," Endo replied.

Himeka put a spoonful of chicken soup powder into a pot of boiling water. Then the android asked, "Which ingredients do you want?"

"How many may I have?"

"As many as you want, as long as they are from this cart."

"I'll have beef and vegetables." He deliberately did not tell the android which vegetables to use.

The android looked at the ingredients, paused for a moment, and asked, "What type of vegetables?"

The android hadn't stalled. It knew what to ask and do. Endo was impressed.

He replied, "Bean sprouts, lettuce, tomatoes, and green onions."

"Testing their programming?" said Dr. Hayase.

"You've programmed them very well," Endo said.

Himeka dropped the beef and vegetables into the pot. Then she added noodles to the broth. Endo observed Himeka's smooth, natural movements.

As Himeka stirred the boiling broth, Toshiko took Dr. Hayase's order.

"Toshiko, I'll have miso broth with sliced pork, carrots, and broccoli," Hayase ordered.

"Very good, ma'am," Toshiko said. The android quickly threw the ingredients into a pot of boiling water.

Dr. Hayase drank some coffee. "Please forgive me for a meal as simple as instant noodles. We hired an executive chef from a five-star hotel, but she won't arrive until next week. Hence, we couldn't program her expertise into Himeka and Toshiko before your visit. On the other hand, we computer science students lived on instant noodles, didn't we?"

"What university student didn't?" Endo said.

"You see they can make *ramen*. You can program them to do anything," said Hayase. "Think of their military uses. They can dispose of bombs without risking human lives. They can dive into the ocean and stay underwater longer than a human can. They can fly to altitudes where the air is thin, but they won't pass out from lack of oxygen."

Himeka and Toshiko poured the *ramen* into bowls and served them to Endo and Hayase. Then the androids walked to the other side of the room and stood still.

"So what courses will you take in your third year?" Hayase asked during lunch.

"Robot design, an electrical engineering course, systems design, and the history of Russian-Japanese relations," said Endo.

"The history of Russian-Japanese relations? Is that an elective?"

"It's an elective for other robotics students, but it's required for student reservists."

"Good for you," said Hayase. "We need more military personnel. North Korea is frightening, isn't it? Do you intend to make a career in the military?"

"No, I'll be a part-time officer, a reservist. After I graduate, I want a regular job in robotics," Endo said.

"That's a good idea. The robotics industry will be a thousand times larger when you graduate. By then, androids like Himeka and Toshiko will be a part of everyday life."

After Endo and Dr. Hayase finished lunch, the androids returned to clean up.

Endo handed his bowl to Toshiko and joked, "That was very good. Have you considered starting your own restaurant?"

Toshiko stared at him. The android stayed silent for a moment. Then it smiled and said, "What type of broth do you want? Chicken, beef, pork, or miso?"

"I didn't expect anyone to ask that question, so it's not in her database," Hayase said. "However, she still has billions of gigabytes of unused memory for any responses you want to save."

"I wonder if it has a response to the next comment." Endo looked at Toshiko again and said, "Thank you. Lunch was very good. I enjoyed it."

"You're welcome," Toshiko said. "We always strive to please our clients."

Then Toshiko smiled.

Endo gasped.

"It smiled," he said.

"The new jaw mechanism has a wider range of movement than the L-1's does. In addition, the new artificial skin is more flexible than the old type," Hayase explained. "Now they can simulate a smile, a frown, or other expressions."

However, their eyes remained dull and emotionless, Endo noticed. The eyes had not evolved.

Hayase stood up and told the androids, "Ladies, take the cart back to the kitchen and wash the dishes."

"Yes, of course, ma'am," the androids said in unison.

Their electronic voice and plastic skin reminded Endo that Himeka and Toshiko were machines despite their smiles. Still, the smile lingered in his mind. It both excited and disturbed him.

Hayase's pocket computer buzzed. "Excuse me," she said as she took the telephone call.

"Yes, I'll come downstairs and meet him," she said. "Send two recreational models to entertain him."

*Recreational models*, Endo wondered?

Hayase ended the call, looked at Endo, and shrugged.

"Time passes quickly, doesn't it?" she said. "Unfortunately, I'm very busy today, and it's time for my next meeting. He's a buyer from Germany."

Endo nodded. "I understand."

"It's too bad that I couldn't give you a tour of the production area. Will you visit us again?"

"Yes, of course. I would like to see the factory."

"Good," said Hayase. "I'll arrange a tour during the school year. We should have it on a weekend so you can get it approved as part of your military training."

"I'll see if I can arrange that with Lieutenant Commander Kirino."

Hayase gave an envelope to Endo. It was made of thick, expensive paper and had the bright blue V logo.

"This is a memory card with information about the L-2," Hayase said. "It contains specifications, endurance test results, and videos of the android at work. For your convenience, the card also has government tender documents with information about Victor Robotics already filled in."

Endo opened the envelope. The memory card was attached to a postcard showing an L-2 Kazusa android in the Victor Robotics office uniform. The android was smiling, but again, its eyes looked glazed.

Words under the android's photo read: "My name is Toshiko. Program me to do anything you want."

"Do you have any questions?" Hayase asked.

"No, not now," Endo said. "Thank you for lunch, thank you for your hospitality, and thank you for this information. I'll certainly read it and report it to my superior officers."

"I'll let you go write the report for Professor Kirino," said Hayase. "It was a pleasure to meet you. If you have more questions, please contact me. And let's bring you back for a tour of the android factory."

As Hayase led Endo to the door, the two androids returned.

"Ladies, please say 'bye to Midshipman Endo," Hayase said.

Toshiko and Himeka bowed, smiled, and said, "Thank you for visiting, sir. Please come again."

Endo stared at the androids' smiles.

"Thank you," he said.

******

As he rode the train back to Etajima, Endo looked at the postcard again. If it weren't for its skin and its eyes, the android Toshiko would look human.

Indeed, Dr. Hayase treated her androids as if they were human. She addressed them as "ladies" and gave them names. She dressed them in office uniforms as if they were her human workers.

Endo had treated the Maritime Self-Defense Force's androids as machinery. He gave them numbers, not names. He never called them with honorifics and titles such as "sir" or "mister."

But he had dressed them in naval uniforms. Endo thought nothing about it until Kirino compared it to putting clothes on a vacuum cleaner.

*I could have left the androids in their ugly factory coveralls,* Endo thought. *Instead, I dressed them like myself. Why did I do that?*

Then the answer came to him.

He must have seen some humanity in the androids. His mind told him they were machines. But his heart told him they were people. It was hard to resist. They looked human, after all.

Why did androids have to look human? Why couldn't they look like vacuum cleaners or rice cookers? Why did they have artificial skin instead of a metal shell? Why did their bodies have the human shape? Why did they have two arms and two legs and a neck and a head? Why did they walk upright?

Endo looked across the train and saw a young girl playing with a doll. The girl's mother handed her a small box of doll clothes. The girl carefully slid a red coat off the doll and put a girl's sailor suit on it.

People had been making dolls for thousands of years. And people had been dressing dolls for just as long. Did humans feel compelled to create machines in their own image?

He laughed silently to himself. He and Dr. Hayase were like children playing with dolls.

Endo read the message on the back of the postcard:

*The L-2 android is the highest achievement in android science. It can talk with people, make decisions, know when to ask more questions, and perform complicated tasks. Such are the most amazing signs of their artificial intelligence.*

He disagreed. The most amazing sign of their artificial intelligence was their smile.

It both excited and disturbed him.

# CHAPTER 4

# The Android Society

Back at Etajima, Endo wrote his report about the L-2 androids. He ended with the conclusion:

*The L-2 android probably could perform duties that are risky to human life, for example, explosives disposal, dives in dangerous underwater environments, and extravehicular activity in space. Its capabilities must still be determined by test trials, but no previous robot or android has shown the potential for taking over high-risk duties from humans.*

*The L-2 is expensive and requires much specialized programming, but if it can be programmed for high-risk duties, it can reduce human casualties and their associated medical, insurance, and death benefits costs.*

*Recommendation: Ask Victor Robotics to lend five L-2 androids to the Maritime Self-Defense Force; program them to swim, dive, and deactivate seaborne explosives; and put them through test trials in high-risk duties.*

*If test trials of the L-2's are successful, purchase L-2's for military use.*

After sending the report to Lieutenant Commander Kirino, Endo opened an email from the University of Tokyo. The email described the registration process for the second semester. His summer of military service was ending. A week later, he would be at the university again.

**

Endo went to the robot storeroom to check the androids' batteries. The L-1's stood in a line, like sailors at an inspection.

He opened the backs of their heads, pulled out their recharge cables, and plugged them into electrical outlets in the wall. It would take three hours to fully recharge their batteries.

Endo looked at the androids as they absorbed the electricity. If not for their shiny skin and unblinking eyes, they would look completely human. But with cables running from their heads to the wall, they certainly looked like machines.

Recently, a TV talk show host said that he thought androids were "weird" and "creepy." He had several household robots, but he didn't mind them. Androids were different, though. Their unblinking eyes, shiny skin, and stiff movements bothered him.

Androids didn't bother Endo. He felt great pride in his little squad. They had come to him with only basic programming. Yet in just a few weeks, he had trained them to do many duties, from moving furniture to cooking rice. They worked all over the school, they never complained, and they always obeyed orders.

The more Endo worked with androids, the more they fascinated him, the more he liked them.

But he couldn't forget the L-2 Kazusa's smile. Androids didn't bother him, but that smile did. He didn't know why.

******

As he walked down a hallway, Endo saw a message on the viewscreen:

*SPECIAL FILM SOCIETY SCREENING*
*Movie director Morita Chiko has graciously allowed us to screen his new animated movie* Imperial Space Marines Battalion Musashi *before its release to theaters. This is a rare treat of a first-run movie in our school.*
*This screening is Mr. Morita's token of his admiration for the brave sailors of the Imperial Japanese Navy and the Japan Maritime Self-Defense Force, yesterday, today, and tomorrow.*
*Unfortunately, due to work commitments, Mr. Morita cannot attend the screening, but he hopes you will enjoy the movie in his absence.*
*TONIGHT, 19:00, AUDITORIUM 12, YAMAMOTO HALL.*

Endo hoped the new movie would be better than *The Navy vs. the Night Monsters*. However, he went to see it with low expectations so that he would not be disappointed.

The movie lived down to his expectations. The audience laughed and jeered throughout it, more than they had during the American science fiction movie.

"Is Morita serious?" Endo asked Oshii after the movie ended.

Oshii gave a movie magazine to Endo. The cover showed Morita Chiko and an animated character, an Imperial Space Marine.

"You can keep this," Oshii said. "I read the article. Who knows if he's serious or not? His parents were left-wing university professors, but he talks fondly about the old Imperial military. Of course, he can't have any memories of it."

"Thanks, I'll read it on the train to Tokyo," said Endo. "My uncle is a video distributor, and he says the industry gossip is that *Imperial Space Marines Battalion Musashi* will get nominated for a Japan Academy Award for animation."

"I don't think it'll be for screenwriting, not with dialogue like this," said Oshii.

He repeated lines from the movie: "*The enemy has a thousand more laser cannons than we do, but they are no match for our bushido spirit, the unbending steel of our swords, and our oath to die for the Emperor! May the flowers of victory grow from soil fertilized by our blood! Banzai!*"

"Hah, hah, banzai, banzai!" Endo repeated. "That's just before the scene where the space marines use samurai swords to attack the alien laser artillery."

"Yeah, and they win with only a ninety-nine percent fatality rate!" Oshii said.

As they walked down the hall, they approached a viewscreen. The TV news was on it.

"Look, they're showing the Minister of Agriculture," said Oshii, "and my father's with him!"

The news showed Akahime Kintaro, the Minister of Agriculture, and Oshii's father walking through a wheat field near Kitami, Hokkaido. The sky was blue, and the Sun shone on the golden wheat. A wind blew the wheat gently.

Oshii's father gave a sickle to Akahime. With a loud cry, he slashed through the wheat. Oshii's father and the Minister's entourage applauded. Akahime laughed as he picked up the stalks.

"Mr. Oshii, thank you for showing me your farm," Akahime said. "I'm happy to see our farmers producing such bumper crops."

Oshii's father grinned, bowed, and shook hands with Akahime. The Minister faced the reporters next.

"Japan has made great advances in agriculture in the last forty years. Now we grow enough to feed our nation, and we have a surplus too," he said. "That's important because we need agriculture for more than food. We also need agriculture for national security."

Then Akahime announced, "If the North Korean government will stop its acts of aggression against Japan, Japan will send wheat as humanitarian aid to the North Korean Red Cross. We will help our neighbors in their time of need, but first, they must stop provoking us.

"The wheat must go to the North Korean Red Cross for use by the civilian population. We will not tolerate any of our wheat going to the military...

"I emphasize that our farmers will receive fair prices for their crops..."

Endo said, "The government thinks it can prevent a war by giving food to North Korea. Will it work? We've tried that before, and they still threaten us."

"Wow, my father's on national TV," Oshii remarked. "I've got to call him. See you later."

Oshii rushed back to his quarters. When Endo turned away from the viewscreen, he saw Kirino coming. Endo saluted the Lieutenant Commander.

"Mr. Endo, I hope you have enjoyed your summer with the Maritime Self-Defense Force," Kirino said.

"Yes, I did, sir," Endo replied. "The work experience was invaluable."

"Good, good," said Kirino. "Thank you for the report about the L-2 androids. I called Mr. Katsura today. He agreed to lend us five androids for military test trials. They'll arrive by the end of the week."

"That's excellent news. Thank you for accepting my recommendation," said Endo.

Kirino pointed at the movie magazine. "Unlike Mr. Morita, I don't think our men's fighting spirit is enough to win a war. We're a modern military in a modern world. The nation with the highest fighting spirit starts the war, but the nation with the highest technology ends the war. That's how Greater East Asia War started and ended."

**

The L-2 androids arrived on Endo's final day at Etajima. His last duty was to uncrate them, activate their basic programming, and give them to the supervision of other midshipmen.

Oshii helped him yank the lid off the first crate. Translucent plastic sheeting, like a white shroud, covered the android. Endo tore the plastic away.

"Oh, this must be a mistake," he said.

"Why would they send female androids to the Maritime Self-Defense Force?" Oshii asked.

"I don't know."

Endo had not expected a female model. He recognized its face. It was an L-2 Kazusa.

Endo heard footsteps coming. Lieutenant Commander Kirino stomped into the room.

"Officer on deck!" Endo said. He and Oshii snapped to attention and saluted.

"As you were, gentlemen," Kirino ordered. "Ah, the new androids have arrived."

He walked in front of the androids as if he were inspecting a squad of sailors.

"Sir, these are L-2 Kazusa female androids," Endo said.

"I can see that," said Kirino.

"Our previous androids have been male."

"I ordered female androids this time."

"You ordered them, sir?" said Oshii. "Why do you want females?"

"The females are smaller than the males," Kirino explained. "A small machine is best for crawling or swimming through tight spaces. I want an android that can enter any cave, tunnel, shipwreck, or spaceship, on the ground or in the water."

******

Endo and Oshii waited in the train station's café. Endo was going back to Tokyo, and Oshii was going back to Sapporo.

"Look at the waitress, so to speak," Oshii said.

The waitress was an L-2 Kazusa android wearing a pink uniform. Its badge read "Etajima Station Coffee House." The human waitresses wore the same uniform and badge.

The android swayed its hips as it walked through the café. As it talked to customers, it flipped its hair.

"It's livelier than some real girls," Oshii joked.

"The owner must have programmed it to be flirty and energetic," Endo said. "A lot of time and effort went into that program."

"Ah, too bad the eyes don't have any expression, the voice sounds like a synthesizer, and the skin feels like a doll's," Oshii lamented. "If it weren't for these things, that android would be sexy."

Endo chuckled. "Oshii, you pervert! If androids looked more human, people would find another use for them."

"Maybe some people already have. I saw on the news that *otaku* buy twenty percent of the female L-2's."

"Hah, hah!"

The android set down their coffee and two slices of chocolate cake at their table.

"Please enjoy your meal, gentlemen," the android said in its electronic voice. "If you need anything else, please ask."

Oshii said, "Excuse me, but this is a chocolate cake. I ordered a banana cake."

"Please enjoy your meal, gentlemen. If you need anything else, please ask," the android repeated.

"Uh, I ordered a banana cake," Oshii insisted.

The android smiled at him and sauntered away.

"It's smart enough only to listen to your order and repeat it to the human staff," Endo said. "If the humans give it the wrong cake, it won't notice."

Oshii grunted. "Then I'll have to take the cake back myself."

He took the chocolate cake to the counter. Within minutes, he returned with a banana cake.

"You were right, the café owner gave the wrong cake to the android," Oshii said.

The android passed them again as it carried drinks to another table.

"Our waitress is the tenth L-2 we've seen in the station," Oshii observed.

"They're cleaning the washroom, pushing luggage, sweeping the floor, and waiting at tables," Endo said. "They've been on the market for only a few months. Before long, they'll be everywhere."

An L-1 female, wearing janitor coveralls, carried a garbage bag past them. It shuffled clumsily out of the café.

"Look at the difference between the waitress and the janitor. I bet the L-2's will outnumber the L-1's within a year," Oshii predicted.

"It's the machine version of natural selection, survival of the fittest, Darwinian evolution," said Endo. "When a superior machine appears, people stop buying the inferior machines and start buying the superior one. As the inferior machines get scrapped, people replace them with superior machines. The number of superior machines increases, and eventually, the inferior machines disappear."

"Or they go into museums, like dinosaur bones."

"Exactly, like dinosaur bones."

"I bet you'll see lots of androids at University of Tokyo, robotics center of the world," Oshii said. "As for me, I'm going back to cows and wheat at Hokkaido University."

"The *Yomiuri Shimbun* says your agricultural school is getting a lot of money from the government," Endo said.

"Yes, now that agriculture is considered vital to national security," said Oshii. "However, I'm not sure whether we're supposed to grow food for ourselves or for our enemies."

"Speaking of enemies," began Endo, "I heard a rumor about the Student Reservist Corps at Hokkaido. Is it true that you guys ran a simulated attack against Russia?"

"Oh? Where did you hear this?"

"From another midshipman at the school. He also said the report of the Hokkaido exercise isn't on the student reservist intranet, and he's right. The intranet has reports of exercises at other universities but not the one at Hokkaido."

"Well, that's true, it wasn't posted on the intranet, but it's not a big secret either," Oshii said. "Yes, we did run a simulated invasion of the Northern Territories."

"Why Russia? There's no threat from Russia."

"There was no real reason. Our instructors chose Russia randomly. We could just as easily have attacked China, North Korea, the United States, or even South Africa."

"Why wasn't the report posted on the intranet?" Endo asked.

"I don't know for sure, but it's possible that the instructors are late in writing the report. They're very busy people," Oshii said. "I'll ask when I get back there."

Endo drank some coffee. "Maybe the rumor is exaggerated. Maybe it was just a role-playing game."

"No, it wasn't just a bunch of guys rolling dice and moving miniature figures. It was a professional war game," said Oshii.

He described the exercise. "We used map tables, three-dimensional models of the islands, and computer simulations of the invasion. We simulated everything: aerial bombings, amphibious landings, offensives on the islands, a missile attack on Vladivostok, and Russian counterattacks. We even forecast civilian casualties. Teams of reservists worked in different rooms and buildings to simulate the physical and communications separation of different units during a war. The computer created random weather conditions, casualty rates, and enemy movements. Professors from the National Defense Academy observed us. It went on for two days."

"That's impressive," said Endo. "At Tokyo, we all sat in one room, our instructors were retired officers, and our exercise lasted twelve hours. Our simulation wasn't as large as yours."

Oshii smiled. "They must be training the Hokkaido students to be the elite of the Self-Defense Forces."

"Hah! It's hard to think of any reserve unit being an elite force," Endo said. "I find the choice of Russia rather odd. Are you sure your instructors chose Russia randomly?"

"That's what they told us."

"I may be wrong, but in an exercise as large and elaborate as yours, the choice of enemy is deliberate. Someone in the Self-Defense Forces wanted to see how a war on Russia would play out."

"You think so?" Oshii took a sip of coffee. "Well, there could be a good reason for that. Russia is illegally occupying the Northern Territories."

"Russia has been occupying the Northern Territories for over a hundred and fifty years, but we can't go to war for those islands. It's against Article 9. Simulations about Russia are usually defensive exercises with Russia attacking Japan," Endo said.

He continued. "In any case, it's North Korea, not Russia, that's dangerous now. At other universities, the exercise was an air attack from North Korea."

"Yes, I read the reports," said Oshii. "Why would Hokkaido University be different? I don't know."

"How did the exercise end?"

"We lost. The Russians pushed us back to Hokkaido."

**

As Dr. Hayase had promised, Victor Robotics invited Endo to see the android factory on a Saturday in December. He got the visit approved as part of his reservist training.

This time, he went to the penthouse suite of Katsura Kenji, president and chief executive officer of Victor Robotics. An L-2 Kazusa ushered Endo into the office.

Unlike Dr. Hayase, Katsura decorated his office with relics of pop culture: movie posters, pages from manga, anime toy figures, and model spaceships. Katsura's kitsch contrasted starkly with Hayase's fine art.

Katsura Kenji looked just like he did on TV. He had long, prematurely grey hair. His black suit had a stand-up collar. He wore white running shoes, his trademark fashion *faux pas*.

"Mr. Endo, I'm pleased you could visit us again," he said.

"Thank you for inviting me," said Endo. "Will Dr. Hayase be joining us?"

"Unfortunately, no," Katsura said. "She's performing at the Crown Prince's Command Performance for Youth. She plays the violin."

"Ah, I should've guessed that," Endo said, remembering the paintings of violinists.

Katsura looked at his watch. "I think she's on TV right now," he said. "I enjoy hearing her perform. Perhaps we can spare a few minutes. Do you mind if we watch her first?"

"No, not at all."

"Good. Please sit down."

Katsura told his L-2 Kazusa, "Robot, activate the television."

The android looked at the television, which suddenly turned on, showing a documentary about pandas.

"How did it do that?" Endo asked.

"My android has a TV remote control," Katsura said. "I can add special features. They cost extra for customers, of course."

"Which station do you wish to see?" the android asked.

"NHK 5," Katsura replied.

The android looked at the television again. The channel changed to NHK 5, which was showing the Crown Prince's Command Performance for Youth.

The command performance was a variety show attended by the Imperial Family. Its proceeds went to children's and teenagers' charities. The Crown Prince founded the annual show and based it on the long-running Royal Variety Performance in Britain. Unlike the British show, which was always on an evening, the Japanese show was on a Saturday afternoon so a young audience could watch it.

The show's host, the idol singer Momoi Kazusa, pranced across the stage. Her short silver dress glittered under the lights.

"Next, we have the leading robot designer in Japan, if not the world," Momoi announced. "We've heard about Victor Robotics, and we've heard about her androids. Indeed, Dr. Hayase Midori makes the most beautiful girl androids in the world. That's because they're modeled on me!"

The audience laughed, and Momoi raised her arms in triumph.

"We don't usually hear about Dr. Hayase's other talents, though. She also plays the violin. She's a concert level violinist, and she's performed for the Emperor and visiting heads of state in private recitals.

"Today, she'll perform from *Coppélia,* a ballet by Léo Delibes," she concluded, mispronouncing the French composer's name.

"*Coppélia.* I should have guessed," said Katsura.

As the audience applauded, Dr. Hayase walked onstage, carrying her violin. She wore a blue dress and looked elegant, as always.

She smiled, curtsied to the audience, and played an excerpt from the famous ballet. After she finished, the audience applauded again.

"That was sweet wasn't it?" Katsura said. "She could just as easily be a concert violinist rather than an android designer."

"Beautiful performance," said Endo. "She's a woman of many talents."

Katsura said to his android, "Robot, deactivate the TV."

The L-2 Kazusa turned off the television by looking at it.

"Now back to business," Katsura said. "Mr. Endo, thank you for recommending the L-2 to the Maritime Self-Defense Force Officer Candidate School. I got a message from Professor Kirino today. The L-2's have successfully completed their test trials."

"They have? That's wonderful!" said Endo.

"Yours were the first L-2's to enter military service," said Katsura. "Now the door is open for the L-2. Another hundred androids will join the Maritime, Land, and Air Self-Defense Forces next month."

"That sounds funny," Endo said. "Androids will join the Self-Defense Forces. The way you say it, it sounds like they are humans enlisting in the military."

"It does sound like that, doesn't it?" said Katsura. "What I meant was that the Self-Defense Forces bought another hundred androids."

Katsura stood up. "Shall we visit the android factory?"

"Yes, let's go," said Endo.

"Robot, open the door," Katsura ordered.

The L-2 Kazusa looked at the door, and it swung open.

"Another remote control," Katsura explained.

**

Katsura guided Endo through the android factory. Endo saw arms, legs, heads, torsos, eyes, cables, microchips, batteries, and many other components stacked in bins and trays. The workers wore white coveralls, picked up the parts, and took them to assembly areas.

"We don't use an assembly line. Instead, our teams construct a complete android from start to finish," Katsura said. "Everyone feels like they've created a whole machine, not just attached the same part over and over again. It's good for staff morale and product quality."

A naked male android walked around while its assembly team applauded. Katsura smiled and waved at the workers.

"That's our latest L-2, the Sesshu," Katsura said. "There's demand for male models too. Some people like a mix of females and males in their workplaces."

"Just like human society," said Endo.

"We modeled the L-2 Sesshu on the footballer Suzuki Sesshu, who was voted Japan's Sexiest Man by the readers of *JJ* magazine," Katsura said. "The women like a handsome android."

The workers shooed the L-2 Sesshu back into an assembly area and dressed it in coveralls.

Katsura and Endo walked past a long row of areas where workers assembled the L-2's. Each time a naked android walked out of its area, its assembly team applauded and chased it back to put clothes on it.

"I'm glad our employees have fun," said Katsura. "Now that you've seen the android factory, let's go to the design department next."

Endo saw a bin full of Kazusa heads, each with its eyes already inserted. The eyes had that wide-open look, and Endo felt as if they were all staring at him. The sight unnerved him until he reminded himself that they were just machine parts.

**

In Endo's second summer at Etajima, an alarm summoned all the midshipmen to Yamamoto Hall. Superintendent Akama announced that Marshal Kim Jong Ok, North Korea's Supreme Leader, was dead.

The North Korean generals had called the Supreme Leader to an emergency meeting at military headquarters. They had captured a Japanese spy, they told him. She was a beautiful woman, a swimsuit model trained for espionage. Would the Supreme Leader want to personally interrogate her? Maybe he could convert her to the Juche Ideology? Marshal Kim rushed to the headquarters.

The generals led him into the interrogation cell. Instead of a Japanese spy, he found a court martial of generals. They tied him to a chair and tried him for treason. Then they shot him. The trial and execution had taken only twenty minutes. Excerpts of the trial kept playing on North Korean TV. A video of the execution appeared on the internet.

The military junta killed the rest of the Supreme Leader's family. The Kim Dynasty, the hereditary Communist rulers of North Korea, was finished.

The Japan Self-Defense Forces went on alert. Endo dropped his robotics work and trained to fire coastal artillery at any North Korean ships that would approach Etajima.

Defense officials debated the use of the Reserves. They had created the Reserves to perform support and garrison duties while the regular Self-Defense Forces were fighting. Now the Minister of Defense wanted to send the Reserves against the invaders. The Opposition argued that the Reserves were not trained well enough for combat.

Then the alert ended as suddenly as it had begun. The North Korean junta signed peace treaties with Japan, Russia, and China.

Since the treaties were signed only two weeks after the coup, Opposition members of the Diet asked whether the government had negotiated with the North Korean generals before they killed Kim. The Prime Minister denied any such thing, as did the Presidents of Russia and China.

Air Koryo, North Korea's national airline, began regular flights between Pyongyang and Zurich, Switzerland. A BBC TV reporter secretly shot videos of North Korean generals carrying briefcases to Swiss bullion dealers. A week later, European banks were selling gold bars stamped with the national emblems of Japan, Russia, and China. The Auditor General of Japan reported that the National Treasury had sent three thousand ounces of gold to the Cabinet Intelligence and Research Office. No government official could explain the transfer. Rumors spread that the three powers had bribed the generals to overthrow their Supreme Leader.

Under the treaties, the three powers gave food, money, and industrial advisors to North Korea. The government bought tons of wheat from farmers like Oshii's father.

In exchange for the aid, North Korea destroyed its nuclear weapons, adopted capitalism, opened its economy to foreign investment, and promised a stable military dictatorship.

As fireworks lit up the night sky of Pyongyang, North Korea began its peaceful transition from communism to fascism.

**

Although the Korean Crisis was over, the Minister of Defense announced that the Self-Defense Forces Reserves would continue to expand. Student reservist programs would start in more universities, Reserve units would get more equipment and funding, and more reservists would be recruited. TV commercials encouraged salarymen and secretaries to become part-time soldiers, sailors, and airmen. The Ministry of Defense created various incentives for reservists, such as increased benefits and new medals.

The Opposition denounced the plan as a return to Imperial militarism. The Minister argued that other democracies, like the United States and Britain, have military reserve forces.

Endo stayed in the student reservist program until he graduated from university. When he became a Bachelor of Science in Robotics, he also became an Ensign of the Maritime Self-Defense Force Reserve.

After the university graduation ceremony, the Student Reservist Corps held a reception for the graduates. Some of them wore civilian business suits. Others wore their military uniforms.

Endo's girlfriend, Masako, wore a short red dress and matching bolero jacket, the same clothes she had worn on their first date.

Endo showed his diploma to Masako. She cooed as she read it and touched the university seal.

"It's so beautiful," she said. "Look at the colors, the calligraphy, and the seal."

She hugged and kissed Endo. "Oh, Hideki, I'm so proud of you."

Officers from the three Self-Defense Forces were at the reception too. Endo saw Lieutenant Commander Kirino talking to some Ground Force officers.

Since it was March, Kirino was wearing the navy blue uniform. It was more formal than the summer working uniform of white shirt and pants. Gold stripes encircled his tunic's sleeves, and he wore a tie with his shirt. As always, he wore his three rows of ribbons.

Endo snapped to attention and saluted when Kirino approached him.

"You don't have to salute. You're wearing civilian clothes," said Kirino.

"Sorry, sir. I did it out of habit."

"You can salute me tomorrow at the commissioning ceremony. You'll officially become an ensign then."

Masako said to Endo, "*I* don't have to salute you, do I? Can I wear your hat instead?"

Endo and Kirino laughed.

"Lieutenant Commander, may I introduce my friend Honda Masako to you?" said Endo.

"I'm pleased to meet you, Miss Honda," said Kirino.

Masako curtsied as she shook Kirino's hand. "I'm pleased to meet you too, sir."

"A curtsy?" said Kirino. "How quaint, how charming."

Masako smiled. "I'm studying European history. Their women used to curtsy. They still do when they meet royalty."

"One should treasure such traditions. When do you graduate?"

"Next year."

"A year will pass quickly."

"Oh, I hope so. I've had enough of university. I have a job offer to teach history at the Gakushuin after I graduate," said Masako.

"The Gakushuin? Excellent," said Kirino.

The Gakushuin or Peers School was a school originally founded for educating the children of the nobility and the Imperial Family. Now it taught wealthy commoners as well as princes and princesses.

"One more year, and I'll be in the real world again, as much as another school can be the real world," Masako said.

An L-2 android waiter came, carrying a tray of drinks. Masako grabbed a glass of wine and toasted, "Here's to the real world!"

Kirino and Endo quickly grabbed some wine and cheered "*Kampai!*"

Masako said, "Oh, there's Ryoko. I want to talk to her. I'll leave you two alone to talk about naval matters. Don't worry, I'll be back."

She went across the room to meet her friend. Ryoko was with an officer in an Air Self-Defense Force uniform.

Kirino glanced at the airman. "Mr. Endo, do you know that fellow?"

"Yes, that's Yi Akira, a student reservist. I hear he's a descendant of the Joseon Dynasty," replied Endo.

Kirino looked impressed. "He's royalty?"

"Korean royalty," Endo added. "Maybe I should say former royalty? They don't rule a country anymore."

"He's still royalty. If only our Imperial Family could serve in the Self-Defense Forces," Kirino said wistfully.

Endo chuckled. "Look at him. He can't wait for the commissioning ceremony to wear his uniform."

"That's why I asked if you know him."

"He wants to go career in the Air Self-Defense Force."

"So he's going into full-time service, eh? I'm glad we're keeping at least one of you," said Kirino.

"I'll still be in a Reserve squadron in Tokyo," Endo promised.

"Will you reconsider?" Kirino asked. "You have another chance to join. The Ministry has extended the deadline to transfer from the Reserve to the regular force. We'll reimburse you for one hundred percent of your tuition."

"Thank you, sir, but I prefer to serve in the Reserve," Endo said.

"Ah, yes, get a civilian job with lots of money and be a part-time sailor too. The best of both worlds, I guess," said Kirino.

He drank some more wine. "Some people tell me that I should've done that too. A robotics engineer like me should be able to make twice what I make in the military, they say."

"I'm sure you made the decision that's best for you," Endo said.

"What's good for one person isn't necessarily good for another person," Kirino said. "Sure, I could've worked for a robotics company, and I could've made more money, but I love the military life. I love the order, the discipline, and the pride. I love to see the flag rising up in the morning, to hear the bugle, to know that we defend our nation. If I could choose again, I would still go full-time military. It's a family tradition."

Endo remembered Kirino's office, practically a museum of the Lieutenant Commander's family serving in the navy since the Meiji Era.

Kirino finished drinking his wine and put the glass down. "What's the civilian job you're going to?"

"I'm going to be a software designer at Victor Robotics," said Endo. "Dr. Hayase offered me a job a month ago."

"That's the best android company in the world. I'm happy that you'll be working there."

"Thank you for allowing me to work with androids. The experience got me the job."

"And now you'll be designing androids for the Self-Defense Forces. Ensign, you better make them good or I'll bust you down to seaman!"

**

Endo designed android algorithms at Victor Robotics. It was an exciting time in the android industry. Competitors sold new androids of their own, and Victor Robotics created new programs for the L-1 and L-2. Victor Robotics hired creative, talented people, and Endo enjoyed working with them.

Endo had been at Victor Robotics for a year when his father suffered a heart attack. The senior Mr. Endo recovered, but he didn't feel up to running his restaurants anymore. Since they made more money than his son's job, he was reluctant to sell them to a stranger. He asked his son if he wanted to take over the business. The offer was tempting.

Endo sadly gave his resignation letter with both hands to Dr. Hayase. She read it and put it on her desk.

"I'm sad to see you leave, but I understand the great opportunity that awaits you," she said.

She smiled and continued. "I have eaten in your father's restaurants several times. The food is delicious."

Endo hadn't known that Dr. Hayase had been his father's customer. "Thank you," he said.

"I bear you no ill will, Mr. Endo. Rest assured that you are leaving our company on friendly terms," said Hayase.

"I'm honored to have worked here," said Endo. "I've known this company since my days as a midshipman."

"I know you have," said Hayase. "Thanks to you, there are two hundred L-2's serving in the Self-Defense Forces now. Japan has more military androids than any other country in the world."

Endo nodded. "I'm happy that our androids have performed well for our military and civilian customers. People are using them more and more."

"Yes, my androids can do anything," said Hayase. "Admiral Endo, you know where to come if you need androids."

**

The Endo restaurants included the family's first *ramen-ya* in Akihabara, the American House of Hotdogs in Tokyo Tower and Sunshine City, Heian Shiro in Chiyoda, and Salzburg-Ya in Ikebukuro. Each had its own theme and cuisine. The old *ramen-ya* sold noodles in a modest setting. At American House of Hotdogs, Elvis Presley songs played while people ate hotdogs, hamburgers, and hot turkey sandwiches. Heian Shiro was the posh restaurant that served Japanese cuisine. Salzburg-Ya was decorated like an Austrian castle, and its waitresses wore dirndls and served roast pork, goulash, and apple strudel.

Heian Shiro and Salzburg-Ya had androids. The technology had advanced greatly since Endo's father bought a cooking robot for the *ramen-ya*. Now androids were washing dishes, carrying supplies, and moving furniture.

Very few restaurants used androids as waiters, though.

"I've seen only one restaurant that used an android to wait on customers," said Endo. "It was a café at a train station. It had an L-2 Kazusa wearing a little waitress uniform."

Masako nodded as she drank her wine. She watched the waiters carry food through Heian Shiro. Their red jackets and white gloves marked the restaurant as the place for Tokyo's elite.

Endo and Masako came here for dinner each Friday. Masako liked the food, the Heian Period décor, the *kanji* calligraphy, the paintings of *daimyo,* and the fast and polite staff. Both the cuisine and atmosphere were suited for a teacher of the Gakushuin.

Endo liked dining at Heian Shiro because he was its boss, so dinner was free.

"Did I ever tell you about the time Ryoko and I went to a restaurant that had an android waiter?" Masako said.

"No. What happened?" asked Endo.

"It was back when we were students..."

******

"We went to a restaurant called Yankee Town," Masako said. "It served American food, hamburgers, spaghetti, pizza, clam chowder, mashed potatoes, stuff like that. I liked the Milwaukee-style pizza. Masako liked one of the waiters. She though he was cute.

"The cute waiter wasn't there that day. The manager said the fellow had gone to his sister's wedding. Instead, an android took our order.

"It was the first time I had seen an android interacting with the customers. Androids were usually kept in the kitchen or the back room, out of our sight. It was an L-2, of course, because no L-1 could carry on a conversation. And it was male like the other waiters at Yankee Town.

"I had seen L-2's on TV, but I had never seen one up close before. They were just coming out. I was curious, so I kept looking at it when I ordered my food. That's when I first saw that its eyes always looked straight ahead and never moved or blinked.

"The plastic skin reminded me of a doll I had when I was a child. I reached out and touched its hand. Yes, it felt like a plastic doll's, but it was flexible.

"When it said, 'thank you, ma'am', I laughed. The machine voice sounded ridiculous. I thought the android was funny, like something out of a science fiction movie.

"When I laughed, Ryoko gave me a strange look, as if she didn't understand what was so funny.

"Then the android asked Ryoko for her order. She flinched when it turned to her. She looked down at her menu and didn't look at the android at all. When the android said 'thank you, ma'am', she smiled, but it wasn't a happy smile. It was the smile that she gives when she's nervous.

"She was in a good mood earlier. She had finished her last mid-term exam, and her boyfriend was coming for the weekend. I asked her what was wrong.

"'They're creepy,' she said. 'I don't like androids. They're just creepy.'

"That surprised me. She grew up around robots. She had a small self-guided vacuum cleaner in her apartment. Her parents had sent a robot cart to carry her luggage.

"She said, 'A household robot's not the same. My vacuum cleaner is cute. Androids aren't cute. They look like freaks.'

"During dinner, I looked at the other tables. Most people treated the android like a human, talking naturally to it. Some even addressed it with polite honorifics. Others treated it like a household robot, just giving commands to it. A few people looked nervous or shied away from it. There was a range of reactions.

"Ryoko and I ate dinner quickly and didn't linger in the restaurant. She was so relieved when the cute waiter came back. The android returned to kitchen, and we never saw it in the dining room again."

**

"Well, I guess an android's no substitute for a cute guy," said Endo.

Masako smiled. "Yes, cute guys were Ryoko's big priority."

The waiter brought plates of multicolored sashimi, braised tofu, steamed vegetables, and udon noodles to their table.

"It smells delicious, as always," Masako said. "Which chef made it?"

"Mr. Harimoto with assistance from the L-2 Sesshu," Endo replied.

**

Six years after their wedding, Masako gave birth to their daughter, Ami. The Endos had to choose a shrine for Ami's *hatsumiyamairi*, the first shrine visit.

Endo had resigned his commission from the Maritime Self-Defense Force Reserve, but he joined a naval veterans' society. He wanted to take Ami to Yasukuni Shrine.

"I know several officers whose children had their *hatsumiyamairi* at Yasukuni," he said. "For military men, it's an honor to have one's child blessed there."

"Well, I prefer Meiji Shrine," said Masako. "It's a beautiful shrine, it's prestigious, and it's the shrine of the most important emperor."

"Spoken like a history teacher for aristocrats and princes," Endo remarked. "I have nothing against Meiji Shrine, but as an ex-Self Defense Forces officer, I have some privileges at Yasukuni. The priests will make time in their schedules for us."

"I have some influence at a shrine too," said Masako. "The new priest at Meiji is an alumnus of the Gakushuin. He welcomes Gakushuin teachers and encourages them to bring our students there. He'll make time for us."

They debated the merits of Yasukuni Shrine versus Meiji Shrine. Eventually, they agreed on Yasukuni. It satisfied Endo's pride in the Maritime Self-Defense Force and Masako's desire for a shrine with history.

They didn't know whether it would satisfy Masako's father, a liberal economics professor.

**

The priest wore a red Heian court robe and a tall black headdress. He recited prayers in archaic Japanese, asking for the *kami* to bless and protect Ami. He asked them to help her grow up healthy and happy. As he spoke, he waved a *haraigushi*, the sacred wand. Its zigzag paper streamers rustled in the air.

With her husband, parents, and in-laws, Masako sat on a mat and held Ami in her arms. The priest knelt in front of them and waved the *haraigushi* over the baby's head. Then he waved the wand over her parents' heads.

A *miko* carried a tray of *tamagushi*, small sakaki tree branches attached to zigzag paper streamers. She gave the *tamagushi* to the priest, who gave them to the family. Together, Endo and Masako placed the *tamagushi* on a table in front of the altar. They bowed twice, clapped twice, bowed again, and returned to their places at the mat. Next, Endo's parents offered their *tamagushi* to the *kami*, followed by Masako's parents.

After the ceremony, the Endos went into an office where the priest inscribed Ami's name in a book, formally registering her at the shrine.

The priest gave a round brass amulet to Endo. It bore the cherry blossom emblem of Yasukuni Shrine.

"This *omamori* is for little Ami," the priest said, smiling. "The *kami* enshrined at Yasukuni will protect her. What better blessing can a girl receive than that of two and a half million heroes?"

Endo took the *omamori* and dangled it in front of Ami. The ringing of its small bell did not wake up the girl.

Masako's father, an economics professor at Osaka University, took the *omamori* and looked at it.

"I don't mind your choice of Yasukuni, but I'm not sure what to tell the faculty club," said Professor Honda.

Mrs. Honda poked her husband. "Hush, dear husband. Not today. Save it for the university.

"The Greater East Asia War used up so many men. I'm sure many of them served honorably. It's not only the war criminals who are enshrined here."

Mrs. Honda took Ami from Masako's arms. "Ah, my dear granddaughter, may the *kami* protect you."

As they left the priest's office, Endo saw a male L-2 android sitting in a room. The android attached paper streamers to sakaki branches while a *miko* watched.

"Hurry up," said the *miko*, who looked about sixteen years old. "We have another three babies this afternoon."

The robot said nothing and continued tying the streamers to the branches with hemp string.

"If you're not going to talk to me, at least work quickly," the *miko* complained.

**

Salzburg-Ya had a TV behind the bar. To enhance the restaurant's Austrian theme, Endo turned on the TV if a Germanic opera or ballet was on. Tonight, NHK 8 was showing Mozart's *The Magic Flute.*

The TV popped on to Fuji News Network, not NHK. But he did not change the channel because he saw a familiar face.

Dr. Hayase Midori and the television actress Suzuki Halko were in a kitchen. A female android wore a white chef's costume and mixed ingredients in a bowl. A crowd of people watched the android. Some were reporters. Others were famous chefs and food critics whom Endo recognized from cooking shows.

The words "*Special News Documentary: The Android Baker*" appeared on the screen.

"Coco, what are you making?" Dr. Hayase asked.

"I'm making a Black Forest cake," the android replied.

The reporters gasped and murmured. Coco had replied in a natural, human voice.

Suzuki Halko giggled. "It sounds just like me."

"Can you hear the difference?" Hayase asked. "Coco's voice is not created by a voice synthesizer. Rather, she can mimic a human voice. Her voice is modeled on that of Miss Suzuki."

"What a beautiful voice," a reporter said.

"Thank you," Suzuki Halko and Coco answered in unison. Suzuki laughed, and Coco smiled.

Another reporter asked, "Dr. Hayase, is Suzuki Halko the only person whose voice will be on the L-3's?"

"We have contracts with several famous actors and singers to provide voices," said Hayase. "We will unveil the other L-3 models over the next few months."

The audience murmured again. A British woman, carrying a BBC microphone, asked, "Dr. Hayase, did you tell the android which ingredients to use? Or did the android know by itself?"

"Why don't you ask the chef?" said Hayase. She turned to Coco. "Did I tell you which ingredients to use for the Black Forest cake?"

"No," replied Coco.

"Did you know which ingredients to use?"

"Yes."

"How did you know which ingredients to use?"

"The ingredients are listed in a recipe for a Black Forest cake by Hans Zuber of the Walper Terrace Hotel, Berlin. The recipe is saved in my desserts folder."

The BBC reporter asked, "Coco, what are the ingredients?"

Coco paused for a moment. "The ingredients of what?"

"Of the Black Forest cake."

The android looked up from the mixing bowl. "Two hundred and seventy-five grams of sugar, two eggs, one hundred and forty-grams of flour, fifty grams of unsweetened cocoa powder, half a teaspoon of baking powder, one teaspoon of baking soda, four hundred grams of pitted cherries..."

The guests laughed and applauded. As Coco poured the batter into a cake pan, Dr. Hayase answered more questions about the android.

"The L-3 can process a thousand times more algorithms than the L-2 can," she said. "The L-3's artificial intelligence is much more comprehensive than those of our previous levels. Coco has the accumulated experience and knowledge of twenty-three bakers, including Sir Simon Caruthers, former executive chef of the Royal Family of Great Britain."

An Englishman in a blue suit stepped out from the crowd of guests. He waved at the camera.

"I'm very flattered that I'm one of the chefs whose expertise is in Coco's artificial intelligence database," said Caruthers in English. "The A.I. research was quite extensive. Dr. Hayase and her team interviewed and observed me every day for three months."

The scene changed to a video of Caruthers putting cherries on a tart. Sensors were taped to his hands, arms, and forehead.

The documentary's narrator said, "This is a scene from the development of Coco's artificial intelligence. As Sir Simon Caruthers makes a cherry tart, sensors on his hands, arms, and forehead transmit his every action and movement to supercomputers. This muscle memory will be saved and programmed into Coco."

In the background, computer monitors showed animated graphics of his hands and arms moving. As Caruthers moved, Coco repeated the same actions a few feet away.

The documentary returned to the cooking demonstration. Suzuki Halko went to Coco and looked at the cake batter.

"Miss Suzuki, how do you feel about your android twin?" an NHK reporter asked.

Suzuki smiled. "She's going to be the best chef in all Japan!"

The guests laughed.

"After Coco finishes the cake, each of you will sample it," Hayase said.

The guests nodded in approval. Coco put the cake into the oven. The documentary showed scenes of Coco at work.

The narrator said, "We watched the android put the cake in the oven, and we watched the whole process to ensure that nobody slipped in a ready-made cake. What we got was what the android made. The cake was finished an hour later, and we each received a slice."

The next scene showed Dr. Hayase and Suzuki Halko giving slices of cake to the guests. All looked happy as they ate.

A man in a garish yellow, red, and black costume looked serious as he chewed. He was Iron Chef German, from the latest revival of the cooking competition show.

"It's moist and has a delicate texture. It's very delicious," said Iron Chef German. "It's comparable with what I've tasted in Vienna and Berlin.

"Hmmm, will androids be competing in Kitchen Stadium?" He thumped his fist against the table. "*Achtung!* I look forward to the challenge!"

"Remarkable!" said a Christian priest. A caption on the screen named him as Father Xavier Ito from the Pontifical Institute of Computer Science and Robotics.

"It's performing more than unskilled work like washing dishes or pushing carts," said Father Ito. "Cooking is a skill, an art. It requires more than training. It requires experience and intuition and personal artistry. The android has mastered it."

Coco smiled and bowed to the priest. "Thank you, sir," it said.

"Did it recognize that I complimented its cooking?" Ito said incredulously.

Hayase nodded. "I programmed her to respond to comments from the diners. Coco's capacity to respond to situations is a thousand times higher than the L-2's. Depending on your budget, your L-3 can be programmed as extensively as you wish."

Another familiar face appeared on TV: Lieutenant Commander Kirino! The onscreen caption identified him as the Director of Android Warfare, Joint Staff Office, Japan Self-Defense Forces.

"With extensive programming, the L-2 could carry on a good conversation, but the L-3's capabilities are much better. It can recognize figures of speech if programmed to do so," Kirino observed.

"Figures of speech will be included in its basic Japanese language module," said Hayase. "We're still working on artificial intelligence to comprehend nuances, but I think we'll eventually develop it."

Kirino nodded. "By the way, that cake was delicious. Maybe we could use an L-3 in the ship's galley."

Caruthers gave his empty plate to Coco. The BBC reporter asked him, "Sir Simon, how does the cake taste?"

"It tastes excellent, fit for the King of Great Britain," he said, grinning. "After all, it's really I who made it."

He glanced at Coco. "My mind is in that machine. Incredible."

"There were twenty-two other bakers too," Iron Chef German reminded him in English.

Caruthers laughed. "I'll see you in Kitchen Stadium!"

Suzuki Halko hugged Coco.

"Isn't she wonderful? She's almost human," the actress said.

The camera zoomed in on a close-up of Coco. The android smiled, and Endo saw that its facial movements looked more realistic than the L-2's. Dr. Hayase had surpassed her past advances in articulated jaw and facial mechanisms.

However, with its shiny skin and unmoving eyes, Coco could never pass as a human.

**

Endo wanted to expand Salzburg-Ya's sales by offering to deliver food to customers. He didn't think that Austrian food was popular enough to justify a full-time delivery driver. However, he didn't want to rely on freelance drivers because they weren't always available when he needed them. Always the robotics pioneer, he bought an L-3 Halko and sent it to deliver food in the neighborhood.

Like the waitresses at Salzburg-Ya, the L-3 Halko wore a dirndl with a white blouse, green bodice, white apron, and short red skirt. It smiled to people it met on the street, and it talked with customers. It soon became a local celebrity.

The Salzburg-Ya android appeared on TV and newswebs. One TV report showed the android delivering pastries to an office worker, chatting with her, swiping her money card through a portable reader, and saying good-bye.

People came to Salzburg-Ya to see the android, and business boomed. Endo stopped sending the android out to deliver food. Instead, he re-programmed it to take orders in the dining room. It became the first android waitress in Endo's restaurants.

One night, Endo watched a young couple pose for photos with the android.

"You're the cutest robot I've ever seen," the man said as he shot a photo of his girlfriend and the android.

The android bowed. "Thank you. I appreciate the comments."

"You're such a sweet person," said the girlfriend.

She playfully poked the android in its arm. The android laughed.

"Hey, let's get dessert," said the man.

The woman sat back in her chair. She pointed at the menu and asked, "Which is sweeter? The *linzer torte* or the apple *strudel*?"

"The *linzer torte* is sweeter," said the android.

"In that case, I'll have the apple *strudel*," the woman said.

"And I'll have the *knoedel*," said the man.

Victor Robotics' waiter software impressed Endo. It was extremely intelligent. It let him program the android to know information about each food item and answer questions about them. The L-3 could do much more than listen to orders and repeat them to the chef.

"Very good choices," the android said before going to the kitchen.

Later, after the couple had finished, Endo said good-bye to them as they left.

"By the way, may I ask if you liked being served by the android?" he asked.

The man nodded. "Yes, *she* served us well. If I asked a question about the food, she knew the answer."

"Excellent, thank you."

"She has such a sweet voice. I didn't feel like I was talking to a machine," the woman added.

Masako came from the Gakushuin. After watching the android for the night, she talked to Endo.

"People are treating the android like a human," she observed. "They're talking to it, joking with it. They're more chatty and friendly to it than they are with the human waitresses!"

"It's the human voice, advanced conversation skills, and artificial intelligence," said Endo.

"But it's missing one thing," said Masako.

"Oh? What is it?"

"You're going to laugh at this. How about giving it a name?"

"A name? As if it's human? It's a machine," said Endo.

"Other androids have names, like Coco, the baker. More people will identify with the android if it has a name. Its publicity value will increase," Masako said.

The next morning, Endo named the android "Heidi."

"It's named after a character from a children's book," said Endo.

"*Heidi*, by Johanna Spyri," said Masako.

"Yes, you guessed it."

"In the book, Heidi is Swiss, not Austrian."

"Well, she's from the Austrian part of Switzerland, isn't she?"

******

Endo, Masako, and Ami strolled through the shopping mall before New Year's Day. Androids of all sorts worked there. Some looked like funny animals, others looked like humans, and some looked like cartoon robots.

An android Viking waved a plastic sword in front of a restaurant. Some schoolgirls giggled as they watched the Viking. It had a blond beard, horned helmet, and leather tunic.

The Viking bellowed, "Come to Hashimoto Buffet! Pillage our dessert table!"

"Hah, hah, I didn't know Vikings spoke Japanese," Masako commented.

Outside a computer store, a male android answered a customer's question. "Since your pocket computer is a Fuji XJ52, it requires a service pack upgrade to download videos from North America," it said.

Endo looked at the store's window. "Look, android software for accounting! I can program Heidi to help Kaneko."

"Kaneko will appreciate it. He's always wanted an accounting clerk," said Masako.

In addition to accounting, there was software for many duties, such as French cooking, cleaning washrooms, singing popular songs, guarding buildings, sewing clothes, repairing shoes, and translating languages. Victor Robotics made software for people who didn't have the time or knowledge to program androids by themselves.

As they stood in line to pay for the accounting software, they watched a salaryman in front of them. He was telling his pretty female android which shares he wanted to buy and sell on the Tokyo Stock Exchange.

The android nodded and said, "I'm transmitting your trade orders now, sir."

A moment later, she touched the salaryman's pocket computer. Its monitor lit up.

"That is a message from your broker. She is acknowledging that she has received your trade orders," the android said.

Female androids worked the cash registers. Endo let one swipe his money card and wrap the accounting software in paper.

As they left the store, they saw other female androids walking with security guards, beckoning customers into stores, reciting their restaurants' menus, and modeling clothes.

"Why do most androids look like attractive women?" Masako asked.

"Because most android engineers are men who didn't date much in high school," Endo replied.

"What about Dr. Hayase Midori? She's not a man."

"No, but Katsura Kenji, the President of Victor Robotics, is. So are many of the designers who work for Dr. Hayase. They're men who spent their youth watching anime about beautiful android girls."

"Like you, eh?" said Masako.

Endo laughed. "Unlike them, I found a real doll. I didn't have to make one."

Masako laughed. Then she glanced to the side.

"Oh, here comes an android that doesn't look like a pretty girl," she said.

An android panda walked on its hind legs to them. "Hitoshi Toys has a special sale today! Half price on Christmas toys!" it announced.

Ami jumped and clapped her hands. "Can I go with the panda?"

"Amazing, she's just five years old, and she's not afraid of an automated panda. Not all children are like that. When I was small, big animal costumes scared me," Masako said.

"An entire generation is growing up with robots and androids everywhere," said Endo.

The panda walked back to Hitoshi Toys, greeting humans along its way.

"He's going away!" cried Ami.

"Let's follow him," said Endo.

They went into the toy store. There they met Santa Claus and his elves. Ami jumped and laughed as she played with the androids.

**

But not everyone liked androids. Vandals had been attacking androids since the L-1 appeared, but with the L-3 becoming commonplace, violence on androids rose. In Tokyo, twenty incidents occurred in one year. Yokohama had one very bad year, when thirty-one androids were damaged. In a society that prided itself with having less crime than other countries did, many Japanese worried about the rising vandalism on androids.

In eighty percent of the cases, the vandals blamed androids for taking their jobs.

On an NHK talk show, Masako's father, the economics professor, discussed the effects of androids on the economy.

"The number of jobs is actually increasing. Not only is the android industry itself creating jobs, but spin-off industries are emerging and hiring people," said Professor Honda.

"There are businesses that make artificial intelligence software. There are businesses that maintain and repair androids. There are even android beauticians and hairdressers now. There's even a boom in industries that aren't directly related to androids. For example, sales of clothes, shoes, and jewelry have increased because people want to dress up their androids.

"Yes, some people lose their jobs when a new technology appears. It happened when cars replaced horse carts, and demand for carts and horse whips fell. It also happened when computers became widespread in the twentieth century. In both situations, jobs disappeared, but new ones appeared, and the overall number of jobs increased. Most people can find new jobs in the new economy."

The Minister of Economic Development nodded in agreement. He said, "We are also the world's leading exporter of androids. Androids have improved our balance of trade with other countries. I'm proud of our android industry."

The NHK talk show host mentioned that a second category of people were attacking androids, causing twenty percent of the incidents.

"When questioned by police, these people say that they don't like androids because they think androids are strange and creepy," she said.

The Minister of Economic Development said, "Unfortunately, some people have trouble adjusting to an android society."

# CHAPTER 5

# Yuko

Victor Robotics created two more levels of androids. Level 4 or the L-4 was supposed to have higher artificial intelligence than the L-3. However, due to faulty hard drives made in North Korea, many L-4's lost memory. Victor Robotics recalled and replaced them with L-3's.

Level 5 or L-5 had eyes that moved, blinked, and gave the impression of humanness. Combined with a mouth that could smile and frown, the L-5 mimicked all human emotions. Katsura Kenji called the L-5 "the closest science has come to creating an artificial person."

The L-5 did not sell well, though, and Victor Robotics stopped producing it after a year. As with the L-4, Victor Robotics recalled all the L-5's and replaced them with L-3's. The company focused on producing and selling L-3's again.

**

Endo went to the Yokohama Robot and Android Fair for the first time in years. The number of android companies had doubled since his last time at the fair. Their booths filled the entire Pacifico Yokohama convention center. Hordes of androids walked among the humans.

Victor Robotics, the leading producer of human-like androids, had its L-3's dressed as security guards, waitresses, lab technicians, farmers, and other workers. Shoen Computers, which specialized in amusement park androids, staged a musical show starring its funny animals. Kobayashi-Daimyo Industries unveiled the first *pachinko* machine that could talk about sports, rock music, and movies with its player.

Not all the companies were Japanese. The American company Hyperion showed off the Hyperbot, its competition against the L-3 in North America. The Russian Federal Space Agency brought a prototype cosmonaut android. Neither machine was as advanced as the L-3 despite their creators' reverse engineering of the Japanese android.

As he left the funny animals show, Endo saw Dr. Hayase Midori. He recognized her even though he hadn't seen her in nineteen years. She still looked svelte and elegant, though her hair had gone partly grey.

"Dr. Hayase, Dr. Hayase!" he called to her.

She turned around. At first, she looked puzzled, but then, she recognized him.

"Ensign Endo," she said, smiling.

"I'm only Endo Hideki now. I resigned from the Maritime Self-Defense Force years ago," said Endo.

"Sorry, I didn't know. It's been a long time since I've seen you."

"Yes, many years have passed, but I've seen you in the news from time to time."

"And I've seen you in the news too," Hayase said. "You had one of the most popular android waitresses in the country, Heidi, the one in the Austrian costume. She was quite famous for a while."

Endo chuckled. "That was a long time ago. Heidi still works at Salzburg-Ya in a variety of jobs."

"She's still running? Wonderful! You can tell Victor Robotics made her," Hayase said. "I really must thank you again. First, you made androids popular with the military. Next, you made the L-3 popular with the service industries."

She looked at the snack bar. "Come, will you have a tea with me?"

They went to get tea and cookies and discussed how their lives and careers had gone.

"...and my daughter Ami is twelve years old now," said Endo.

"She must make you very happy," said Hayase.

"Yes, she does," said Endo. "What about yours? I remember reading about her birth in the newspaper."

"Unfortunately, Rei died of cancer shortly after her eighteenth birthday," Hayase said.

"I'm very sorry to hear about that," said Endo. "Please forgive me for asking."

"I don't feel any offense or discomfort. Unlike her birth, her passing was not mentioned in the media. You had no way of knowing," said Hayase.

She drank some tea and changed the subject. "So what brings you to the Yokohama Robot and Android Fair?"

"I've opened a maid café," replied Endo.

"A maid café? Really?"

"Yes. They're popular again, a sort of retro pop culture phenomenon. The *otaku* and other Akihabara types love them. Mine is called the Nikkou Café, and I'm looking for an android to work in its kitchen. I figure an L-3 could do it."

"Let me make you an offer," said Hayase. "Do you want an android for free?"

Endo put down his cup of tea. "Oh? What are you saying?"

"You're looking for an android. I'll give you one. You don't have to pay for her."

"What model is this android? L-3?"

"Better than that," Hayase said. "She's got a new form of artificial intelligence, the world's first advanced learning program. You can train and teach her like you would with a human being. She can also observe people and things and learn on her own."

"I've never heard of anything like this. If it's that advanced, why aren't you selling it?"

"She's a prototype that never went into mass production. Only one was made. Mr. Katsura doesn't want to sell this model. He wants to destroy the prototype. But why waste a perfectly good android? I owe you so much. You can have her for free."

"That's a very generous offer, but you must want something in return," Endo insisted.

Hayase nodded. "I don't want much, but I regret that I must ask you to accept three conditions. I hope they won't be a burden for you."

"What are they?" Endo asked.

"First, don't let Mr. Katsura know that you have her."

"I suppose there's no harm in not telling him. What's the next condition?"

"Don't get a license for her," Hayase said.

"But if I don't, I could get fined by the Android Licensing Authority," Endo warned.

"Don't worry, the licensing inspectors won't notice her," Hayase reassured him.

Endo knew that the licensing inspectors would find a new android. They swept through Akihabara and asked to see the licenses each month. There was no way he could hide an unlicensed android.

Nonetheless, he asked, "What's the third condition?"

"This is the most important condition." Dr. Hayase's face turned serious. "Never tell her who gave her to you. Even if she asks you repeatedly, never tell about me."

"What if she asks?"

"Tell her that you found her wandering on the street after she suffered a disk error. Or tell her another story. Whatever you say, never tell her about me."

Endo thought that these were strange terms, but how could he refuse an android from the world's best android designer?

"Okay, I'll agree to those conditions," he said.

"Do you solemnly swear never to tell the android about me?" Hayase insisted.

"I solemnly swear," said Endo, though he wondered why Hayase wanted these conditions.

**

A week later, an attractive girl came into Nikkou Café. She looked about eighteen years old and wore a white blouse and black skirt.

Another job applicant, thought Endo. This one wore black and white clothes, as if to show that she already liked the colors of the French maid costume.

"Excuse me, are you Mr. Endo?" she asked.

"Yes," Endo replied.

"You are the person I am supposed to meet."

"I am? What is your name?"

The girl bowed deeply. "Yuko. I'm pleased to meet you."

"I'm pleased to meet you too. What is your surname, miss?" Endo asked.

Yuko gave him a blank stare before saying, "It's just Yuko."

"How interesting," said Endo. He didn't want to address Yuko by her given name. It would be impolite to use given names without a close relationship between them.

"Miss Yuko, do you have any previous experience working in a restaurant?" Endo asked.

"No," said Yuko, shaking her head.

"Oh. That's not all important. Many a young lady's first job was as a waitress. We can train you."

"I'm eager to learn."

"That's good." Endo picked up a form and a pen from the bar counter. "Please fill in this job application and return it to me."

Yuko read the application, wrote on it quickly, and handed it back to Endo.

"That was fast," Endo commented. He had expected the girl to go away and return with the application later.

Yuko grinned.

Endo looked at the application in disbelief. The girl had filled in only her name: Yuko.

"You've left most of the form blank," he said. "Don't you have a home address?"

"No," Yuko replied.

"Don't you have a school?"

"No."

"Or any previous job experience?"

"No."

"So why do you want to work here?" Endo demanded.

Yuko smiled. "I was programmed to come here. You are my new master."

"You were *programmed* to come here? Oh, no, this can't be true."

Endo went behind Yuko and said, "May I open the back of your head?"

"Of course, master."

"Excuse me."

He tugged on her hair. The panel lifted up, and he saw a small monitor and a row of data ports.

"You're an android," Endo said.

"Yes, I am."

He plugged his pocket computer into a data port and typed a command. Information about Yuko appeared on both his pocket computer and the monitor in her head:

MODEL: L-6 Prototype

OWNED BY: Endo Hideki

SERIAL NUMBER: deleted

PRODUCTION DATE: deleted

FACTORY: deleted

PATENTED BY: deleted

LICENSE NUMBER: none

Endo disconnected his pocket computer and closed Yuko's head. The android turned around and smiled at him.

"You must be the android sent by —" he said before stopping himself. He remembered his promise to Dr. Hayase.

"Yes, someone sent me to you."

"Who sent you?"

Yuko shook her head. "I don't know. That data was deleted from my memory."

"Do you know who your owner is?"

"You are my owner," Yuko replied.

"Who owned you before me?"

"I have no record of my previous owner."

"Who created you?"

"Data about my creator has been deleted from my memory, though I have data fragments about her."

"May I touch you?" Endo asked.

"Yes, master."

Endo put his hand around Yuko's wrist. Her skin felt soft and warm. Yuko didn't have the cold, plastic feel of an android.

"You skin feels human," Endo said, surprised. "How is that possible?"

"It's a new polymer," Yuko explained.

She twisted her wrist out of Endo's grip and held his hand, palm to palm.

Ami came into the café. She gasped when she saw Endo and Yuko holding hands.

"Father?" she blurted.

Endo pulled his hand away from Yuko's. "Ami, come here! This is incredible!"

"What's so incredible?" Ami asked, looking warily at Yuko.

"This is Yuko. She's an android."

Ami looked skeptical. "Is that so?"

"Yes, it's true," said Yuko.

Endo opened the back of Yuko's head again. Ami stared in shock at the monitor and data ports.

"This is impossible," Ami said. "She looks so real!"

"I want to see what programs and data she has," Endo said. "Let's take her to the office."

**

They sat Yuko in a chair and connected her to a computer. Ami typed some commands, and program names scrolled up on the computer's monitor.

"That's her programs drive," said Ami.

"She has programs for basic functions and household chores, the typical software for a servant," Endo observed. "Now *this* is interesting. She's got programs for social graces and etiquette, music, and playing the violin."

Ami laughed. "Maybe we can get her to perform in the café."

Endo pointed at some program names. "She's got many other programs too, ones I can't identify. What are they?"

Yuko looked at the monitor. "Those are new programs created by my learning program."

"Your learning program creates new programs?" Endo said.

"Yes, master," said Yuko. She turned to stare at the wall again.

"I didn't think artificial intelligence had gotten so advanced," said Ami.

"If it has, nobody knew about it," Endo said. "Let's look at her primary storage."

Ami typed more commands, and the information appeared.

"Look at that! She has one hundred yottabytes of random access memory!" Ami said.

"One hundred yottabytes? Isn't a yottabyte a one with twenty-four zeroes after it?" said Endo incredulously.

Ami nodded. "Ten to the twenty-fourth power. She can run hundreds of programs simultaneously."

"Like a human mind and body," Endo commented.

He looked at Yuko. The android sat silent and still.

"Let's look at her memory drive," Endo suggested.

Ami typed the commands. Names of data files appeared on the monitor.

"That's interesting," Ami said. "She has no complete memory files from yesterday or earlier. Her earliest recorded experiences start today. Is she straight from the factory?"

"I don't think so. Perhaps someone deleted all her memory files from before today," said Endo.

"Let's check for errors and fragmentation on her memory drive," Ami suggested.

She typed another set of commands. The monitor filled with a grid of squares. Most of the squares were blue, but some red ones were scattered through the grid. Information about data fragments appeared on a sidebar.

"She did have old files from before today, and someone deleted them, but it wasn't a clean wipe. Look at all those data fragments. She's got a lot of them," Ami observed.

"Maybe she has a disk error," Endo guessed.

"She has no disk errors at present," Ami said. "It's strange that she has so many data fragments, though. She must have a defragmentation tool. Why hasn't she defragged herself?"

Endo said to Yuko, "Do you have a defragmentation tool?"

Yuko replied, "Yes, I do."

"Have you been using it?"

"Yes, I have. It runs on a daily cycle."

"And yet those old fragments are still there," said Ami.

"Let me try something. Give me the chair," Endo said.

He sat down and typed a series of commands. Names of files appeared.

"What are you doing?" Ami asked.

"I'm searching the data fragments for the old memories, any memory," Endo replied. "Ah, here's the oldest fragment. Let's open it and see what's in it."

A video image appeared on the monitor. It was the face of a woman, but it constantly broke into pixels, and its colors were faded. The words "SOURCE DATA IS CORRUPTED" appeared.

"Who's that?" Ami asked.

Yuko said, "That is my creator."

"Now do you remember who she is?" said Ami.

"No, that data is lost. This incomplete file is my only record of her," said Yuko.

"Father, do you recognize her?" Ami asked Endo.

"No, I don't know who she is," Endo said.

Actually, he recognized the woman despite the poor video quality. She was Dr. Hayase Midori. He didn't like lying to his daughter, but he had made a promise to Hayase.

"There's sound on it," Ami said. "Turn up the volume."

Endo raised the volume, and they heard violin music. When the music ended, the woman clapped and said, "Good girl, good girl."

Ami asked Yuko, "This is a memory from your point of view. Were you playing the violin?"

"Yes, ma'am, I was," Yuko said.

"Can you remember anything else from that day?"

Yuko shook her head.

"You played the music well. What was it?" asked Ami.

"I'm matching it to recordings in my music database," said Yuko. "It's from the ballet *Coppélia*."

They heard the footsteps and chatter of the maids arriving for work.

"I've got to get the café ready for business," said Endo, rising to leave the office. "Do you know how to run a diagnostic on her?"

"Of course, I can, father," said Ami. "I'm not a little baby anymore. I'm twelve years old."

**

The café filled with customers and French maids, and another day began at the Nikkou Café. Business ran routinely until after the lunch period. Then Ami and Yuko came out of the office. Yuko was wearing a French maid uniform.

"She's changed clothes," Endo remarked. "Did you dress her?"

Ami giggled. "Yes, I thought she would look good as a maid. Isn't she cute?"

She said to Yuko, "Greet him as if he were a customer."

Yuko curtsied to Endo. "Welcome home, master. My name is Yuko, and I'm here to serve you."

"You taught her the maid greeting," Endo said.

"She should train to be a maid," said Ami. "She's too pretty to stay hidden in the kitchen."

"I don't know if we should have her in the open. I don't want people to know we have a secret, custom-built android."

"Nobody will know. Look at her. She looks human. She fooled me."

"She looks human, but she doesn't have a lot of life experience."

"And Heidi the L-3 does?"

"Everyone can see that Heidi is an android. Yuko is different. She can pass for human physically. But does she have the life experience to pass for human socially?"

"Maybe not, but what better way for her to gain life experience than from working at the front, with the customers and the maids?" said Ami.

Sora approached them. "Oh, a new girl," she said.

"My name is Yuko. I'm pleased to meet you," said Yuko.

"My name is Sora. Welcome to Nikkou Café. Now, if you'll excuse me, I'll make a parfait for table twelve," said Sora.

She went behind the bar and scooped vanilla ice cream into a parfait cup. Next, she poured chocolate sauce on it.

"Oh, the cherries are over there," Sora said, looking at a jar at Yuko's end of the bar.

Without warning, a customer came to Sora to talk about his bill.

Ami took the parfait cup and passed it to Yuko. "Finish making the parfait while Sora sorts out the customer's bill."

"Yes. What do you want me to do?" said Yuko.

Ami pointed at the jar of cherries. "Put a cherry on it."

Yuko nodded, twisted the lid off the jar, and dumped all the cherries onto the ice cream.

Sora stared in shock as the cherries flowed over the bar. Yuko looked at her, then at Ami, and grinned.

"She's still in training," Endo explained.

"Does that mean she can stay?" said Ami.

******

"...and that's how Yuko came to us," Endo said.

Ishiro nodded. "That's quite a story."

"The past four years have been fascinating," said Endo. "Yuko is always learning something new. She learned how to dance by going to ballet classes with Keiko and Kagami. She learned how to cook by working with the kitchen staff. She learned how to make small talk by talking with the maids and Ami."

"She really gets along well with them," Ishiro said.

"She gets along well with everyone, especially my daughter," said Endo.

He picked up the photo of Ami and Yuko again. "About six months after Yuko arrived, Ami began calling her 'older sister.' She and her 'older sister' go to many places together: to the movies, to the shopping mall, to the park. Now that they're the same height, Yuko even wears Ami's clothes.

"The funny thing is that as Ami grows older, Yuko stays looking eighteen years old. She'll look the same forever. Eventually, Ami will look older than her 'older sister.'"

Ishiro began a lecture. "Androids don't show their age, although it is possible to replace the android's exterior covering with a wrinkled version to simulate the effects of aging skin. Indeed, a professor at Kyoto Institute of Technology wrote a paper that proposed how aging could be simulated on androids. Not only would the skin need to be replaced, but the metal casing of the head would need to be resculpted. Then there's the hair, which should look grey, but that's not a problem because android hair is easily replaced. The voice, however, would need to be changed because a person's voice changes as he ages. However, having proposed procedures where aging could be simulated, the professor acknowledged that most owners would prefer to keep their androids looking young and pretty. There's also a Swedish researcher who thinks —"

Endo interrupted him. "Yes, I know all about that."

"Then you know that the Swedish researcher thinks that the simulated aging of the appearance of androids does not improve human acceptance of androids in the workplace," said Ishiro.

Endo held up his hand. "I heard about that. There's no need to go any further, Mr. Sato."

"However, there are Japanese studies that show results contrary to the Swedish study," Ishiro continued. "At Chiba University —"

"Thank you, but there's no need, Mr. Sato."

"At Chiba University —"

"Stop, Mr. Sato!"

Ishiro became silent. Endo, finally relieved, could talk again.

He said, "I'm not interested in making Yuko look older. I've got at least six more years before people notice that she hasn't aged since she started working here.

"What interests me is what she's learning. She wants to learn about love now. I don't know what's going to happen or what she'll do. I'm also concerned that she's chosen to learn about love with you."

Ishiro fidgeted nervously in his chair.

"You didn't have any physical action with her, did you?" Endo asked.

Ishiro giggled. "Uh, no, sir! I didn't get that far."

"Good. You're not ready for that yet."

# CHAPTER 6

# You're Fired!

Ishiro debated with himself for two weeks. During the day, he went to his job at Ashi Android Scrapyard and thought about Yuko. His mind had nothing else to do while pulling androids apart. At night, he went home to his parents. He knew not to talk about his problem with them. They would not be sympathetic. Instead, he listened to their constant whining about his failed jobs and low wages. He could escape from them briefly in his bedroom, but he could not escape from his thoughts of Yuko. At night, he lay restless in bed.

Yuko was the best girl he had met in years. She was fun, she was pretty, and she was smart. Best of all, she wanted to go on a second date with him.

But Yuko was not a real girl. She was a machine. Ishiro's family would ridicule him mercilessly if they knew he was in love with an android. What type of person preferred a machine over a human? Would they think Yuko was a toy for lonely men? Would they call him a pervert? At the very least, they would call him a loser, as they always did.

He knew the limitations of androids, even advanced ones like Yuko. Yuko said she had enjoyed their date. Had she genuinely enjoyed it or was she programmed to say so? As a single man, he wished her feelings were real. But as a computer science graduate, he knew Yuko was programmed to say what pleased her customers.

He dreamed about Yuko one night. They were in a love hotel. Their room smelled of roses. As he waited in bed, Yuko danced sensuously and stripped off her French maid costume. Now she wore only a lacey black bra, bikini panties, and stay-up stockings. With a seductive look in her eyes, she climbed into bed and caressed him. They embraced, and she gave him a long, wet kiss. Ishiro had never felt so much bliss with a girl before.

"Please take my bra off, master," Yuko pleaded.

He fumbled with the bra strap.

Yuko said, "It unhooks in front."

"*So desu ka*," he said as he shifted to face her again.

He grasped the bra's clasp and leaned to kiss her again. Suddenly, he felt an electrical shock on his lips.

Electricity surged from the bra clasp into his hand. He tried to break free, but Yuko grabbed and hugged him. The pain felt like a thousand hot knives stabbing every part of his naked body.

Yuko's skin melted away to reveal an all-metal casing, shiny like silver. Without a face, the android's eyes and teeth looked grotesque.

The android hugged Ishiro tightly. He could not break free. The electricity kept flowing. As Ishiro squirmed and struggled, his skin sizzled, and he smelled his own flesh burning.

Ishiro woke up suddenly, horrified by his fantasy.

**

He finally made up his mind and returned to Nikkou Café.

Yuko was playing with a hula hoop. The other maids clapped and cheered as she swayed her hips. A customer snapped a photograph of her. Finally, the hula hoop slid down and clattered on the floor.

When Yuko saw Ishiro, she rushed to him, bowed, and curtsied. Her mix of Japanese and European gestures amused Ishiro.

"Welcome home, master," she cooed. "It's been a long time since I've seen you."

"It's nice to see you again, Yuko," said Ishiro.

"Where have you been, master?"

"Uh, I was busy. I was thinking about things."

"You've come to the right place to relax. I'll take care of you."

Yuko led him to a table. "What do you wish to drink?"

"Uh, an iced tea," said Ishiro.

"I'll be back soon," Yuko said before going to the bar.

When she returned with his drink, Ishiro said, "Yuko, there's something I want to ask you."

"Yes, master?"

"I had a good time with you on Christmas, and I hope you had a good time too."

"Yes, I did. Dinner with you was very nice."

"Even though you didn't eat everything?"

"A dinner date is about more than the food. It's also about your companion. That's a line I read in a women's magazine that Sora gave me. Does it sound romantic?" said Yuko.

"It does, I guess," said Ishiro.

"You were saying you wanted to ask me something, master?" said Yuko.

"Uh, blah, ugh, ah, duh!"

Ishiro uttered nonsense syllables. He suddenly couldn't say anything. He had been ready to ask Yuko for another date, but now that the time had come, he lost his nerve. The panic had caught up with him.

Asking a real girl for a date was hard enough. Asking an android was worse.

Yuko leaned over and gazed seductively into his eyes.

"Yes, master?" she said.

Ishiro finally said, "Will — will you go out with me again?"

"Yes! I was hoping you would ask me for another date," said Yuko.

"You were?" Ishiro said, astonished.

"Remember, I have more research to do, like what occurs inside a love hotel."

Mr. Endo was passing the table at that moment. Ishiro saw him grimace at the words "love hotel."

"Have you been thinking about going to a love hotel with me?" Yuko asked.

Ishiro laughed nervously. "Hah, hah, I had a dream about it. It was just a dream, though. It's not as if I seriously planned to go to one. No, don't misunderstand me! It's not that I don't find you attractive, but, uh, ah —"

"You were dreaming about us going to a love hotel?" Yuko looked intrigued. "What did we do in the dream?"

"Uh, uh, nothing. Really nothing."

"What is it? Tell me, tell me," Yuko urged.

"Are you sure you want to go to a love hotel?" said Ishiro.

"Why not? Sora goes to a love hotel with her boyfriend every week. That must be a good place to create love."

"Uh, uh, uh, uh —"

"Sora told me that she and her boyfriend need to use a love hotel. They both live with their parents, so they have no other place to create love."

"Uh, it's just that I've never gone to one with an android," Ishiro muttered.

"Do you think I will be a satisfactory lover, master?" Yuko asked.

"Yes, yes," said Ishiro.

"Then let's go," Yuko insisted.

"Yes, yes."

Ami came to the table and said, "Hey, Mr. Sato! Welcome home."

Yuko turned to Ami. "Mr. Sato and I are going to a love hotel."

Ishiro wanted to flee when he saw Ami's face. The girl smirked at him.

"Still thinking about doing it?" she said to Yuko. "Are you sure?"

"Yes, I'm sure we will do it."

"Even though you're not human?"

"Yes, I'm sure he wants to do it. Mr. Sato dreamed that he went to a love hotel with me," Yuko boasted.

Ami turned to Ishiro. "Did you really dream about her?"

"Uh, yes, I did," he admitted. He did not say that the fantasy had ended in horror.

Ami laughed and spanked Yuko's butt. The android squealed and jumped.

"You're such a seductress!" Ami said. "You're invading his dreams now!"

Yuko giggled. "Thank you, younger sister!"

Ami kissed Yuko on the cheek and looked at Ishiro again. He wished she would stop smirking.

"I think you two will have lots of fun. Enjoy the love hotel," she said, leaving the table.

"Which love hotel shall we visit?" Yuko asked.

"I don't know," said Ishiro. As much as he liked Yuko, he didn't feel right going to a love hotel with her. He hadn't even gone to one with a real girl. Was he ready to go with an android?

Maybe he should suggest a less intense experience for their second date. However, he couldn't think of anything other than dinner.

He asked, "Can we have dinner first? I know you don't eat anything, but you can, uh, watch me eat while we talk. That went well last time, eh?"

Yuko nodded. "Having dinner first is a good idea. It must be a sort of preparation for people to create love. Almost everyone goes to dinner as a first step in a date. Only Mikita starts a date in a love hotel."

"I didn't know that," said Ishiro. He was amazed that Yuko knew so many personal details about the maids.

"When and where shall we have dinner?" Yuko asked.

"How about tomorrow night?" Ishiro suggested. "Are you working then?"

"I don't need to be. Sora said she wants to work an extra shift for the money, so there will be enough maids here tomorrow. I can take the time off. When shall I meet you?"

"Six o'clock again?"

"Fine with me. Where shall I meet you, master?"

Ishiro shrugged. "We've already tried Picolit-Ya, the Italian restaurant. It was good, but do you want to try something different? Do you have other ideas?"

"I don't eat food, so I don't have much experience or knowledge about restaurants. I was hoping you would teach me about them," said Yuko.

"I'm not an expert on them either," Ishiro said. "Other than Nikkou Café, Picolit-Ya is the only restaurant I know."

"Mikita likes her boyfriends to take charge of things and make the decision," Yuko said.

The maids had already taught her how to prod men into doing work, Ishiro realized. He better suggest a restaurant.

"Let's meet at Picolit-Ya again, tomorrow night, six o'clock," he said. An old idea was better than no idea.

"Excellent, master," said Yuko. "I'll ask Sora and Mikita what to bring to the love hotel."

**

As he put on his blazer, Ishiro watched a special news bulletin on TV. The Emir of Purist Arabia had insisted on addressing the Japanese people. Japanese TV networks would broadcast his message tonight, but first, they recapped the crisis between Japan and Purist Arabia.

The Vernacular Wars started as fratricidal wars between Moslems and spread to include other peoples. Four years ago, Wahhabi Purists killed the Saudi Royal Family and took over Saudi Arabia, now called Purist Arabia. In Sudan, the Purists won the civil war. Purist Arabia and Sudan formed the Holy Alliance for Monotheism. The Holy Alliance immediately made demands on the United States, Great Britain, and Jordan. It wanted the United States to outlaw American Moslems from reciting the Koran in English. It wanted Britain to arrest its Ahmadiyya Moslems, whom the Purists had condemned as heretics. It wanted Jordan to overthrow its queen. All three countries rejected the demands, and the Vernacular Wars broke out.

The wars pushed countries to develop energy sources other than oil from the Middle East. NASA built the first satellite system to collect solar energy, convert it to electricity, and transmit it to Earth via microwave beams. The United States sold space-generated electricity to some countries but denied it to others.

At first, Japan bought small amounts of American space-generated electricity without decreasing its oil imports from Purist Arabia. Then Prime Minister Fujiwara announced that Japan would build its own energy satellite system.

The news showed an excerpt from Fujiwara's speech in the Diet last year. The Prime Minister said, "Japan will generate its own energy in space. Our goal will be self-sufficiency, to no longer depend on either the Arabs or the Americans for our energy. Our dependence on foreign oil led us into the Greater East Asia War. Let us not rely on others for our energy anymore. Energy self-sufficiency is the road to peace.

"The government's goal is to redevelop our infrastructure to reduce oil imports by fifty percent within ten years. We want to be completely self-sufficient in energy needs within twenty years. These goals will be major challenges for our industry, technology, and economy, but we Japanese have achieved great changes before. Think of the Meiji Era..."

The news showed Japanese rockets launching into space. Each rocket carried a satellite of the new energy system.

Purist Arabia objected to the energy satellite system, but it did not stop exporting oil to Japan. The Purists needed money for the Vernacular Wars. However, Umar al-Tabuk, Chief Imam and Emir of Purist Arabia, called the Japanese ambassador and demanded to address the Japanese people. If he did not get air time, he would double the price of oil to Japan. Tonight, he would talk to the Japanese, live from Murabba Palace in Riyadh.

The broadcast from Riyadh began. The Emir wore a *thobe* or ankle-length shirt and a *ghutra* or headdress, all in white. Behind him hung the Purist Arabian flag, which looked like the old Saudi flag but in red and gold instead of green and white.

The austere, stern man stared into the camera. As he spoke, an interpreter translated his Arabic into Japanese:

"People of Japan, I send greetings from the people of Purist Arabia. Tonight I speak on an important matter, the survival of nations, yours and mine.

"The United States and several other countries, including yours, are using space-generated electricity. The Americans invented it. As we all know, nothing good comes from America the Great Satan. The Americans invented space-generated electricity to control other nations.

"Ah, but what if you develop your own satellite system to create electricity? Is that not freedom from the Americans? That is what your government tells you, but do not be deceived. It is not freedom. The more you adopt American ideas, the more you become like Americans, and the easier it becomes for them to control you. Their hedonism, pornography, immorality, and selfishness will seep into your culture. Why are you imitating the barbarians who dropped two nuclear bombs on your peaceful cities?

"I do not accuse the Japanese people of promoting American ideas. Instead, it is your government's fault. First your government bought space-generated electricity from the Americans. Now your government wants to create its own electricity in space. Can you not see that Prime Minister Fujiwara is a slave of America, always doing what the Great

Satan demands? Reject American ideas and those who adopt them. Reject Fujiwara.

"There is another reason to reject space-generated electricity. It reduces the need for oil, and thus, reduces the income of the Holy Alliance for Monotheism. The Holy Alliance is the only force that can fight against imperialist America. However, we need money to continue fighting."

The Emir smiled. "Our *jihad* is an ethical war fought on behalf of all peace-loving peoples. That is why many countries, including Somalia, Indonesia, Pakistan, and Venezuela, are allies of the Holy Alliance. Do not think we are fighting to defend only ourselves. We also fight on behalf of all victims of American aggression. We fight to avenge the destruction of Hiroshima and Nagasaki. Yes, my friends, we fight for you too.

"Finally, there is a third reason to reject space-generated electricity," said al-Tabuk. His face turned stern again.

"Oil is a gift from God to Islamic countries. It is the major source of income for several Moslem states, including Purist Arabia. If worldwide oil consumption falls, many people will become poor. Many will die of starvation. The survivors will live in utter poverty, vulnerable to the Americans and Zionists.

"After careful consideration of the facts, the Supreme Court of Purist Arabia has issued a *fatwa* declaring that an energy method is immoral and racist if it reduces the consumption of oil. If you adopt space-generated electricity, you will be committing genocide against Moslems."

Al-Tabuk's voice grew louder. "Stop obeying the Americans! Avenge the destruction of Hiroshima and Nagasaki! Overthrow Fujiwara and reject space-generated electricity!

"People of Japan, heed my advice, for if you don't, your immoral actions will condemn you, and God will punish you without mercy! God is great!"

The message abruptly ended with Japanese words written in white on a green background:

AVENGE THE DESTRUCTION OF HIROSHIMA AND NAGASAKI!
REJECT SPACE-GENERATED ELECTRICITY!
OVERTHROW FUJIWARA, THE SLAVE OF AMERICA!

The news switched to a group of Japanese politicians and professors in an NHK studio. They all looked stunned.

Prime Minister Fujiwara spoke first. "I wish to reassure the international community that Japan does not want revenge for Hiroshima and Nagasaki. That war occurred almost two hundred years ago. Japan always looks to the future and enjoys a long and peaceful friendship with the United States and other countries."

"For the Purists, history is never in the past. They're always angry about a historical insult," said a woman off-screen.

The TV camera turned to the woman. Ishiro recognized her as Masako, Mr. Endo's wife. The caption said she was a history teacher at the Gakushuin, the elite school for the nobility.

Masako continued. "The Purist Islamic ideology is based on avenging historical insults from unbelievers. They view human society as split between believers and unbelievers with no compromise possible between the two.

"Japan used to have good relations with both the Western countries and the Moslem states. Now the Purists are forcing us to take sides."

"What about the idea that space-generated electricity is immoral and racist?" a reporter asked.

The camera shifted to Professor Honda of Osaka University. Ishiro had never met him, but Ami had mentioned that the economics professor was her grandfather, Masako's father. How odd it was to have a father and daughter on the same panel.

"The real issue isn't morality or racism. The real issue is income," said Honda. "Purist Arabia has no major industry other than oil. If Purist Arabia can't sell oil, it has nothing the world wants. The Saudis and Purists have not followed the lead of other Arabs. When alternative energy sources became feasible, other Arab countries diversified their economies. They knew they couldn't depend on one industry forever. For some reason, the Saudis and Purists couldn't see the future coming."

"Maybe the Purists intend to bully the world to buy their oil forever," the reporter suggested. Several panelists nodded.

Kotohito Kuni, the Minister of Defense, said, "Purist Arabia is expanding its military to intimidate other countries. The Saudi Arabian navy had ten cruisers. Now the Purist Arabian navy has three aircraft carriers, fifteen cruisers, twenty destroyers, and twenty frigates."

"Do you think Purist Arabia will attack us?" the reporter asked.

"Purist Arabia is threatening us," said Kotohito. "I'm glad that we've intensified our own re-arming. We might need every bit of military strength."

Professor Honda shook his head while his daughter nodded hers.

"No, I disagree. Purist Arabia will not attack Japan," Honda insisted. "We can't convert the entire country to space-generated electricity overnight. We'll still be using oil for decades. In the meantime, Purist Arabia needs our money. Purist Arabia will not attack us while we still buy its oil."

Masako looked at her father. "Sorry, but I respectfully have to disagree with you. The English have a saying about the dog that bites the hand that feeds it. Historically, the Purists have attacked the people who buy from them. In the twenty-first century, Saudi Arabia and the United State were major trading partners, yet the Saudis funded terrorists who attacked Americans. The most notorious Purist was Osama bin Laden, whose family became wealthy by trading with the Americans —"

Ishiro reluctantly switched off the television. He wanted to continue watching the crisis, but he had a date with Yuko.

**

Ishiro arrived at Picolit-Ya and looked around. He didn't see Yuko. Instead, he saw Endo sitting by himself at a table. Endo stood up and waved at him.

A gnawing feeling grew in Ishiro's stomach. He felt anxious and fearful. Why was Yuko's owner here?

"Mr. Endo, what a pleasant surprise to see you here," he said. It was a partial lie. He felt surprised, but he did not expect anything pleasant.

"I hope you'll join me," said Endo. "Come, sit down."

Ishiro sat down and looked warily at Endo. The former naval officer looked calm, even friendly. Nothing in his face, his posture, his gestures, or his words showed anger.

Ishiro's experience with Yuko had taught him that looks could be deceiving. Endo's calmness unnerved Ishiro more than open hostility would.

The waiter came and asked, "May I get you some drinks, gentlemen?"

"Mr. Sato, please let me be your host tonight," said Endo. "Order anything you want."

"I'll have a cola," Ishiro mumbled.

"The Suntory malt," Endo ordered.

The waiter went to the bar, leaving the two men alone. Ishiro waited for trouble to start.

"You must be surprised to see me here. Were you expecting Yuko?" said Endo.

"Yes, I was expecting her," Ishiro said bitterly. He was annoyed that Endo asked the question when he already knew the answer. "How did you know?"

"Yuko told me. She asked for the evening off. This time, I asked who she was seeing."

"And she told you."

"Don't blame her for her absence. I ordered her to stay home. Yuko is an android, so she's programmed to obey her owner. Real girls aren't so easy to command, do you agree?"

"Uh, yes, I agree."

"Still, that shouldn't stop you from seeking one."

Ishiro felt hot with embarrassment.

The waiter returned with their drinks and said, "Gentlemen, are you ready to order your meals?"

"We're still deciding," said Endo. "Give us a few minutes."

After the waiter left, Endo drank some of his beer and said, "That felt good."

Ishiro did not touch his cola.

Endo said, "I should have foreseen that a man would want to court Yuko someday and she would agree to go out with him. I should have known that it was inevitable with her. I'm sorry that you had to be the first man."

"I — I do not regret my date with her, sir," Ishiro said.

"No, you don't regret the first date, but you'll regret the second date with her," Endo warned. "I apologize for Yuko's humanness and any problems that she may have caused you. She can fool anyone into thinking that she's human, and I can see how a man can become attracted to her. But despite how she looks and acts, Yuko is not human. It's not right to treat her as such. It's wrong to go on dates with her."

Ishiro felt his heart pump faster. Mr. Endo had challenged him. He could not surrender! He had to argue and defend himself.

"But she has extremely advanced artificial intelligence," Ishiro protested.

"It's *artificial* intelligence," Endo said. "It's not real intelligence."

"So what is intelligence? Is it any different if it gets stored in a hard drive instead of a brain? And she's got a learning program. That's something that makes her almost human."

"Being *almost* human isn't the same as being human. She's still not human."

"She certainly acts like one. You have to agree on that," Ishiro retorted.

"It's all computer programming," Endo said. "Even what she learns on her own is turned into programs, routines, and algorithms. She can act independently as far as her artificial intelligence will allow, but she's only mimicking human behavior."

Ishiro glanced at the other people in the restaurant. "What about them? How do humans learn to do things? How do humans learn how to behave? They watch other people, and they imitate them, and people tell them what to do and how to do it, and they get conditioned to know what's good and bad behavior. Every human learns by observing and mimicking other people. That's what Yuko does. That's how her learning program works. She's just like a human."

Endo nodded. "I see we both took psychology courses in university, so I think I know what you're saying. You're saying that Yuko undergoes the same learning processes that humans have."

"Yes, that's right!" Ishiro said.

"Does that make her human?"

"If it doesn't, what else can?"

"A human being is made of more than intelligence," said Endo. "A human also has emotions or feelings."

"Ah, but Yuko shows those too," Ishiro pointed out. "Didn't you say that watching Yuko develop is like watching another daughter grow up?"

Endo smiled weakly. A wistful look appeared in his eyes.

"Ah, yes, she is like another daughter to me. I confess that I too have fallen under her spell.

"But as much as I like her, I always remember that she's a machine. Machines can think like us, but they can never *feel* like us. When Ami feels happy or sad or angry, I know that her feelings are real. When Yuko smiles or frowns, I doubt that she really feels anything. She's mimicking human behavior because her artificial intelligence tells her it's the appropriate response to the situation. Yes, she's like a daughter, but she's not a real girl."

Endo took a sip of his beer and looked pensive.

"But if she has no feelings, why are you trying to protect her?" Ishiro asked.

Endo shook his head. "Mr. Sato, I'm not trying to protect Yuko. I'm trying to protect *you*. Your feelings are the ones at risk. If you pretend that Yuko is a real girl, you'll love her, and she'll act as if she loves you, but she'll only be imitating other girls. She has no emotions and will never return your love in a meaningful way. When you finally realize that you've been playing with a machine, you'll regret the time that you've wasted with her. Can you deal with such disappointment?"

"Maybe I won't be disappointed. Who can predict the future? Who can predict how I will feel?"

"You studied computer science in university. You know what androids really are. Don't tell me you haven't thought about the problems you would have with Yuko. You must have thought about them."

"Yes," Ishiro admitted, remembering his own doubts about Yuko.

Endo asked, "After you found out that she's an android, did you doubt whether you should continue dating her?"

"I suppose I did," Ishiro mumbled.

"I know you did," said Endo. "Also think about this: Yuko can never have children. You might not want children now, but you'll change your mind when you get older. She has the anatomy of a woman, but it's an imitation. She will never reproduce."

"*So desu ka*," said Ishiro.

"Mr. Sato, my staff and I think that you're a fine gentlemen. The maids are grateful that you appreciate and respect them," said Endo. "Please do not think that I dislike you. But I feel that I should advise you against courting Yuko. You would be much better off seeking a human girl."

Ishiro nodded. "Mr. Endo, what you have said is sensible."

Endo smiled. "I'm sorry to have bothered you."

"No, everything is fine."

The waiter returned and asked, "Are you ready to order, gentlemen?"

Endo looked at Ishiro. "Mr. Sato, please have dinner with me. I would like us to remain friends."

"I hope you forgive me if I don't feel hungry tonight," said Ishiro. "Perhaps we can have dinner another time."

Endo nodded. "I'm not in the least offended. Yes, we must have dinner another time. Will I see you again?"

"Yes, you will. I'll see you at the café, at the very least," said Ishiro before he stood up and bowed.

He left without drinking any of his cola.

**

In the morning, as usual, Ishiro went to his job. It would be just another boring day at Ashi Android Scrapyard, he thought.

"Hey, Sato, look what I just bought!" yelled the owner, Ashi Yasuo.

An L-2 Kazusa walked into the room. Its plastic skin had lost its shine, so now it looked dull. Its hair was frayed and sticking out in places. However, it still moved smoothly.

It wore a pink waitress uniform, wrinkled as if it hadn't been ironed in years. Its badge read "Etajima Station Coffee House."

Ashi patted the android's shoulder. "A good buy at five hundred thousand yen, don't you think? It comes from a coffee house at Etajima Train Station. Its owner finally upgraded to an L-3."

"I'm surprised it's still working," said Ishiro.

Ashi opened the android's head and pointed at the display. "Wow, it's twenty-five years old. Its owner took very good care of it."

The L-2 looked at Ishiro, smiled, and said, "Please enjoy your meal, sir. If you need anything else, please ask."

"It needs to be reprogrammed, of course," said Ashi.

"You want to reprogram it, not scavenge it?"

"This one's still working. It's too good to tear apart for scrap. We can use it for labor. Besides, it's a conversation starter. When was the last time you heard an android talk with an electronic voice?"

Ishiro stared at the android. It looked like a life-size doll worn out from excessive play.

**

Ashi programmed the L-2 Kazusa to sort android parts into piles. He kept the L-2 in its waitress uniform because he didn't want to buy new clothes.

Ishiro was glad that the android continued to wear its old clothes. He liked the uniform's tightness, which hugged the android's curves. He liked its low-cut neckline, which revealed the android's deep cleavage. He liked its short skirt, which showed off the android's attractive legs.

Ishiro stared at the android when it bent over at the waist to pick up some scrap cables. It had a cute, round rump. Victor Robotics designed the most attractive androids.

Ishiro couldn't control his hunger any longer.

"Come here, robot," he called to the android.

The L-2 Kazusa put down the cables, stood up, and strutted to him. It stared at him with its empty eyes.

Ishiro put his arms around the L-2 and kissed its lips. They felt like cold, hard plastic. The android stayed still and did not move.

"Open your mouth a little," he whispered.

The android obeyed, and Ishiro pushed his tongue into its mouth. He felt for the android's tongue, which served no real purpose except to make the android seem more human.

The android's tongue tasted like dry rubber. Androids did not eat, and their voices came from hidden micro-speakers, so they had no saliva in their mouths.

Kissing the L-2 was like licking a rubber glove. Though he hated the taste, Ishiro kept probing the android's mouth with his tongue.

"Pervert! Pervert!"

He pulled himself away from the android and turned around. Mr. Ashi was frowning at him.

"What are you doing?" Ashi cried. "Do you think this behavior is acceptable in my shop?"

"Please, Mr. Ashi, I can explain," Endo pleaded. "You see, I was just testing if it could respond to human interaction. Uh, ah, its programming —"

Ashi growled, "You weren't testing its programming. You were satisfying your own urges."

Ishiro shivered as Ashi approached him. The boss scowled.

"This equipment isn't here for your pleasure," Ashi continued. "You've misused and abused company equipment."

"Please, sir, I apologize!"

"I don't want to hear your whining! You're fired! Get out of here immediately!"

Suppressing a sob, Ishiro ran out of the room.

**

Ishiro stared at his dinner as it turned cold. He had no appetite.

"It's not often you don't eat," his mother said. "Usually, you eat everything in sight even though you do the least work."

His father said, "So you lost another job."

"I don't know how you can lose a part-time job with minimum wage, no benefits, and no chance for promotion," his mother said. "It's not as if there were many other people competing for your job, were there?"

Ishiro remained silent.

"Hey, son, your mother asked you a question!" his father scolded. "Answer it."

Ishiro's mother repeated, "It's not as if there were many other people competing for your job, were there?"

"No, mother, there were not many other people competing for my job," Ishiro said.

"I think there was *nobody* else who wanted your job," said his father.

His mother picked up Ishiro's plate of uneaten food. "Look at you, wasting this good food!" She sighed loudly and shook her head.

Ishiro fled into the living room. Although he could still hear his parents grumble about him, at least he wouldn't have to look at them.

His father was the chief accountant of Dynamo, a large department store in the Ginza. On the wall was a golden plaque, the Dynamo Employee Service Award. The company president had given it to the senior Mr. Sato to recognize his excellent management of the accounting department.

His father had brought the plaque home to show to his family. At the time, Ishiro felt very proud of his father. Now he wished his father would hang the plaque in his office instead. Shouldn't it been seen by his employees, not by his family?

Other family mementos decorated the living room. A display case held photos in shiny silver frames. Some were photos of his younger brother, his wife, and their son and daughter. They were smiling, as they should be. Ishiro's brother was a rising news writer for Fuji News Network. His business card was also framed in silver.

It wasn't his brother's fault that the card was on display at home rather than in a client's pocket. When their mother had asked for a card, his brother could not refuse her. Indeed, he was happy to oblige.

A silver thousand-yen coin also sat in the display case. His mother, a sculptor, had designed the coin to commemorate the start of the Emperor's reign. The design, showing the chrysanthemum above the Imperial Palace, was voted "Coin of the Year" by the American Numismatic Association. His mother's work was famous around the world.

Ishiro retreated to his bedroom and shut the door, sealing off his parents' voices. Now temporarily safe, he shuffled through a pile of manga and anime DVD's, looking for something to pass the time.

A DVD box fell on the floor. It was entitled *For the Glory of the Emperor*. A handwritten message on it read:

"Stop loitering in Akihabara! Do something useful with your life, boy! Banzai! General Morita Chiko."

It was the DVD from General Morita. With nothing better to do, Ishiro played it on his computer.

Old newsreel footage showed Japanese soldiers invading Manchuria; planes bombing Pearl Harbor; and ships firing on the enemy at sea. As military marches played, General Morita's voice praised the old Imperial Army and Navy.

"Only military rule can restore the glory of the Emperor," Morita announced.

The video switched from old newsreels to new animation. Characters from *Time Warp at Midway*, *Nuke the Yanks*, and *Imperial Space Marines Battalion Musashi* praised the re-arming of Japan.

"Banzai! Banzai! Banzai!" they cheered.

A succession of right-wing militarists appeared, each urging the Japanese people to restore military rule and worship the Emperor as a living *kami* again. The video ended with the national flag fluttering to the tune of "Kimigayo."

Ishiro got off his chair and stood at attention.

**

"You want to join the Navy?" said Endo.

Ishiro didn't know why Endo looked so surprised. What was wrong with joining the Navy?

"Yes, I want to join the Navy, sir," Ishiro announced. He stood up straight. "I want to be an officer, like you were."

"Regular Navy or Naval Reserve?"

"Regular Navy."

"Full-time service for a minimum of five years," said Endo. "Are you sure you want to do this?"

"Yes, I am. Why should I not?"

"Today's Navy is different from the old Maritime Self-Defense Force," said Endo. "The government might change the Constitution. You might wind up at war."

"But you had the Korean Crisis," Ishiro reminded him. "Weren't you preparing to fight then?"

"Yes, I served during the Korean Crisis, but we were going to stay on the defensive if North Korea attacked. We were not supposed to go on the offensive or invade Korea. The mood of the government is different now. The re-arming has intensified greatly in the past four years. It's no secret that the military is preparing for war on Purist Arabia."

"Like you, I will fight if necessary," said Ishiro.

"Other things have changed since my day," Endo said. "The Navy has brought back physical punishment. It's like the Imperial Navy again. Do you think you can handle getting flogged with a stick?"

Ishiro took a deep breath. "Yes, I can. It makes the sailors tougher."

"That's easy to say if you're holding the stick, not receiving it. As a new recruit, you won't be holding the stick," said Endo.

"I'm sure I won't be punished," said Ishiro. "I never received any detentions or demerits from elementary school to high school. Every teacher said I was a model pupil. I was never once punished for bad behavior. Indeed, my grade ten teacher said that if all students behaved as well as I did, she wouldn't be so eager to retire. In grade eleven, my chemistry teacher said —"

"I get the idea," said Endo, cutting Ishiro off. "But it's not just the physical punishment. There's also the physical education: sports, martial arts, wilderness training, combat training, gym training. That's just to start. I bet the physical training will be tougher than anything you've had in school. Were you the athletic type? Did you do well in phys-ed?"

"Uh, actually, I asked for and received an exemption from phys-ed in middle and high schools," Ishiro admitted, "but I'm not disabled or ill. I'm sure I can pass the physical and undergo the training."

"There are courses for officers, on military subjects such as history, battle planning, engineering, math, science. The list goes on. I'm sure you were good in school, but can you handle the workload?"

"I can. I always got high marks in school. I got awards in grade nine chemistry, grade ten computer science, grade ten math, and grade eleven physics. I also got my I.Q. tested, and unlike the majority of students at my high school, I tested so high that I was recommended for —"

"I'm sure you're a smart person," said Endo, interrupting Ishiro again. "But the Navy isn't like high school or university. You can study and pass exams, but can you follow the discipline? Can you obey orders and be on time all the time? Don't expect to be the one barking orders. You'll be receiving them."

"At every job I've had, I obeyed one boss or another," said Ishiro.

"But in the Navy, if you annoy your boss, he'll hit you with a stick, try you by court martial, or give you a dishonorable discharge," Endo warned. "You just can't quit as if nothing happened, and he just can't fire you and let you go."

"I don't know what you're implying, but I'm sure the Navy will want me," Ishiro said defiantly.

"Again I ask, are you really sure you can handle the Navy?" Endo said.

"Yes, sir," said Ishiro.

"But why, Mr. Sato? Why join the Navy?"

"Are you saying the Army and Air Force are better?"

"Of course not!" Endo blurted. "What I'm asking is why do you want to join the military?"

"I need to do something worthwhile with my life," said Ishiro. "I don't want to be stuck in dead-end jobs that go nowhere. I need to do something important. Defending our country seems like an honorable profession. You, as a former naval officer, agree, don't you?"

Endo nodded. "I cannot disagree about that. The Navy is an honorable profession."

"Do you regret serving in the Maritime Self-Defense Force?" asked Ishiro.

"No, I don't regret it at all," Endo said.

"Then why don't you understand why I want to join the Navy?" said Ishiro.

"I have nothing against the Navy or any branch of the military. Indeed, I'm proud of my time in the Maritime Self-Defense Force," said Endo. "It's just that I'm wondering if it's right for you. It's physically and mentally tough. It's highly organized and disciplined. Can you handle all that?"

Ishiro snapped to attention. "Of course I can, sir!"

Endo nodded. "Very well, ensign. When will you be going?"

"I go to Etajima two days from now."

"Two days from now? That soon? They're taking new midshipmen in January?"

"Yes, they are. New classes of midshipmen begin all year round."

"Incredible," said Endo. "In my day, the new classes started in the summer and the fall. Nobody started officer training in the winter."

"The Navy wants more officers," said Ishiro.

Endo nodded. "Our military forces are growing rapidly with all the war threats."

He saluted Ishiro, who promptly returned the salute. Endo smiled weakly.

"Good luck in the Navy, Mr. Sato. Please visit us when you're on leave. If you need to talk to an old sailor, just call me," he said.

"Thank you very much, Mr. Endo. I'll be sure to contact you."

"I hope you find the Navy to be a rewarding experience. I'm not talking about your pay. I'm talking about the rewards of pride and self-satisfaction and *esprit de corps*. That's what I got out of the Maritime Self-Defense Force Reserve."

"Again, many thanks, Mr. Endo. I will not disappoint you."

Endo bowed to Ishiro, deeper than ever before. The sign of respect surprised him.

"Now please excuse me, I want to check on the kitchen," said Endo.

Endo left Ishiro by himself at the bar. He was not alone for long. Yuko and Ami came with empty glasses. The android maid squealed when she saw Ishiro.

"Welcome home, master!" she said. "Have you been well?"

"Yes, I have, Yuko," said Ishiro. "Ah, I have something to tell you."

"Yes, master?"

"I'm going to join the Navy."

"Will you be going away?" asked Yuko.

"Yes, but I'll come back and visit from time to time," said Ishiro.

Ami laughed. "When you visit us, wear your sailor uniform. I like the sailor uniform."

She punched Yuko in the arm. "And I think Yuko will look cute wearing your sailor hat, so bring that too!"

"Give me your pocket computer," Yuko told Ishiro.

"Sure," said Ishiro. He didn't know why she wanted his pocket computer, but he gave it to her.

Yuko typed words into it.

"What are you doing?" asked Endo.

"I'm giving you my email address and telephone number," said Yuko.

"I installed an email system and telephone in her," Ami explained. "If you send email or voice messages to her, they'll go to her communications drive, literally into her head."

"I can phone and send messages to her?" said Ishiro.

"Oh, yes, I'm sure she'll want to talk and exchange messages with you," said Ami.

Yuko handed the pocket computer back to Ishiro. "These are my email address and telephone number. Please keep in touch, master."

"Thank you, Yuko," said Ishiro. He felt mystified.

Did Ami program Yuko to give him her telephone number and email address? Or did Yuko feel a real need to stay in contact with him?

**

Ishiro had correctly predicted his parents' reaction.

"You in the Navy?" said his father. "Is this a joke?"

"It's no joke," Ishiro said.

His father sighed. "You could have had a good career in banking or business or robotics, but you lost each job you had. If you weren't fired, you quit. If you're going to make an effort now, why not get a civilian job?"

"There's nothing wrong with the Navy. It's an honorable profession."

"Most military jobs are underpaid compared to civilian jobs. The Navy will be a tough job for low pay. Is that a logical choice for someone with a good education?"

"I have a university degree, so I'm eligible for officer training," said Ishiro. "I can go into a specialized area like information technology, robotics, or electronic warfare. No civilian company will promote me to manager in less than five years, but I can be an officer after a year in the Officer Candidate School. My pay as an officer will be comparable to that of a bank supervisor."

His mother joined the debate. "The recruitment ads say military people are supposed to be brave, strong, smart, organized, and disciplined. They want people who like teamwork. They want people who keep trying and don't quit. Are you really sure you'll like the Navy?"

Ishiro stayed silent. He didn't like what his mother was implying, but he couldn't think of a sarcastic comeback.

Finally, he simply said, "I don't know why you object."

"Are you so stupid that you can't understand us?" said his father. "Do you really think you can succeed in the military?"

"You can't keep a minimum-wage job, but you think you can be an admiral?" his mother added.

His father laughed. "I didn't think they promoted people for surrendering the ship!"

"But at least we can trust our son to uphold Article 9!" his mother joked.

"Shut up!" Ishiro screamed. "Just shut up!"

The living room suddenly became silent. His parents stared in shock at him.

"I have a chance to do something with my life," Ishiro declared. "Now I will do it."

His father frowned. "If the Navy rejects you, you'll come back like a dog with his tail between his legs."

"Is that what you want?" said Ishiro.

"It's not what I want. It's what will happen. I'm being realistic. Ishiro, get a civilian job. Maybe you can start at the bottom and work you way up a company."

"It's time to try something different," Ishiro said.

"Did you get this idea from watching anime?" his mother asked. "Did that idiot anime artist tell you to join the Navy? You know who I mean."

"I don't know who you mean," Ishiro said. He knew she was talking about General Morita.

"That guy who dresses in a stupid general's costume."

"No, he didn't talk me into joining the Navy. He prefers the Army. Why else would he dress like a general?"

"You'll come back. You'll wash out," his father predicted.

Ishiro suppressed the urge to shout. Instead, he muttered, "And if I don't wash out?"

"Then you'll become a low-ranking swabbie, always washing the ship's toilets, always earning less than the janitor in my department store."

Without saying a word, Ishiro stormed to the door.

"Wait, Ishiro! Don't leave!" his father said.

Ishiro left the house and did not look back despite the shouts behind him.

# PART 2

# THE NAVY OFFICER

# CHAPTER 7

## *Otaku* Boy

Midshipmen came to the Naval Officer Candidate School from varying backgrounds. Some were graduates of the National Defense Academy and the National Defense Medical College. Others were student reservists from civilian universities. There were also seamen and non-commissioned officers who showed potential for promotion. Finally, there were university graduates with no prior military training. Ishiro fell into the last group, which formed the 4th Regiment of the Brigade of Midshipmen.

Due to American influence, the Brigade was organized like its counterpart at the United States Naval Academy. The Brigade was divided into regiments, which were divided into battalions, which were divided into companies, which were divided into platoons, which were divided in squads.

Each squad had five midshipmen. In addition to Ishiro, Squad 11 had: Kwon, a woman banker of Korean descent; Miyahara, a policeman from Kyoto; Yamaguchi Yumi, a Roman Catholic girl from University of the Sacred Heart; and Kamio, an accountant of a bicycle manufacturer. Together with five other squads, they formed the 2nd Platoon.

In contrast to civilian universities, the Naval Officer Candidate School had a brutal orientation week for new students. The midshipmen got phys-ed, lectures, and combat training in the first day of Hell Week. By dinnertime, they had already received an order to submit their first academic assignment, an essay due on the third day. All this work occurred before they were formally admitted to the school. The entrance ceremony was four days away.

On day two, Squad 11 assembled for inspection in Tsushima Gymnasium. It was a gigantic building, part of the rapid expansion of the military. It had indoor obstacle courses, running tracks, and simulations of outdoor terrains so the Navy could train officers all year round.

Lieutenant Shujimi, the 2nd Platoon's trainer, paced between the rows of midshipmen. No specks of dust or wrinkles marred his blue uniform. He wore two rows of ribbons, and his gold buttons and badges shone like the Sun. He stood straight as a flagpole.

When he was a civilian, Ishiro would feel awe at seeing such military perfection. However, now in the Navy, he felt fear when he saw Shujimi. The lieutenant eyed the midshipmen like a wolf stalking chickens.

Ishiro had heard that the 4th Regiment received the harshest trainers because its midshipmen had no previous military training.

Shujimi looked disdainfully at his recruits. "What a bunch of winners you are! Some of you didn't play sports in high school or university. Some of you didn't even take phys-ed. And this is sweet: Some of you don't know how to swim! I should quit the Navy because it sends me human junk like you!"

Ishiro felt a chill run down his spine. Shujimi kept walking between the rows of midshipmen.

"In its great haste to expand the military, the Ministry of Defense has lowered its standards for recruits. That's how stupid pigs like you get here!" Shujimi said.

The lieutenant pointed his swagger stick at Ishiro.

"You! What is your name?" Shujimi demanded.

The question puzzled Ishiro. His name was on his name tag, plainly visible to everyone. Why did Shujimi need to ask his name if he could see the answer?

"Sato Ishiro, sir, as is written on my name tag," Ishiro answered.

"Just stating your name will suffice, Mr. Sato," Shujimi said. "What is your progress in completing the battle analysis essay due tomorrow?"

Ishiro reported, "Sir, I went to find the map of Port Arthur in the library like you said we should, and that took an hour because I'm not familiar with the map room. Then I had to find the part about the torpedo boats in Admiral Togo's report. That took about another hour because it wasn't in an obvious place in the report. And then I wrote about Admiral Dewa's reconnaissance mission, and that took forty-five minutes, and then I —"

Shujimi slapped Ishiro across the face. "You haven't answered my question!"

Ishiro's cheek stung from the slap. He fought back his tears. He dared not cry in front of the whole platoon.

Mr. Endo had not been joking when he said the Navy had brought back physical punishment!

"Sorry, sir!" said Ishiro.

Shujimi slapped Ishiro again. The sound of the slap echoed in Ishiro's ears. The pain shot through his head.

"You still haven't answered the question, *otaku* boy!" Shujimi shouted.

Ishiro said, "Well, like I said, I looked for the map of Port Arthur, and I found Admiral Togo's report, but I had to search through it to find the part about the torpedo boats, and then I —"

"Shut up, shut up, shut up!" Shujimi screamed. "I didn't ask how long you've wasted on your stupid essay! Sato, remove your headgear!"

Ishiro took off his cap.

Shujimi knocked his knuckles on Ishiro's head. "You're a perfect example of the type of idiot created by universities! Put your headgear back on!"

The lieutenant turned to Miyahara. "You! Miyahara! Tell me your progress on the essay!"

"Sir, I have completed seventy-five percent of the essay and expect to submit it by deadline!" Miyahara declared.

Shujimi shook his swagger stick at Ishiro's face. "That's how to answer a question, *otaku* boy!"

**

The 4th Regiment's physical training had begun on day one. As always, the Navy used physical training to weed out weak recruits. Shujimi pushed and insulted his midshipmen mercilessly.

Having avoided phys-ed throughout high school, Ishiro struggled to keep up with his fellow midshipmen. He jogged at the rear of the company. He lost his kendo match. He fell into a mud puddle in the obstacle course. Everyone else, even the girls, knocked him to the floor in hand-to-hand combat. These were just the first two days!

The third day was excruciating. The platoon jogged around Tsushima Gymnasium twice, ran in one spot for thirty minutes while holding rifles above their heads, practiced kendo for two hours, and did fifty-push ups, all before lunch. Gasping and panting, Ishiro finished his push-ups after everyone else had.

As Ishiro crouched on his hands and knees, Shujimi rapped his swagger stick on Ishiro's shoulder.

"No, don't stand up," Shujimi ordered. "Assume the push-up position."

Shaking with fear, Ishiro obeyed.

"*Otaku* boy, you were three minutes behind the rest of your company!" Shujimi yelled. "In a real battle, what will happen if you lag three minutes behind everyone else?"

"Uh, uh, uh — we become late for dinner, sir?" Ishiro muttered.

Shujimi pressed his foot on Ishiro's back and pushed him to the floor. Ishiro groaned as he lay face down.

"Look up, look at your shipmates!" Shujimi yelled.

Ishiro looked at the midshipmen. They stared with disdain at him.

"In an emergency, when every second counts, when every action is a matter of life and death, your shipmates will die because you were slow," Shujimi said. "Do you want them to die?"

"Sir, no, sir!"

"Do you want yourself to die?"

"Sir, no, sir!"

"Then don't lag behind anymore!" Shujimi shouted.

He took his foot off Ishiro's back and ordered, "Give me another twenty push-ups!"

**

The entrance ceremony occurred at the end of Hell Week. Before the ceremony, midshipmen could resign without penalty. Thirty-eight people, one quarter of the 4th Regiment, resigned and went home.

Shujimi had asked Ishiro if he wanted to resign, but Ishiro chose to stay. As hard as officer training was, he didn't want to go back to salvaging android parts.

But more importantly, he didn't want to go home and hear his parents berate him for quitting again, even if they opposed his joining the Navy.

As he put on his uniform, he marveled that the school had not expelled him already. He was at the bottom of his platoon in physical education. However, he did pass, though barely.

"We've got a war coming," Shujimi had told him. "We'll take anyone now."

The new midshipmen's families and friends filled the audience area of Taisho Auditorium. A band played military music as the midshipmen marched in.

Rear Admiral Kirino, Superintendent of the Naval Officer Candidate School, went to the lectern. The national and naval flags hung behind him.

The Superintendent wore the new ceremonial uniform, a dark blue tunic with a closed collar. Gold stripes encircled his sleeves. Although it was a new uniform, it was actually a revival of the past. It was reminiscent of Admiral Togo, the old nobility, and Imperial ceremonies. No naval officer had worn such a uniform since the Showa Era.

"4th Regiment, sit down!" Lieutenant Shujimi shouted.

The midshipmen sat down, and Kirino began his speech. "Our nation faces uncertain times. Foreign powers threaten our neutrality. As much as we wish to avoid war, war may be coming to us..."

After Kirino's speech, Midshipman Yamaguchi stood up. A random draw had selected her to read the midshipmen's oath. The honor was so important that she had practiced the oath ritual for an hour last night.

Carrying a scroll under her left arm, she marched to the lectern, saluted the Superintendent, and unrolled the scroll. The midshipmen stood up.

Yamaguchi read the oath: "I swear I will abide by Japan's Constitution and laws, the international laws of armed conflict, as well as the rules of the school...I will obey the Prime Minister and my officers and defend the nation to my utmost ability...I, Yamaguchi Yumi, and one hundred and fourteen others."

The midshipmen bowed. Shujimi shouted, "4th Regiment, at attention!" They snapped to attention.

The band played the national anthem, "Kimigayo." Then the Superintendent dismissed the assembly, the band played military tunes again, and the midshipmen marched out.

Ishiro looked at the audience as he left the auditorium. He did not see any familiar faces.

He had not expected to see anyone he knew. His parents refused to come to the entrance ceremony. Mr. Endo wanted to come, but the café's business kept him in Tokyo.

He had thought about inviting Yuko but did not. Other midshipmen had parents, siblings, and sweethearts cheering them on. He would look like a loser with only an android to encourage him.

Nobody from the outside had come to see him join the Navy. He was on his own.

**

Kamio's background intrigued Ishiro. The accountant had been in General Morita's National Bushido Guards Regiment.

While in line for lunch, Ishiro asked, "Why did you come here? I thought you guys got to train with the military?"

L-3 androids dished curry beef onto plates. It was Friday, the traditional day for curry.

"We do train with the military, but it's with the Army," Kamio replied. "General Morita thought we should get naval training too, so I volunteered for the Naval Officer Candidate School."

"And wound up in the 4th Regiment," said Ishiro. "I guess the National Bushido Guards Regiment doesn't count as prior military training."

"Unfortunately, it doesn't. It should, though. The Ministry of Defense knows that we train with the Army. It would've been nice to skip basic training and go straight to the military courses."

They joined the rest of their squad and waited for Lieutenant Shujimi. They could not eat until he gave the order.

Shujimi went from table to table, chatting with each squad in his platoon. Finally, he got to the Squad 11's table.

"Today, we'll do things differently," he said. "I will give the order to eat after you have bet your lunches."

The midshipmen looked baffled. Shujimi gazed at them and explained the bet.

"I will ask you a question about the Midshipmen's Manual. You should have memorized the required facts by now," Shujimi said. "You have a choice of betting your own lunch only or the lunch of your shipmates.

"If you bet your own lunch and answer my question correctly, everyone eats. If you bet your own lunch and answer my question incorrectly, you lose your lunch, but your shipmates may eat theirs.

"If you bet your shipmates' lunches and answer my question correctly, everyone eats. But if you bet your shipmates' lunches and answer my question incorrectly, you get to eat lunch, but they don't. Do you understand the rules?"

"Yes, sir," they replied.

"Okay, let's start," said Shujimi. He looked at Kamio. "Kamio! Will you bet your own lunch or your shipmates' lunches?"

"I will bet my own lunch, sir!" Kamio replied.

"Very good. Question: What is length of a nautical mile in meters?"

Kamio replied, "One nautical mile is equal to one thousand, eight hundred, and fifty-two meters, sir!"

"That is correct, Mr. Kamio," said Shujimi. "Very good."

Ishiro began eating his lunch. Then he saw the worried look on Kwon's face.

"I have not given the order to eat," said Shujimi. "Are you hungry, Mr. Sato?"

"Uh, no, uh, I mean, yes, sir," Ishiro replied with his mouth full.

"Sato, let's play another round," Shujimi demanded. "Will you bet your own lunch or your shipmates' lunches?"

"I will bet my shipmates' lunches, sir," said Ishiro.

They looked nervously at him. Ishiro smiled weakly, hoping to reassure them.

"Question: How many of the school's buildings are named after admirals?" Shujimi asked.

"Seven," Ishiro replied.

"Seven, eh?" said Shujimi. He looked at Kwon. "Miss Kwon, do you agree?"

Kwon answered, "No, sir. There are nine buildings named after admirals."

"That's correct, there are nine," said Shujimi.

Ishiro's shipmates stared silently at their food.

"Everyone, pass your plates into the center of the table," Shujimi said. "Mr. Sato, you may eat your lunch. Squad 11, the rest of you will carry on with other duties."

Except for Ishiro, Squad 11 quietly left the table. Shujimi smiled and shook his head.

"Do you know what you've just done?" Shujimi asked.

"I just won the bet, sir," Ishiro replied.

"Yes, that's right, you won a bet." Shujimi pointed at the plates of beef curry. "You can eat their food too, Sato. Don't let good food spoil. Enjoy your lunch."

"Thank you, sir," said Ishiro.

Shujimi went to the next squad and asked its members to bet their lunches. Ishiro watched the game for a moment. Then he ate his lunch.

Ishiro savored the curry beef. The long, exhausting morning had made him hungry, so he ate a second plate of curry, one left by his shipmates. Halfway through his third helping, his stomach felt full.

It was the best lunch he had ever had. He had outsmarted Lieutenant Shujimi.

**

When Lieutenant Commander Hirano entered the classroom, the midshipmen stood up, bowed, and saluted her.

Hirano opted to wear a skirt instead of pants with her uniform. Unlike the older faculty members, she wore only four ribbons. But she wore the badge of the new Military Law Corps, the silver cherry blossom with the word "Justice" in red.

The petite woman looked more like a bus attendant than a Navy officer, but her biography in the Midshipmen's Manual listed her formidable achievements. She graduated at the top of her class from Kinki University's School of Law. She worked in criminal law for two years, defending wealthy executives charged with white collar crimes. Then she joined the Navy and prosecuted the Indonesian spy Juk Sutarta. She was Ishiro's age and already a lieutenant commander and law professor.

She pointed her pocket computer at the classroom's viewscreen. Pictures and photos of Japan's imperial wars appeared: Imperial soldiers fighting the Satsuma samurai at the Battle of Shiroyama in 1877, Japanese ships sinking Russian ships at Battle of Port Arthur in 1904, sailors on parade at Yasukuni Shrine in 1931, soldiers celebrating the fall of Singapore in 1942, and various soldiers, sailors, and airmen in formal uniforms and medals.

Kamio smiled and nodded at the images. Miyahara and Kwon showed no emotion. Yamaguchi stared keenly at the screen. Ishiro felt the same surge of pride that he had felt when he watched General Morita's anime.

"The glory of the Greater Japanese Empire," said Hirano. "Who cannot feel proud when seeing our history shown like this?"

But grimmer images appeared: piles of corpses in Nanking in 1937, a ditch full of dead Chinese civilians in Xuzhou in 1938, dead Canadian prisoners of war in Hong Kong in 1942, and a Japanese soldier beheading a kneeling Australian prisoner in New Guinea in 1943.

Miyahara stared stone-faced at the atrocities. Kwon shook her head at the photos of mutilated Koreans. Yamaguchi briefly glanced away from the screen. Ishiro wondered what Hirano was trying to prove. They were going to be Japanese Navy officers. Shouldn't Hirano be instilling them with pride and glory?

"Unfortunately, we cannot feel proud about all of our military history," said Hirano.

She let the midshipmen stare at the photograph of the beheading of the Australian. "War is the uncivilized last resort of civilized people. The uncivilized aspect is the killing. The civilized aspect is the laws of war. There are international laws and treaties that govern how we wage war on each other.

"It should not have mattered to our forebears whether the imperial wars were justified or not. That is for the politicians and historians to debate. What should have mattered to our forebears is how they conducted themselves in war. Undeniably, many military personnel served with honor. But equally undeniably, many others committed war crimes and caused great shame for future generations of our people.

"War is always violent and deadly. However, there are limits on what we can do. Torture, rape, forced labor, human experimentation, and killing of civilians and prisoners of war are not acceptable."

Hirano switched off the viewscreen. "That's why you'll be learning military law. Not only will you be required to obey the laws of war, but you must also ensure that the people you command obey the laws too. Japan is a modern democracy, and thus, we have the honorable duty of upholding the laws of war."

She looked at her laptop and said, "I trust that you all read the assigned articles about the treatment of civilians. I'll give you a hypothetical situation, and you'll tell me how to deal with it.

"You're on a reconnaissance party in a town where fighting is going on. You and your party are hiding behind some bushes and awaiting an enemy squad to pass by. Your job is to observe the enemy and report back information about them. However, a child is playing in the bushes, sees you, and runs away. What should you do?"

Miyahara put up his hand, and Hirano looked at her photo I.D. chart. "Yes, Mr. Miyahara?" she said.

"Ma'am, the child is a civilian and noncombatant. We should let the child escape," said Miyahara.

"But she could tell the enemy about your position and jeopardize you and your mission," Hirano said. "Would you still let her escape?"

"Ma'am, that's a difficult situation, but we shouldn't do anything illegal like shoot her or capture her," said Miyahara. "We should let her escape."

Hirano looked at her photo I.D. chart. "Mr. Sato, what do you think?" she asked.

"I think this situation could never happen, ma'am," said Ishiro.

Hirano looked puzzled. "Why do you say that?"

"Ma'am, if fighting were going on in the town, a child would not be roaming free and playing in the bushes," Ishiro explained.

"Well, for the sake of the exercise, let's assume that this child finds you."

"But ma'am, that's unrealistic. The child's parents would not let her run around by herself."

"What if the child's parents are dead?" said Hirano.

"You didn't mention that in the question."

"Okay. Assume the child's parents are dead. Then what would you do?"

"Well, if the child's parents were dead, she would not be so happy as to play in the rubble. It's still an unrealistic situation, so hence, I would say there is no answer to your question, ma'am," said Ishiro.

Hirano sighed. "Next question..."

Ishiro felt the warm glow that came from knowing he had argued against the best and won.

**

At each meal, Shujimi asked the midshipmen some questions. Ishiro's shipmates always bet their own meals. Ishiro always bet his shipmates' meals. He cost them seven meals over two weeks.

One night, he feasted on Chinese-style roast duck, a special treat. The chef had found culinary school interns to work for a week, and they practiced their gourmet cooking. Ishiro liked the duck so much that he devoured three helpings, all forfeited by his shipmates.

When Ishiro returned to his room, his shipmates were waiting for him. Their presence was unusual. Kwon and Yamaguchi lived in the women's wing. Miyahara and Kamio shared the room with him, but after dinner, Miyahara usually went to the library, and Kamio usually went to the pistol range.

Miyahara approached him. Unlike Ishiro, Miyahara had a strong body, stood straight, and always looked determined. Ishiro admired the former policeman's toughness. He wished he could be as physically imposing as Miyahara.

"Was dinner good?" Miyahara asked.

Ishiro nodded. "It was delicious. I think those cooking interns are superb. Bringing them here is a good idea. An academic exchange with a civilian school builds trust between civilians and the military. In a democracy, the elected government controls the military. This is quite different from the situation in the twentieth century, when —"

"Sato, stop it," Miyahara demanded.

Kwon and Yamaguchi came forward. Kamio swung behind him.

"They're leaving tomorrow," said Miyahara. "I would like to eat some of their cooking and build trust between civilians and the military, as you say."

"I'm sure you will try some of their dishes," said Ishiro. "Uh, you're going to dinner tomorrow, right?"

He eyed his shipmates nervously as they surrounded him.

Miyahara smiled wryly. "Yes, I'll go to dinner tomorrow. The question is whether *you'll* be there."

"Uh, ah, uh, why wouldn't I be?" Ishiro muttered.

"Tomorrow is Sunday. You can volunteer to serve at the Christian chapel and skip dinner," Yamaguchi suggested.

"I'm not Christian. Why would I want to serve in their chapel?" Ishiro asked.

"So the rest of us can eat," Miyahara said.

Ishiro suddenly realized why his shipmates were upset.

"You can buy food at the quartermaster," he suggested.

"What if I don't want to eat instant *ramen* and *onigiri*?" said Miyahara.

"What if I want to eat in the wardroom?" said Kwon.

Ishiro shrugged. "Hey, uh, you've always had the opportunity to bet my meal."

"But we'll never do that," said Kwon.

"No, a good officer doesn't starve his shipmates to feed his own fat stomach," Miyahara said.

"You have to understand mathematics," Ishiro argued. "If I bet my own meal, there is a fifty percent chance that I will lose it. But if I bet your meals, there is a hundred percent chance that I will keep my meal.

A good military officer knows when to take advantage of a situation and chooses the strategy with the highest probability of success."

Kwon groaned. "Success? How does losing our meals count as success?"

"I've won every bet," Ishiro reminded them.

"No, you've lost every bet, you idiot!" Miyahara said. "You keep giving the wrong answers, and we keep starving!"

"It depends on how you define success," said Ishiro.

Kamio, who was standing behind Ishiro, gently pushed him closer to Miyahara.

"I chose the strategy with the highest chance of success," Ishiro insisted. "That's what we should do. We're naval officers."

"If you're a naval officer, why don't you just memorize the Midshipmen's Manual like the rest of us?" Kwon demanded.

"Even if I did, there's always a chance that I might not know the answer. There's never one hundred percent probability of answering the question correctly. Betting your shipmates' meals still has the best chance of success regardless if you answer the question correctly or not," Ishiro explained.

Kwon moved her lips, as if to say something, but Ishiro continued. "It's regrettable that sometimes I don't give the correct answer, but all of you could have bet like I did."

Miyahara snarled, "You'll be the worst officer in the Navy! You'll never win any battles! You'll only kill your own crew!"

Miyahara fist suddenly hit Ishiro between the eyes. Ishiro staggered backwards, but Kamio caught him and pushed him forward into Miyahara's arms.

"Is your belly full of roast duck, you pig?" said Miyahara.

He punched Ishiro's stomach. Ishiro howled and bent over. The two women snickered.

Ishiro let out a long, piercing cry.

"What's going on in there?" someone yelled.

As Lieutenant Shujimi rushed into the room, Kwon shouted, "Officer on deck!"

Except for Ishiro, the midshipmen snapped to attention. Holding his stomach, Ishiro slowly stood up.

"What's going on here?" Shujimi demanded again.

Nobody answered.

Shujimi looked suspiciously at Ishiro.

"Good! I'll carry on, and I suggest you carry on too," he said as he walked to the door.

Ishiro cried, "He hit me!"

Shujimi turned back to the squad. "Did someone say something?"

"He hit me!" Ishiro repeated.

"Say, 'He hit me, *sir*!'" said Shujimi.

"He hit me, sir."

"Who hit you?"

"Miyahara."

Shujimi looked at Miyahara. "Is that true, Miyahara?"

"Sir, yes, sir!" Miyahara declared.

Shujimi shrugged and said, "All new recruits get a little excited. Gentlemen, if you can resolve the issue and promise to settle future disputes peacefully, I'll consider the issue closed and carry on."

The lieutenant turned to the door again, but Ishiro spoke up.

"Excuse me, sir," he said, "but the Midshipmen's Manual states that no midshipman shall assault another midshipman except when required for training or educational purposes. Any accusation of assault between midshipmen must be investigated by a training officer or member of the faculty. If the investigation proves the accusation, the midshipman who committed the offense will receive physical administrative punishment or expulsion from the school, whichever is the pleasure of the investigating officer or faculty member."

The squad members glared at Ishiro, but he did not waver. He knew the rules and upheld them, which is what a naval officer should do.

Shujimi rapped his swagger stick into the palm of his hand.

"Physical administrative punishment," he muttered. "Indeed, the Midshipmen's Manual has such a rule. Sato, are you saying that I am required to conduct an investigation into an assault?"

"Yes, sir!" said Ishiro.

Miyahara's eyes blazed with hate, but Ishiro pretended not to notice.

"For the record, Sato, has a midshipman assaulted you?" Shujimi asked.

"Yes, sir," said Ishiro.

"Who do you accuse of assaulting you?"

"Midshipman Miyahara, sir."

Shujimi asked Miyahara, "I have to ask again, this time for the record. Did you hit Midshipman Sato?"

"Sir, yes, sir!" Miyahara replied.

Shujimi sighed. "Miyahara, report to my office at seven hundred hours tomorrow. Come right after breakfast. Don't do anything violent or rash tonight."

"Yes, sir."

"Good. See you in the morning."

Shujimi turned to Ishiro and said, "If only you would memorize the other sections of the Midshipmen's Manual, like everyone else."

Ishiro's stomach turned. Why was Shujimi annoyed with him? He wasn't the one who had hit another midshipman. Indeed, he was the one who got hit. He was the one who knew the rules of the school. He was the one who wanted people to follow the rules. Shujimi should be praising him, Ishiro thought.

"Squad 11, carry on," Shujimi said as he walked away.

The squad rushed out behind him, leaving Ishiro alone. Just before lights out, Miyahara and Kamio returned to the room, but they did not speak to Ishiro.

**

In the morning, Squad 11 lined up on the artificial grass of Tsushima Gymnasium. Shujimi stared grimly at them.

"Miyahara, step forward!" Shujimi ordered.

Miyahara came forward and stood at attention.

"I have investigated an accusation against Midshipman Miyahara and found that he committed an offense against rule of conduct number twenty-four, which you can find in the Midshipmen's Manual," Shujimi announced. "The offense was hitting another midshipman when not required for training or educational purposes. The penalty is either physical administrative punishment or expulsion from the school.

"After considering the situation and Midshipman Miyahara's record, I assign him administrative punishment of two blows of the swagger stick."

He held up his swagger stick and said, "Miyahara, turn and face your shipmates and stand with your legs apart!"

Miyahara turned and spread his legs. Shujimi swung his swagger stick so quickly that it whistled as it sliced through the air. It smacked onto Miyahara's buttocks.

The squad members grimaced at the sight and sound of the flogging. Miyahara stayed silent. His face remained blank, like stone. No tears flowed down his cheek.

Shujimi hit Miyahara's butt again. He did not flinch or make any noise.

Ishiro wondered how Miyahara could stand the pain. The former policeman must be very strong.

Shujimi put the swagger stick under his arm. "Midshipman Miyahara, stand at ease. Midshipman Sato, come forward and stand at ease."

Ishiro nervously obeyed the order. It made no sense to call him forward, he thought. He wasn't the one who needed a flogging.

"Midshipman Miyahara, bow to Midshipman Sato and apologize as we had discussed," Shujimi ordered.

Miyahara bowed and said, "Midshipman Sato, I regret hitting you in anger last night. Please accept my apology."

Ishiro said nothing.

"Sato, stop smiling!" Shujimi yelled. "Sato! Bow to Midshipman Miyahara, accept his apology, and tell him you bear no grudges against him."

"Sir, since I'm the person who suffered the offense, shouldn't I be the one who decides whether or not to accept the apology?" Ishiro asked.

"Just do it!" Shujimi ordered.

Ishiro bowed slightly, not as deeply as Miyahara had. "I accept your apology and bear no grudges against you."

"Very good," said Shujimi. "I consider this matter to be finished. I expect that this squad will not discuss it anymore. Squad 11, do you understand me?"

"Yes, sir," they replied in unison.

"Sato, Miyahara, return to your positions in the squad," Shujimi ordered.

After Sato and Miyahara rejoined their squad, Shujimi addressed them.

"There will always be disagreements between members of a ship's crew, but the crew must resolve its differences and work efficiently and effectively together. Otherwise, they will lose their ship and die together."

Ishiro wondered how any ship could sail, much less fight, with officers like Miyahara. Miyahara should be expelled from the service, he thought.

******

After another morning of physical training and a radio communications course, the squad went to the wardroom for lunch. As usual, they waited for Shujimi to ask questions about the Midshipmen's Manual.

"Kwon, will you bet your own meal or your shipmates' meals?" Shujimi asked.

"I will bet my own meal, sir," Kwon said.

"What is the Japanese Monument at the United States Naval Academy?" Shujimi asked.

"Sir, it is a stone pagoda presented by the family of Saito Hirosi, Japanese Ambassador to the United States," Kwon answered.

"Good, that is correct," said Shujimi.

He looked at Ishiro. "Sato, will you bet your own meal or your shipmates' meals?"

"I will bet my shipmates' meals, sir," Ishiro said.

The squad members murmured.

"If you wish," said Shujimi. "Which Japanese ship came within twenty kilometers of Wonsan during the Korean Crisis?"

"Sir, she was the submarine *Marquis Saigo*," said Ishiro.

Shujimi waited before speaking. Then he said, "Yes, you are correct. Squad 11, you may eat. Enjoy your lunch."

After Shujimi left, Kamio said, "Sato, you bet our lunches again. Why do you continue?"

"Like I keep saying, it's the best bet from a strategic point of view. I've explained it before, do I have to explain it again? Here, I'll draw an outcome table," said Ishiro with his mouth full of food.

"No, that won't be necessary," Kamio said.

Ishiro took a pen out of his pocket and started drawing on a napkin. "But it won't take long to show you. First we draw a box like this —"

"No, that won't be necessary," Kamio repeated.

"I want to explain how mathematics shows the optimal strategy," Ishiro insisted.

"Well, at least this time you studied the Midshipmen's Manual," said Kamio. "That's an improvement, isn't it, fellows?"

The other squad members nodded silently and continued eating.

Kamio smiled. "See, they're impressed by your most recent progress. Keep studying the Midshipmen's Manual. That's the best strategy."

"But what if Shujimi asks a question whose answer I don't remember, even if I study the Manual? Nobody has one hundred percent recall," Ishiro said.

Somebody kicked Ishiro's shin under the table. The pain shot through his leg. Miyahara and Kwon sat across from him, so one of them had done it, but neither looked at him.

"Keep studying the Midshipmen's Manual. Trust me, that's the best strategy," Kamio repeated.

Ishiro wondered if Kamio was too dumb to understand probabilities and outcome tables. After all, Kamio was an accountant, not a computer scientist.

He wondered who had kicked him. What ingrates, he thought. He had made the best bet *and* won their meals for them. What more could they want?

**

On the evening of February fourteenth, the mail delivery android knocked on Ishiro's door. "Permission to come aboard, sir," it asked.

Ishiro looked up from his books. Nobody else was in the room to let the android enter. Miyahara and Kamio had decided to study for tomorrow's navigation test in the library.

"Yes, permission granted," he said.

The android, a male L-3, entered the room and said, "One package for Midshipman Sato Ishiro."

"Over here," said Ishiro, rising from his chair.

The android gave the package to Ishiro, bowed, and left. Ishiro looked at the return address. It was from Nikkou Café in Tokyo.

He tore off its wrapping and looked at the box. It was red with the gold words "*Honmei Choco*."

Ishiro's heart beat quickly. This was the special, often expensive, chocolate that girls give to their sweethearts or prospective boyfriends.

He opened the box. It contained a heart-shaped chocolate and a small hologram projector.

He pressed the projector's button. A shimmering image of Yuko appeared. She wore her maid costume. The sounds and music of the maid café played softly on the hologram's soundtrack.

The holographic Yuko bowed and curtsied before talking.

"Happy Valentine's Day, master!" she said. "Please accept this *honmei choco*. It's from Mamoru Candy Palace, just around the corner from our café. Sora recommended the shop, and Ami helped me choose the chocolate. I hope you like it, master. It's the first time I ever bought chocolate for anyone."

He knew Mamoru Candy Palace. All the maids loved its confections, and their boyfriends bought their White Day chocolates there.

Ishiro took a deep breath and smelled the sweet scent of the chocolate. He imagined Yuko recording the hologram and wrapping the chocolate at the café.

The holographic Yuko smiled. "Ami showed me a documentary about the Navy, so now I know that your education will be difficult and strenuous. I won't use your time any longer. Please study and work hard, and when you get your leave, please visit me."

After the hologram faded, Ishiro broke off a piece of the chocolate and ate it. It tasted exquisite and melted in his mouth.

Duty called, however. He put the hologram projector and chocolate away and returned to his books. Although he still maintained the academic grades to stay in the school, he was the bottom-ranked midshipman in the platoon. He excelled in subjects like navigation, naval engineering, electronics, and calculus. Just like at university, the science and math subjects were his best. However, he scored at the bottom of his platoon in physical training. He was always the last person to finish any obstacle course or running track. He was always the loser in kendo and judo.

He scored equally low in history, military law, political science, sociology, and battle analysis. He received only the minimum passing grades on these subjects. His poor performance surprised him because he considered himself an expert on history and law. Indeed, at an anime convention a few years ago, he had talked about Korean history for two uninterrupted hours when someone asked where to buy a Korean anime disc.

A new email message appeared. It was Lieutenant Commander Hirano returning his military law essay. Ishiro read her message in shock:

"Your essay did not answer the question at all. Grade: 20/100, Failure."

How could she give his essay a failing grade, he wondered? He had practically copied the entire first four chapters of the textbook! Certainly he had written something that answered the question.

He had to memorize more facts, write more words on the tests and papers, he reasoned. He knew he couldn't take the top position, but he might get out of the last position.

He had a girlfriend to impress now.

**

After the navigation test, the midshipmen went to the wardroom for lunch. As Ishiro reached the door, Lieutenant Shujimi approached him.

"Sato, come with me," Shujimi said.

"Huh? It's lunchtime, sir," Ishiro said.

"I know that. You're skipping lunch today."

"What?"

"That's 'What, sir?'" Shujimi corrected him. "Follow me."

"But I'm hungry, sir."

Shujimi slapped the back of his hand across Ishiro's face. The midshipman squealed in pain and touched his cheek.

"Buy an *onigiri* at the quartermaster later," Shujimi ordered. "Come with me."

Ishiro watched his shipmates enter the wardroom. They did not look back at him. Still feeling his cheek, he followed Shujimi to the Memorial Pavilion.

The Memorial Pavilion was covered in gold leaf, and it gleamed in the sunlight. Built after the Korean Crisis, it was a three-story building with a pagoda roof, like the Golden Pavilion in Kyoto. Unlike the Golden Pavilion, the Memorial Pavilion did not have a *fenghuang* or Chinese phoenix on its top. Instead, the emblem of the Navy, an anchor with a cherry blossom, sat atop of the Pavilion.

Shujimi stopped at the entrance of the Memorial Pavilion, bowed, and entered. Ishiro did the same. Everyone had to show respect for the dead before entering the Pavilion.

Inside were models of ships and aircraft, old flags, and photographs of naval battles. An open book sat on a marble pedestal at the center of the floor.

"Look how thick the Book of the Naval Kami is," said Shujimi. "That book contains the names of all sailors who died in war, peacekeeping missions, disaster relief, and peacetime duty. The book is open, always waiting for the horrible duty of receiving more names.

"Sato, I fear you will cause the next names to be written in that book. Your squad mates are afraid that you'll get them killed. However, you can prevent their deaths. You can resign from the school."

Ishiro muttered, "I don't know what you mean, sir."

"A ship's crew needs to work together to fight, to win, and to survive," Shujimi said. "You're not a team player. You work only for yourself."

"That's not true, sir," Ishiro protested. "I've participated in every group exercise and drill. You check our attendance, so you know that."

"I know you've been participating in group exercises, but have you really been working with the rest of your squad? I say not."

"Sir, I still don't know what you mean."

"Sato, you're ruining your squad," Shujimi said. "You maintain the minimum scores to stay in the school, but you're also pulling down the squad average. You bet your shipmates' meals at no risk to yourself but at great risk to them."

"Are they still complaining about the food game?" Ishiro said incredulously. "I disagree with them. I think that I am acting as a naval officer should. If there is an option that combines a high value outcome with a high probability of success, one should take it. That's how battles are won, sir."

"No, they're not! *Otaku* boy, you haven't won a single bet, game, or challenge since you came here. That's because you're selfish. If you led your crew in battle, you would still be alive, but they would all be dead. You can save yourself, but you can't win a battle."

"In the All-Japan Videogame Convention, I won every match in the Battleship game," Ishiro retorted. "I can win battles, sir."

Shujimi grunted. "This is real life, not a videogame, *otaku* boy! The battle isn't between you and a computer. It's between you and your crew on one side, the enemy and his crew on the other. When your ship gets sunk, your shipmates won't have three more lives, and neither will you!"

"Sir, I don't agree with what you're saying about me!" Ishiro said.

"Then you should resign and leave."

"No, sir!"

"Listen to me," Shujimi urged. "If you resign today, I'll make special arrangements so you won't suffer any penalties. I'll talk to the Superintendent. You're not going to get a chance like this after February. How about it, son? Will you resign?"

Ishiro declared, "No, I will not resign, sir. I wish to stay and become an officer of the Japanese Navy."

"If you don't resign, I'm stuck with you," Shujimi complained. "I wanted to expel you in Hell Week, but the Superintendent didn't let me. The only reason why you're still here is because recruitment is low. The Superintendent has to keep even losers like you."

"Sir, I'm not a loser," Ishiro said.

"Yes you are. Do I need to criticize your other failures?" Shujimi said. "First, you're lousy at phys-ed. You're last in every physical test. You should practice and train more in your spare time."

Ishiro nodded silently.

"Second, you're sloppy and have a record number of dress code violations. Look at the top button of your jacket!"

"Yes, sir," Ishiro muttered as he quickly buttoned up his jacket.

Third, you hog every conversation," Shujimi continued. "Yesterday in the navigation course, you kept talking and would not let the other midshipmen speak. I wanted to —"

Ishiro said, "But that's because I know the right answer. The others don't always get it right."

Shujimi poked Ishiro with his swagger stick. "Don't interrupt me again, *otaku* boy!"

Ishiro gasped.

"Shut up and listen. What I'll say next is the most important," Shujimi advised. "The Navy is all about teamwork. Teamwork requires you to control your mouth. When you talk, give useful information. Make your comments relevant to the topic under discussion. Don't do all the talking, but do all the listening. Do you understand?"

"Yes, sir," Ishiro mumbled.

"Bow to the Book of the Naval Kami. Then return to Yamamoto Hall for your afternoon classes. Do not stop for lunch in the wardroom," Shujimi ordered.

Ishiro turned, bowed to the book, and fled from the Memorial Pavilion. He wiped a tear off his cheek as he ran to Yamamoto Hall.

He had a few minutes before the military law class, so he went to his room. There he devoured the *honmei choco* heart. In this bitter moment, he needed the chocolate's sweetness.

The Navy wasn't like Akihabara. Everyone was mean at the Naval Officer Candidate School. Life would be much easier if he resigned. He didn't need a job. He could become a NEET: Not in Employment, Education, or Training. Like them, he could devote every day to reading manga and watching anime. Unfortunately, his parents would nag him, and he would have to beg for their money. However, his parents were small pains compared to Lieutenant Shujimi.

But he couldn't resign from the Navy. He couldn't go back to civilian life. The NEET lifestyle had one drawback: NEET's never had girlfriends. Would Yuko want him if he came back as a total failure?

# CHAPTER 8

# The Game

At the end of February, the 4th Regiment had its first major exercise, a naval battle against Purist Arabia on the Sibuyan Sea in the Philippines.

"Your first exercise will be a tabletop simulation because only an idiot would give real ships and weapons to losers like you," Shujimi told his platoon.

The game was elaborate. The squads worked in separate rooms in Yamamoto Hall, Taisho Auditorium, and Tsushima Gymnasium to simulate the separation between ships. Computer models of the Sibuyan Sea appeared on their computers. The controllers' room acted as "Navy headquarters" and fed weather conditions, sonar readings, images of ships, and enemy movements to the computer network.

Squads 2 and 11 went to Yamamoto Hall, classroom 7. Each squad had its own table of maps and computers. A large screen dominated one of the room's walls. Computer animation showed ships moving across the Sibuyan Sea. Chatter from Navy headquarters came over the large screen's speakers.

Shujimi led some professors into the classroom. They wore Navy, Army, Air Force, and Coast Guard uniforms.

"Professors from the National Defense Academy, all three officer candidate schools, and the Japan Coast Guard Academy will observe this exercise," Shujimi told the midshipmen. "Look sharp and perform well.

"Since Indonesia is an ally of Purist Arabia, the Purists may send its forces from Indonesia into the Sibuyan Sea, where they can attack the Philippine island of Luzon."

He went to Squad 11's table. "Squad 11, you are the corvette *Osaka Maru*. Miyahara is your skipper. You know your roles, so carry them out."

He went to the other table. "Squad 2, you are the light cruiser *Sakura Maru*..."

After Shujimi and the professors left, the game began. Weather reports, ship positions, intelligence on the Purist Arabian and Indonesian navies, and messages from Navy headquarters came to the squads by email, the large screen, and pocket computer calls.

"Hey, we don't invade the Philippines this time," said Yamaguchi as she unfolded a map on the table.

Kwon looked up from her computer. "We're not supposed to invade anyone anymore. Maybe we'll do better on the side of the democracies. We lost with the dictatorships last time."

Kamio said to Ishiro, "Purist Arabia won't attack us while we buy its oil. Russia is our real enemy. We should be practicing to liberate the Northern Territories."

"But relations with Purist Arabia are getting worse each day," said Ishiro.

"That's what the government wants you to think. Fujiwara and his Cabinet are Russia sympathizers."

Miyahara said, "Sato, Kamio, what are you chattering about?"

"Uh, just weather reports, sir," Kamio replied.

"Any information about enemy ship positions?"

"No, sir, nothing yet."

Miyahara pointed at the large screen. "Look at that. It's showing just our ships. We're blind at the moment."

On the large screen, the Japanese ships sailed in three groups. Battle Groups 1 and 2 each had an aircraft carrier surrounded by her escort ships. Battle Group 3 had the *Osaka Maru*, *Sakura Maru*, and other corvettes, frigates, and destroyers. The Purist Arabian fleet stayed invisible.

"Communications ready?" Miyahara asked.

"Ready, sir," said Yamaguchi.

"Weapons systems ready?"

"Ready, sir," said Kwon.

"Sensors ready?"

"Ready, sir," said Kamio.

"Electronic warfare ready?"

"Ready, sir," said Ishiro.

"And as captain, I take care of navigation," said Miyahara. "We're ready. Where are the Purists?"

Soon afterwards, the enemy ships appeared, one at a time, on the large screen. Some of them moved towards the northernmost Japanese carrier group.

Yamaguchi's pocket computer rang. She answered it, listened, and reported, "Message from the *Hosho*. An enemy ship just opened fire against her."

On the large screen, Purist ships approached the aircraft carrier *Hosho* and her escorts. Information about cannon fire and guided missiles appeared on the midshipmen's computers.

"Battle Group 1 is under attack," said Miyahara.

"Nothing about torpedoes," Ishiro observed. "I guess the Purists have no submarines."

"I wouldn't be so sure, not yet," said Kamio. "They could be hiding somewhere."

Minutes later, the Purist began attacking the Battle Group 2, the second carrier group. They kept away from Battle Group 3 and the *Osaka Maru*, though.

"Hey, where did that come from?" Kamio blurted. He stared at his computer. "An aircraft just flew over our ship."

"It's showing up on my computer too," said Kwon.

"Not mine," said Ishiro.

"Not mine either," said Kwon.

"They're intentionally confusing us," said Miyahara.

Kamio's pocket computer rang. After listening to it, he said, "The *Sakura Maru* called. They see it too."

"Prepare weapons and track it," Miyahara ordered.

"Yes, sir," Kwon replied.

Ishiro looked at Kamio's computer. The sensors showed an airplane flying over their group of ships.

"Is it hostile or friendly?" Miyahara asked.

"Something's wrong. I can't tell from the radar info," said Kamio.

"Could it be one of ours?" asked Ishiro.

"Kamio, go on the deck and check it visually," Miyahara said.

"Yes, sir," Kamio replied as he clicked on a "VISUAL" button on his screen.

A photograph of a Purist Arabian fighter jet appeared.

"It's hostile, sir!" Kamio announced.

"Kwon, bring it down. Sato, jam its communications," Miyahara ordered.

"Yes, sir," Kwon and Ishiro said as they typed commands at their computers.

Ishiro sent hundreds of jamming signals. In a real battle, some of the signals would end the enemy's radio communications if they hit the right frequencies. Other signals would crash the enemy's wireless internet if they got through the firewalls and hit the right IP addresses.

Animated gunfire appeared on their computers; Kwon was firing the ship's guns. The plane got hit and crashed into the sea.

"Yay, we got it!" said Kwon.

Miyahara smiled. "Good. Keep watching for others."

"That enemy plane did nothing. I think it was an easy kill for our benefit," Kamio whispered.

"Maybe," Ishiro replied. "Let's see what happens next."

A message appeared on the large screen: "To Battle Group 3: Do not approach or engage the enemy unless you are fired upon. Ship captains, your course directions will come momentarily..."

The exercise went into its second hour. Ishiro constantly monitored enemy radio and internet activity so he could disrupt them. However, the exercise's controllers sent no information about jamming results, so he didn't know if his electronic warfare was working.

"In a real battle, you don't know if everything you did was successful," Miyahara explained.

The battle concentrated on the two carrier groups. Battle Group 3 stayed relatively safe, close enough to watch the enemy but far enough to avoid fighting.

"It's funny that we should be fighting our simulated battle here," said Kamio, glancing at the table map. "Didn't we lose to the Americans here in the Greater East Asia War?"

"Yes, that was the Battle of Leyte Gulf, the largest naval battle in history," said Ishiro. "It occurred in October 1944. The Americans had invaded Leyte, and we sent almost every ship we had to defeat the invasion. The large battle can actually be divided into four battles, the battles of the Sibuyan Sea, the Surigao Strait, Cape Engaño, and Samar..."

Ishiro launched into a lecture about the Battle of Leyte Gulf.

"Sato, shut up and pay attention to the enemy! Don't talk so much!" Miyahara ordered.

Ishiro stopped talking. Then his pocket computer rang. He answered it.

"This is the *Adachi* to the *Ota*," a woman said. "*Ota*, tell your captain —"

"*Adachi*, this is the *Osaka Maru*, not the *Ota*," Ishiro interrupted her.

The caller kept talking. "We've got a sonar reading of a large unidentified object at latitude twelve degrees, fifty minutes, and zero seconds north, longitude one hundred and twenty-two degrees, thirty-five minutes, and zero seconds east. Write that down. I repeat, latitude twelve degrees, fifty minutes, and zero seconds north, longitude one hundred and twenty-two degrees, thirty-five minutes, and zero seconds east. We don't know what it is. It might be a whale, it might be a ship, or it might be nothing. Over."

The call ended, leaving Ishiro puzzled. The message wasn't meant for him. He had eavesdropped on a message from the *Adachi* to the *Ota*.

He looked at the large screen. The *Ota* was close to the coordinates he had scribbled on a piece of paper. There were no enemy ships close to the *Ota*, though.

Perhaps it was just a whale or a false reading, Ishiro thought.

Five minutes later, Miyahara got a message from the controllers' room.

"Navy headquarters just sent another course change," he said as he typed on his computer. "Changing course now."

Battle Group 3 was splitting into two groups, one with the *Osaka Maru*, the other with the *Ota*. The *Osaka Maru* was sailing to join the aircraft carrier *Hosho* in the fight.

A new ship suddenly appeared beside the *Ota* on the large screen.

"Hey, did you see that?" said Yamaguchi.

"What is it?" Miyahara asked.

"New sonar reading," Kamio said. "It's an enemy submarine coming from nowhere!"

The *Ota* disappeared from the large screen.

"What happened?" Miyahara asked.

"Sir, I'm getting a message from Navy headquarters," Yamaguchi reported. "The *Ota* has been sunk by an enemy submarine at the coordinates latitude twelve degrees, fifty minutes, and zero seconds north, longitude one hundred and twenty-two degrees, thirty-five minutes, and zero seconds east."

Now Ishiro knew that the *Ota* had not been the only ship at those coordinates.

**

Squad 11 sat around a table to discuss the exercise. Shujimi recounted the results of the battle. Japan's two aircraft carriers survived, but twenty other ships sank. The Purists lost one aircraft carrier and ten smaller ships, but their troop transports got to Leyte. Japan had failed to prevent the Purist invasion of the Philippines.

Shujimi asked, "Did anyone receive a message about an object near the *Ota*?"

The squad members said nothing.

Then Miyahara said, "No, sir, we didn't receive any such message."

"Wrong, you did. I was monitoring communications at the controllers' room," said Shujimi. "I know one of you received a call on his pocket computer."

The squad members said nothing.

"If I don't get an answer, I'll have to punish the whole squad," said Shujimi, holding his swagger stick. "Afterwards, the miscreant will suffer far worse from his shipmates than from me."

Ishiro silently raised his hand.

"Sato, do you have something to say?" Shujimi said.

"Yes, sir," said Ishiro.

"What is it?"

"I overheard a call between the *Adachi* and the *Ota* about a large object, sir."

Miyahara turned to Ishiro. "Sato, you received a call, and you didn't tell me or Yamaguchi?"

"I want to clarify that I did not receive a call. Since the call wasn't intended for me, it is improper to say that I received it. Rather, I *overheard* it," Ishiro said.

Shujimi crossed his arms. "The *Adachi* and *Ota* were in another building. Please explain to your shipmates how you overheard them."

"My pocket computer rang, and I heard their call," Ishiro replied. "I tried to explain to the caller that she had phoned the *Osaka Maru*, but she wouldn't listen."

"What did she say in the call?"

"She gave the coordinates of an unidentified object near the *Ota*, sir."

"I see," said Shujimi. "What did you do with the coordinates?"

Ishiro's temperature rose. He blurted, "Uh, ah, well, ah, duh, oh "

"I need an answer," Shujimi demanded.

"I didn't do anything with them," Ishiro admitted.

His squad mates stared ruefully at him.

"So you got the call," said Shujimi. "Did you try to contact the *Ota*?"

"No."

"No? Why didn't you contact the *Ota*?"

"I wasn't supposed to get the call. I simply overheard it. I presumed the *Ota* received the call," Ishiro said.

"Except that she didn't," Shujimi revealed. "None of the *Ota*'s crew got that call. *You* got the call. In other words, you heard about a possible hostile object and its coordinates, and you didn't contact the ship closest to it."

Ishiro's shipmates looked sullen. He sensed their disdain for him.

"You're an idiot, *otaku* boy!" Shujimi said. "When you have nothing important to say, your mouth never stops! When you have something important to say, your mouth stays shut! You are the *otaku* boy of complete failure! You're stupid, ignorant, incompetent, selfish, disrespectful, lazy —"

"That's unfair, sir!" Ishiro argued. "I was never supposed to receive that call. It was meant for someone else."

"But you did receive the call," Shujimi reminded him.

"But in real life, I wouldn't have received that call," Ishiro complained. "The exercise was illogical."

"Illogical? Is war ever logical?" said Shujimi. "In battle, anything can happen. What if the *Ota* missed the message due to enemy interference? What if the *Adachi* had sent the message to the wrong frequency or the wrong email address? Anything could have happened. You should have informed the *Ota*, or at least your own captain, of any important information you learn."

Ishiro felt sick, ready to vomit. He wanted to flee from Etajima.

"But it wasn't my job to communicate with other ships," Ishiro pleaded. "I was assigned to jam enemy communications. It was someone else's job to communicate with our own ships."

The squad members glared at him. Shujimi shook his head.

"Are you blaming someone else?" Yamaguchi said.

"Uh, ah, no, but you've got to admit that it shouldn't have been my responsibility," said Ishiro.

Shujimi groaned. "*Otaku* boy, you'll never understand the Navy, will you? It doesn't matter what your job is. In a crisis, everyone has to do whatever it takes to survive and win. We have to work as a team, not as isolated individuals. You have disappointed not only your squad but also the entire 4th Brigade, especially the crew of the *Ota*."

Ishiro breathed shallowly, hardly drawing in air. He was sure the lieutenant would expel him. He needed to defend himself.

"Sir, your exact words to me two days ago were, 'Don't do all the talking, but do all the listening.' In the exercise, I followed your directions exactly," Ishiro declared.

Shujimi grinned, but the hostility in his eyes showed his true feelings.

"Yes, *otaku* boy, I did say that," Shujimi agreed.

He slammed his swagger stick on the table and stood up. The squad rose to their feet immediately.

"This meeting is over," Shujimi said. "All of you except Sato are dismissed."

The rest of the squad left the room. Ishiro wished he could leave too.

"*Otaku* boy, you think you're very smart, don't you?" Shujimi said.

"Yes, I am, sir," Ishiro said. "I have a university degree in computer science from University of Tokyo. In high school, I got the highest marks in my class for math and computer programming. I qualify for membership in Mensa, an international high-I.Q. society. In addition, I —"

"Enough, I'm confident of your above-average intelligence," said Shujimi. "The private sector has great demand, as well as great salaries, for people with high I.Q.'s. Will you resign from the Navy and return to civilian life?"

Ishiro shook his head. "No, I will not, sir."

"Why not?" Shujimi said. "Your shipmates hate you, the professors hate you, and I hate you. Why do you remain?"

"Sir, I've got nowhere else to go," Ishiro admitted. "I've tried everything else and failed. Please, sir, I need to succeed here. It's my only chance."

Shujimi looked stern. "The Navy is not a daycare center for the rejects of society. We're here to throw out losers like you, not take them in."

Ishiro looked down at the floor.

"*Otaku* boy, will you resign?" Shujimi asked.

"No, sir," said Ishiro.

"*Otaku* boy, I'm going to ask the Superintendent if he can meet us, you and me. For some reason, he's interested in your case. Check your pocket computer for the day and time," Shujimi said.

"Yes, sir," Ishiro said softly.

A pain gnawed at his stomach. He knew why Shujimi wanted him to meet the Superintendent. The Superintendent approved all expulsions from the school.

**

Before lights out, he looked at the hologram of Yuko again. He longed to see her pretty face and hear her sweet voice.

Not long ago, he doubted if she could feel real emotions. But something had made her send the *honmei choco* to him. Did she choose to send the chocolate? Or did Ami program her to do it?

Perhaps Yuko was waiting for a message from him. He sent an email to her:

*Dear Yuko,*

*Thank you for the honmei choco heart. It was the sweetest chocolate I had ever tasted. You are the most beautiful girl I have ever met.*

*All is going well at the officer candidate school. I promise to visit you during my leave, whenever I get it. Please say hi to Mr. Endo, Mrs. Endo, Ami, and the maids for me.*

*Sincerely,*

*Ishiro*

**

The order to report to the Superintendent's office came in the morning. After lunch, Ishiro went to the office, where Kirino was waiting for him.

Superintendent Kirino's office was like a museum of the Japanese Navy. It had model warships, medals, badges, rank insignia, and photos of naval officers from the Meiji Era to the present day. Also on the wall were a naval officer's sword and the signal flag for "Z." Ishiro guessed that the Navy was not a mere job but a holy calling for the Superintendent.

Not every artifact was related to a ship or an admiral. He had three model androids, L-1, L-2, and L-3 female types in Navy uniforms. They were promotional items given by Victor Robotics. The Midshipmen's Manual said that Kirino had been Director of Android Warfare at the Joint Staff Office.

Ishiro and Shujimi stood in front of Kirino's desk. They watched him read an electronic report on his computer. The silence made Ishiro nervous.

Kirino looked up and said, "Lieutenant Shujimi?"

Shujimi snapped to attention and asked, "Yes, sir?"

"Thank you for your report about Midshipman Sato."

"You're welcome, sir."

The Superintendent asked Ishiro, "Midshipman, have you ever been diagnosed with a mental illness or a learning disability?"

"No, sir," Ishiro muttered.

Shujimi grunted. "His medical and psychological entrance tests showed no evidence of a mental illness or learning disability."

"Then there is no excuse for Midshipman Sato's poor performance," Kirino said.

"In my opinion, his performance is due to rudeness, bad manners, and social ineptitude."

"Then I agree with you that a charge of gross negligence is justified."

"Thank you, sir," said Shujimi.

"Uh, ah, I don't mean to be rude, actually, I don't think I am, uh, ah, rude at all," Ishiro stammered.

"Shut up!" Shujimi ordered.

Kirino scowled at Ishiro. "Midshipman Sato, Lieutenant Shujimi is charging you with gross negligence. You may choose to be tried by a court martial. However, I must advise that your chance of an acquittal is small, based on reports I've received from the lieutenant and other professors. Do you wish to be tried for gross negligence by a court martial?"

Trial by court martial sounded painful and humiliating to Ishiro. He did not know its alternatives, but anything seemed better than a trial.

"No, I do not wish to be tried by a court martial, sir," Ishiro said.

"A good choice in this case," said Kirino. "If a court martial were to find you guilty, you would go to military prison, and after your release, be expelled from both the Navy and this school."

"Sir, I think leaving the school is inevitable for Midshipman Sato," Shujimi said. "We should consider letting him resign and waiving the penalties."

Ishiro glanced at the floor. Resignation looked good now. He actually felt relieved, as if the Navy were letting him be a failure. Nobody had given him such permission before.

"I'll resign, sir," Ishiro said quietly. "Please give me the resignation form, and I'll seal it."

Kirino shook his head. "No, let's not talk about resigning yet."

"Sir, with all due respect, if he wishes to resign, we should grant his wish," said Shujimi.

"I know, I read that in your report. But there's a war coming, and I need all the meat I can get," Kirino said.

"But sir, Sato is unfit for a position of authority. He's not officer material," Shujimi protested.

"I agree that he seriously lacks the qualities of an officer at present," said Kirino. "However, can administrative punishment help him learn those qualities?"

"I doubt it, but we can try it if you wish."

"What do you recommend, lieutenant?"

"Two whacks of a swagger stick on his buttocks, sir," Shujimi suggested.

Kirino nodded. "An excellent idea. That might force him to think about his shortcomings and modify his behavior. If it works in training dogs, it can work in training *otaku*. Thank you, lieutenant."

Ishiro couldn't believe them. They wanted to flog him!

Kirino said, "Midshipman Sato, for your gross negligence in simulated battle, which in actual battle would have caused the loss of a vessel and all her hands aboard, I order you to receive administrative punishment of two blows of a swagger stick. Do you have anything to say, Mr. Sato?"

"I did nothing wrong, sir," Ishiro protested. "I was only following Lieutenant Shujimi's advice to me."

Kirino stood up and glared into Ishiro's eyes.

"The punishment is increased to four blows," said Kirino.

"Wait! You can't arbitrarily increase the punishment," Ishiro complained.

"The punishment is increased to eight blows."

Shujimi smirked. He looked genuinely happy.

"But I just resigned!" Ishiro said.

"I don't see any resignation letter here, do you?" said Kirino.

"But you heard me! Just give me the resignation form," Ishiro begged.

Kirino said, "Do you think you can escape punishment by quitting?"

"Superintendent, may I speak to the boy?" Shujimi asked.

Kirino nodded.

"Midshipman Sato, I offered you three chances to resign, but you refused them all. You cannot resign now. You must face the consequences of your actions like an adult," said Shujimi.

Kirino said, "Thank you, lieutenant, those are my thoughts too."

He sat back down and looked at the daily schedule on his computer. "The punishment will occur in front of the 2nd Platoon, 4th Regiment, during roll call tomorrow morning."

"Yes, sir," said Shujimi.

They weren't going to let him resign, Ishiro realized. They were going to keep him just to flog him. His hopes of returning to civilian life, afloat only a minute ago, sank quickly.

"No, I want to resign right now!" Ishiro insisted. "If I leave, you won't have to put up with me anymore!"

"The punishment is increased to sixteen blows," Kirino ordered.

"But sir —"

"Sato, stop talking and listen to me!" Shujimi said. "You're smart in math. Do you see a mathematical pattern in the increases of your punishment?"

"Uh, yes, sir, each new quantity is twice the previous quantity," Ishiro observed.

"Good," said Shujimi. "Do you wish to continue discussing your punishment? Before you answer, think for a moment, but not too long."

Ishiro sighed. "No, sir."

"No, sir, what?" Shujimi demanded.

"No, sir, I do not wish to continue discussing my punishment," Ishiro answered.

Shujimi smiled again. "I finally found out how to shut your mouth, *otaku* boy!"

**

Between reveille and roll call, Shujimi thrust a piece of paper at Ishiro.

"What is this, sir?" Ishiro asked.

"It's a waiver absolving the Navy from any temporary or permanent scarring, temporary or permanent injury or disability, temporary or permanent mental illness, or death due to physical punishment," Kirino explained. "Stamp it with your *inkan* seal."

"What happens if I don't seal it? Can the punishment proceed?" Ishiro said.

"In that case, the punishment will be doubled to thirty-two blows. If you survive, you survive. If you die, your death will be recorded as a training accident."

Ishiro's hand shook as he pressed his *inkan* on the paper. He hoped that he would not suffer any of the terrible injuries listed on the waiver.

The punishment came during morning roll call, as Kirino had ordered. Shujimi ordered Ishiro to stand in front of the whole platoon.

Shujimi announced, "Midshipman Sato, for his gross negligence in simulated battle, which in actual battle would have caused the loss of a vessel and all her hands aboard, will receive administrative punishment of sixteen blows of a swagger stick by order of the Superintendent."

He turned to Ishiro and ordered, "Midshipman Sato, turn and face your shipmates and stand with your legs apart!"

Ishiro spread his legs and braced for the first blow. But it didn't come. Instead, he heard footsteps.

He turned and saw an L-3 android, one of the pretty female models by Victor Robotics. Since Kirino banned androids from wearing military uniform, it wore a short black dress and boots.

It also carried a swagger stick.

"You're in for a treat," Shujimi whispered. "A midshipman programmed it to flog people."

"Which midshipman?" Ishiro asked.

"Miyahara."

In the front row, Miyahara stood at attention and stared at Ishiro. Ishiro felt queasy.

The swagger stick whistled as it slashed through the air. Then it smacked on Ishiro's buttocks.

Ishiro screamed on the first blow. He burst into tears on the second blow. He fell to his knees on the third blow.

"Stand up!" Shujimi ordered.

Ishiro wiped the tears from his face and stood up. The android struck him again. He cried and leaned forward.

"Stand up straight!" Shujimi ordered.

Ishiro straightened his back and felt the swagger stick's sting again. The pain shot through his body. He cried out.

"Shut up!" Shujimi ordered.

The android struck the sixth blow, the seventh blow, the eighth blow...

The platoon stared at him. Nobody looked at him with sympathy. The public humiliation intensified the pain.

The Navy was a nightmare. It was nothing like Ishiro had expected. It didn't resemble the Navy in General Morita's anime, like *Time Warp at Midway*, *Imperial Space Marines Battalion Musashi*, or *Nuke the Yanks*. He should have heeded the warnings of his parents and Mr. Endo.

Finally, the android hit the sixteenth blow. Panting and sobbing, Ishiro fell to the ground.

Shujimi tapped his swagger stick on Ishiro's shoulder. "Did I order you to lie down?"

Ishiro stayed on the ground and wept. Shujimi frowned and kicked the midshipman's shoulder.

"Stand up, *otaku* boy!"

Ishiro stood up but slouched. Filled with pain, he staggered back to his squad.

Shujimi ordered the platoon to disperse. As the others walked away, he kept Ishiro back.

"*Otaku* boy, if you resign now, I'll talk to the Superintendent again. Do it soon," Shujimi said.

**

Throughout the morning, Ishiro heard hushed comments uttered behind him:

"Isn't that the guy who was flogged for gross stupidity?"

"Look, there's Sato the loser! No, don't look at him."

"Did you see him cry? Like a baby, he couldn't stop."

"I hear that his squad is at the bottom of the 4th Regiment because of him. They won't win any awards."

"I'm glad he's not in my squad."

Miyahara, Yamaguchi, and Kwon refused to talk to him at lunch. Only Kamio talked to him.

"Purist Arabia is far away and has no ambitions for Asian territory," Kamio said. "Russia, however, is close by and wants to control its neighbors. And Uncle Joe is still up there while we put up space electricity satellites. I bet we'll be at war with Russia within five years."

"*So desu ka,*" Ishiro said as he chewed his food.

After the day's last class, he printed the resignation letter, pressed his *inkan* on it, and gave it to Kirino's administrative android.

Kirino acted quickly. Before lights out, a message appeared on Ishiro's pocket computer. Kirino wanted to see him tomorrow.

The Superintendent never saw the midshipmen when approving their resignations. What did Ishiro do wrong now?

**

Ishiro stood while Kirino sat behind his desk. The Superintendent did not give the order to sit down.

Kirino held up Ishiro's resignation. "Is this your letter and your *inkan* seal?"

"Yes, sir," Ishiro replied.

Kirino put the letter down. "Shujimi wanted to expel you in Hell Week, but I told him to keep you. Yes, it's true, there's a war coming, so I need more meat for the sharks. And recruitment is not as high as the Department of Defense wishes. But there's another reason why I've kept you."

He took a letter from his desk drawer, stood up, and gave it to Ishiro. "Sato, you should read this."

Ishiro felt the smooth linen texture of the paper. It was thick and firm, like a ceremonial scroll. Its author had shunned email, written on expensive paper, and sent it by the traditional post office. Its message must be important.

He read the words, written in bold black ink:

*Dear Superintendent Rear Admiral Kirino,*

*I regret that I have not attended the Maritime Self-Defense Force old comrades' reunions over the past five years. My restaurants keep me occupied too much. It is too long since I have seen you, but I hope to attend next year's reunion. Of course, if you come to Tokyo, you are very welcome to visit me and dine at any of my restaurants. Masako sends her regards.*

*I'm writing to you about a midshipman named Sato Ishiro, who will be entering the Naval Officer Candidate School this week. I have known Mr. Sato for two years, as he is a regular customer at one of my restaurants.*

*On the surface, Mr. Sato may not seem like officer material. He is socially awkward, tends to talk too much, focuses on the minor and irrelevant aspects of a conversation, and concentrates intensely on a narrow range of interests, mostly computers and anime. I suspect that his behavior is caused by lack of life experience that other people his age normally acquire. I cannot speculate as to how this occurred. I tried to dissuade him from joining the Navy, but he insisted on going.*

*However, under the surface, he has many fine qualities. He is very knowledgeable in computer science and robotics, respects our military traditions, is honest, works hard, and wants to be useful to society. He likes to help people so long as he can do so within his range of interests and competence. For example, he tutored one of my employees in trigonometry so that she could graduate from high school. He gave his services to her without any expectation of reward, material or immaterial.*

*I do not ask for any special treatment or favors for Mr. Sato. Indeed, I wish you to treat him as harshly as you would any other midshipman and expel him from the school if he is beyond hope of training.*

*I do ask that you take the opportunity to correct his flaws if possible so that his extensive talents will not go to waste. I agree that the Navy does not need failures, but at the same time, it is also the place where a boy can grow to be a man. You and I both know that.*

*If you have any questions or wish to discuss this matter, please contact me at any time. I wish you all the best and hope to see you at the next old comrades' reunion.*

*Sincerely,*

*Endo Hideki, Lieutenant Commander, Japan Maritime Self-Defense Force Reserve (retired)*


"Well, do you have anything to say?" Kirino asked.

"Wow, I never knew Mr. Endo had a rank as high as lieutenant commander," said Ishiro.

Kirino looked shocked. "You fool! Is that all you got out of that letter? I should expel you from the school right now!"

Ishiro looked at the floor. "I apologize, sir."

"Darn right that you should apologize! A recommendation from Lieutenant Commander Endo Hideki is no trivial matter," Kirino said. "Endo was one of the best robotics students I ever had. He was a pioneer in android warfare. His impressive achievements began as early as his midshipman days. He accomplished much in his military career. I wished he had joined the regular force, not the Reserve."

Ishiro nodded. "Yes, sir, I understand."

"No, you don't understand, but I'll give you a chance to," said Kirino. "Sato, keep that letter from Mr. Endo. Read it over and over until you know what it means. Think about the advice that Lieutenant Shujimi, your professors, and your shipmates have given you. Think over and over until you understand what they were saying. Learn whatever it takes to become a man and an officer. You have a month to prove yourself."

"Sir, I just resigned," Ishiro reminded him.

"Oh, yes, that." Kirino picked up the resignation. "Do you want to take it back? The choice is yours."

*Mr. Endo wrote a letter to support me,* Ishiro thought. *If I were to return to Nikkou Café now, he would view me as a great disappointment and a failure.*

*And how would Yuko view me? She's not a real woman, she's an android, but she's a different kind of android. Would she see me as a loser?*

"I would like to take my resignation back, sir," Ishiro decided.

Kirino returned it to him. "Okay, mister. Remember, you have one month to prove yourself. That's one month to improve your performance scores. If Lieutenant Shujimi doesn't give you a satisfactory rating by then, you'll be expelled from the school."

"Thank you, sir," said Ishiro.

"Don't thank me. Thank Lieutenant Commander Endo Hideki," Kirino said as he sat back down. "Now stop wasting my time. Dismissed!"

# CHAPTER 9

# Reprogram Yourself

NAVY TELECOM CONTROL: *You are calling on a secure network. The Japanese Navy will record your telephone call for security monitoring.*
ENDO: Hello, Nikkou Café.
ISHIRO: Mr. Endo?
ENDO: Yes, that's me.
ISHIRO: Mr. Endo, this is Sato Ishiro. Do you remember me?
ENDO: Mr. Sato! Of course, I remember you. How are you?
ISHIRO: I'm still at the Naval Officer Candidate School.
ENDO: That's good. I'm glad you chose the Navy. What can I do for you?
ISHIRO: Remember, before I left, you said that I could call you?
ENDO: Uh, yes.
ISHIRO: Is this a good time to talk?
ENDO: Yes, I can talk now. How may I help you?
ISHIRO: Sir, I need your advice about how to stay in the school. I'm afraid that I'll be expelled.
ENDO: Oh, that's unfortunate. Do you really want my advice? Remember, I warned you that former military officers can be brutally frank.
ISHIRO: You're the only person I know who has gone through the school and the Navy.
ENDO: Okay, I'll talk to you. First, you must ask yourself: Do you really want to stay in the Navy?
ISHIRO: I do, sir. It's the only place I've got left. I can't get a job anywhere else. I used to work for Dai Tokyo Taikun Financial Group as a computer systems analyst, but for some reason, the company fired me. Then I was an IT support analyst at Chugoku Telecom, and I got fired. Then I was in retail sales at a computer store, but I got fired there too. Then I worked at Ashi Android Scrapyard, but the owner fired me — unfairly, I'll say. He said I was misusing the equipment, but it's an android, it's built to resemble a human, and I didn't damage any components, and —
ENDO: Okay, okay. Which are your best courses?

ISHIRO: Physics, computer science, navigation, and robotics and android science. I do well in the science and computer subjects.

ENDO: I always knew those are your strong points. The Navy needs people who know those subjects. Which are your poorest courses?

ISHIRO: I'm not doing well in the combat training, phys-ed, and seamanship courses, but at least I'm scoring the minimum grades to stay in. But I think the Navy has relaxed the standards for physical training. I hear the Navy needs more people.

ENDO: Well, for whatever reason, you're still passing those courses. What about the academic subjects?

ISHIRO: For some reason, I'm failing in history, political science, military law, and naval battle analysis. I don't know why my marks are so low. I know these subjects thoroughly. Just yesterday, in military law class, the professor said my class participation was dismal, but I did talk in the class discussion.

ENDO: Who is the professor?

ISHIRO: Lieutenant Commander Hirano.

ENDO: She's famous, and I hear she's good. What happened?

ISHIRO: I talked about the software design of robot submarines. Nobody else knew anything about that software. But Professor Hirano didn't like my comments.

ENDO: How does software design for robot subs relate to military law?

ISHIRO: Professor Hirano asked a question about robot subs.

ENDO: What was the question?

ISHIRO: If a self-guided robot sub fires a missile that sinks a civilian ship, who is responsible for the incident? Is it the officer in charge of the robot subs? Is it the person who programmed the robot sub? Is it the company that made the robot sub? Or is it the company that made the robot sub's software?

ENDO: Interesting.

ISHIRO: She asked me what I thought.

ENDO: And what did you say?

ISHIRO: I said that two companies, Victor Robotics and Mitsubishi, have been developing software for robot subs. They're civilian contractors, of course. Mitsubishi uses the so-called risk-based algorithm, whereas Victor Robotics uses the so-called visual identification system. Hence we have two competing systems, and the Navy is testing both of them. The advantages of the risk-based algorithm are —

ENDO: Sato, she didn't ask about mathematical algorithms.

ISHIRO: But I think the development of robot sub software is important.

ENDO: Sato, I think the professor only wanted you to tell who you think should be held responsible for sinking the civilian ship. I don't think she cared about the development of software for robot subs.

ISHIRO: But for a comprehensive answer —

ENDO: Sato, you asked for my advice, so don't argue with me. Listen to me. You've got to reprogram yourself.

ISHIRO: What?

ENDO: I'm talking to you in a language that you understand. There's a bug — maybe several bugs — in your mental programming, so reprogram yourself.

ISHIRO: What do you mean?

ENDO: When someone asks a question, answer it. Make your answer short and to the point. Don't ramble about something irrelevant.

ISHIRO: Everything I say is true.

ENDO: It may be true, but nobody asked for it. You're only showing off.

ISHIRO: But what I say is important --

ENDO: Sailor, did you ask for my advice or not?

ISHIRO: Uh, I did.

ENDO: Then listen to me. Sailor, this is your next order: Work with your shipmates, not against them.

ISHIRO: Huh? I don't work against my shipmates.

ENDO: I think you do. You argue over unimportant issues with them, and you take easy ways out that help yourself but get them in trouble.

ISHIRO: But, but, but -- are you talking about the food game? How did you know about that?

ENDO: I also know about the simulation exercise. The one time when you should've spoken up, but you kept quiet.

ISHIRO: What! Who told you about that?

ENDO: I have contacts in the school.

ISHIRO: Who is it? Superintendent Kirino?

ENDO: It doesn't matter. Listen to me. You've got to learn the right time to speak and the right time to stay quiet. You've got to learn teamwork with your shipmates. Teamwork is what a ship's crew does.

ISHIRO: I don't know why you are saying this —

ENDO: If you want to stay in the school, reprogram yourself. If you don't, you'll be expelled from the Navy, and you'll return to taking computers apart in a used computer store.

ISHIRO: That can never happen to me.

ENDO: I thought you said you had no other career choices.

ISHIRO: I can never return to taking computers apart because I never had a job like that. I took *androids* apart.

ENDO: Please excuse me, but I've got to get back to work.

ISHIRO: Did I say something wrong?

NAVY TELECOM CONTROL: *Your telephone call has reached the maximum time allowable for first-year midshipmen. You will be disconnected now.*

# CHAPTER 10

# The Summer Cruise

The next morning, Shujimi held a surprise quiz for Squad 11. They stood at attention as he paced in front of them.

"Sato!" said Shujimi. "Sun Tzu, the Chinese military theorist, wrote a book entitled *The Art of War*. He wrote that all war is based upon something in particular. What is that thing?"

Ishiro had not read *The Art of War* even though it was required reading for the military theory course. He stayed silent.

"Sato, I can't wait forever!"

Ishiro uttered a stream of nonsense syllables.

"I didn't understand a word you said, you moron!" Shujimi said. He put his swagger stick under Ishiro's chin. "Tell me, *otaku* boy, is this a joke?"

"No, sir!"

"Give me an answer. That's an order. If you don't give me an answer, I'll cancel all your food rations for today!" Shujimi threatened.

"Sir, all war is based on — fighting," Ishiro guessed.

Shujimi withdrew his swagger stick and grunted.

"Wrong! According to Sun Tzu, all war is based on deception," Shujimi said. "Sato, you are prohibited from receiving food rations today."

"No! Sir, you can't do that!" Ishiro cried.

"What?" Shujimi shouted. "Who says I can't?"

"Sir, with all due respect, cutting my rations is unfair," Ishiro pleaded. "You asked a question, you ordered me to give you an answer, and I gave you one."

"But it was the wrong answer," Shujimi said.

"You ordered me to give you an answer, but you didn't say it had to be a *correct* answer," Ishiro explained. "I followed your order exactly."

Shujimi smiled and nodded. "Mr. Sato, once again, you've used your impeccable logic to win another argument."

"Thank you, sir, thank you very much!" said Ishiro. He relished the praise from Shujimi. The lieutenant had never said anything good to him before.

Shujimi hit Ishiro's shoulder with his swagger stick. Ishiro cried out.

"I'm still removing your rations," Shujimi said. "I'm punishing you for being a smart ass."

Ishiro was horrified. A day without food! How would he survive?

"I'm sending an order to the wardroom and the galley to withhold serving you today," said Shujimi. "Use your meal times to meditate about your stupidity."

The lieutenant turned to Miyahara. "Miyahara, if any member of Squad 11 gives any food to Sato today, even as little as a gram of candy, report that person to me immediately. Is that understood?"

"Yes, sir," said Miyahara. He looked at the rest of the squad. "Don't worry. I'm sure nobody will give him anything."

**

A day without food made Ishiro think.

*Reprogram yourself.*

*I'm punishing you for being a smart ass.*

Endo's and Shujimi's words stuck in Ishiro's mind. Ishiro thought about them constantly. He thought about them as he read and reread Mr. Endo's letter to Superintendent Kirino.

How could he, Sato Ishiro, an overachiever in math and science in high school, a graduate of University of Tokyo, be such a failure? What made him so different from Endo, Kirino, or Shujimi, all smart university graduates, all successful naval officers?

Hunger pangs made him think.

Endo, Kirino, and Shujimi not only survived but thrived in the Navy. In contrast, Ishiro was failing.

Three officers versus one midshipman: the odds were against him. Their naval careers proved that they knew how to succeed. Ishiro finally admitted to himself that their advice was probably good.

It was he, not everyone else, who had to change.

*Reprogram yourself.*

He had to summon every ounce of willpower for the most difficult task in his life: changing himself. He had to fight against his urges. Could he do it?

He looked at the letter from Endo. He had to do it for him. He couldn't bear the shame of failure after Endo had written to Kirino to support him.

He looked at a photograph of Yuko on his desk. He had to do it for her, especially for her.

Ishiro went to the Memorial Pavilion and stood in front of the Book of the Naval Kami. He bowed twice, clapped twice, and bowed once more.

Then he prayed to the war dead. "Please give me the strength to listen to the advice of my officers and change my ways. If you help me, I will serve the Navy with honor."

It was the first time in his life he had ever prayed to any *kami*.

As he left the Memorial Pavilion, he felt the cold air of late winter, but he saw the Sun shine through a break in the clouds.

**

As always, Squad 11 awaited Lieutenant Shujimi's order before eating breakfast. As always, Shujimi asked questions from the Midshipmen's Manual and made them bet their meals.

"Miyahara, will you bet your own meal or the meals of your shipmates?" Shujimi asked.

"Sir, I'll bet my own meal only!" Miyahara replied.

"Okay. What is the M-E-P-I?" Shujimi asked, saying the Latin letters in English.

"Sir, MEPI is the Middle East Pakistan Indonesia submarine communications cable."

"Very good," said Shujimi. "Remember that cable's name, especially in its English acronym. It carries telecommunications between Purist Arabia, Sudan, Somalia, Pakistan, and Indonesia, all countries in the Purist camp."

He looked at Ishiro. "Sato, will you bet your own meal or the meals of your shipmates?"

"Sir, I'll bet my own meal," Ishiro replied.

His shipmates looked shocked.

"If you wish," Shujimi said. "Question: How many cruise missiles can the *Taisho* Class submarine carry?"

"Sir, the *Taisho* Class submarine can carry three hundred cruise missiles."

Shujimi nodded. "You are correct." He stood up to leave. "Okay, all of you can eat."

Kamio leaned over to Ishiro. "Hey, Sato, you took a risk today. Good for you."

Miyahara grunted. "It took you long enough to learn."

Ishiro nodded silently as he ate his breakfast.

**

In the military law class, Lieutenant Commander Hirano asked Yamaguchi, "Suppose you see some hostile persons who do not wear the regular uniform of an enemy country. They may be in civilian clothes. Under what circumstances will they qualify as combatants and prisoners of war under international law?"

"Ma'am, they have to be under command of a person responsible for his subordinates, have a distinctive emblem that is recognizable from a distance, carry their arms openly, and conduct their operations in accordance with the laws and customs of war," said Yamaguchi.

"Very good," said Hirano. "Those qualifications were laid out in the Hague Convention of 1907. Defining lawful combatants versus spies and terrorists will be important in any conflict involving the Purist countries. The Purists often use fighters who do not qualify as combatants under international law."

She looked at Ishiro. "Sato, suppose you find hostile people in a territory that has not been occupied. They spontaneously take up arms against you. They wear civilian clothes, and they have no armbands or badges or other identifying emblems. Should you consider them to be combatants?"

"Only if they carry their arms openly and respect the laws and customs of war, ma'am," said Ishiro.

"That's from the Hague Convention of 1907. What if they conceal their weapons or hide bombs under their clothes?"

"Then they are terrorists and do not qualify to be treated as combatants or prisoners of war, ma'am."

Hirano nodded. "Again, that's an important distinction if we engage the Purists."

She pointed her pocket computer to the classroom's viewscreen, and a historical photograph appeared. It showed New York's World Trade Center on fire after hijackers had crashed airliners into its towers.

"One of the most well-known photographs of the twenty-first century," said Hirano. "The Al-Qaeda hijackers are legends in the Purist countries. The Purists hail Al-Qaeda's founder, Osama bin Laden, as their greatest military hero since Saladin, who beat the Europeans in the Crusades. Purists say that the planes' hijackers were lawful combatants. But they don't qualify as such under international law. They didn't carry their arms openly, they didn't wear uniforms or identifying emblems, and they deliberately targeted civilians. They did not respect the laws and customs of war. The same goes for Purists who blow themselves up in buses or open fire in shopping malls. Don't listen to those left-wing university professors who describe them as a revolutionary, anti-capitalist army."

The midshipmen laughed. Kwon put up her hand. Hirano nodded at her.

"Ma'am, at the Dubai Peace Conference, the Emir of Purist Arabia told Prime Minister Fujiwara that Purist suicide bombers have the same samurai spirit of our kamikaze pilots. The Prime Minister objected to the comparison," said Kwon.

"Thank you for mentioning that," said Hirano. She pointed her pocket computer to the viewscreen, clicked on some buttons, and the image changed to a black and white photo of a smiling man. He wore a flight suit and a white headband with a disc, the design of the national flag.

"Ensign Ogawa Kiyoshi, the kamikaze pilot who crashed into the aircraft carrier *U.S.S. Bunker Hill*," said Hirano. "Can someone tell me why the Prime Minister would object to comparing Ensign Ogawa to *these* men?"

Hirano changed the image to faces made infamous by the history books: the nineteen hijackers who attacked the United States on September 11, 2001.

Ishiro put up his hand.

"Mr. Sato?" said Hirano.

"Ma'am, the Japanese kamikaze flew military aircraft and attacked military targets. The Al-Qaeda terrorists hijacked civilian aircraft in flight, killed the crew and passengers, and attacked civilian targets," said Ishiro. "Clearly our kamikaze conducted themselves according to the laws and customs of war, whereas Al-Qaeda did not. The Prime Minister was right to object to the comparison."

Hirano gave him a small smile. "Correct. Thank you, Mr. Sato."

"You're welcome, ma'am!" said Ishiro.

The law professor looked at her watch and said, "Class is dismissed. For next class, read the chapter about prisoners of war."

The midshipmen went to their next class. As they walked through the hall, Kamio said, "Sato, what happened? You actually made sense today."

**

White Day, when men give gifts to their sweethearts, was coming, one month after Valentine's Day. Ishiro went to the quartermaster, but she had no White Day chocolates. The Naval Officer Candidate School was a military academy with no use for frivolous candies. Even worse, the quartermaster had run out of ordinary chocolates and did not expect a new supply.

"The Navy is saving its chocolate for serving personnel," she explained. "Wait until you go to sea, then you'll get your chocolate ration."

Ishiro wrote an email message to Yuko:

*Dear Yuko,*

*Please forgive me for not sending you any chocolate, not even an ordinary chocolate bar, for White Day. The school is a strict military academy without such luxuries. Also, midshipmen are not allowed to leave the school grounds until the summer, so I cannot go to the town to buy chocolate.*

*Naval officer training is going very well, and it's only three months until the summer cruise. It's not a cruise like a vacation aboard a pleasure boat, but rather, an assignment aboard a warship. I hope to get a very important ship, like an aircraft carrier.*

*Hopefully, I'll get some leave after the cruise and can come visit you. Give my regards to the maids, Ami, and Mr. and Mrs. Endo.*

*Sincerely,*

*Ishiro*

He sent the message to Navy Telecom Control. Five minutes later, Navy Telecom Control replied that a military censor had cleared his message and it had been sent to Yuko via email.

After receiving the censor's clearance, Ishiro remembered that Yuko could not eat, so she would not care for White Day chocolate anyway. He silently cursed himself for his stupidity. Yuko would think he was an idiot and laugh at him.

But perhaps she would not laugh at him? It depended on how Ami or Mr. Endo had programmed her.

Now he felt even more stupid than before. All of Yuko's behavior was programmed algorithms, not genuine emotions. Why did he keep treating Yuko like a real girl?

**

A day after White Day, he received a video message from Yuko. It started with Yuko smiling at the camera. She wore the French maid costume. She was in the café's back room, with the lockers and the e-bulletin viewscreen. Since it was quiet, she must have made the video outside business hours.

Yuko bowed to the camera. "Good morning, master. Thank you very much for your email message for White Day. I was so happy to receive it. It was the first time anyone has sent me greetings for White Day."

Ishiro felt relieved that Yuko did not mind the lack of chocolates. Not all girls would understand.

An off-screen voice said, "Hey, you're supposed to say you received many chocolates from other men. Make him jealous!"

Ishiro recognized the voice as Ami's. She must have held the camera.

Yuko giggled. "Oh, younger sister, you didn't program me to lie and be deceitful. Is that what other girls do to boys?"

"Well, not me, but Mikita says that's what we should do," Ami said.

"Will you program me to lie to boys?"

"Not now. Maybe when you meet a rich man. Go on."

"It's not as fun without you here, master," Yuko said. She pouted and stroked her hair. "I know that each customer has his favorite maid, and we maids have our favorite customers too. You're my favorite."

She looked slyly at the camera. "When you come back, I'll be waiting for you at the Nikkou Café. You know where to find me. I know what you want, and I can give it to you."

She slowly licked her lips. The camera pulled back, and Yuko posed by curving her body and putting her hand on her hip.

Ami laughed, and Yuko giggled, ending her seductive stare and pose.

"Where did you learn to talk and lick your lips and pose like that?" said Ami.

"I learned the talking and lip-licking from Mikita. I learned the posing from Kagami," Yuko replied.

"Mikita the seductress and Kagami the showgirl," Ami said. "What fine role models for an innocent android! I should send you to a Christian girls' boarding school, but I heard those girls are sleazier!"

Yuko laughed and looked intently at the camera. "Everyone here wishes you great victory in the Navy. You'll be the first admiral to visit us, I'm sure! Good luck, master, and I'll see you soon!"

As the video ended, Kamio entered the room. "Hey, Sato, is that your girlfriend?" he asked.

Ishiro turned around. "Yes, she is."

"Wow, she's beautiful," said Kamio. "Every guy should have a girl like her at each port."

Ishiro nodded. "I'll be happy with just one girl like her at one port..."

*...even if the girl is an android,* he silently reminded himself.

**

Ishiro dreaded the weekly performance review with Lieutenant Shujimi. The training officer always criticized and insulted him.

Shujimi looked at his pocket computer. "Hmmm, there's a slight increase in your overall rating. Are you actually Sato Ishiro, the *otaku* boy? You're not an android sent to replace him, are you?"

Ishiro bristled at the sarcasm. "Yes, I am the real Sato Ishiro, sir."

"That's too bad. An android would score better than you in physical and military tactical training," said Shujimi. "The phys-ed instructors say you're playing better in team sports, but your phys-ed grades are still at the bottom of the platoon. Here's a comment from a phys-ed instructor: 'Midshipman Sato is still the clumsiest person in the platoon. It's a miracle if he doesn't trip over his own feet.'"

Ishiro bit his lip and fought the urge to cry.

Kirino continued. "Your military tactical grades are just as low as your phys-ed grades. You really need to improve in basic seamanship. You're still maintaining the minimum grades to stay in, though. That's what happens when we lower the standards to graduate more officers. The Navy needs more meat for the sharks."

"I see, sir," said Ishiro.

Kirino read more reports on his pocket computer. "The professors are no longer rating your classroom participation as poor. You've gone up to mediocre. Here's a comment from Professor Hirano: 'He finally shut up and let the other midshipmen talk.'"

"Thank you, sir," said Ishiro.

"Your navigation professor says you actually answered a question in less than one hundred sentences, and even better, your answer was related to the question. That's quite an accomplishment, eh, *otaku* boy?"

"Thank you, sir."

"Regarding written assignments and tests, your scores in military law and history have gone up too," said Shujimi.

"Thank you, sir," said Ishiro, basking in the rare praise.

"You're still at the bottom of the class, although you've gone from poor to mediocre," said Shujimi. "I don't know why the Superintendent doesn't expel you, but he must have a reason. Don't disappoint him. Continue to improve, Sato."

Ishiro nodded. "Yes, sir, I will."

"Your weekly review is over. You're dismissed."

Ishiro stood up, saluted, and left the small meeting room. He sighed in relief as he went to the shooting range.

For the first time, Shujimi had said something positive at the weekly review.

**

Each night, some midshipmen gathered to watch the news at the television lounge. Tonight, Kamio and Ishiro joined them.

The news was grim. Terrorism was resurging in the Vernacular Wars.

Purists killed a Moslem American doctor and a bookseller in Baltimore. The bookseller was not Moslem, but he had touched a copy of the Koran with his bare hands when stacking books in his store. The doctor had treated the bookseller and his family for twenty years and refused to give up his non-Moslem patients. Secret Purists had been watching them for months. When the bookseller went to his doctor, the Purists stormed into the medical clinic and opened fire with assault rifles. The police eventually killed the Purists in a shoot-out but not before TV stations had shown their victory speech.

In Jordan, Purists stabbed a schoolteacher who told her pupils that Queen Areej was right to tolerate all sects of Islam in her kingdom. The Queen's refusal to persecute so-called heretics and apostates angered the Purists. Queen Areej attended the teacher's funeral. Only jail guards attended the killers' funerals.

In Germany, a woman imam named Amira Edip started a Reformation by nailing demands to a door of a mosque. Moslems all over Europe were denouncing the Purists and demanding reforms from their religious leaders. Police arrested two men who carried knives to Imam Edip's lecture in Berlin.

Not all the Vernacular Wars were between terrorists and civilians. When the Holy Alliance for Monotheism decided to conquer foreign territory, old-fashioned wars, with armies and navies and air forces, broke out too. In the latest news, Egypt and Israel launched another attempt to recapture the Suez Canal from Purist Arabia. For two years, Purist Arabia had controlled the canal and sent its warships and Somali privateers into the Mediterranean. Control of the canal let Purist Arabia and Sudan invade Cyprus and Malta. The Somalis devastated commercial shipping as far as Spain. The first Egyptian and Israeli attempt to recapture the canal had failed. Could they succeed this time?

The Cypriots were faring better than the Egyptians and Israelis. The last Purist Arabian and Sudanese troops surrendered in northern Cyprus. The TV showed fireworks and celebrations all across the island. The Purists had done what nobody else could do in Cypriot history: unite the Turks and the Greeks. The Turks sided with the Greeks rather than live under the Purist version of Islam.

The Fuji News announcer said, "And next, we'll interview Dr. Nitta Takashi, the Japanese member of Irene 3, the international mission to Mars."

"How incredible, there's actually news other than war and terrorism," said Kwon.

Fuji News cut to a commercial for Victor Robotics. It showed androids diving into the ocean.

Miyahara drank his apple juice. "Let's see what Dr. Nitta says. Irene 3 actually got back alive."

Ishiro nodded. "Given the record of the Mars missions, that's cause for celebration."

"Space missions are often named after European gods," Miyahara observed. "Yamaguchi, you know about European mythology. What does 'Irene' mean?"

"Irene is the Greek goddess of peace," Yamaguchi replied. "There's a special reason for naming the Mars missions after Irene. Mars is named after the Roman god of war. The space agencies wanted to show that they can explore Mars together in peace. Symbolically, they are bringing peace to war."

"The planet of war is Earth, not Mars," said Miyahara.

"Spacers know that all too well," said Yamaguchi. "They want joint space missions to inspire our world to live in peace. Unfortunately, it doesn't always work."

Ishiro reached for the peanuts. "With all the wars going on, how can anyone explore space?"

"But people always do," said Yamaguchi. "Americans went to the Moon when the United States was fighting a war in Vietnam. It seems that space exploration thrives in troubled times, as if people are looking for a better planet."

Miyahara smiled. "Ah, Miss Yamaguchi, you're insightful and poetic as always. It must be that Roman Catholic education."

"Thank you, Mr. Miyahara," said Yamaguchi.

Kwon suddenly stood up and said, "Officer on deck!"

Superintendent Kirino walked in, and the midshipmen stood up at attention.

Kirino raised his swagger stick. "As you were, everyone. As you were."

He sat down and reached for a bowl of *arare*, the bite-sized crackers. "I just want to get out of my office for a few minutes and see the latest news. There's so much going on in the world these days."

"News about the Japanese astronaut on Irene 3 is next," said Miyahara.

"Ah, that should be interesting," said Kirino. "He's a nephew of an officer I trained years ago. I see the uncle every year at the Maritime Self-Defense Force old comrades' reunion. Good old Oshii Toshio, the farmer from Hokkaido."

The Fuji News announcer said, "Dr. Nitta Takashi was the Japanese member of the Irene 3 mission to Mars. Dr. Nitta is a psychiatrist. His job was to provide medical services and study the effects of deep space exploration on the crew. But out there, he saw something that nobody can explain."

**

The news show recounted the history of the Irene missions. Irene 1 orbited Mars to collect data about the atmosphere and surface. The spaceship lost all contact with Earth, and the flight controllers feared that disaster had struck.

A week later, they regained contact with Irene 1. The crew said that they had found a small asteroid inhabited by the ghosts of their dead relatives. When the crew lost contact with Earth, the ghosts left the asteroid and boarded the ship. They urged the crew to stay around Mars, but the mission commander ordered an early return to Earth. Then the ghosts vanished as suddenly as they had appeared.

The flight controllers reviewed all video and audio recordings made aboard the ship. The recordings showed the crew talking to empty air, to people who weren't there. Nobody could explain why the crew saw ghosts.

Other videos showed the asteroid. Unlike Phobos and Deimos, which were shaped like potatoes, the asteroid was a sphere. Its perfect shape was odd for an object of its size, only half a kilometer wide, much smaller than the moons. It reflected even less light than did Phobos, one of the least-reflective bodies in the solar system. Spectrograph readings showed it to be carbonaceous chondrite, like the two moons and D-type asteroids.

However, the videos did not show any people on the rock. Its dark grey surface had only a few craters.

Nobody had seen this rock before. Was it like Phobos and Deimos, an asteroid that Mars had captured in its gravity? Was it a third moon? Astronomers tried to observe it from Earth, but they couldn't find it.

Irene 2 went to explore the two moons of Mars. But the mission commander reported a third moon. Video transmissions showed a dark spherical rock. Excitement grew on Earth and aboard Irene 2. This must be the mysterious asteroid found by Irene 1.

Irene 2's commander said, "Oh my God, there are girls on the rock! I can hear them sing!"

It took twenty-two minutes for his radio signal to reach Earth. Mission Control replied, "Irene 2, please explain your last message and send a video of the rock."

They waited twenty-two minutes for the message to go to Mars. Then they waited another twenty-two minutes for a reply. No reply ever came. Irene 2 and her crew had disappeared.

Later, unmanned probes went to Mars, but none could find any trace of Irene 2 or the asteroid.

At the European Space Agency, a Greek astronaut nicknamed the rock "the Siren Stone." In Greek mythology, the sirens were seductresses who sat on seaside rocks, sang to sailors, and lured them to shipwreck. Rumors began that there were several Siren Stones in deep space. People blamed them for the disappearance of Irene 2.

Irene 3 went to gather data for planning a future landing on Mars. Again, the crew saw a mysterious asteroid in orbit. Communications was lost for an hour. When it resumed, the commander said he had moved the ship into a different orbit, away from the Siren Stone.

The recap of past missions ended, and the scene turned to a field of wheat with a red *torii* gate. The news reporter stood with Nitta Takashi in front of the *torii*. In the background was a Shinto shrine, also painted red. The sunlight, the blue sky, and the golden wheat added to the scene's beauty.

A man in a grey kimono stood beside the shrine and watched the TV crew from a distance.

"That's not a spaceport. Where is it?" Ishiro asked.

"I've been there before," said Kirino. "It's his uncle's farm in Hokkaido. That's his uncle, Oshii Toshio, standing in the background."

"Why would they interview him at his uncle's farm?"

"Maybe it has some relationship to the Siren Stone? The farm is reputed to be haunted."

"The farm is haunted, sir?" Ishiro said.

"Let's listen," said Yamaguchi.

The reporter wore a stylish dress, white with a red sash around her waist. Wearing the national colors was the latest fashion trend for young women.

She asked Dr. Nitta, "What happened around Mars?"

Nitta was a handsome man in his thirties. He wore a blue flight suit with the logo of the Irene missions: the Greek goddess Irene holding the red planet Mars.

"We went into orbit around Mars on schedule, and then we saw the asteroid," Nitta replied.

"Was it the Siren Stone?" asked the reporter.

"It was a perfect sphere, half a kilometer in diameter, so it matched the descriptions from Irene 1 and 2," said Nitta.

"How did you and your fellow crew members react?"

"We were all surprised even though we knew that both Irene 1 and Irene 2 had reported the rock. Nothing can prepare you for seeing something so mysterious."

"What happened next?"

"We flew alongside the rock so we could observe it. Then we lost contact with Earth. That's when we heard the voices."

The reporter looked intrigued. "You heard voices?"

"Yes, over the radio," said Nitta.

"Who were they? What did they say?"

"One of them told our geologist Jerome Carmichael that he was his grandfather. Another one told Commander Marberg that she was his ex-wife, who died a year ago. Everyone heard from someone from the past."

"Who did you hear?"

"A friend who died in a swimming accident five years ago," said Nitta.

"How eerie," the reporter remarked. "What did you do next?"

"We looked at the asteroid, and we saw people standing on it. They were people we knew but who had died years ago. The people — the ghosts — asked us to come to the asteroid and meet them," said Nitta.

"Incredible! This happened to Irene 1 and probably to Irene 2. Did anyone go down to the asteroid?"

"No, nobody did. Commander Marberg forbade extravehicular activity. He didn't want to take any risks after the disappearance of Irene 2. We did, however, aim our sensors at the rock to try to get data about it."

"What did you detect?"

Nitta shrugged. "Unfortunately, some of our sensors failed while we were following the rock. We had just video and radio working. The other sensors didn't work again until later."

"How eerie," the reporter repeated. "Then what happened?"

"After an hour of observing the rock, Commander Marberg thought we had taken enough risks. He was especially worried about the malfunctioning sensors. He moved the ship into a different orbit, away from the Siren Stone."

"And that's when you regained contact with Mission Control?"

"That's right. That's also when the sensors began working again."

"Mission Control viewed audio and video recordings made aboard the ship during the blackout with Earth. The flight controllers say you and your crewmates are talking to people who don't exist, and no people appear on videos of the asteroid," said the reporter.

Nitta looked pensive. "I know that's what the recordings show. I reviewed them too. Neither I nor my fellow crew members can explain them."

"As a psychiatrist, you must be curious about what happened," said the reporter. "Do you have a theory?"

"Unfortunately, I don't," Nitta said. "The best theory is that the asteroid affects our minds. That theory doesn't really explain anything, though. Nobody knows how the asteroid does it. Nobody knows anything about the asteroid."

"Is your Martian experience why you came here?" asked the reporter as she looked at the shrine.

"Yes, that shrine has its own haunted rock," said Nitta. "Perhaps I can find an explanation of the Martian ghosts here."

"At the place where the ghosts gather on Earth," said the reporter.

They walked to the shrine, where they greeted the man in the grey kimono.

The reporter said, "This is Oshii Toshio, owner of the farm and caretaker of Ghost Rock Hokora."

Oshii bowed to the camera.

"Oshii was a midshipman," said Kirino. "He built that shrine after inheriting the farm from his father."

Ghost Rock was a *hokora*, a small shrine dedicated to the local *kami*. Many *hokora* stood by roadsides, in fields, in forests, on hills, or anywhere someone wanted to honor a *kami*. Many were unassociated with larger shrines. Ordinary people built them as expressions of their folk religion.

In front of the shrine were two short Chinese lions and a lantern. They had the color of white marble but looked like fiberglass lawn ornaments from a gardening store. Oshii had obviously built the shrine with little money, but it looked pretty and well-kept.

Ghost Rock Hokora's single structure was a small *honden*. It was the size of a tool shed and had a sloping roof. White *shide*, zigzag paper streamers, hung from a rope strung horizontally above the door.

The *honden* was the shrine's most sacred spot. Ghost Rock's *kami*, the spirits of the local dead, were enshrined inside the *honden*. The *honden* also contained the *goshintai*, an object that the *kami* entered during rituals. Thus the spirits could take a material form.

While Ghost Rock looked like most small shrines, it had one major difference. Its door had a window. At Ghost Rock, ordinary people could look at the *goshintai*. At most shrines, only the priests had that privilege.

What was the *goshintai*? In most shrines, it was a mirror, a tribute to the mirror used to lure the Sun Goddess Amaterasu out of her cave. But at Ghost Rock Hokora, it was a black rock.

The TV image showed the black rock as the reporter said, "There is the famous meteorite."

Oshii put a bowl of rice in front of the shrine. The rice was an offering to the *kami*, the ghosts of the dead.

He faced the shrine and bowed twice, clapped twice, and bowed once more.

The reporter asked, "Mr. Oshii, please tell us about the history of Ghost Rock Hokora. Many shrines are centuries old, but Ghost Rock is only ten years old. Yet it's a popular local shrine despite its young age."

"The shrine is only ten years old, but its history actually began sixty years ago," said Oshii. "That's when a meteorite fell on this wheat field."

"The rock inside the shrine?" said the reporter.

Oshii nodded. "Yes, that's the meteorite. Local people came to look at the rock, and some said they saw the ghosts of their dead relatives. Before long, people were visiting the rock and hoping for one last conversation with their loved ones."

"How did your family react?"

"At first, my grandfather was happy to let people go on his field, but he grew tired of them. He didn't try to stop them, though. My father also didn't like the trespassers, but he eventually got used to them. The traffic gets heaviest during *Bon*. Fortunately, the rock landed close to the road, so people don't have to walk through too much wheat."

The reporter asked, "Has anybody tried to steal the meteorite?"

"Incredibly, nobody has tried to steal it," Oshii replied. "My grandfather and father took no steps to protect the rock, but it stayed here. I guess the local people are all law-abiding folk. Either that or the rock is too heavy for anyone to carry."

"For whatever reason, I'm glad it's still here. It's such a local legend. After all these years, why did you build a shrine?"

"The place deserves a shrine. Some people believe that ghosts are attracted to the meteorite, so it's a *goshintai*. If that's so, there should be a shrine here. I didn't want to move the rock, so I built the shrine above and around it."

The reporter approached the shrine. "It must be the only shrine with a window. It's not normal to let people look into the most sacred spot. Why did you put in a window?"

"I know the window is unorthodox," said Oshii. "Some priests have objected. They remind me that I'm not a trained Shinto priest and my little shrine is not a member of the Association of Shinto Shrines. I don't mind, nor does anyone around here. I'm just a farmer practicing the folk Shinto of the common people.

"The meteorite lay out in the open, visible to everyone for fifty years. I didn't think it would be right to conceal it."

"*So desu ka*," said the reporter. "I must ask the next question. Have you ever seen a spirit of the dead?"

Oshii shook his head. "No, I've not been so fortunate. I used to set up my telescope beside the meteorite and look at the stars when I was young. In all those years, I never saw a ghost. But I believe the ghosts are here. Other people have seen them."

"That's a fascinating history," said the reporter. "May I honor the *kami*?"

"Yes, please do."

The reporter turned to the wooden offering box. In past centuries, worshippers would toss coins into the box. This box had openings for the coins but also had a card reader attached to it.

She swiped her money card through the card reader and pressed some buttons to transfer money from her card.

Kirino grinned. "If people are going to trespass on his property, he might as well get money from them. It was a shrewd idea to build the shrine."

Facing the *honden*, the reporter bowed twice, clapped twice, and bowed again. After honoring the *kami*, she turned back to Dr. Nitta.

"Do you think you'll find an explanation of the Siren Stone here?" asked the reporter.

"The meteorite is like the asteroid around Mars. People see ghosts of their relatives around it," said Nitta. "If there's an answer to what's going on around Mars, this seems to be the best place on Earth to find it."

**

In June, the midshipmen received their orders for their "summer cruises," their first assignments aboard a ship. Both Ishiro and Kamio were assigned to the corvette *Ota*.

"Hey, that's the ship that sank during our exercise," said Kamio.

Ishiro bristled at the reminder of his incompetence. "Sank in a computerized simulation, that is."

"Ah, cheer up, Sato, it should be fun. We'll be cruising on the Inland Sea. We'll be going to Itsukushima, Hiroshima, Matsuyama, Kobe, and various ports and islands in between. At least we're not going to Antarctica like Miyahara is."

"Is that because nobody wants us on an important mission like that? Antarctica isn't pleasant, but senior officers will respect Miyahara after his cruise. He'll be bringing supplies to a research station and conducting scientific experiments. Meanwhile, we'll be patrolling tourist attractions."

"The Navy has many different missions," said Kamio. "Look at our cruise this way: We'll be defending the home islands. Isn't that the noblest duty of the military?"

"I guess so," said Ishiro.

Although Ishiro was glad to avoid Antarctica, he felt bitter about the assignments. Miyahara, his nemesis, was on track to become an admiral. Ishiro would be lucky to command a tugboat.

**

The *Ota* approached Itsukushima, also known as Miyajima, the Shrine Island. Standing on the deck of the ship, Ishiro saw the famous *torii* of Itsukushima Shrine. The large wooden gate rose majestically in the water and looked bright red in the sunlight.

Kamio came on the deck. "Sato, look at Itsukushima. It's a holy island with hundreds of *kami*. There are many shrines and temples there. The island reminds me of our traditions and our civilization. I cannot help but feel pride when I see Itsukushima. Do you feel that pride too?"

"Yes," said Ishiro, in awe of the red *torii*, the blue sea, and the green mountains.

"Sato, you're interested in General Morita's anime, aren't you?" said Kamio. "You always talk to me about *Time Warp at Midway* and *Nuke the Yanks*."

"I like his anime, and I'm impressed that you know him. I met him only once, during a demonstration of the National Bushido Guards Regiment," said Ishiro. "You've met him many times, I imagine."

"Indeed I have. Would you like to meet the General tomorrow?"

"Tomorrow? You must be joking! How? Where?"

"The command group of the National Bushido Guards Regiment will be meeting on Itsukushima. Yes, right on the holy island. Our shift gets shore leave tomorrow afternoon, the same time as the meeting. I would be happy to invite you to meet the General."

"That would be wonderful! He's the reason why I joined the Navy."

"Then you will come with me?"

Ishiro nodded. "Yes, yes, of course."

"Good," said Kamio. "I'm sure you'll like the General and the command group. They're all very worthwhile men."

Kamio's face turned serious. "Don't tell our shipmates. Not everyone is sympathetic to General Morita and his goals."

"They don't like anime?" Ishiro said.

Kamio chuckled. "Hah, hah, I haven't heard that reason before!"

Ishiro stared silently at Kamio.

Kamio looked baffled. Then he smiled weakly. "Oh, you weren't joking. Uh, correct, not everyone likes anime. We anime fans should keep our interests to ourselves, eh? Sato, don't say anything to our shipmates. If anyone is nosey enough to ask, just tell him that we're visiting a minor shrine. Understand?"

"Yes."

"Good," said Kamio before he returned below deck.

Ishiro looked at the *torii* in the water and the shrines on the island.

**

Ishiro and Kamio's cab passed numerous Shinto shrines, Buddhist temples, pagodas, stone monuments, sacred gardens, maple forests, and green hills. On Itsukushima, humanity did not overpower nature. Instead, the human and natural worlds blended together in harmony. Ishiro, who

173

had spent his whole life in urban Tokyo, had never seen such scenery before.

The ancient book *Nihon Shoki* tells that the Sun Goddess Amaterasu sent her grandson Ninigi-no-Mikoto down from heaven to rule Japan. Ninigi-no-Mikoto's great-grandson, Emperor Jimmu, became the first human ruler of Japan. Under the concept of *dōzoku*, the whole Japanese nation belongs to a great cluster of extended families with the Imperial Family as the main house. Thus all Japanese are descended from the *kami* who created Japan, and thus, all Japanese are descended from the divine forces of nature.

Ishiro, like all Japanese, knew of the divine descent of his people, but he had spent no time contemplating it. Except for his prayer in the Memorial Pavilion, he had never been spiritual in a serious way. But now, surrounded by natural beauty, he felt a warm closeness to his divine ancestors.

*If the Yamato race was born on islands so beautiful, certainly we are children of the gods,* Ishiro thought.

The cab drove them to a one-story building. Its sign read "Daimyo Mori Banquet Hall." A billboard had tattered posters promoting the hall as a place for wedding banquets, business meetings, and parties. The small parking lot had a statue of a samurai on horseback, made of white concrete pitted by the weather.

They entered the hall. Its walls were decorated with paintings of samurai and their lords, the *daimyo*. A suit of samurai armor stood in a corner, and swords hung near the bar.

Kamio pointed at a portrait of a *daimyo* in a brown kimono. "That's Mori Motonari, who defeated the Ouchi Family at the Battle of Itsukushima. Since nobody is allowed to die here, priests had to perform extensive purification rituals to cleanse the island after the battle."

Ten young men chatted at a table covered by a white tablecloth. Half of them wore the Regiment's Russo-Japanese War costume, but the others wore current Army, Navy, and Air Force uniforms.

"Some of them are in national military uniform," Ishiro observed.

"They're like me. We have men in each military service, all as officer candidates or junior officers," Kamio explained.

Portraits of the Emperor and Amaterasu the Sun Goddess hung on the wall behind the table. Ishiro had never seen the two pictures side by side before.

"This place is so military, so traditional, so medieval," Ishiro said.

"You sound disappointed," Kamio noticed. "Were you expecting something else?"

"Anime posters, anime action figures. He did make *Time Warp at Midway*."

"The General is not only an animator. He is also a patriot."

Female L-3 androids served food and drink to the Bushido Guardsmen. The androids wore kimonos and sported the latest hairstyles, combining the old and the new.

"Of course, we would prefer to be served by real girls, but the work of our Regiment requires secrecy," Kamio said. "Hence, we use androids and erase their memories after each meeting."

The Bushido Guardsmen noticed Kamio, and in turn, each one approached him and saluted. Ishiro realized that Kamio held an important position in the command group.

"Who is your guest?" they asked.

"Please allow me to introduce Midshipman Sato Ishiro, my comrade from the Naval Officer Candidate School and shipmate aboard the corvette *Ota*," said Kamio.

Ishiro felt elated that Kamio introduced him as a comrade and shipmate. No other midshipman at Etajima had shown him such friendship.

"The General's video *For the Glory of the Emperor* inspired Ishiro to join the Navy," Kamio added.

"Excellent, excellent," each Bushido Guardsman said as he greeted Ishiro.

Kamio guided Ishiro to a seat. An android waitress brought beer, sashimi, sushi, and soba noodles to them.

Ishiro whispered to Kamio, "Who's paying for all this?"

"The General has wealthy benefactors, patriots who believe in restoring Japan and the Emperor to their past glory," Kamio replied.

Ishiro nodded and began gobbling the food.

A bugle blared, and the Bushido Guardsmen stood up. Ishiro watched them, and then he stood up too.

"Sato, hurry up and swallow your food. Don't chew in front of the General," Kamio whispered.

A Bushido Guardsman carried the national flag into the room. The bugler came next, playing a march. The General walked at the end of the procession.

General Morita Chiko, grim-faced as usual, went to the head of the table. When the bugler stopped playing, he turned around to face the portraits of the Emperor and the Sun Goddess Amaterasu.

"All bow to the images of the Emperor and Amaterasu!" he ordered.

Everyone, including the androids, bowed three times to the portraits.

The General sat down and said, "You may sit. I apologize for being late. I had to discuss certain matters with Defense Minister Kotohito. I'm glad that you followed my orders and started the meal without me. I wouldn't want any of you to go hungry due to my tardiness."

He looked at Kamio and asked, "Mr. Kamio, who is your guest?"

Kamio stood up and said, "General, please allow me to introduce Midshipman Sato Ishiro, my comrade from the Naval Officer Candidate School and shipmate aboard the corvette *Ota*."

Ishiro stood up and bowed to the General.

"Mr. Sato, patriotic young men like you are welcome for the social part of the meeting," said Morita. "I hope that you'll forgive us when we ask you to leave for the business part. I hope that you understand."

"Yes, that is fine with me, sir," Ishiro said with his mouth full of food.

Morita grimaced. "Don't the military academies teach you not to speak with your mouths full of food? It's hard for me to understand what you're saying."

"Sir, I do not intend any offense," Ishiro said while chewing.

"Hurry up, chew and swallow!" Morita demanded.

Ishiro swallowed his food.

The General stared at him and said, "You look familiar. Have we met before, Mr. Sato?"

Ishiro nodded. "Yes, sir, in Akihabara. You were making a speech on the street about a year and a half ago. You gave me a DVD of *For the Glory of the Emperor*."

"Ah, yes, the *otaku*," Morita remembered. "I see you have taken my advice and committed yourself to defend our nation. That's good. You may sit down now."

The Bushido Guardsmen continued their meal, with conversation flowing across the table. They talked about various subjects, including sports, their military training, and the General's anime. Ishiro delved eagerly into the talk about anime. He talked so much that the General interrupted him several times.

"Stop talking, boy!" Morita ordered. "You don't need to retell the plot of each episode of *Time Warp at Midway*. Did you forget that I wrote them?"

"I'm sorry, sir," said Ishiro before changing the topic to *Imperial Space Marines Battalion Musashi*.

Despite Ishiro's repeated attempts to talk only about anime, the conversation inevitably turned to politics.

"The Emperor is a descendant of Amaterasu," General Morita declared. "A living *kami* is much more suitable than an elected politician to be the heart and soul of the nation."

"Fujiwara is a conservative. Give him time, and he will turn command of the military over to the Emperor, won't he?" said a University of Tokyo student.

An Army lieutenant shook his head. "Prime Minister Fujiwara will never relinquish the role of commander-in-chief. Like all politicians, he wants the power for himself."

"Yes, like all politicians," Morita agreed before sipping his beer.

An Osaka University student said, "Even having the Emperor as a ceremonial commander-in-chief, like the King of Great Britain, would be fine. I think we could accept such a position for the Emperor, could we?"

"Hah, spoken like a left-winger from Osaka University!" the Army lieutenant joked. The men laughed and teased the student by calling him a communist. The student smiled, knowing they were just joking among comrades.

"But the idea has come up before," said Kamio. "One of the Fujiwara's Diet Members wanted to introduce a bill to amend the *Self-Defense Forces Act* to make the Emperor the ceremonial commander-in-chief. However, Fujiwara ordered him to withdraw the bill."

"Fujiwara is an idiot," an Air Force cadet complained after drinking more beer.

"No, do not speak so disrespectfully of the Prime Minister," General Morita said. "He has done much to revive our national glory. He greatly accelerated the re-arming of the nation. He restored the traditional names of our military forces. He has declared his willingness to send troops into battle."

The Air Force cadet stood up, bowed, and said, "I'm sorry for the rash comment, sir."

Morita motioned to him to sit down. "Having said all that, I think Fujiwara needs to do more and reassess his priorities. He needs to restore the Emperor as commander-in-chief. He needs to repeal Article 9. And he needs to realize that our real enemy is Russia, not Purist Arabia. It is Russia, not Purist Arabia, that occupies the Northern Territories."

A Navy ensign asked Ishiro, "Midshipman Sato, do you agree that the Emperor should be commander-in-chief of the armed forces?"

"I agree, sir. His role should be as the General showed it in *Time Warp at Midway*," said Ishiro.

The General looked at Ishiro and nodded.

******

When the androids stopped bringing food, Morita said, "The social part of the meeting is over. The business part is next. Mr. Kamio, please ask your guest to leave us now."

"Yes, sir," said Kamio as he stood up. He motioned to Ishiro, who stood up too.

The General typed a command in his pocket computer. An android walked to Ishiro and held out a gift-wrapped box to him.

"Take it," said Morita. "It's a modest gift from the Regiment."

Ishiro took the box and stared at it.

"You may open it now if you wish."

Ishiro tore off the wrapping paper and opened the box. He gasped as he pulled out a small figurine.

"This is Captain Uchiha of the Imperial Space Marines!" he exclaimed. "He's wearing the Martian terrain battle uniform. This is the exclusive resin figure from the San Diego Comic Con! All one thousand sold out on the first hour of the show, mostly to Americans."

Ishiro bowed deeply to the General. "Sir, I cannot accept this gift! It's a Comic Con exclusive. It's much too valuable."

"Please take it, midshipman," said Morita. "That's an order."

Ishiro bowed again. "Thank you, sir, thank you!"

The Bushido Guardsmen applauded, and Kamio glanced at Ishiro.

"Sato, I'll walk you to the door. Follow me," he said.

They went outside the building, and Kamio used his pocket computer to call for a cab. Ishiro kept examining the figurine.

Kamio asked, "Did you enjoy the lunch?"

"Oh, yes, yes," said Ishiro. "I did, very much. The people are pleasant and smart. And I got a resin figure."

"Good, good," said Kamio. "Perhaps you will consider joining the National Bushido Guards Regiment? We're always looking for good men, especially those in the military."

"You think I qualify to join?"

"You'll be a Navy officer, so not only do you qualify to join, but you also qualify for the command group."

"That's impressive! But can we be in both the Navy and the Regiment at the same time?"

"Not officially, but the Minister of Defense has given us his tacit approval. Kotohito has long allowed the Regiment to train with the Army. He's also aware that several members of the Regiment are officers in the military. Think of the Regiment as a patriotic organization, and you'll see no conflict of interest."

"But you told me not to tell our shipmates that we were going to this meeting," said Ishiro. "Why should we keep it a secret?"

"That's complicated," said Kamio. "The armed forces, especially the Navy, have some leftists in the ranks: socialists, communists, anarchists, republicans, pacifists, and atheists. The all deny the divinity of the Emperor. There are not many of them, but it takes only a few to cause trouble. Needless to say, such people are not sympathetic to the General and the Regiment."

"*So desu ka*," said Ishiro. "I understand now."

The cab came and picked up Ishiro. As he rode back to the dock, he imagined himself wearing a Russo-Japanese War uniform and marching with General Morita in Akihabara.

**

A month later, the *Ota* docked at Hiroshima. Ishiro and Kamio went ashore and visited a bookstore.

They walked past shelves of books on right-wing politics. There were books about Russia's illegal occupation of the Northern Territories, the benevolent colonial rule of Korea, and the holy war against China and the United States. Military marches played on speakers.

A man came to them and said, "The General is waiting in my office. It's the door beside the poster of Tojo."

"Thank you, sir," said Kamio.

As the man went to help customers, Ishiro asked, "Who was that?"

"He's the bookstore's owner. He's also a benefactor of the Regiment," Kamio said. "We can hold the ceremony here without being disturbed by leftists."

They met General Morita and two Bushido Guardsmen in the owner's office. The General looked stern and formal again.

The General and his two men wore the Regiment's Russo-Japanese War uniforms, but Ishiro and Kamio wore Navy uniforms. However, the General had told them that Navy uniforms were appropriate for the ceremony.

"Midshipman Sato, do you believe that the Emperor is a living *kami*?" Morita asked.

Ishiro had never thought about the Emperor's divinity until now. Itsukushima and General Morita had changed him.

"Yes, I do, sir," he replied.

"Do you revere the Emperor?"

"Yes, I do, sir."

"Do you wish to see the Emperor restored as commander-in-chief of the military?"

"Yes, I do, sir."

"Do you wish to join the National Bushido Guards Regiment?"

"Yes, I do, sir."

"Look at the *kamidana*," said Morita, referring to the miniature Shinto altar sitting on a shelf.

The *kamidana* was made of wood and looked like a shrine building. It even had its own little *torii*. Zigzag strips of white paper hung from a sacred rope strung across its front. Two white vases each held an artificial sakaki branch. An offering of rice sat in front of a round mirror.

A miniature national flag stood on its roof. A toy tank sat under the *torii*. Toy soldiers of the Greater East Asia War stood guard around the altar. The war toys puzzled Ishiro. He had never seen them with a *kamidana* before.

The Bushido Guardsmen held a bowl of water up to Ishiro. Ishiro ritually washed his hands and wiped them with a towel from Kamio.

"The *kamidana* contains an *ofuda* from the Ise Shrine, the shrine of Amaterasu the Sun Goddess, the mother of the nation and the divine ancestor of the Emperor," said Morita. "Do you understand the importance of the *kami* honored here?"

Bewildered by the solemnity of the moment, Ishiro softly muttered, "Yes."

"Then face the *kamidana*, bow twice, clap twice, and bow once more."

Ishiro obeyed the order.

Morita gave him a piece of paper. "Face the *kamidana* and recite this oath."

Ishiro recited the oath. "I, Sato Ishiro, do, of my own free will and without coercion, in the presence of the Sun Goddess Amaterasu, join the National Bushido Guards Regiment and pledge myself to fight against all domestic and foreign enemies of the Emperor and his nation, to revere the Emperor as a living *kami*, to restore the Emperor to his rightful position in Japanese society, to defend the Imperial way, to uphold and practice *bushido*, and to obey General Morita Chiko as commander of the Regiment."

He bowed towards the *kamidana* again, breathed deeply, and glanced around. His fellow Bushido Guardsmen looked grim. What had he done wrong now?

Morita said, "Welcome aboard."

Kamio and the other two Bushido Guardsmen applauded. Ishiro saluted them and the General, and they returned his salute.

The afternoon sunlight burst through the window and lit the office. Amaterasu is smiling, Ishiro mused.

The General asked one of his officers, "In which direction is Tokyo?"

The Bushido Guardsman took a compass out of his pocket and pointed. "Northeast, sir!"

"All face the Imperial Palace!" Morita ordered.

They turned towards Tokyo, stood at attention, and shouted:

"Long live the Emperor! Banzai!"

"Long live the Emperor! Banzai!"

"Long live the Emperor! Banzai!"

# CHAPTER 11

# Simple Gifts

Ishiro performed well on the cruise mostly because it emphasized technical training. He thrived away from the classrooms, the lecture halls, the gymnasium, the kendo hall, the football field, the obstacle course, and the firing range. He did not have to compete against other midshipmen in phys-ed and combat. And he did not have to impress professors in discussions on war theory, military law, history, political science, and leadership. Instead, he could concentrate on maintaining and using a variety of equipment: engines, air vents, heating systems, radios, sonar, radar, computers, androids, guns, and many more gadgets. He always preferred working with machines over people, and the ship was one large system of machines.

One of the ship's L-3 androids suddenly stopped moving one day. Ishiro knew how to diagnose the problem, remove and replace the damaged hard drive, and load programs onto it. When the executive officer thanked him, Ishiro knew he could fit into the Navy.

******

The Inland Sea was renowned for its beautiful islands, coasts, and cities. To Ishiro, his cruise seemed far removed from the Vernacular Wars. But events were pushing Japan and Ishiro closer to war.

On August fifteenth, the anniversary of Japan's surrender in the Greater East Asia War, the National Bushido Guards Regiment paraded at Yasukuni Shrine. General Morita stood atop a box and declared, "The true enemy is Russia, not Purist Arabia. The re-arming of the nation is in vain if we fight the wrong enemy. Our true enemy is the one that occupies our sacred soil, the Northern Territories." The parade ended as usual, with the singing of the "Kimigayo."

Few people paid attention to Morita. Most Japanese were more interested in their space-generated electricity system. Each month, another rocket took a satellite into space. Construction of the microwave receiver stations finished in September. All phases of the project were on schedule. The system would start up on January second, as planned.

Modern science combined with ancient ritual when the last satellite was launched. Priests from Ise, the shrine of Amaterasu, waved *tamagushi* and blessed the satellite and its rocket in the name of the Sun

Goddess. Engineers placed an *omamori* and a picture of Amaterasu inside the satellite.

Hundreds of people gathered at Tanegashima Space Center to watch the rocket launch. They waved national flags, which looked like hundreds of red Suns. As Prime Minister Fujiwara watched the rocket climb into the sky, he said, "Now we will harness the power of the Sun."

Purist Arabia proposed a resolution to the United Nations Security Council:

"Whereas the people of Purist Arabia depend on the export of oil, a gift from God, for their survival, energy methods that reduce the consumption of oil are forms of racism and insults against Islam."

The Security Council, except for Sudan, rejected the resolution. The Purists took the resolution to the General Assembly, where it was rejected by all members except Purist Arabia and its allies.

Islamic scholars in Egypt, Jordan, Turkey, Iran, Morocco, and the Gambia criticized Purist Arabia for misusing their religion. Since Egypt, Jordan, and Turkey were at war with Purist Arabia, their criticism did not surprise the Purists. The criticism from Iran wasn't surprising either, given the Iranian disdain for the Purists. But the criticism from neutral Morocco and the Gambia surprised the Purists. Purist Arabia's Supreme Court issued *fatwas* for the deaths of the Moroccan and Gambian scholars. Purist agents killed twenty of them within a week.

Unable to get support outside of the Holy Alliance, Purist Arabia prepared its people for *jihad* against Japan. In October, Umar al-Tabuk, Emir of Purist Arabia, said on As-Sahab TV, "When Mohammed returned to Mecca, he smashed the pagan idols in the Kaaba and killed the infidels. It is our duty to smash idols and the people who worship them."

Immediately after the Emir's speech, As-Sahab TV showed a documentary called *Japan, Empire of Pagans and Idolaters*. It showed Shinto and Buddhist deities: a famous painting of Amaterasu the Sun Goddess, woodblock prints of the *kami* Izanagi and Izanami, Buddha statues in various temples, and even the Maneki Neko, the Lucky Cat. The narrator said, "Most Japanese are followers of Shinto or Buddhism or both, cults that worship millions of idols. Like the Hindus, they are a race of pagans."

*Japan, Empire of Pagans and Idolaters* ended with an old video of the Buddhas of Bamyan. Centuries ago, Buddhists carved two giant statues of the Buddhas Vairocana and Siddhartha into the side of a sandstone cliff in Bamyan valley, Afghanistan. The United Nations declared the statues to be a World Heritage Site. But the U.N. could not protect the Buddhas from the Taliban. The statues had stood for over one thousand and five hundred years. They disappeared after a few weeks of artillery fire, tank barrages, and dynamite blasting. After their destruction, Mullah Mohammed Omar, Emir of Afghanistan, said, "Moslems should be proud of smashing idols. It has given praise to God that we have destroyed them."

"Let us joyfully continue the holy mission of smashing the idols and their worshippers. *Allah Akbar!*" the narrator said over scenes of the Buddhas of Bamyan exploding.

As-Sabah TV aired another documentary, *The Japanese: A Lost Tribe of Israel?* Its narrator concluded, "The great similarities in Japanese and Jewish rituals, culture, and language lead to one inescapable conclusion: The Japanese are descended from one of the Lost Tribes of Israel. Therefore, they are Zionists as well as pagans."

Jihadists abducted a Japanese journalist in Purist Arabia and cut off his head. A video of the beheading aired repeatedly on As-Sabah TV. The Purist TV network had been showing beheadings of foreigners since the early twenty-first century.

Ramzi Jarrah, the Purist Arabian Ambassador to Japan, went on Japanese TV to say, "Your journalist was not killed by anyone authorized by my government. However, since the Japanese people are enemy pagans, the Purist Arabian people sympathize with the justifiable indignation of the holy warriors who killed him."

A reporter asked Jarrah, "If your government did not authorize the killing, will it arrest the killers and bring them to justice?"

The ambassador shook his head. "What good can that do? Arresting the holy warriors will not bring your journalist back to life. What's done is done. It's God's will. You should learn to forgive and forget."

In Tokyo, crowds gathered in front of the National Diet Building. They held signs reading "REVENGE AT ALL COSTS" and "REPEAL ARTICLE 9." But other demonstrators urged peace with Purist Arabia, even if it meant abandoning space-generated electricity.

Prime Minister Fujiwara ordered all Japanese citizens to leave Purist Arabia, Sudan, Somalia, Pakistan, Indonesia, and Venezuela. Only the diplomatic staff stayed behind. Fujiwara still hoped to negotiate peace with the Purists.

Nonetheless, preparations for war gripped Japan. The Navy launched a new warship, the Army bought fifty tanks, and the Air Force bought twenty fighter jets. Purchases of equipment and supplies rose.

Military salaries increased, and every shopping mall had a recruitment booth. But enlistment fell below the government's target. The Minister of Defense wanted five hundred new recruits in the summer. By the end of August, he had gotten three hundred of them.

When Ishiro returned to Etajima in September, the Navy shortened the training period for midshipmen. Ishiro's class, originally scheduled to graduate in February, would now graduate in December.

"None of you guys would have passed in the old days," Shujimi growled at the 2nd Platoon. "You're still here because we're so desperate that we'll take any loser."

The officers and professors constantly talked about war. Yet, as Ishiro counted the weeks until graduation, he did not think of war. Instead, he thought about the last week of December, when he would get leave and visit Yuko.

**

Ishiro invited his parents to his graduation. They did not reply to him until the day before the ceremony. Their email read:

"Your brother will be receiving a broadcasting award on that same day, so we regret that we will not be able to attend your graduation. However, please visit us when you get shore leave. Your loving mother."

*Your loving mother*. How ironic, Ishiro thought.

**

On the last day of classes, Lieutenant Shujimi stopped Ishiro in the hall. Ishiro dreaded these conversations. What did Shujimi want now?

"Congratulations, *otaku* boy. You escaped the washout list," said Shujimi. "You survived after all."

"Thank you very much, sir," said Ishiro, relieved that Shujimi wasn't going to criticize or beat him.

"You *should* thank me." Shujimi held up his swagger stick. "I literally had to beat some sense into your idiot head."

"Uh, thank you, sir."

"I heard you performed well during your cruise, eh?"

"So the *Ota*'s captain tells me, sir."

"Good, good. Your success on the cruise was all due to technical merit, though. It had nothing to do with leadership. I don't think you're ready to command sailors, to lead them in a battle. You're an officer due only to your university degree and your technical expertise."

Ishiro's relief faded. He fought the urge to flee.

Instead, he said, "The Navy needs officers with education and technical expertise, so hopefully I can bring those to the job, sir."

Shujimi grinned. "A good answer. If you weren't an android sent to replace the real Sato Ishiro, I would be impressed."

"Uh, ah, thank you, sir," said Ishiro, uncertain if Shujimi had just praised or insulted him.

"You're right, the Navy needs officers with education and technical skills," said Shujimi. "Give two hundred percent of all your knowledge and skills to the job.

"But don't ever think you know everything. Watch, listen, and learn from your fellow officers. Pick up their good habits. You can learn much from other people. You've come this far. You can go further if you want."

"Yes, sir," said Ishiro.

**

The graduation occurred on December twenty-eighth, between Christmas and New Year. Since it was December, the graduation ceremony was held in Tsushima Gymnasium rather than outdoors.

The ceremony began with a parade by the midshipmen. A band played "Gunkan March." A color party carried the national and navy flags, and the audience waved small versions of the flags. The red Sun was everywhere.

Superintendent Kirino told the graduating class, "I will not bore you with the usual pep talk. You know what threats await our nation, and I know that you are very well trained to fight those threats.

"Hopefully, war will not occur, but in case it does, I expect you all to fight bravely and honorably. Each of you knows the meanings of bravery and honor.

"To fight honorably, we must practice both the *bushido* of our ancestors and the laws of war from The Hague, Geneva, and the United Nations. Since we may be fighting our first war in two centuries, the whole world will be watching us. Let us not give them any reason to question our honor."

After the speech, the midshipmen received their diplomas one by one and became ensigns, the lowest rank of commissioned officers.

When Ishiro received his diploma, he felt a rush of joy. Now he was an officer, which meant that nobody could hit him anymore. He no longer feared Lieutenant Kirino's swagger stick.

At the end of the ceremony, in a tradition of naval academies around the world, the new ensigns threw their hats into the air.

Relatives and friends rushed to the field to meet their new naval officers. Kwon and her boyfriend hugged and kissed while her parents looked on awkwardly.

Miyahara told his wife about penguins. He was wearing a medal ribbon for Antarctic service. Ishiro glanced away from the Miyaharas. He felt annoyed that Miyahara had already earned a medal. That man might actually rise to be an admiral.

Yamaguchi gave her camera to Ishiro. "Hey, Sato, will you take a photograph of me and my parents?"

"Yes, of course," said Ishiro.

He looked at the image in the camera's display. Yamaguchi's parents were wearing their best clothes. Their smiles showed their pride in their daughter. Ishiro couldn't help thinking about his absent parents.

Then he realized that they were probably smiling and posing for photos too, with his younger brother, the award-winning news writer for Fuji News Network, whose business card was framed in silver in the family house.

After taking the photo of the Yamaguchis, Ishiro wandered through the crowd, hoping to see anyone familiar.

"Ah, Ensign Sato!" said General Morita Chiko, coming forward to greet him. Ensign Kamio followed the General.

"General, sir!" said Ishiro as he saluted.

Among the modern Navy uniforms, Morita looked out of place in his Russo-Japanese War uniform. Still, he carried himself like a soldier in the way he stood and walked.

"Congratulations," said Morita. "I'm very proud that another member of the National Bushido Guards Regiment has been commissioned in the armed forces."

"Thank you, sir," said Ishiro.

"The command group of the Regiment sends its regards to you gentlemen," said Morita. "They look forward to seeing you again."

Kamio said, "I apologize for having missed the last two command group meetings. Unfortunately, the timing and location of my military duties do not always allow me to attend the meetings."

Ishiro had gone to only one command group meeting, the one where he had to leave before the business session. He had not been able to meet the command group since his induction into the Regiment at the bookstore.

"I too am sorry for not attending the command group meetings," said Ishiro.

"There is no need to apologize, gentlemen. I know that military duty comes first. What priority can be higher than defending the homeland?" said Morita. "I'll try to schedule meetings around your leaves so each serving officer can attend at least two meetings per year. I'll also try to hold meetings in cities where you're stationed."

"That would be much appreciated, sir. I would like to meet the command group again," said Kamio. "These are trying times for our nation. I think our organization can do much to revive the national spirit."

Morita nodded. "We will do something to inspire the people. I'll let you know more about it in the New Year. Now, if you'll excuse me, I need to return to Tokyo. I have a meeting with the Imperial Household Agency."

The Imperial Household Agency controlled the Emperor's and Imperial Family's every move. Ishiro was awestruck.

"How did you get a meeting with the Imperial Household Agency? Why are you meeting them?" asked Ishiro.

"Some officials within the agency think as we do," said Morita. "We will discuss the future of the Emperor system."

Ishiro and Kamio exchanged salutes with Morita, and the General left to catch a train to Tokyo.

Kamio introduced his parents to Ishiro. They were a wealthy couple who supported right-wing organizations. Kamio's father was a car company executive who had invested in the latest movie of *The Forty-Seven Ronin*. His mother was a hospital administrator who wore the badge of the Military Families Association.

"I'm so proud that my son will be defending our nation," said Mrs. Kamio. "The Purist Arabians will regret what they did to our journalist."

"Thank you, mother," said Kamio. "The Purists will indeed pay for the murder."

"General Morita thinks Russia should be our first priority," said Ishiro.

"I know what your General says, but we can't let Purist Arabia go unpunished," said Kamio the father. "We should defeat Purist Arabia first, and later, use our war experience to retake the Northern Territories from Russia."

Mrs. Kamio nodded. "That's a good strategy. Practice on the weaker enemy first and then fight the stronger enemy. We did that with China and Russia in 1894 and 1904."

They talked about the impending war and their future postings. The Kamios left for dinner, and Ishiro continued looking for anyone familiar.

"Ensign Sato!"

"Mr. Endo!"

"That's Lieutenant Commander Endo."

Ishiro saluted and greeted Mr. Endo and his wife Masako. Mr. Endo was wearing a Navy uniform with the sleeve stripes of a lieutenant commander.

"This is a surprise. I didn't know you were coming," Ishiro said.

"Yuko said you were graduating today, so I let the managers run the restaurants on their own and came here to see you graduate," said Endo.

"And the Gakushuin has its December break now, so I can come too," said Masako.

"That's nice," said Ishiro. "Yuko really told you I was graduating?"

"Yes, she did. She told us about an email you sent her," said Endo.

"Wow. Thank you for coming. Is that your old uniform?"

"It's my old uniform, but this armband is new." Endo pointed at a white and black armband. "I'm in the Supplementary Reserve now."

"Very good, sir," said Ishiro.

"I'm glad I still fit in my old uniform. Some guys in the Supplementary Reserve are too fat to wear their old uniforms now."

"A bunch of old guys playing soldier again," said Masako.

"No, I'm playing sailor," Endo corrected her.

"It's the same thing if you don't ever go on a boat," said Masako. She looked at Ishiro. "You know the joke about the Supplementary Reserve, don't you? Their job is to surrender after the regular military and the reserves are defeated."

Endo chuckled. "The Supplementary Reserve isn't as useless as that. I just inspected an air raid shelter in Akihabara. And I taught basic first aid to some high school kids. And best of all, the uniform got me into this graduation ceremony without an invitation."

"I guess we're comrades in arms now," said Ishiro.

"Hah, if the military ever issues arms to the Supplementary Reserve," said Endo. "I'll be lucky to get a sword."

"Where are your parents?" Masako asked.

"They did not come," Ishiro muttered.

"Oh, I'm sorry to hear that," Masako said. Then she smiled. "Well, then you'll be at liberty tonight?"

"Yes, ma'am."

"We're staying at the Okimi Hotel. It's booked full of families of the graduates, but my husband managed to get us a room because he's in the Supplementary Reserve. Will you have dinner with us?"

"Thank you, I would like that very much," said Ishiro.

As they walked to the exit, Endo said, "I hope I was able to help you when you called."

"You did indeed, sir. You were very helpful," said Ishiro.

"Good, good. You must tell me about your cruise. It was the Inland Sea, wasn't it? Did you work with any androids?"

**

They had dinner in the Okimi Hotel. It was a plain hotel, between low-grade and luxurious. Its guests were usually visiting military officers, contractors working for the Navy, and new midshipman on the eve of their first day at the school. Lieutenant Commander Endo remarked that its guest rooms reminded him of junior officers' quarters in the old days — dull and austere but clean and comfortable.

Tonight, its restaurant was filled with new Navy officers and their families. The air smelled of both Japanese and European food, and L-3 android waitresses scurried between the dining room and the kitchen.

They talked about the cruise on the Inland Sea, the androids aboard the *Ota*, and the threat of war with Purist Arabia. Inevitably, the conversation turned to the maids of Nikkou Café.

"So what's been happening with the maids?" Ishiro asked.

"Where do I start?" said Masako. "We can start with Rena. She left the café to work as a secretary at a big law firm."

"Good for her," said Ishiro. "I'll miss seeing her at the café, though."

Masako waited for the L-3 android to take away her soup bowl. "Kagami quit too. She's playing Minnie Mouse at Disneyland now."

Ishiro chuckled. "Kagami as Minnie Mouse? That's hilarious!"

"I couldn't believe it either," said Masako. "It's hard to imagine Kagami as a cute cartoon character. I always thought she would be dancing in a black leather bikini behind a death metal band."

"There's another dancer too," said Ishiro. "Keiko."

"Ah, Keiko," said Masako. "She works only two days a week at the café now. On the other days, she's dancing with the Paris Ballet Company of Tokyo."

"Really? That's wonderful! She always wanted to dance with a classical ballet company."

"She's rehearsing for a ballet called *Coppélia* now. Before that, she danced as a peasant girl in another ballet, *Giselle*. My daughter and Yuko saw *Giselle* and told me that Keiko performed very well."

"Oh, about Yuko, how is she doing?" Ishiro asked.

"Her learning program still continues to amaze me," said Endo. "Just last week, she learned how to ride a bicycle."

Ishiro said, "She's riding a bicycle? That's amazing. She's such a surprising girl."

"Android," Endo reminded him.

"Oh, sorry, android," said Ishiro.

Masako took a sip of wine and asked, "What will you be doing next?"

Ishiro nodded and chewed his food. He did not reply immediately.

Masako smiled. "Just take your time, Sato. Don't talk while you're chewing. A Navy officer has to have the manners of a gentleman."

Ishiro swallowed his food before saying, "I've got two weeks leave, and then I'll report for six months duty aboard the submarine *Yayoi*."

Endo looked fascinated. "The *Yayoi*? She's a *Taisho* Class ship. You'll be on one of the largest submarines in the world. I wish I could sail aboard the *Yayoi*. It'll be a remarkable experience."

"I'm looking forward to it, sir," said Ishiro.

******

After dinner, they went to the hotel lobby. In the morning, Endo and Masako would take the train back to Tokyo. Ishiro would finish some paperwork at the school and follow in another train two hours later.

"The Navy has been a positive influence on you," said Masako. "The girls will be very impressed to see you now."

"Oh?"

"You carry yourself differently. The way you walk and stand is more confident."

"And you didn't ramble endlessly about anime and computers," Endo remarked.

"Well, it's not as if I haven't seen any anime," said Ishiro. "Last week Midshipman Kamio and I saw the anime version of *Runaway Horses* by Morita Chiko, based on the novel by Mishima Yukio. It's only two years old, and already, the film critics think it's a modern classic. I tell you, the art style was bold and dark, and the voice actors were overacting a bit, but that's just to emphasize the strong beliefs of the characters in the original novel. I heard that Anime America, an anime fans' convention in the United States, had the English voice actors meet the Japanese voice actors at a special panel discussion, and they talked about "

"Ah, that's fine, I'll read about it on the internet," Endo interrupted him.

He had controlled himself throughout the day, but when he heard the word "anime," Ishiro had weakened. It had been weeks since he had unloaded verbally on Kamio, but Kamio had steered the conversation away from anime. Instead, they ended up talking about General Morita's parades at Yasukuni Shrine. Ishiro felt a slight pain in his bowels. His pent-up urge had no release.

He took a deep breath and regained control of his mind and body. "As you wish, sir," he said.

"My wife and I need to retire soon so we can catch the early train," said Endo. "Sato, it's been a pleasure hosting you to dinner. Drop in the Nikkou Café during your leave."

Ishiro saluted. "Yes, sir, I will."

Endo returned the salute. "Very well, Ensign Sato, carry on."

As Ishiro walked out of the hotel, he thought he heard Endo say, "He was talking like an *otaku* again."

"I think he relapsed," said Masako.

Ishiro returned into the chilly December air. As he boarded the bus to the school, he felt a warm glow. *The girls will be very impressed to see you now.*

Would Yuko be impressed? He wanted to know.

******

At Nikkou Café, in the late afternoon of December thirty-first, Ami changed into a silver minidress, her party clothes for the evening. As she unpacked noisemakers, she watched Mikita argue with a boyfriend.

Mikita pouted and said, "I catch you flirting with other girls, and *you're* the one who feels wronged?"

"I only talk to girls. I don't do anything else with them, but you go on dates with other guys," her boyfriend protested.

"Is that what's bothering you?" Mikita said. "Well, I think you're jealous."

"You think I shouldn't be? I gave up all other girls for you."

"That's what you should do if you want me."

"But you're still dating other guys. You're not even denying it."

Mikita smiled. "But I'm just seeing them very casually. Those guys mean nothing to me."

The boyfriend looked more agonized than angry. "Do you think that makes it right?"

Mikita sighed. "Oh, dear, oh, dear. How can I prove that you are the only one for me?"

She grabbed the second button of his school uniform and yanked hard. The button came off instantly. She grinned slyly at the shocked look on his face.

"Oh! You want my button?" he said.

"Yes, I want *your* button because you're the only one for me," Mikita purred.

Caught by surprise, the boyfriend smiled and stammered, "Oh, ah, that's wonderful! I love you too!"

"Well, I don't know what to do. You doubted me," Mikita said, pouting again.

"Oh, no, I never doubted you," said her boyfriend.

Mikita quickly suggested, "You know how you can make it up to me? Meet me at our love hotel at six-thirty. Then take me to Heian Shiro and buy me dinner at seven-thirty."

"Heian Shiro? That's a very posh restaurant," the boyfriend said.

"Am I not worth every yen?"

"Yes, yes!"

"It's New Year's Eve, so make a reservation. Now get going! I have to finish my shift," Mikita said. She grabbed his shoulders, pulled him close, and kissed his lips. "See you tonight."

Mikita gently pushed him out of the café. Ami shook her head, surprised by how the maid controlled the young man.

Yuko went to Mikita and asked, "Why did you take the button off his uniform?"

"When a boy loves you, he gives you the second button of his school uniform because that's the button closest to his heart," Mikita explained.

"I see. Is he supposed to give it to you or are you supposed to take it from him?"

"He's supposed to give it to me, but I have to take charge with that guy. I usually don't go out with guys like him. He's too shy and reserved. But he comes from a wealthy family, he's smart, and he might get a good job. I should keep my options open."

Mikita pulled a clear plastic sandwich bag from her apron. The bag was full of buttons. She dropped the latest one into her collection.

Ishiro, wearing his Navy uniform, walked in.

Mikita gasped. "It's been almost a year! Welcome back, Mr. Sato!"

Ami said, "I think he's Admiral Sato now."

Yuko threw herself at Ishiro, and he stumbled backwards. She hugged him tightly.

Her warmth felt human. But Ishiro knew that Yuko didn't have warm blood. The heat came from her processors and motors. The illusion was convincing, though.

Ishiro had seldom hugged his past girlfriend. He felt uneasy with public displays of affection. He laughed nervously and pushed Yuko away.

"Master, welcome back!" said Yuko. She didn't seem to notice that Ishiro had squirmed out of her embrace.

"Who programmed you to hug me like that?" Ishiro asked.

"I learned it on my own by watching American romance movies," she replied.

"Romance movies?"

Yuko nodded. "It was Mikita's idea. She thought I could learn about love by watching movies."

Yuko took off her barrette, plucked the naval cap off Ishiro's head, and put it on. "This is a nice cap. Does it look good on me?"

Mikita laughed. "Such a happy reunion. Now please excuse me. I have to get changed to see my boyfriend tonight. Have fun. See you later."

As soon as Mikita left, Ami said, "I'll leave you two alone." She went into the office.

"Where are you staying in town?" Yuko said. "Are you staying with your parents?"

The question saddened Ishiro. He shook his head. "No, I'm not staying with them. I'm staying at the naval base."

"Do you have to go back to the naval base tonight? Can you stay for our New Year's Eve celebration?" Yuko asked hopefully.

"That's why I came here," said Ishiro.

Still wearing the naval cap, Yuko led Ishiro to a table in her section.

"It's New Year's Eve, so we have the *osechi* box tonight," Yuko said, referring to the traditional foods of the New Year Festival. "Do you want a box?"

"Yes, of course, and a sweet tea," said Ishiro.

Minutes later, Yuko returned with his tea and a two-tiered lacquered box. Ishiro lifted the top tier and gazed at the different items, all in their own small compartments. There were herring roe, black beans, sardines, egg custard, sweet potato and chestnuts, rice cake, fish paste cake, shrimp, sea bream, seaweed, tofu, and sashimi.

In past centuries, women made *osechi* before New Year's Eve so they would have enough food without cooking for the first few days of the New Year. Now robots made *osechi* at food factories, and grocery stores sold millions of boxes of it.

Mr. and Mrs. Endo came to greet him. As on Christmas Eve, Endo wore a business suit, and Masako wore the kimono with Christmas symbols.

Endo saluted Ishiro. "Ensign, it's nice to see you again."

"Yes, sir, it's nice to be back at my favorite café," said Ishiro.

"Even after your cruise on the Inland Sea, this is still your favorite place," said Masako. "Thank you."

**

The regular customers congratulated Ishiro on his new career.

"Hey, Sato, you look really smart in that uniform! At first I didn't recognize you," said a banker. "Are there many girls in the Navy?"

"There are some. Maybe forty percent of the personnel are women," said Ishiro.

The banker giggled. "Just like on *Moé Girls Fleet*, a new dating sim I just bought! You have to try it sometime."

Ishiro smiled and nodded silently. The banker was addicted to dating sims and hadn't gone on a date with a real girl for seven years.

Another *otaku* asked if the Navy had a gift shop that sold plastic model kits of ships and planes. He built models that won awards at science fiction conventions. Ishiro had seen photos of the man's apartment before. It was crammed with models of planes, ships, spaceships, and robots.

The Navy did have a gift shop, and Ishiro promised to send its mail-order website to him.

As on Christmas Eve, the maids and customers blew on noisemakers and threw paper streamers into the air at midnight. Pop songs blared on the speakers. Some of the maids played with hula hoops. Ami and Yuko danced on the stage.

Mr. and Mrs. Endo handed gifts to the customers. Ishiro howled with delight.

"Wow, it's an Ogon Bat miniature figure!" he said as he took the small plastic toy.

Ogon Bat, Japan's oldest manga superhero, was making a comeback in the live-action movie *Ogon Bat Returns*. Due to his naval duties, Ishiro couldn't watch it in a theater, but Kamio had given him an illicit video of it.

"Thank you, thank you very much!" Ishiro said.

After dancing on the stage, Yuko sat down at Ishiro's table. She looked longingly into his eyes.

"Master, I'm very happy that you've returned. Will you be staying long?" she asked.

"No, I've got a posting. I'll be at sea for six months starting on January eleventh," Ishiro replied.

"Oh, we don't have much time together. Let's go on a date later today."

The offer surprised Ishiro. He hadn't expected Yuko to be so bold to ask for a date.

"But last time we were supposed to go on a date, Mr. Endo ordered you to stay home," Ishiro said. "Can you go on a date now?"

Yuko grinned. "Ami reprogrammed me so that she could countermand her father's orders. Then she programmed me to ask you for a date and go with you if you agree."

"Oh, I see. Does Mr. Endo know about your reprogramming?"

"No, he doesn't, and Ami programmed me not to tell him."

"Oh, that little sneak!"

"Well, master, shall we go on a date on New Year's Day?" Yuko asked.

Ishiro nodded. "Yes, Yuko. Let's do it. But what shall we do? You can't eat dinner."

"It's New Year's Day. How about *hatsumode*?" Yuko suggested. "I've never gone on a *hatsumode*."

*Hatsumode* was an old tradition, the first visit to a shrine in the New Year.

"You want to visit a shrine?" said Ishiro.

"Why not? Everyone else does."

"I don't. The shrines are very crowded, and I don't like being around so many people."

Ami suddenly appeared beside him. "Hey, admiral, you're not giving the right answers to a girl! I think you should say yes."

"Uh, sure, I'll take you to a shrine," Ishiro said.

Ami giggled and went away.

"Thank you! I want to know what a *hatsumode* is like," said Yuko. "Which shrine should we visit?"

Ishiro and his family hadn't gone on a *hatsumode* for years, and when they did, they had visited a nondescript shrine near their house.

Then he remembered a shrine that appeared often in General Morita's anime.

"Yasukuni," said Ishiro. "I'm a Navy officer, so I should visit Yasukuni Shrine before I go away."

He thought about the idea and sighed. "But wait. Mr. Endo is an officer again. He'll be there too."

"No he won't," said Yuko, smiling. "This year, the family is going to Meiji Shrine at Mrs. Endo's request."

"Great! Can you meet me at Ichigaya Station at two o'clock in the afternoon?"

Yuko put the naval cap back on Ishiro's head. "Yes. See you in the afternoon, master."

**

In some religions, a dead person's soul goes to a heaven. In Buddhism, a dead person is reincarnated, lives, dies, and is reincarnated again until he achieves enlightenment, goes into the state of nirvana, and finally breaks out of the cycle. Shintoism, however, has a different view of the afterlife.

In Shintoism, the deceased person's *kami* does not go to a heaven or to nirvana. Instead, it stays in the world, where it becomes unquiet because it has suffered death, the ultimate uncleanness. An unquiet *kami* roaming the world could cause trouble for the living.

Since Buddhism offered reincarnation, many Japanese held Buddhist rituals for their dead relatives. But other Japanese enshrined the *kami* of their dead in Shinto shrines, where they could be pacified by offerings, entertainment, and rituals to honor them. If the living were fortunate, they might turn the *kami* into a benevolent spirit, one who would help them in their current lives.

In the Meiji Era, Japan became an imperial power, first by uniting the country in a series of civil wars, then by wars against its neighbors. In the centuries when Japan was isolated, Japanese wars were feudal struggles between *daimyo*, fought by samurai. Japan had not seen war deaths on the scale of the Napoleonic Wars or the American Civil War. In the Meiji Era, Japan fought modern wars for the first time, with mass armies and mass deaths. The *kami* of the war dead multiplied rapidly into the thousands. In the twentieth century, they grew into the millions.

The war *kami* were especially troublesome. Dead soldiers were young people killed in their prime, before they had the chance to fulfill their lives. When they returned to Japan, they would seek revenge on their own people, not on the enemy who had actually killed them. The living had to pacify millions of unquiet spirits.

In 1867, the Japanese government created several war memorial shrines to enshrine and honor the war *kami*. In 1875, all the war *kami* were brought together at a shrine on Kudan Hill. It sat between the poor and rich neighborhoods of Tokyo, as if to unite the war dead of all social classes.

The Meiji Emperor visited the shrine to honor all the war dead, not just the nobility. For the first time, a peasant received the gratitude of the Emperor. For the first time, the Japanese felt like equal citizens of a nation, not lords and peasants of a feudal society.

The shrine was called "Yasukuni," meaning "the peaceful country." It was not just one building, but rather, a large complex of many buildings, monuments, statues, gardens, and wooded areas.

Ishiro met Yuko at Ichigaya Station. She wore a red coat. It was the first time Ishiro had seen Yuko wear clothes other than her maid costume.

"That's a nice coat," said Ishiro.

"Thank you," said Yuko. "Ami lent it to me. She said I should wear it if I'm going outside."

"Really? Do you feel the cold weather?"

"No, the temperature doesn't affect me. I could wear anything — or nothing at all." She smiled. "But Ami didn't think I should wear my maid costume at a shrine."

"I agree with her. That wouldn't be right."

"But I'm wearing my uniform underneath." She opened her coat to show her maid costume.

Ishiro chuckled, and Yuko quickly buttoned up her coat.

"I'm in uniform too," said Ishiro. He was wearing his naval uniform with an officer's overcoat.

He wasn't the only person in uniform. Other soldiers, sailors, and airmen walked along the streets. Ishiro had never before seen so many military personnel in Tokyo.

They entered Yasukuni from the south gate, where two stone mythical lions guarded too large wooden doors. A grey metal chrysanthemum hung on each door.

L-3 androids in security uniforms stood by the footpath and watched the people stream past them. On a busy day like today, the shrine needed extra security.

Ishiro and Yuko joined a crowd surrounding a *temizuya*, the stone purification basin. People were scooping up water from the basin and washing their hands with it. Ishiro waited for a ladle to become free, took it, scooped some water, and poured it on Yuko's hands. Then he washed his own hands.

"You're supposed to rinse your mouth too," said Ishiro. He scooped more water, held the ladle above his head, and looked up. "Pour it into your mouth but don't let your lips touch the ladle."

He poured the water into his mouth, kept it briefly, and spit it into the trough for waste water.

"Most people aren't rinsing their mouths," Yuko observed.

"The tradition is disappearing over time," said Ishiro.

"Let me try it." Yuko took the ladle, scooped up some water, poured it into her mouth, and spit it out.

She smiled. "Thank Victor Robotics for designing waterproof androids."

"The Navy has plenty of them," said Ishiro.

"But not like me."

Many people walked on the path to the center of the shrine complex. Most wore civilian clothes, but many wore military uniforms, including Supplementary Reserve armbands.

They went to a dark wooden building with a peaked roof. It was the *haiden*, the hall of worship. Only priests and invited guests could enter it. Regular worshippers stood outside it to honor the *kami*.

The worshippers crowded around the wooden offering box in front of the *haiden*. Too many people were waiting to use the money card reader, so Ishiro tossed a coin into the box. The sound of metal hitting wood repeated as other people threw their coins.

Ishiro looked ahead. The walls of the *haiden* were open, so he could see through to the other side and what lay behind the building. It was the *honden*, visible from a distance but closed to the public. The *kami* of the war dead dwelled there.

He took a deep breath as he stared at the *honden*. The simple building struck him with awe. He was looking at the souls of over two million people who had died fighting for their Emperor.

Ishiro handed his naval cap to Yuko. He bowed twice, clapped his hands twice, and bowed once more.

Yuko gave the cap back to Ishiro and performed the ritual too. They walked away from the *haiden*.

"Did you pray to the *kami*?" Yuko asked.

"I asked them to keep us safe if a war breaks out," said Ishiro. "I'm not religious, but it can't hurt to ask them, I guess. What did you pray for?"

"I didn't pray. I'm an android."

"You didn't pray, but you performed the ritual for honoring the *kami*."

"It's a cultural tradition. People do it."

A male L-3 android in a kimono gave them a schedule of the shrine's festivals. When Ishiro thanked the android, it bowed.

Yuko pointed at a wooden booth. "What's over there?"

A stern-faced *miko* stared at them as they approached the booth. Lucky charms and amulets were laid out in front of her.

"That's an *omamori* for victory," said Ishiro, pointing to a cloth amulet. It was red with the shrine's *mon* in gold.

"I'll buy one of those," said Yuko, picking up the victory *omamori*. She gave a money card to the *miko*.

"Where did you get the money?" Ishiro asked.

"From Ami," replied Yuko. "She gives me money from time to time."

"That's very nice of her."

"She's a good programmer," Yuko said as she took the money card back from the *miko*.

She opened Ishiro's overcoat, unbuttoned the top button of his jacket, and put the *omamori* into the left breast pocket of his shirt.

"Keep this close to your heart. Victory for you, master," Yuko said.

"Thank you, Yuko," said Ishiro as he buttoned up his jacket and overcoat. "I'll always keep it with me."

They walked through the grounds. There were statues dedicated to military horses, dogs, and carrier pigeons. They saw a statue of a kamikaze pilot and an old tree planted by a Luftwaffe general.

At a sculpture of a battleship, an old man approached them. He wore the hat of the Naval Veterans Association.

"I was in the Maritime Self-Defense Force," the man said. "I'm so happy to see a young naval officer here."

"Where did you serve?" Ishiro asked.

"I was a petty officer aboard the destroyer *Empress Jingu*. Now I'm in the Supplementary Reserve. How about you?"

"I just graduated from the Naval Officer Candidate School."

"Very good! And it's great that you brought your girlfriend." The man turned to Yuko. "You must be very proud of him."

Yuko nodded. "Yes, I'm very proud of him."

"Sorry for interrupting. I hope you don't mind an old veteran like me. I'll let you young folks go on your way." The man bowed to them. "Have a good day."

As the man walked away, Yuko said softly, "People think I'm your girlfriend."

"There's nothing wrong with that," said Ishiro.

Yuko smiled, grabbed his wrist, and led him away. They walked to the main path and passed the statue of Omura Masujiro, the founder of the modern Japanese Army.

They stopped at the fountain honoring soldiers who had died of thirst. The fountain gave Ishiro a sobering thought. Combat was not the only way to die in war. There were many other ways, like thirst, starvation, disease, and accident. What if one of his submarine's torpedoes exploded in the launch tube? What if the engine broke down?

Near the fountain were stones from battlefields like Manchuria, Indonesia, the Philippines, Saipan, and Iwo Jima.

"People died at each of these places," Ishiro said. "That's horrible. War is horrible. I hope we don't get into one."

"I hope so too, master. You humans are not as repairable as androids," said Yuko.

Ishiro chuckled. "Come on, let's look around the neighborhood.

******

Ishiro and Yuko saw a musical instruments shop. Its window had a poster of a ballerina in costume from *Coppélia*, by the Paris Ballet Company of Tokyo.

"Keiko's in that company, isn't she?" Ishiro asked.

Yuko nodded. "Yes, she's a dancer in the *corps de ballet*."

"Is that a French word? What does it mean?"

"It's the group of dancers who do not perform solos."

A robot stood outside the shop. It was a low-end model, capable of only a few repetitive tasks. It looked like a man in a tuxedo and played a violin.

"I've heard that tune before. What is it?" Ishiro asked.

"It's an American song called 'Simple Gifts' by the composer Joseph Brackett, which was also used in the ballet *Appalachian Spring* by another American composer, Aaron Copland," Yuko replied.

"Wow, you know a lot about Western classical music," said Ishiro.

Yuko pointed at the ballet poster. "My creator liked classical music. She programmed me to play the violin and downloaded many music files to me, including *Coppélia*. This poster reminds me of her."

"Was she a dancer?"

"I don't know. I have only data fragments about her. I used to ask Mr. Endo who she was, but he said he didn't know. He said I suffered a disk error, strayed away from my owner, and wandered into his café. I stopped asking him after a while."

"Do you often wonder who she was?" Ishiro asked.

"Yes," said Yuko.

"Why?"

"Ami has Mrs. Endo. And you have a mother, right?"

"Uh, yes, but our relationship isn't the same as the one between Ami and Mrs. Endo," said Ishiro.

"At least you know who your mother is. I have no related machines, not even other androids of my model. My creator is my closest equivalent of a mother, but I don't know who she is," Yuko said.

"Is that something you want to know?"

"Yes. My learning program directs me to find the answer. So far, I have been unsuccessful."

She sounded sad and full of longing for her lost mother. Ishiro felt sorry for her. But his mind knew that she was a machine imitating human emotions.

Or was she?

"Yuko, can you truly *feel* emotions?" he asked.

"I have extensive social skills software. I am programmed to behave appropriately for the situation in which I am in," she replied.

That reply did not answer his question. He decided not to pursue the subject.

"Listen to that robot," he said, changing the subject. "I think the shop owner didn't program it to play anything else."

"I can play something else," Yuko offered.

She took the violin away from the robot and played another tune. Ishiro thought the melody was sweet and let her perform for a couple minutes.

But he had to interrupt her. "Yuko, maybe you better finish before the shopkeeper comes out!"

Yuko finished playing and put the violin back in the robot's hands. Ishiro clapped, and Yuko smiled and curtsied.

The robot began playing "Simple Gifts" again.

"What did you play?" Ishiro asked.

"A selection from *Coppélia*," replied Yuko.

"You played another part of *Coppélia* at the Christmas show last year, didn't you? What's that ballet about?"

"It's about a scientist named Dr. Coppélius, who invents a mechanical doll named Coppélia."

**

Finally, they came to Nikkou Café in the late afternoon. Yuko smiled and pressed herself against Ishiro. Again, the maid's brazenness startled him.

"Thank you for taking me to the shrine on my first *hatsumode*," said Yuko.

"Didn't Mr. Endo ever take you on a *hatsumode*?" Ishiro asked.

"No, the family didn't take me along. Mr. Endo didn't know if he should take an android to a shrine," said Yuko.

"There are androids working at the shrine," Ishiro said.

"Mr. Endo has an ambivalent attitude towards androids."

"It wouldn't have mattered. Nobody knew you were an android. You fit in well with humans."

"Thank you, master. I'm glad that I can pass for a real girl."

They stared at each other. There was an awkward silence.

"Well, I guess this is the end of our date," said Ishiro. "I'll be going away on the eleventh, and, uh, I don't know if you'll be busy between now and then, but do you want to see me again?"

"Of course, master," said Yuko. "I'm still researching about love. I want to visit a love hotel and learn what happens inside it. Will you take me to a love hotel?"

Ishiro laughed nervously. Yuko was beautiful, and her hands felt smooth and soft. But he remembered the hard plastic lips and dry rubber tongue of the L-2 at the android scrapyard. He didn't want to repeat that experience.

"Why are you laughing?" said Yuko. "Do you not think that I can perform like a real girl?"

She threw her arms around his shoulders and pushed her tongue into his mouth. She gave him a deep, wet kiss. Ishiro was astounded by how soft and wet and natural Yuko felt. She felt nothing like the L-2 android.

"Master, you're supposed to put your arms around my lower back," Yuko whispered.

"*So desu ka,*" Ishiro mumbled as he hugged her.

203

"That's better," she said before kissing him again.

What would passersby think of this shamelessly public kissing, undoubtedly learned from American movies? Ishiro gently pushed Yuko away.

She looked at him with hungry eyes.

"Oh, what the hell," he muttered. He kissed her deeply, driven by pent-up urges.

When they stopped kissing, Ishiro said, "You feel so human and natural."

"My lips, tongue, and mouth are made of new polymers that feel like human tissue, and my mouth is lubricated to simulate human saliva," Yuko explained.

"Your mouth is lubricated?" Ishiro said incredulously.

"I'm also lubricated in other places to make me more desirable to humans," said Yuko.

Ishiro chuckled. "Oh, which other places?"

Yuko smirked. "I'll show you at our next date."

She opened his overcoat, grabbed the second button of his uniform, and yanked it off. Ishiro gasped.

Yuko clutched the button in her hand. "I have to go now. The night shift is starting. But yes, let's go on another date, master."

As she sauntered into the café, she looked back and gave him a sly grin.

She must be learning about love and dating from Mikita, Ishiro guessed. Mikita was a dubious role model, but she would not train Yuko to be boring. That was the positive side.

On the negative side, now he had to replace the button on his uniform or suffer punishment from his captain.

**

On the next day, January second, Prime Minister Fujiwara stood in a microwave receiver station. While the nation watched on TV, he pressed a button, and satellites turned solar energy into electricity and sent it to Earth in microwave beams.

"Now we have the energy of the Sun," he announced.

The war began two hours later. Rockets and bombs exploded simultaneously in eleven Japanese embassies around the world. Gunmen shot a group of Japanese tourists in Egypt before dying in a gunfight with police. Terrorists bombed a Japanese car factory in the United States. A Sudanese knifeman stabbed a Japan Airlines pilot at London Heathrow Airport.

No target was too small, and not all victims were Japanese. In Paris, Islamic militants crashed a car into an anime toy shop owned by an

Algerian couple. In Toronto, Canada, a suicide bomber killed everyone in a sushi restaurant run by Koreans.

The Purist Arabian Ambassador to Japan spoke on TV again. "Neither the Purist Arabian government nor its people are involved in these incidents. However, we sympathize with people who oppose paganism and racism."

**

That night, Yuko suddenly stopped walking while waiting on tables. She stood still, and her eyes looked glazed.

"Yuko, what's wrong?" Ami asked.

"I'm receiving a telephone call in my head," said Yuko. "It's from Mr. Sato."

"Oh? What does he want?"

Yuko spoke in Ishiro's voice. "Yuko, this is Ishiro."

"Master, how nice to hear from you," Yuko replied.

Ishiro spoke through Yuko again. "The Navy has cancelled all leaves, and we're all confined to the base. I can't come out."

"Oh. Can we go on another date before you leave?"

"Don't worry. I'm sure we will. I just don't know when right now."

"Master, please be careful."

"Don't worry, Yuko, I will. I have to go now. The captain is a really tough woman. She wants to inspect the ship in the morning."

"Good night, master."

"Good night, Yuko."

The call ended, and Ami hugged Yuko.

"Don't worry, everything will be fine," Ami assured her.

**

On the morning of January third, two gunmen stormed through the University of Tokyo campus. They killed ninety people in a shooting spree, took over a building, killed forty hostages, and died when police besieged them. They were students from Sudan who were studying international politics.

When the police searched the students' apartment, they found ammunition inside diplomatic bags of the Sudanese Embassy. Diplomatic bags were not searched when they entered the country. Sudanese diplomats had used them to smuggle weapons to the students.

Prime Minister Fujiwara called the Japanese Embassy in Khartoum to tell the ambassador to leave. A man answered the telephone and said in English, "Fujiwara-san, go watch the television. Your spy nest is destroyed, and your spies are dead. *Allah Akbar!*"

The prime minister turned on the TV and watched in horror as Sudanese hordes stormed the embassy. As-Sabah TV broadcast the beheadings of the ambassador and his staff.

Fujiwara ordered the Sudanese Ambassador to leave Japan immediately. The Army and police rushed to the embassy to expel the Sudanese. The street filled with armored vehicles and police cars.

Ambassador Omar Adwok carried a handgun out of the embassy. Police officers and soldiers watched him warily as he stepped on the street. He was no longer within the embassy compound. Now he was holding a gun in Japanese territory. It was a violation of the law.

Adwok told the TV reporters, "I have diplomatic immunity. I can wave this in your faces, even open fire, and you can't touch me."

"Our ambassador had diplomatic immunity too, and your country murdered him," said an official from the Ministry of Foreign Affairs.

Adwok spat on the street. "He was a pagan spy. He deserved to be beheaded like a pig!"

Behind him, his staff stared stone-faced at the soldiers and police.

The ambassador got into his limousine, and the Foreign Affairs official slammed the door shut. Ten police cars escorted the Sudanese motorcade to the airport.

Ramzi Jarrah, the Purist Arabian Ambassador, denied that his country had any involvement in the University of Tokyo massacre. "However, we will not condemn the actions of the Sudanese government and people. They have every right to defend their religion against pagan oppression."

**

On January fourth, thousands of people gathered in front of the National Diet Building. Their chanting filled the air:

"Punish Sudan!"

"War against Purist Arabia!"

"Remember the embassy in Khartoum!"

"Revenge at all costs!"

Someone unfurled a banner reading "Repeal Article 9." Military marches blared from black vans. A solemn procession carried photographs of the University of Tokyo victims.

General Morita and the National Bushido Guards Regiment held a parade. As usual, he granted interviews to reporters.

"General, you were opposed to war against Purist Arabia and Sudan," a reporter asked. "Why are you here?"

"The international situation has obviously changed," Morita replied. "The massacres of our students and our embassy staff are unforgivable. We must punish the Sudanese."

"What about Purist Arabia?"

"Purist Arabia and Sudan are allies. They work together. The Purist Arabians deny they are involved in attacks on us, but soon, the truth will come out, and when it does, we will crush the Purists!"

Not everyone urged war. A small group of pacifist students staged their own demonstration. They held a banner reading "Use Oil for Peace."

A young woman stood on a chair and shouted, "Our own government is at fault. There's nothing wrong with using oil, there's nothing wrong with importing oil. We should scrap the space-generated electricity system!"

The crowd's jeers drowned out the rest of her speech.

"How can a student say that after the university massacre?" someone shouted.

"Go to Purist Arabia!" another person yelled.

"Deport her to Sudan!"

"Traitor! Traitor!"

The people swarmed around the pacifists and pushed them away. The police watched and did nothing.

Ami and Yuko were shopping nearby when they heard the noise. They went to the National Diet Building. People held national flags all around them.

"I've never seen anything like this before," said Ami. "This seldom happens in Japan."

"I've never seen a demonstration of any sort," Yuko said. "This is a learning experience."

A government spokesman appeared on the steps of the National Diet Building. Loudspeakers carried his message to the crowd.

"The Diet has voted to exercise the nation's right to self-defense by ordering a military mission against Sudan," he announced.

The crowd roared with approval. The sound was deafening. Ami imagined that it must sound like a volcano eruption.

"We're at war with Sudan!" a woman shouted.

"It's only a matter of time before we'll be at war with Purist Arabia too. Destroy them both!" said a man wearing the Military Families Association badge.

Another man grunted. "Hah, notice how the government calls it a 'military mission' instead of a war."

The national flags waved vigorously, like thousands of red Suns dancing.

An old man held out small flags to Ami and Yuko. He wore the hat of the Naval Veterans Association.

"Do you want these flags? Take them, they're free," he said.

"Thank you," said Ami. She took the flags and gave one to Yuko.

The man looked curiously at Yuko. "Hey, didn't I see you with your boyfriend at Yasukuni on New Year's Day?"

"Ah, that's right, I remember you," said Yuko. "How are you?"

The man smiled. "I am fine. I'm too old to serve in the Navy again, but I can come out to support the people. Is your boyfriend here?"

"Boyfriend?" Yuko said.

Ami giggled, and Yuko smiled and nudged her in the elbow.

"Oh, *him*. No, he's not here," said Yuko. She waved her flag. "He's at the naval base."

"Ah, of course, I should have known that! He's where he's needed. If he were here, I would congratulate him wholeheartedly. He has the honor of defending our nation against the Sudanese."

Yuko turned to Ami. "Will Ishiro be sent into the war?"

"He's on the largest submarine in the fleet. He'll definitely go into the war zone," Ami realized.

**

On January fifth, Ishiro phoned Yuko from the naval base. Right after sending her telephone number, instead of a ring tone, he heard Yuko say, "Hello, this is Yuko." Androids answered their internal phones immediately.

"Yuko, this is Ishiro," he said.

"Master, how nice to hear from you again," said Yuko.

"Yuko, can you talk now?"

"Yes, I can."

"My ship is leaving earlier than originally planned. You probably heard that on the news. It'll be a big propaganda event. We're leaving the day after tomorrow," Ishiro said.

"Oh, then I won't see you until you return from sea," said Yuko. She sounded disappointed.

"They're letting the friends and families of the crew say goodbye tomorrow," said Ishiro. "Go to the naval base. Go to dock fifteen. There's a gate there, and they'll let me see you outside the gate. Can you come between one and three o'clock in the afternoon?"

"Mr. Endo will be at Heian Shiro tomorrow. I can sneak out."

"Good. I'm sorry for the short notice. Everything is so rushed now."

"I understand."

"Yuko, I'll see you tomorrow. I have to go now. 'Bye."

"Have a nice day, master."

**

On the afternoon of January sixth, Ishiro stood outside dock fifteen. Behind him was the gate, and behind the gate was the submarine *Yayoi*. A large naval flag fluttered from a tall flagpole near the submarine.

All around him, his shipmates chattered with their friends and family. A sister gave her brother, a petty officer, an *omamori* for good luck. A navigator told her boyfriend to take care of her cat. Commander Fukuda, the executive officer, talked to his wife and son. A sailor posed for photos with his girlfriend.

A band played military marches, and Red Cross nurses gave candy to the children. It was like a carnival, with laughs and jokes in the air. People knew it was their last celebration before they went to war.

Ishiro's pocket computer beeped. He opened it and read a new email:

"Dear Ishiro, you know how your brother feels about the war, so please do not feel personally insulted if we do not come to the naval base. In addition, more than a day's notice would have been welcome. Good luck on your voyage. Please visit us when you get shore leave. Your loving mother."

Although he felt he needed to invite them, he hadn't expected them to come.

"Master!"

Yuko approached him. Ishiro chuckled because she was wearing her maid uniform.

"Master, I'm so happy to see you before you leave," said Yuko.

"And I'm so happy that you came," Ishiro said.

Yuko gave a bag to Ishiro. "This is a present for you."

Ishiro pulled the gift out of the bag. It was a national flag with words handwritten in black ink. The largest words read, "We pray for your good luck." The other words were names: Keiko, Mikita, Sora, Ami, Yuko.

"A good luck flag!" Ishiro remarked. "Thank you, Yuko. Please thank the girls for me."

"I'll tell them. They're all very proud of you."

Yuko put her arms around his shoulders. Ishiro put his hands on her waist and slid them around her back.

The maid giggled. "Your hands are in the correct position this time. Good, I've programmed you well."

"Yes, you have, my dear," said Ishiro.

"I'll see you again, won't I?"

"Of course, you will."

"Here's a kiss for good luck," said Yuko.

She gave him a long kiss. This time, Ishiro did not care if other people saw them.

# CHAPTER 12

# The Wolf Pack

Ishiro pointed the video camera at Captain Yamane Michiko, commander of the *J.S. Yayoi*.

Yamane was the first woman to command a Japanese Navy submarine. The captain, in her mid-forties, had more grey streaks in her hair than did most women of her age. She had earned her medals in the harshest operations: rescuing Antarctic explorers, evacuating refugees from the Venezuelan Civil War, and finding survivors after the China earthquake.

A week ago, she abruptly ordered the *Yayoi* and four other submarines to leave Mumbai. For reasons known only to her, Navy Headquarters cancelled a joint exercise with the Indian Navy.

Yamane stood beside the viewscreen in the wardroom. Her officers sat at tables behind Ishiro and the camera. An L-3 android gave a glass of water to the captain. Other androids stood in a row and waited for orders. There was enough room for the officers, furniture, video equipment, and androids. *Taisho* Class submarines were spacious compared to older ships.

The officers wore their working uniforms of shirts and pants and ribbons but not jackets and ties. In contrast, Captain Yamane wore her service dress blue uniform, with the jacket, skirt, tie, and ribbons. She obviously wanted to look official when speaking to the crews of five submarines.

Finally, they would learn why they were sailing south into the Indian Ocean.

"I bet it's about the cargo ship that sank," whispered Ensign Yamaguchi as she walked past Ishiro.

Yamaguchi Yumi, from Ishiro's squad at the Officer Candidate School, had boarded the *Yayoi* in Mumbai. She was a communications officer now.

"The other ships are ready. Captain, you may start anytime. Ensign, be ready for the captain," said Commander Fukuda, the executive officer.

"I'm ready to start," said Yamane.

"Yes, ma'am," said Ishiro. He pushed a button and began broadcasting to the other stations in the *Yayoi*, such as the engine room, the missile rooms, the crew's quarters, the galley, and the sickbay. The broadcast was also going to the other four submarines.

Yamane looked at the camera. "To the crews of the *Yayoi*, the *Jomon*, the *Kofun*, the *Asuka*, and the *Nara*, thank you for attending this briefing. I am Yamane Michiko, captain of the *Yayoi* and commander of our wolf pack.

"Eight days ago, unidentified ships attacked and sunk the Japanese merchant ship *Sanshain Maru* in the Indian Ocean, west of Indonesia, south of the Maldives. All hands and the cargo were lost. The attackers did not fly any flags or have any identifying names, words, or symbols on their ships. The *Sanshain Maru* tried to communicate with her attackers by various means — radio, signal flags, signal lights — but received no reply.

"A crew member of the *Sanshain Maru* transmitted the following video to the Navy while under attack."

Yamane pointed her swagger stick at the viewscreen, and a video played. The image was shaky, shot by a handheld camera. It showed a freighter and three other ships at sea. Bursts of cannon fire came from the freighter, and two of the ships launched missiles. The soundtrack was full of shouting by the *Sanshain Maru*'s crew.

"Those are the ships that sank the *Sanshain Maru*," said Yamane.

An explosion sounded, and the video suddenly lurched as the *Sanshain Maru* listed. Smoke billowed across the ship's deck. The crew screamed.

"That was a torpedo hit," Yamane said.

The screen turned into static.

"That was a missile hitting the camera," said Yamane. "The *Sanshain Maru* was sunk by a squadron consisting of an armed freighter and three cruiser-size ships. Commander Fukuda will now brief us on what Naval Intelligence has learned about the attackers."

Fukuda aimed his pocket computer at the screen, and its image split in two. The right side showed a grey ship, the freighter from the video. The left side showed a similar ship painted orange and white.

"The ship on the left is the South African freighter *Van Riebeeck*. Somali privateers hijacked her four years ago," said Fukuda. "The ship on the right is freighter in the video. She's the same ship but painted grey."

Another set of photos appeared. On the right were the other three ships on the video. On the left were identical ships. Two were flying the Purist Arabian flag, and one had the Sudanese flag.

"Two of the ships on the left are cruisers of the Purist Arabian Navy, specifically the *Bin Laden* and the *Mullah Omar*. The third ship is the

Sudanese Navy cruiser *Al-Bashir*. If you remove their flags and markings, they would look just like the ships that sank the *Sanshain Maru*," said Fukuda.

The ship photos disappeared, to be replaced by the badge of the Naval Intelligence Branch.

Fukuda said, "Although the ships are hiding their identities, Naval Intelligence Branch is certain that the Purist Arabian, Sudanese, and Somali navies control them.

"However, the enemy has forgotten that ships without flags are either stateless or pirate ships, and the Navy has every right to stop and search them."

Captain Yamane said, "But we're not going to stop and search those ships. We're going to sink them."

**

After the briefing, each submarine's captain revealed the plan of attack to the officers.

Germany and Japan had different tactics of submarine warfare in the twentieth century. In the Atlantic, German U-boats formed "wolf packs" and sank merchant convoys and their military escorts. In the Pacific, Japanese submarines went on long-range reconnaissance and only occasionally attacked ships. The Japanese did not use their submarines to their full potential as weapons. But now, Yamane's five submarines would attack the enemy together.

But before moving on the enemy, the *Yayoi* dived to the bottom of the sea.

In the *Yayoi*'s command and control center, crew members looked at video monitors showing the scene outside. A petite female figure, clad in a red swimsuit, swam to an undersea cable and placed a bomb on it.

"That's a good android," said Commander Fukuda. "You've programmed it well, Sato."

"Thank you, sir," said Ishiro.

"Let's wait until it succeeds in its mission before we congratulate each other," said Captain Yamane.

"Of course, ma'am," Fukuda agreed.

The android swam back to the submarine. Ishiro excused himself and went to the airlock. When he arrived there, sailors were helping the android into the ship. Ishiro gave it a towel, and the android wiped itself dry.

Ishiro said into his pocket computer, "Sato here. Sakura is aboard the ship."

"Good," replied Fukuda. "Captain, shall I give the order to surface?"

"Yes, Mr. Fukuda," said Yamane.

"This is the executive officer," said Fukuda. "Surface, surface."

Ishiro said to Sakura, "That was the longest time you've ever been underwater. Run a diagnostic and check for damage."

"Yes, sir," said Sakura.

The android stood still for a moment. Then it said, "Scan finished. No damage detected."

Sakura was an L-3 Extreme Environments Type. With its shiny skin and lifeless eyes, Sakura could not be mistaken for a human being. Instead, the android looked like a pretty doll. But Sakura was more than ornamental. The L-3 Extreme Environments Type could work anywhere from outer space to the ocean floor.

"I'm glad that you're not damaged. You performed very well out there."

"Thank you, sir," said Sakura. Its lips smiled, but its eyes lacked expression, like the eyes of all L-3's.

"Follow me," Ishiro ordered.

They went to the command and control room. Video monitors showed the undersea cable receding into the background.

"Detonate the explosive," Yamane said.

A weapons specialist pressed a button and sent a very low frequency signal to the bomb. A segment of the undersea cable exploded. Its pieces drifted in a cloud above the ocean floor.

"I think it's severed," said Fukuda.

Yamane nodded. "We'll know soon."

As the *Yayoi* rose, she released a tethered buoy to the surface. The buoy picked up radio and satellite signals and sent them through the tether down to the submarine.

Messages appeared on communications officer Yamaguchi's monitor. She looked up at Fukuda.

"Sir, the Electronic Monitoring Branch reports that internet and telephone communications have gone down between Purist Arabia, Sudan, Somalia, Pakistan, and Indonesia," she said.

"We've severed MEPI," Fukuda said.

Yamane smiled. They had cut the Middle East Pakistan Indonesia submarine communications cable.

"*Now* congratulations are in order," said Yamane.

Fukuda turned to Ishiro. "Sato, you and the android have done an excellent job."

"Thank you, sir," said Ishiro.

Sakura bowed her head and said, "Thank you."

Yamane asked Yamaguchi, "Has the Electronic Monitoring Branch heard anything interesting on Purist TV and radio? I wonder what their governments are saying about losing their telecommunications."

"Negative, there's no information about the Purist reaction," Yamaguchi replied.

"The Purist governments might be in shock at the moment. We may get more news when we arrive at the surface."

Fukuda looked at Sakura. The android was still wearing its wet swimsuit.

"Oh, Sato, put some clothes on the android."

"Yes, sir," Ishiro replied.

As Ishiro led Sakura away, Captain Yamane stared at the water swirling on the video monitors.

"When we get to the surface, we'll see if the Russians fulfill their part of the deal," she said.

**

When the *Yayoi* reached the surface, antennae rose from her conning tower. No longer under water, the crew could pick up high frequencies, including television signals.

Fukuda turned a video monitor's channel to As-Sabah, the Purist Arabian TV station. As-Sabah showed Umar al-Tabuk, Chief Imam and Emir of Purist Arabia. He looked excited as he talked.

Sakura sat down beside Ishiro. The android was wearing a naval uniform without rank insignia. Against Superintendent Kirino's wishes, the Minister of Defense had decreed that all military androids would wear uniforms.

"Sakura, translate his speech from Arabic into Japanese," Ishiro said.

Sakura translated al-Tabuk's words. "The infidels have not completely cut off communications with our brothers. Just a few minutes ago, I talked to the Emir of Sudan by radio. And we can still broadcast and receive television signals. The Americans, Crusaders, Zionists, pagans, heretics, and apostates are utterly incompetent, and in the end, they will suffer defeat greater than —"

Suddenly, the picture turned to static. Yamaguchi read another message on her monitor.

"Captain, the Electronic Monitoring Branch reports that ten communications satellites, fourteen spy satellites, and eight weather satellites, each belonging to a Purist country, have been destroyed within the last ten hours. The last satellite was destroyed just seconds ago," she said.

"Thank you, Uncle Joe!" said Yamane.

"Let's see what else is going on in the world," said Fukuda. He changed the channel to NHK News.

In Moscow, Anton Alexandrov, the President of Russia, greeted Prime Minister Fujiwara in a room with rococo patterns, paintings of czars and generals, and a gigantic golden eagle on the wall.

"For an important occasion like this, we must use the most opulent room in the Kremlin," Alexandrov said in English.

"Yes, this is a historical first between our two countries," Fujiwara replied, also in English.

They went to a table and signed the new defense agreement.

"We welcome Japan as our partner in the war against the Purists," Alexandrov told the reporters.

"Together, we will free Asia from Purist oppression," Fujiwara said.

Ishiro wondered what General Morita thought about the Japanese-Russian alliance. The General always urged Japan to fight Russia for the Northern Territories. Now Fujiwara was shaking hands with Alexandrov.

In other news, Purist Arabia and its allies were suffering from a massive communications failure. Their communications satellites and MEPI had suddenly disappeared, so international telephone calls overwhelmed the remaining cables. Email had stopped flowing between the countries. TV and radio broadcasts were limited to the range of their transmitter towers. The Purists couldn't even get data from their weather satellites. The Purist Arabian military suspected that Uncle Joe, the Russian space weapon, had killed their satellites.

The *Yayoi*'s crew knew other facts not in the news. Not only were the Purists' communications and weather satellites dead, but their spy satellites were gone too. To make matters worse for the Purists, Australian robot planes controlled the air over the Indian Ocean, so the Purists could not send reconnaissance aircraft there. The wolf pack could prowl unseen by its enemies.

American spy satellites tracked the enemy squadron and reported its position to the wolf pack. On monitors in the command and control center, animated graphics of the enemy squadron and the wolf pack appeared on maps of the Indian Ocean.

"Let's move in for the kill," said Yamane.

**

The five *Taisho* Class submarines sailed on the surface, moving steadily towards the enemy.

Ishiro asked Fukuda, "Sir, the three cruisers must be defending the freighter, so there must be something important aboard her. Does Naval Intelligence know what it is?"

"They don't know," said Fukuda.

"It doesn't matter," said Captain Yamane. "We'll sink them and see what floats to the top."

All around the command and control center, crew members worked at monitors and consoles for every system on the submarine, ranging from propulsion to weapons. Ishiro, now an electronic warfare specialist, sat beside Sakura the android.

Although Ishiro's main duty was to deceive the enemy by electronic means, he also got to work with Sakura. Ishiro did not mind being paired with an android.

"The enemy squadron is fifty kilometers away," said an officer watching satellite images. On several monitors, the two ship formations approached each other.

"They'll hear us soon if they haven't already," said Yamane.

The *Taisho* Class submarine used a magnetohydrodynamic drive. The MHD passed an electric current through seawater, which would also go through intense magnetic fields. The electricity and magnetism controlled the water's molecular structure and pushed the water out the back of the submarine, thus propelling her. With few moving parts, the *Taisho* Class submarine was supposedly silent, difficult to detect by sonar.

In reality, the electric current created gases and noise, and the magnetic fields created detectable magnetic signatures. In addition, a fast-moving *Taisho* Class submarine created noise just from her large size.

Since *Taisho* Class submarines couldn't be completely silent, Japanese Navy tacticians devised a new approach to submarine warfare, making the submarines as noisy as possible to deceive the enemy. It was a controversial idea. Some officers rejected it, but others supported it. Captain Yamane wanted to try it. Now the Navy would use it for the first time in actual battle.

Fifty kilometers from the enemy, Yamane spoke to each of her ships. "This is Captain Yamane to battle group. Here is your order: sleeping giant. I repeat, sleeping giant."

Each submarine pushed four small unmanned robot subs into the water. The robot subs surfaced and sailed alongside the wolf pack. Ishiro glanced at a sonar monitor. The vessels looked like sharks surrounded by a school of fish.

Forty kilometers from the enemy, Yamane said, "Okay, let's make some noise."

"Everyone, keep the talk to a minimum and speak softly. We don't want them to hear us speaking Japanese," Fukuda ordered.

Ishiro pushed a microphone to Sakura and said, "Start radio transmission of Urdu deception script two."

Sakura spoke in Urdu with a man's voice. Other male voices replied to her.

Ishiro didn't understand Urdu, but he knew that Sakura was saying, "This is the *Karachi Star* to the *Islamabad Star*. Captain Farheed, we've just spotted an Australian robot plane."

A reply came in Urdu from an android aboard the *Jomon*. It followed a script by the Electronic Warfare Branch. "*Islamabad Star* to *Karachi Star*. We copy, Captain Mirza. Alert the other ships. Our cargo has to reach Indonesia."

Meanwhile, the robot subs made propeller noises, amplified so they sounded larger than they actually were.

Captain Yamane wanted the enemy to think that the Japanese wolf pack was a Pakistani merchant convoy. In the deception, the *Taisho* Class submarines were slow-moving freighters, and the robot subs were small but fast cargo ships.

Thirty kilometers from the enemy, Yamaguchi said, "Sir, we're getting a radio transmission from an enemy ship."

"Yamaguchi, relay the radio signal to Sato," Fukuda ordered.

Yamaguchi routed the signal to Ishiro's earphones. He heard a foreign language.

"Sakura, identify the language and translate it into Japanese," Ishiro ordered.

"It is Arabic," said Sakura. "Translation: We have been listening to your radio. Please identify yourselves."

"Reply in Urdu in a man's voice: We need to find someone who can speak Arabic," said Ishiro.

Sakura spoke to the enemy as Ishiro ordered. Ishiro put the microphone on mute to block the enemy from hearing him and the rest of the crew.

After a minute, Ishiro said, "Speak in Arabic in a man's voice: We are the *Karachi Star* under Captain Mirza. Identify your ship."

Sakura radioed the enemy ship, which replied, "*Karachi Star*, we are friendly towards Pakistan."

"What is the name of your ship?" Sakura asked under Ishiro's orders.

"Just know that we are friendly towards Pakistan," said the enemy.

Over his headphones, Ishiro heard the other androids speaking Arabic and Urdu in male voices, identifying themselves as sailors aboard Pakistani ships.

The enemy radioed the *Yayoi* again. "*Karachi Star*, what is your destination?"

"Our destination is Jakarta, and we're carrying food and supplies to the Indonesian Jihad. What is the name of your ship?" Sakura said for Ishiro.

The enemy sounded happy. "*Karachi Star*, thank you for identifying yourself, and thank you for aiding the Indonesian Jihad. They need help. We support your mission."

Aboard the *Jomon*, disguised as the *Islamabad Star*, an android told the enemy that Australian planes had seen the cargo fleet.

The "*Islamabad Star*" asked the enemy squadron if it could protect the merchant convoy. "We're sailing to join you. Are you armed? Can you provide escort?"

The other androids chattered in Urdu and Arabic about seeing airplanes and fearing that the Australians might attack them.

Twenty-five kilometers from the enemy, Yamane nervously tapped her swagger stick.

"They haven't launched anything at us yet. I hope they think we're a merchant convoy," she said. "Let me speak to our captains on the secure frequency."

Yamaguchi handed a microphone to Yamane. The captain said, "This is Captain Yamane to battle group. Here is your order: Climb Mount Niitaka. I repeat, climb Mount Niitaka."

Under remote control, the robot subs veered away from the wolf pack and sped westward.

Pretending to be captains of the small ships, the androids agreed to flee and leave the slow-moving freighters behind. Yamane wanted the enemy to think that the merchant convoy was splitting in two.

After the robot subs sailed twenty kilometers away, the androids said that the Australians were stalking the small ships instead of the freighters.

The airwaves filled with the chatter of androids speaking in Urdu and Arabic, saying that Australian planes were bombing them.

A robot sub exploded, as planned. The *Nara*, disguised as the *Peshawar Star*, reported that the Australians had sunk the cargo ship *Bahwalpur*.

Another two robot subs exploded. "We're under attack!" yelled an android aboard the *Asuka*. "They just got the *Quetta* and the *Multan*."

"The situation is serious! Australian dive bombers are above us!" another android yelled in Urdu.

Ishiro marveled at the language software in the androids. With no time to train language interpreters before the war, Japan had to rely on androids. The best interpreters could speak five or six languages. The androids could speak up to one hundred languages fluently, so long as a human told it what to say.

"Oh God, will someone help us?" said the *Kofun*'s android. "I don't know who you are, but if you are the Purist Arabian Navy, please help us!"

On the sonar and radar monitors, the enemy squadron turned to the west. As Yamane hoped, the enemy was going to aid the small ships.

"Tell the battle group to dive," Yamane told Fukuda. "Also tell them to release the communications buoys. We have to maintain radio contact."

As the *Taisho* submarines dived, they released tethered buoys and dragged them along the surface. While submerged, they could send and receive radio signals through the buoys.

"Order the battle group to increase speed and retract the buoys when they reach twenty knots," Yamane told Fukuda. "We're going in for the kill."

The wolf pack rushed towards the rear of the enemy squadron.

"Start the close-range electro-magnetic interference," Yamane commanded.

Close to the enemy ships, the robot subs broadcast signals to jam and confuse the enemy's communications and weapons guidance systems.

"Hey, the enemy ships are dropping depth charges on our robot subs," said a sonar operator. "I can hear the explosions."

"They must've figured out the robots aren't Pakistani cargo ships," said Ishiro.

"Let them waste their depth charges," said Yamane.

"Captain, we're close enough to the surface that we'll be vulnerable to their missiles. We should launch our missiles before they launch theirs," Fukuda said. "Give me the order."

"I'll give the order myself," Yamane said.

She took the microphone for the secure frequency. "This is Captain Yamane to battle group. Here is your order: Z-flag. I repeat, Z-flag."

Fukuda added, "This is the executive officer. Crew, launch weapons."

Yamaguchi transmitted the image of the Z-flag to viewscreens throughout the wolf pack. Every Japanese officer and sailor knew the importance of the black, yellow, blue, and red flag.

Each submarine launched ten guided missiles into the air, followed by ten torpedoes through the water.

The command and control crew watched their radar and sonar monitors as the missiles and torpedoes sped towards the enemy.

The enemy ships launched their own missiles against the incoming ones. Twenty attacking missiles got destroyed, but the other thirty hit the ships. Next, all the torpedoes hit their targets. The explosions looked like little bursts of light on the monitors.

"We got some direct hits," said Fukuda.

Yamane ordered the submarines to continue the attack. Wave after wave of missiles and torpedoes shot at the enemy squadron. The enemy ships fought back, but they could not shoot down everything. The wolf pack scored fifty-one direct hits.

The enemy missiles missed the submarines and exploded harmlessly in the water. The robot subs were confusing their guidance systems.

The air filled with the enemy's distress calls, but after two hours, their radios fell silent. The sonar operators heard a new sound from the ships — their hulls cracking.

A sonar operator looked up. "Wow, that freighter is really creaking. She's not going down quietly."

"Ma'am, we're getting pictures from an Australian robot plane," said Yamaguchi.

"Put them on the video monitors," said Yamane.

Aerial views of the enemy ships appeared. The freighter's bow was submerged, and her stern pointed in the air.

"Ma'am, the *Asuka* wants permission to finish off the freighter," said Yamaguchi.

"Permission granted," said Yamane.

Moments later, the *Asuka*'s missile slammed into the freighter at the waterline. Debris exploded into the air. The ship cracked and snapped in two. As the bow sank to the ocean floor, the stern crashed into the water.

One of the cruisers burned. Orange flames and black smoke rose from large holes on her deck. Her hull exploded, and the ship capsized to the starboard.

"Her magazine must have caught fire," Ishiro guessed.

"Where's the crew?" asked Yamaguchi.

"I don't see anyone in the water," Ishiro said. "They're probably still on board."

A second cruiser was sinking. Fire and smoke rose from gaping holes in her hull.

Only floating debris and fiery pools of oil remained of the third cruiser.

Fukuda smiled with grim satisfaction. "We have avenged you, *Sanshain Maru*."

"I want to find out what the freighter was carrying," said Yamane. "Let's go there and see what's left."

******

The *Yayoi* surfaced where the freighter had sunk. Captain Yamane turned to Yamaguchi and Ishiro.

"Yamaguchi and Sato, come topside with me," said Yamane. "If you're going to lead the next generation of sailors, you should learn how war looks and smells."

"Yes, ma'am," said Yamaguchi as another communications officer took her station.

"Sato, bring the android. We might need a language interpreter if we find any survivors," said Yamane. "Bring a rescue tube too."

They went topside with several officers and sailors. Above them, the sky was clear and blue. In the distance, sunlight shone on the deep blue water. It was a beautiful day on the Indian Ocean.

"Oh my God, this is horrible!" said Yamaguchi.

Hundreds of dead bodies floated around the submarine. Some corpses were whole, and others were torn apart. Blood seeped from the bodies into the sea. Between the corpses, small pools of oil burned.

Captain Yamane frowned. "This reminds me of Venezuela. The Bolivarians sank a refugee ship. Three thousand people died."

"What's that smell?" asked Ishiro. The stench was pungent. His stomach churned, and he wanted to vomit, but he controlled himself.

"You smell several things," Captain Yamane said. "First, there's the burning diesel fuel. Thankfully, there's not much this time. Secondly, there are the corpses. Their organs really stink. And there's some burning meat too, bodies that got covered in oil and caught fire."

Yamaguchi coughed. "It stinks, ma'am."

"It'll get worse when they've been rotting for a while," Yamane warned. "Get used to the smell."

A wave sent some bodies slapping against the hull of the submarine.

"I've never seen anything so horrible," Yamaguchi whispered to Ishiro.

Ishiro nodded. "This is like a mass grave in the water."

At varying distances from the *Yayoi*, the other submarines surveyed the destruction. Only one of the enemy cruisers, the capsized one, still floated.

Yamane pointed at a wooden plank, the remains of a crate, floating in the sea. A man clung to the wood. He lolled his head as waves swept over him.

"I think that man's still alive," Yamane said.

She turned to two sailors who carried rifles. "Fix bayonets," she ordered.

Yamane spoke to Ishiro next. "Sato, get the android to capture the survivor."

Ishiro pointed to the sea. "Sakura, do you see that wooden plank?"

Sakura stared at the water. "Yes, sir."

"Swim to the wooden plank. Capture the man holding it and bring him back to the ship. Use the routine for rescuing an uncooperative victim," Ishiro ordered.

"Yes, sir."

The android stripped off its Navy uniform, revealing its red swimsuit. Ishiro slung the rescue tube's rope over Sakura's shoulder. The android stepped to the edge of the deck and dived into the ocean.

Sakura swam to the wooden plank. The man shouted in a foreign language. Sakura grabbed him, but he struggled. The android pried him off the plank and wrapped the rescue tube around him. Then, pulling the man by rope, Sakura swam back to the submarine.

The sailors helped Sakura and the prisoner onto the deck. He coughed up salt water and crouched on his hands and elbows. They pushed him to the deck, tied his wrists behind his back, and pulled him up to a kneeling position.

Ishiro wiped oil from Sakura's face with a handkerchief. The android smiled at him.

"You performed well, Sakura," said Ishiro.

Sakura bowed her head slightly. "Thank you, sir."

The prisoner looked up at his captors. Yamane poked her swagger stick on the man's shoulder.

"Stand up!" she ordered in Japanese.

The prisoner did not move. Yamane smacked the swagger stick across his cheek. The man sprang up and lunged at her.

An armed sailor rammed the butt of his rifle on the prisoner's chin. He howled and staggered, but he regained his balance.

"Stand away from the captain!" the sailor demanded.

The prisoner stood still. Glaring at his captors, he muttered in a foreign language.

He wore a blue military-style shirt with rank insignia on its shoulder straps. A dog tag hung from a chain around his neck. The man was obviously a sailor in a country's navy.

His ordeal had ended any military decorum, though. He had a bloody gash and bruises on his face. Water dripped off him, and his hair and beard were soaked in blood and oil. His shirt was torn and dirty, and one of his pant legs was missing. He wore only one shoe.

Yamane reached for the prisoner's dog tag, but he grunted and flinched. A sailor gently poked his bayonet in the prisoner's ribs. The man became still. Yamane yanked on the dog tag.

"It's written in a foreign language, possibly Arabic," she said. "Sato, bring the android here."

Ishiro led Sakura to the prisoner. Yamane showed the dog tag to Sakura and said, "Identify the language and translate it into Japanese verbally."

"The language is Arabic. Lieutenant Achmet Hasani, Purist Arabian Navy, serial number 100094856," Sakura read from the dog tag.

"He's living proof that Purist Arabia sank the *Sanshain Maru*," said Yamane. "This is better than I expected. I thought we would have to make do with evidence from the bodies and the debris."

She glanced at Sakura. "Ask him in Arabic: Which ship were you aboard? After he replies, translate his answer from Arabic to Japanese."

Sakura asked the question. Lieutenant Hasani looked up, scowled at Sakura, and spoke.

Sakura translated the answer. "I'm not talking to a woman, you mechanical whore."

Yamane sighed and told her sailors, "Force him back into a kneeling position."

They pushed him back to his knees. Yamane lifted Hasani's chin with her swagger stick.

"Look up at me," she commanded in Japanese.

She said to Sakura, "Translate the following into Arabic: Lieutenant Hasani, you've been floating in saltwater for hours. You must be exhausted from dog-paddling with a piece of wood. You've had nothing to eat or drink for a long time. You must be very tired, hungry, and thirsty."

Hasani said nothing.

"Go below and get a bottle of water," Yamane ordered a sailor.

When the sailor returned with the bottle, Yamane poured some water on the deck and thrust the bottle a few inches in front of Hasani's lips. Ishiro saw the thirst in the man's eyes.

When Hasani tried to drink from the bottle, Yamane pulled it away and took a sip of water.

"Mmmm, that fresh water tastes good," she said.

Hasani looked down. He looked beaten and sad.

"Sakura, translate the following into Arabic," said Yamane. "If you answer our questions, we can verify that you are an officer of the Purist Arabian Navy, and we will take you as a prisoner of war and give you water and food. You can sit out the war in peace.

"If you do not answer our questions, we cannot verify that you are a member of any legitimate navy. We will consider you a terrorist or a pirate. In that case, we will throw you back into the ocean. You'll drown, and nobody can prove that we ever found you alive.

"You have two choices. You can talk and live or stay silent and die. You decide."

Sakura translated the demand. Hasani grunted and replied in Arabic.

"I will talk," Sakura said.

"Good," said Yamane. "Translate the following into Arabic: If, at any time before we return to a port, we discover that you have lied to us or concealed the truth, we will throw you to the sharks in the ocean. Do you understand the importance of telling the truth?"

After hearing the question from Sakura, Hasani nodded silently.

"Let's start," said Yamane. "Sakura, ask him in Arabic: Which ship were you aboard? Translate his reply from Arabic to Japanese."

Sakura asked the question, and Hasani replied. The android translated, "I was aboard the *Al-Aqsa Intifada*."

"The *Al-Aqsa Intifada*? Was that the hijacked freighter *Van Riebeeck*?" Yamane asked.

"The freighter was not hijacked. She was liberated from capitalist control," Hasani insisted.

"I see," said Yamane. "There were four ships in your squadron. Tell me the name of each ship and which navy controlled her."

Hasani looked grim. "The *Al-Aqsa Intifada*, a Somali privateer. The *Bin Laden*, Purist Arabian Navy. The *Mullah Omar*, Purist Arabian Navy. The *Al-Bashir*, Sudanese Navy. They're all sunk now, thanks to you."

Yamane glanced at her officers. "Naval Intelligence was correct." They nodded and murmured.

She asked Hasani, "So you were aboard the Somali-controlled freighter, correct?"

"Yes," Hasani said.

"You're a Purist Arabian officer. Why were you on a Somali privateer?"

"The Somalis don't have enough men and have to borrow ours."

"They were using you. You don't have to help them anymore," said Yamane. "What was the purpose of your mission?"

"We were transporting jihadists to East Timor," Hasani replied.

"On which ship were they?"

"The *Al-Aqsa Intifada*."

"You mean you used the freighter as a troop transport?"

"Yes."

"From which countries were the jihadists?" Yamane asked.

"From the Holy Alliance countries."

"How many jihadists were you transporting?"

Hasani sighed. "Six thousand."

Ishiro looked in disbelief at the sea. Six thousand bodies floated out there.

"That's six thousand men who won't be fighting our troops in East Timor," said Yamane. "I think the Army owes us a favor, eh?"

Her officers and sailors nodded in agreement.

"Lock him in the brig," Yamane told an officer. "Everyone, let's return below deck."

Ishiro glanced at the bodies bobbing in the waves. The currents swept them together, and now they were packed like dead fish in a can. They horrified him, but he couldn't stop looking at them.

"Captain, should we look for more survivors?" Ishiro asked.

Yamane shook her head. "No, one's enough."

She went below deck, followed by the other crew members. Yamaguchi paused beside Ishiro.

"Sato, there's no reason to stay out here," she said before going down the hatch.

Ishiro nodded and turned to the android. "Sakura, pick up your uniform. Follow me."

**

The other submarines also picked up a few survivors. They all told the same story. They had served in either the Purist Arabian or Sudanese navy or on the Somali privateer. They were carrying jihadists to fight in East Timor.

The prisoners admitted to sinking the *Sanshain Maru*. Now Prime Minister Fujiwara had proof that Purist Arabia, as well as Somalia, were waging war on Japan.

The Japanese embassies in Somalia and Purist Arabia closed. Unlike in Sudan, the diplomatic staff returned home safely.

Next, the Prime Minister ordered the Somali and Purist Arabian ambassadors to leave Japan. The Somali Ambassador and his staff left quickly without trouble.

The Purist Arabians did not leave. Instead, they barricaded themselves inside their embassy. Nobody inside would answer the telephone, reply to emails, or speak from the doors and windows.

Police cars and armored vehicles surrounded the embassy. For twenty-hour hours each day, police and soldiers watched the building and wondered what the Purists were doing inside.

**

Captain Yamane Michiko became a national heroine. All news media showed her photograph beside those of Fleet Admirals Togo and Yamamoto. Newspapers published full-page photos of Yamane, suitable for framing. For the first time in years, newspaper sales exceeded newsweb downloads.

At the Gakushuin, the principal assembled the students to sing patriotic songs of the Showa Era. As in the past, TV and radio stations broadcast the recital. As Masako listened to her students, she received a message on her pocket computer. The principal wanted her to teach about the sinking of the *HMS Prince of Wales* and the *HMS Repulse* in 1941.

General Morita, always near a TV camera, urged the Prime Minister to promote Yamane to admiral. Then he announced his upcoming anime trilogy: *Ensign Yamane: The Naval Academy Years*, *Commander Yamane: Mission to Venezuela*, and *Captain Yamane: Victory at Sea*.

A toy company made *Yayoi* toys overnight. They sold well, and collectors asked for more toy ships. The company's next toys were the historic battleships *Yamato*, *Musashi*, and *Shinano*. All had been lost in the Greater East Asia War.

In Ginza, NHK's giant screen showed the message:

THE GREATEST NAVAL VICTORY SINCE PEARL HARBOR!

**

Unconfirmed news reports said that the Emperor would appear in public to celebrate the victory. Endo, Masako, Ami, and Yuko set off to see His Imperial Majesty.

Since it was April, the cherry blossoms were blooming. The white and pink flowers were everywhere on the way to the Imperial Palace.

"That's what I love most about the spring," said Masako as they walked past a park filled with cherry blossom trees.

"The cherry blossoms will be blooming at Yasukuni Shrine," said Endo. "They don't live long, so they symbolize the short lives of the soldiers, sailors, and pilots."

"They also symbolize love," Ami added.

"I'll remember that," said Yuko.

An *Asashi Shimbun* photographer stopped them. "You look like a patriotic family — except for the maid, but you're very cute," he said.

Endo wore his Navy Supplementary Reserve uniform. Ami wore a grey Red Cross uniform, which she had recently received after first aid training. Masako wore civilian clothes, but she held a small national flag.

Yuko wore her French maid costume. Ami considered it a fashion statement.

"May I take your photograph, please?" the photographer asked.

"Uh, I'm fine with it, but you should ask the ladies too," said Endo. "Ladies, are you okay with that?"

Ami and Yuko grinned, hugged each other, and jumped up and down. "We're going to be famous, we're going to be famous, we're going to be famous!" they squealed.

"I guess that means yes," said Masako.

"Ah, if you could look this way, please," said the photographer.

They posed for the photo, with Ami and Yuko making peace signs with their hands.

The photographer pressed the shutter button. "Thank you, thank you. Look for it in *Asashi Shimbun*, both the newspaper and newsweb editions."

He showed the photo on his camera's monitor. "Ah, it looks like a historical photo from the Greater East Asia War. I should publish it with a sepia tone. Thank you again!"

After the photographer left, Endo said softly, "Everyone's talking about the Greater East Asia War. That was so long ago. Why don't they talk about a more recent mission, like U.N. peacekeeping in Venezuela?"

Masako shrugged. "Wasn't that mission a total failure?"

They joined the crowd gathering at Kokyo Gaien, the large park in the Imperial Palace grounds. In front of them was the moat. Over the moat was the Nijubashi Bridge to the Main Gate. In the distance were the green trees and white and pink cherry blossoms of the East Gardens.

Thousands of people waved the national flag. Endo had seen more flag-waving in the last year than in the previous decade.

"I can't remember the Emperor making a spontaneous appearance before," said Masako. "His appearances are usually scheduled months in advance."

"We don't even know for sure if he'll be appearing," said Endo.

An old man wearing a Naval Veterans Association hat approached Yuko and Ami. "Hey, we've met before," he said.

"Yes, we have," said Ami. "You're at all the rallies."

"It's the least I can do. I wish I could do more," he said. Once again, he gave national flags to Ami and Yuko. "Please have another flag."

He glanced at Endo. "Ah, who's this fine young officer?"

Ami giggled. "That's my father."

The veteran saluted. "I'm pleased to meet you, sir."

Endo returned the salute. "Thank you, I'm pleased to meet another Maritime Self-Defense Force veteran."

Strangers bowed to Endo and said, "Congratulations, congratulations! Thank you, sir, thank you!"

Ami laughed and said, "Father, they think you're a war hero!"

"Wow, who knew that the Supplementary Reserve was the elite squadron of the Navy?" Endo joked.

Suddenly, the crowd cheered with a deafening roar.

"Look! The Prime Minister and the Emperor are coming out!" said Masako.

Fujiwara and the Emperor walked on the Nijubashi Bridge and waved to the crowd. The Prime Minister wore a business suit, but the Emperor wore a Navy uniform.

"I didn't know the Emperor was in the Navy," said Endo before he stood at attention and saluted.

"No Emperor has worn a military uniform since the twentieth century," said Masako.

"This is exciting!" said Ami as she waved her Red Cross cap at the Emperor.

"What do we say to the Prime Minister?" asked Yuko.

The crowd yelled, "Banzai!"

"Banzai!"

"Banzai!"

"There has been nothing like this since the Showa Emperor rode his horse on the bridge after the fall of Singapore," said Masako.

Lieutenant Commander Endo Hideki, still silently saluting, remembered his days in the Maritime Self-Defense Force. He felt a surge of pride.

But he wished people would stop comparing the current war to the Greater East Asia War.

# CHAPTER 13

# The Brass Button

When the war started, the Navy forbade its ships' crews from having real-time telephone or video calls with civilians. Instead, crew members had to record messages, which military censors checked before sending them to their recipients. The *Yayoi*'s private video booths were always in use, so Ishiro made a voice message instead.

The censors required messages to be under two minutes long. Since he recently realized that he talked too much, Ishiro wrote his message in advance.

He wanted to tell Yuko about the corpses in the sea. They haunted him, and he needed to tell someone. But he knew the censors would not allow him to talk about the enemy dead. Ishiro decided not to mention them, at least not explicitly.

He went into the telephone booth and recorded his message.

*"Hello, Yuko, how are you doing? This is Ishiro. I'm fine, and I'm proud to be aboard the* Yayoi. *You must have heard about my heroic Captain Yamane by now.*

*"The Battle of the Indian Ocean has made me realize that life is fragile. It's possible that I might not return. That has always been the big risk of a military career, so it's no surprise to me. It just seems more realistic now. Nonetheless, I am confident that I'll return to you.*

*"Please promise to do something for me if I do not return. If I do not come back, please get Mr. Endo to have the priests enshrine my kami at Yasukuni Shrine. I want to be enshrined at Yasukuni for two reasons. First, it's the national military shrine. Secondly, and more importantly, it's where we went for our most recent date. I will always remember how pretty you looked in that red coat.*

*"Dear Yuko, I will send you photos and gifts when I am able to do so. I eagerly wait for our next time together. I have to sign out now. I hope all is well with you."*

**

The *Yayoi*'s crew could not enjoy the victory celebrations in Japan. After the Battle of the Indian Ocean, the submarine sailed to Subic Bay in the Philippines to get new supplies. Then she went to Dili, the capital city of East Timor. The Japanese and Australians were fighting the Indonesians there.

The harbor was so full of ships that the *Yayoi* had to stay a distance from the docks. Military boats crisscrossed the harbor, carrying people and supplies between ships and to and from the shore.

Standing on the *Yayoi*'s tower, Ishiro watched the siege. Dili looked calm and undamaged, but he could hear artillery and see smoke beyond the suburbs. Out there, the Australians, Timorese, and Japanese were fighting to keep the Indonesians out of the city.

Fukuda pointed at a small boat flying the Royal Australian Navy flag. "Two hundred years ago, we came here to fight the Australians. Now we're on their side. Isn't that interesting, eh?"

"It sure is, sir," said Ishiro.

Yamaguchi looked through her binoculars. "Ah, there's the Christ the King statue."

At the east end of town, a bronze statue of Jesus on a globe stood atop a hill. After the one in Rio de Janiero, it was the second largest statue of Jesus in the world.

Although most Indonesians are Moslem, most East Timorese are Roman Catholic, due to Portuguese influence. Portugal ruled East Timor for almost three hundred years until Indonesia invaded the colony in 1975 and occupied it for twenty-seven years.

According to Yamaguchi, a graduate of University of the Sacred Heart, the Indonesian government erected the Jesus statue in 1995 as a sign of goodwill from Moslem Indonesians to the Roman Catholic East Timorese. However, the statue was loaded with Indonesian symbolism. It was twenty-seven meters from base to tip because East Timor was Indonesia's twenty-seventh province. The figure of Jesus was seventeen meters tall to symbolize June seventeen, the date when Indonesia formally annexed East Timor. The figure of Jesus, with its outstretched arms, faced Jakarta instead of Dili.

After a bloody occupation, the Indonesians left in 2002. Now they were back in East Timor after massacring the Chinese, Hindus, Buddhists, South Moluccans, Shia Moslems, and other minorities.

"I heard reports that the jihadists vandalized the statue," Yamaguchi said. "I should try to visit it while I'm here."

A boat stopped beside the *Yayoi*. Her skipper yelled, "Is Ensign Yamaguchi ready?"

"Yes, I am, sir," Yamaguchi replied.

"Permission to come aboard granted. Get aboard, ma'am."

The Navy was transferring Yamaguchi to Dili. Her knowledge of the Roman Catholic religion and her proficiency in English were valuable in working with the East Timorese and Australians.

Yamaguchi left the tower and boarded the boat. Then another officer emerged from the boat and climbed onto the *Yayoi*'s deck. Ishiro recognized him immediately.

"Kamio! What are you doing here?" Ishiro yelled.

Kamio saluted and said, "Ensign Kamio Atsushi, requesting permission to come on board."

"Permission granted," said Fukuda, returning the salute.

When Kamio got to the tower, Fukuda said, "Ensign Kamio, present your orders to me."

Kamio projected a hologram of a document from his pocket computer. Fukuda read the orders, which had approval stamps from several Navy officers.

"It matches the document I received. Turn off the hologram," said Fukuda. "Welcome aboard the *J.S. Yayoi*."

A rocket plane roared over them and sped past the city.

"Wow, was that a Mitsubishi Type 50 tactical bomber?" asked Ishiro.

"Yes, it was, from the aircraft carrier *Hosho*," said Kamio. "The air service has been attacking the Indonesians on the ground for weeks."

"That's the *Navy* air service," Fukuda emphasized with a bit of pride. "The Air Force is absent due to a lack of suitable airports. But the Navy can fly anywhere."

Two Australian robot planes buzzed towards the city.

"Drone planes for reconnaissance," said Kamio. "There's a lot of hardware here."

"I wish we could stay and join the fight, but we've got some ships to hunt," said Fukuda.

He spoke into his pocket computer. "This is the executive officer. The last transferee has arrived. Prepare to leave port after we come down."

**

"What a coincidence. First Yamaguchi, now you," said Ishiro. "What brings you aboard the *Yayoi*?"

"I don't know for sure, but it might have something to do with Russia," said Kamio. "The base commander asked me if I had studied some Russian history in university. I told him that's true, and then Navy headquarters ordered me to join the *Yayoi*. It seems that headquarters traded me with Yamaguchi."

"Russia?" said Ishiro. "Aren't we at war with enough countries already?"

They entered the wardroom, where the officers were assembling to meet Captain Yamane. When Yamane arrived, they stood up and waited as she sat at the head of the table.

"Please sit down," she said. "Gentlemen and ladies, we have received a most interesting order. We will proceed directly to Makarov Naval Base on Shikotan."

The officers, disciplined to remain silent, did not speak. However, Ishiro could see the surprise in their eyes.

Before the Greater East Asia War, Japan ruled the Kuril Islands. At the end of war, the Soviet Union occupied the Kurils. The Yalta Agreement gave the Kuril Islands to the Soviet Union. However, Japan claimed that the southernmost islands were never technically part of the Kurils. To the Japanese, Etorofu, Kunashiri, Shikotan, and the Habomai Rocks formed the Northern Territories.

"You're wondering why we are going to the Northern Territories," said Yamane. "The reason is North Korea. North Korea refuses to stop selling weapons to Venezuela. Russia is not formally at war with either North Korea or Venezuela, but thanks to the new defense treaty, the Russians will allow us to use Shikotan as a base for attacking North Korean shipping.

"More details of our mission will come from headquarters shortly. In the meantime, are there any questions?"

"Will we be attacking North Korea directly?" asked a lieutenant. "Our Army is fighting again. If we can land troops in East Timor, we can land troops in North Korea."

Yamane shook her head. "The South Koreans would object to that. They're still sensitive about Japanese troops anywhere in Korea, north or south. However, they will agree to us attacking North Korean shipping."

Kamio stood up and said, "Captain, this is excellent news. We will be the first Japanese military personnel in the Northern Territories in two hundred years. I think we all agree that this is a momentous occasion."

The officers murmured and nodded in agreement. Kamio asked, "Could our presence be a preliminary step to Japan retaking the Northern Territories?"

"Definitely not," Yamane declared. "The Russians have no intention of letting us rule the islands again. Our presence there is only temporary until North Korea stops sending weapons to Venezuela."

They watched an educational video about Shikotan. The island had always been poor, with fishing as its major business. To boost the economy, Russia built a cosmodrome there. Japanese right-wing groups opposed the cosmodrome because it enhanced Russian control over the Northern Territories.

After the briefing, Kamio told Ishiro, "I already know much about Shikotan's history. General Morita has talked about it many times. The Northern Territories is one of his passions."

"However, we're going there to use the naval base, not to capture it," said Ishiro. "It's an interesting treaty, though. We get to use Makarov Naval Base, and we can get the Russians to use Uncle Joe against our enemies. What are the Russians are getting from us?"

In the morning, the TV news showed a Russian military victory. A hundred L-3 androids, wearing Russian uniforms, attacked a Purist Arabian base in Afghanistan. The androids could hardly think and fight like real soldiers, but their assault kept the Purists occupied. Meanwhile, Russian troops moved on the Purist flanks and enveloped them. It was the first pincer movement involving androids in military history.

**

At Nikkou Café, Endo saw Yuko wear a small bright object on a gold chain around her neck. He had not bought any jewellery for the android, so he wondered what it was.

"Yuko, what is that?" Endo asked, looking at the necklace.

"A button, master," Yuko replied.

"A button? Why are you wearing it?"

"I had nowhere to put it, so Mikita gave me a chain so I could wear it around my neck."

"Show me the button."

Yuko took off her necklace and gave it to Endo. He knew immediately that it came from a Navy officer's uniform.

Endo put the necklace back on Yuko. "How did you get the button?"

"I took it from Mr. Sato," said Yuko.

"You *took* it from Mr. Sato? Did he offer it to you?"

"No. I took it from him."

Endo felt curious. "Yuko, come to the office," he said.

Yuko followed Endo into the office. He ordered Yuko to sit beside his computer. He opened her head and switched her to sleep mode. Then he connected her to his computer and checked her memory files.

He saw videos of Sato Ishiro at Yasukuni Shrine. These were recorded from Yuko's point of view. On the audio track, he heard them bantering. They were certainly on a date.

The memory files surprised Endo. Hadn't he programmed Yuko not to go on a date with Ishiro?

He was more surprised to see Yuko pull the button off Ishiro's uniform. It was a courtship ritual for teenagers. For a moment, he forgot that Yuko was an android.

Unlike humans, androids did not desire property. Androids acquired objects in two ways. Their owners could give them things, like Yuko's maid uniform. Other owners programmed their androids to collect things for them. In the Maritime Self-Defense Force, Endo programmed androids to salvage old coins from shipwrecks. In both cases, the android itself did not actually want anything. It was actually the human programmer who wanted the objects.

Yet on New Year's Day, Yuko had taken a button without anyone programming her to do so.

He opened other memory files. One was a video message from Ishiro, asking to be enshrined at Yasukuni if he died. Although Endo worried that Ishiro was pouring his feelings to an android, he admired the young officer's reverence for Yasukuni Shrine. Endo hoped he would never have to carry out Ishiro's wish.

Other scenes shocked him. He looked at videos of Ishiro's eyes and face, very close to Yuko's face, seen from her point of view. The sounds they made were unmistakable. His android and her human friend were kissing.

Delving into Yuko's programming record, Endo discovered that Ami had reprogrammed Yuko to go on a date with Ishiro. The clever girl had also programmed the android not to tell the father about the reprogramming.

But Ami had not anticipated that Yuko would take a button from Ishiro and wear it in public. And Ami had not anticipated that her father would ask Yuko how she had acquired the button. Without programming for these situations, Yuko had simply told the truth.

"Okay, Yuko, I'm going to correct your programming," Endo said. He deleted Ami's programming and reset Yuko to obey his commands. Then he changed Yuko's password, invalidating the old password that he and Ami had shared. Now he alone controlled Yuko.

Endo thought about deleting the memory files of the date at Yasukuni and the farewell at the naval base. Then he decided to let Yuko keep the memories.

"I don't know why I'm letting you remember him," he said even though Yuko was not listening.

When he restarted Yuko, the android asked, "Master, I have been in sleep mode for one hour. I may have shut off abnormally. Do you wish me to run a diagnostic for disk errors?"

"No need for a diagnostic," said Endo. "You're repaired now."

# CHAPTER 14

# The Conspiracy

Venezuela was a socialist dictatorship ruled by the Bolivarian Party. When the Vernacular Wars broke out, the Bolivarians saw an opportunity to defeat their traditional enemies, the United States and Israel. Venezuela became the only officially atheist country to side with the Holy Alliance for Monotheism.

North Korea, a fascist dictatorship, declared its neutrality and sold weapons to both sides, namely Venezuela and China.

When Japan went to war against the Holy Alliance, Venezuela declared war on Japan. Japan demanded that North Korea end its weapons sales to Venezuela. North Korea insisted that, as a neutral country, it could trade with anyone.

When war broke out in Asia, North Korean ships stopped sailing through the Yellow Sea and the East China Sea to reach the Pacific Ocean and eventually Venezuela. Those waters were full of Chinese, Japanese, Australian, Indonesian, Purist Arabian, and Somali ships hunting each other. Now the North Koreans sailed northeast through the Sea of Japan, went through the La Perouse Strait between Hokkaido and Sakhalin, and entered the Pacific Ocean.

The Japanese Navy planned to bottle up the North Koreans inside the Sea of Japan by blocking the Korea Strait in the south and the La Perouse Strait in the north. The Navy had bases at Hokkaido, but with more ships joining the blockade, needed another base. That was Makarov Naval Base on Shikotan.

Makarov Naval Base, built during the Korean Crisis, was the most boring port that Ishiro had ever seen. The base itself consisted of ugly box-like buildings with only a few trees. Its only public art was a bronze statue of Stepan Makarov, the Russian admiral who died when his ship struck a mine during the Russo-Japanese War.

Outside the base was a sleepy fishing village with few sources of entertainment for either Russian or Japanese sailors. The cosmodrome had not attracted as much investment as the Russian government had hoped. However, after the Battle of Baikonour, Russia lost its largest cosmodrome, and Shikotan's residents hoped their spaceport would get more business.

Shikotan Cosmodrome was the smallest spaceport in Russia. It specialized in commercial and government satellite launches. Ishiro wanted to tour the cosmodrome, but it was off limits to the Japanese.

Despite the dull surroundings, Kamio constantly took photographs of the naval base and the village.

"Hey, Kamio, you're acting like a tourist," Ishiro said. "I didn't think this place was so interesting."

"It isn't, but it's important," replied Kamio.

******

The naval war against North Korea began in the air, with the Japanese and Australian air forces bombing North Korea's ballistic missile launch sites. The attack caught the North Koreans by surprise, since North Korea's president was meeting the prime ministers of Japan and Australia in Hong Kong at the time. With North Korea unable to retaliate with missiles, the Japanese Navy began hunting North Korean ships.

In the month of June, the *Yayoi* sank ten North Korean cargo ships and their sixteen naval escorts. The officers gathered in the wardroom to watch Fuji News Network report on their success.

"The *Yayoi* sank another North Korean cargo ship today, thus making her the most successful ship in the Sea of Japan," said the announcer, a woman wearing the badge of the Military Families Association.

"I'm pleased that the news is positive," said Kamio. "Ten years ago, the news media had nothing good to say about the Self-Defense Forces. We're no longer ashamed of military power."

The next news item was the war in East Timor. With the Australians and Japanese blockading the island, the Indonesians could not get supplies and reinforcements. Four months ago, three thousand Indonesian soldiers, mostly ill-trained conscripts, invaded East Timor. Today, only four hundred survived to surrender in Dili.

The news showed the Indonesians, their uniforms reduced to muddy rags, surrendering in mass. They stared with hollow eyes at their Australian and Japanese captors.

Kamio smirked and said, "Hah, six thousand jihadists were going to help these Indonesians. But we sent them to the bottom of the sea. The Army owes us a favor!"

The other officers laughed, but Ishiro nodded in silence. He did not regret sinking the six thousand jihadists. It was war, and they were the enemy. But he wished he hadn't seen their bodies floating in the sea.

After a long description of Indonesian losses of equipment and soldiers, the news announcer took only seconds to say that three hundred and four Japanese soldiers had died in East Timor.

She quickly moved to the next item. Purist terrorists had driven five cars into the Artificial Intelligence Lab, a research center of the Russian Federal Space Agency in Moscow. Each car carried a bomb, and the explosions destroyed the lab and killed some of Russia's best computer scientists.

Katsura Kenji, the President of Victor Robotics, told the TV reporters, "This is a tragedy for the international community of robotics scientists. I'm saddened that Dr. Nikolai Polyakov was killed. I met him at the International Conference on Robotics in Berlin. I'm sending my condolences to his family."

Finally, the news announcer came to the last item. "At the summit meeting with the presidents of China and South Korea, Prime Minister Fujiwara stated that Japan has no territorial ambitions in the war."

The scene switched to a room inside the National Diet Building. With the flags of China, South Korea, and Japan in the background, the three leaders faced the reporters.

Fujiwara spoke first. "I know that other Asian countries are sensitive about Japanese troops fighting overseas, but this war is not a war of imperialism. Japanese troops went to East Timor at the request of the United Nations to prevent genocide. Japan will not occupy or annex any territory.

"Now that East Timor is liberated, we will return control of the country to its people. With equipment and weapons provided by Australia and Japan, the East Timorese will be able to defend their country against foreign aggression.

"Japanese troops will stay only long enough to train the East Timorese Army to use its news weapons...we will not stay any longer than necessary..."

As Fujiwara talked, the presidents of China and South Korea stared impassively at him from behind.

Kamio glared at the TV and grunted. "Look at the coward, giving in to pressure from Korea and China. We could have gained some territory."

"But we're not fighting to gain territory," Ishiro reminded him. "We're fighting because the Purists attacked our people for using space-generated electricity."

"I know, but wouldn't it be wonderful if we had an empire again?" said Kamio with a wistful look in his eyes. "Korea, Taiwan, Manchuria, the Philippines, Indonesia, Burma, Malaysia, Singapore, Indochina, the

Marianas, the Caroline Islands, the Marshall Islands — they were all ours at one time."

**

Ishiro and Kamio got four days of leave in early August. They went to Tokyo, where the National Bushido Guards command group was meeting. This time, they met in a restaurant in a poor district. The building's facade had faded paint and chipped stucco. The words "Saga Restaurant" blinked in failing neon lights.

"The General seems to be nomadic," said Ishiro.

"Why do you say that?" Kamio asked.

"He holds meetings all over the country."

"That's because he has benefactors everywhere. They let him borrow their premises."

A balding man wearing a white chef's uniform greeted them. "Ensign Kamio, it's wonderful to see you again," he said.

"It's a pleasure to meet one of the General's most enthusiastic supporters," said Kamio. "Mr. Saga, may I introduce Ensign Sato Ishiro?"

Ishiro and Saga shook hands. The restaurant owner led them to a private room. Like other places that General Morita borrowed, it was decorated with samurai artifacts, such as pictures, swords, and armor. All the General's benefactors were fascinated by samurai.

Ishiro and Kamio joined the command group at a long table. As before, they wore a mix of modern and Russo-Japanese War uniforms.

Female L-3 androids in restaurant uniforms served drinks and food to them. Just as Ishiro bit into his *yakitori*, a bugle sounded.

Ishiro quickly chewed and swallowed his food and stood up with his fellow Guardsmen. The command group repeated the ritual that opened every meeting. First, a Guardsman carried the national flag into the room, then a bugler followed, playing a march, and finally, the General walked at the end of the procession.

As usual, General Morita went to the head of the table. There he faced the portraits of Amaterasu and the Emperor.

"All bow to the images of the Emperor and Amaterasu!" he ordered.

The Guardsmen and the androids bowed three times to the Sun Goddess and her Imperial descendant. Then Morita and his command group sat down.

"If you follow the news, you know that our Prime Minister surrendered to Chinese and Korean pressure," Morita said.

He pointed his pocket computer at a painting of Saigo Takamori leading his samurai against the Imperial troops at the Battle of Shiroyama. The painting rolled up into the wall to reveal a viewscreen.

Video images of the Japan-China-South Korea summit meeting appeared. The Guardsmen heard Fujiwara declare that all Japanese troops will leave East Timor.

"For the first time in two centuries, Japan had the chance to occupy a foreign territory," said Morita. "Indeed, it is one of our lost colonies. Unfortunately, our Prime Minister will not return it to the Empire.

"To be fair, Fujiwara re-armed our country. That is a great accomplishment. But he has not used the military for the good of our nation. Why should we invade another country if we do not add it to the Empire? Why should we rescue Timorese, Chinese, Hindus, Shia Moslems, and other people who are not subjects of the Emperor?

"It is time for a new Prime Minister, one who will restore the Emperor as commander-in-chief of the military."

"General, are you running for Prime Minister in the next election?" asked Ishiro.

Morita grinned and shook his head. "No, no. I am proposing a more direct way to restore Imperial rule."

"Oh?"

"Sato, unfortunately, you missed the last meeting. The command group agreed to a special mission in case Fujiwara withdrew our troops from East Timor."

"I didn't know that, sir."

"Ensign Kamio tells me that you are a patriot and veteran of the Battle of the Indian Ocean. That's good. I'm sure you want to serve the Emperor and the nation. Is that so?"

"Uh, of course, anything for the Emperor and the nation," Ishiro said. "That's why I joined the Navy and the National Bushido Guards."

"Good, good," said Morita. "At our last meeting, we agreed on the purpose of our mission. Now I have drawn its plan.

"Our Regiment has tripled in size since the war began. We have three hundred members, of which half are men serving in the military. I will divide the Regiment into three units."

Morita clicked on his pocket computer, and a map of Tokyo appeared on the viewscreen. He zoomed in on Minato Ward.

"The first unit will attack the Russian Embassy. They will occupy the embassy just like Russia has occupied the Northern Territories," Morita said. "Inspired by our boldness, the military units of Tokyo will join us in expelling the Russian ambassador.

"Major Watasuki will lead the first unit, consisting of Guardsmen and Army officers in Tokyo."

Watasuki stood and bowed.

Ishiro coughed and put down his tea. Was this a joke? Were the National Bushido Guards planning a war on Russia?

The map of Minato Ward changed to a map of Shikotan. The General zoomed in on Makarov Naval Base.

"The second unit will capture Makarov Naval Base from the Russians," Morita announced. "Navy and Army units in Hokkaido and Shikotan will join us when they see us fighting to reclaim Japanese territory. With their help, we will retake all of Shikotan. Afterwards, the military can use Shikotan as a base for retaking the remaining Northern Territories.

"Ensign Kamio will lead the second unit, consisting of young officers and sailors at Makarov Naval Base and the ships stationed there."

Kamio stood and bowed to his fellow Guardsmen.

Ishiro suppressed a gasp. He didn't know that his friend Kamio would be leading an assault on the Russian Navy.

The viewscreen's map changed back to Tokyo and zoomed in on the Imperial Palace.

Morita said, "The third unit will enter the Imperial Palace and ask the Emperor to be commander-in-chief of the military. After assuming control of the military, the Emperor will appoint a new government."

Fear ran up Ishiro's spine. This was not just a private war against Russia. It was a coup against the Japanese government.

Photos of the Regiment's benefactors appeared. Some were obscure men, like Mr. Saga the restaurant owner. But others were famous businessmen, professors, and publishers.

"These men have graciously volunteered to form a new government if asked by the Emperor, with Mr. Shiga as Prime Minister," said Morita.

Ishiro could not believe it. The president of his old employer, Dai Tokyo Taikun Financial Group, was involved in the coup, as the future Prime Minister, no less.

"Although the Imperial Household Agency will support us, leftists in the Army and Air Force will oppose us," Morita predicted. "The Air Force is especially infested with leftists because of Colonel Yi Akira, the Korean. The leftists will certainly storm the Imperial Palace. The third unit will protect the Emperor, defend the palace, and defeat the leftists.

"I will lead the third unit, consisting of all Guardsmen not assigned to the other two units," he declared. "That is our plan of battle. Gentlemen, do you approve this plan?"

Led by Kamio, the Guardsmen stood up and applauded. Ishiro paused for a moment before joining in the clapping.

"I'm so thrilled," said a Guardsman. "This is just like *Time Warp at Midway*, episode twelve!"

Ishiro remembered that episode, the last of series. The time travelers go back in time and storm the White House in Washington. They don't succeed in killing President Roosevelt, but they die gloriously in battle, and their *kami* go to Yasukuni Shrine.

"Finally, we'll do more than just go on parade! I feel like a real soldier already," another Guardsman said.

"We will become a great empire again!" said an Air Force officer.

"You could have told me you were planning a coup," Ishiro whispered to Kamio.

"I'm sorry I didn't mention this aboard the *Yayoi*. There are some leftists in the crew. I hope you understand," said Kamio.

Morita gestured for the men to sit down. "Before we talk about the tactical details, are there any questions?" he asked.

"Sir, when do we take over the government?" asked Kamio. "Can we do it soon?"

"Your enthusiasm fills me with pride, but be patient," Morita replied. "It would be unpatriotic to overthrown Fujiwara while a war is going on. We will wait until the war is over. But we will not have to wait long. The Americans and British have sunk most of the Purist Arabian and Sudanese navies. The Russians have defeated the Purists in Afghanistan. The Indonesian government has collapsed. Jordan has invaded Purist Arabia. The war will end soon, and then we can strike."

Ishiro raised his hand and asked, "Sir, we are only three hundred against thousands who might remain loyal to the Prime Minister. What if they overwhelm us?"

Morita took a *tanto* knife from his briefcase. He unsheathed the *tanto* and held it up. Light shone off its blade.

"If we do not succeed, I will commit *seppuku* on the Nijubashi Bridge to atone for failing the Emperor," he said.

The Guardsmen murmured. Kamio stood up again, visibly dismayed.

"General, if we fail, let me commit *seppuku* with you!" he begged.

"No, Kamio, you must live to tell the nation why we attempted the coup," Morita insisted. "Your testimony will inspire the people to take up our struggle, and we will win through them."

"But General!"

"No, you must live! That's an order!"

Kamio frowned, bowed, and sat down.

Major Watasuki rose and said, "Let's not talk of defeat! I'm certain that the military and the people will join us, and then we will be the ones who number in the thousands against Fujiwara!"

The Guardsmen cried cheers of "Yes, yes!" and "Banzai, banzai!"

For the rest of the meeting, the unit leaders described their battle plans, with troop movements animated on maps of the Russian Embassy, Shikotan, and the Imperial Palace. The Guardsmen listened intently as androids served food and drink to them. But unlike the others, Ishiro lost his appetite.

**

In their Japanese Navy car, Ishiro told Kamio, "I never expected the National Bushido Guards to do anything like this!"

Kamio steered the car towards the highway. "What do you mean?"

"I never expected to attack the Russians and overthrow the government!"

"We're a patriotic organization. What do you expect us to do?"

"Wear historical costumes, walk in parades, make speeches, and watch military anime," said Ishiro. "That's what I thought we do. That's why I joined."

Kamio grunted. "That's all child's play. The Regiment is growing up. It's time to do the work of heroes."

Ishiro glanced nervously at a police car as it passed them. "I think it's illegal," he said.

"Fujiwara's government is illegal," said Kamio. "It isn't Imperial rule."

"We swore an oath to obey the Prime Minister," Ishiro reminded him.

"The Emperor is above the Prime Minister," said Kamio.

"Only the command group knows about the plan," Ishiro observed. "Is the whole Regiment going to agree with it?"

"We'll tell them of the plan. Those who join us will swear to secrecy and train for the task," said Kamio. "Those who reject the plan will also swear to secrecy but sit out the coup."

"What if they talk to the police?"

"If they break their silence, they and their families will suffer terrible consequences. Not only does the General know where they live, but our benefactors control large businesses and banks, any of which can make life miserable for a traitor's family."

"You guys are serious!" Ishiro said, aghast.

His pocket computer beeped. He turned it on and saw a message from Navy headquarters.

TO ALL PERSONNEL: NON-URGENT NEWS UPDATE: PURIST ARABIANS LEAVE EMBASSY.

Ishiro switched to a TV station. Fuji News Network showed the Purist Arabian Ambassador and his staff leaving their embassy.

"The Purist Arabians have finally run out of food and water after four months barricaded inside their embassy," the news announcer said. "They agreed to leave Japan earlier today. They boarded a Purist Arabian Airlines flight to Riyadh ten minutes ago."

Ishiro switched off his pocket computer and looked at the Tokyo Naval Base, now in front of them.

"Sato, I would like you to take command of the gunboat *Shidehara Kijuro* and bombard Makarov's coastal artillery," Kamio said.

"But won't the *Shidehara Kijuro*'s captain object to us taking his ship?" Ishiro asked. He looked at Tokyo Naval Base, getting closer in front of them.

"Some of his sailors will relieve him of his command on the day of action," Kamio said confidently.

"That's a mutiny," Ishiro snapped.

"It's not a mutiny if the captain is more loyal to Fujiwara than to the Emperor," Kamio insisted.

"But I think the Emperor wants the Prime Minister to run the military. That's the purpose of Prime Ministers, isn't it? Anyway, assuming the mutineers succeed, why choose me to take command of the ship?"

"Because you're an officer, and I know you want to do something important. That's why you joined the Navy, isn't it?"

"Yes."

"Are you with us?" Kamio asked.

"Can it possibly succeed?" said Ishiro.

"That doesn't matter. Are you with us? I need to know now."

"Park the car first."

They drove through the gate of Tokyo Naval Base and to the officers' parking lot. After Kamio parked the car, Ishiro quickly opened the door and left.

"Are you with us?" Kamio demanded, following Ishiro.

"Let's not talk about General Morita's mission on the yard," said Ishiro. "As you say, there are leftists all around us."

"Ah, yes, you're correct," Kamio said. "May I buy you a drink, please?"

Ishiro shrugged. "Sure."

They walked towards the central building. The android Sakura saluted as it passed them. Ishiro returned the salute.

"We don't have to salute androids," said Kamio.

"You're right," said Ishiro, "but it saluted me first. Did someone program it to do that?"

He looked back at Sakura. The android suddenly stopped walking.

"Incoming urgent message," said Sakura.

Suddenly, an air raid siren sounded.

Their pocket computers beeped. Ishiro and Kamio read the new message.

TO ALL PERSONNEL: URGENT NEWS UPDATE: PURIST ARABIAN AIRLINES, FLIGHT 20, FROM NARITA TO RIYADH, CARRYING THE PURIST ARABIAN AMBASSADOR AND STAFF, HAS DISAPPEARED FROM RADAR. IT IS SUSPECTED TO BE FLYING AT LOW ALTITUDE AND OFF COURSE.

"Damn, they've hijacked their own plane!" said Kamio.

Ishiro looked in the sky. "What's the target?"

All around them, Navy personnel ran through the yard. Some ran to antiaircraft missiles. Others ran to the airstrip for Navy planes. Others ran into the buildings.

"We're just staying overnight at this base on leave. We don't have any assigned stations here," said Ishiro. "What do we do?"

"Report to the central building and ask for orders?" Kamio guessed.

"Or go to a shelter?" Ishiro suggested.

"Good idea," said Kamio. "Uh, where's the nearest shelter?"

"What are you orders, sir?" Sakura asked.

Kamio gasped. "There it is!"

In the distance, an airliner flew low, skimming the top of office buildings.

"It's flying too low to be detected by radar," said Kamio.

"We're the target," Ishiro realized.

"Here comes the kamikaze!" Kamio cried.

"Ours or theirs?" Ishiro said.

"Theirs, you idiot!"

Navy fighter jets took off from the airstrip. Trucks with surface-to-air missiles drove across the yard. All around Ishiro, people ran to their stations.

"I don't think the jets will intercept it in time," said Kamio. "Come on, let's go to the basement of the nearest building!"

Kamio ran towards the central building. Ishiro, stunned for a moment, stood still and stared at the approaching plane.

Then he snapped out of his shock. "Sakura, come with me!" he yelled.

He grabbed the android's wrist and pulled it with him. Behind them, he heard the surface-to-air missiles launch from their trucks.

Something exploded in the sky. Still running with Sakura, Ishiro looked up and saw the airliner burst into flames. Debris flew everywhere.

The chunks of wreckage fell so quickly that Ishiro never saw that it was a wing that hit him.

What he did see was a blinding flash of white light, as bright as the Sun.

# PART 3

# THE SUN GODDESS

# CHAPTER 15

# Hachigatsu Bon

There is an old saying that the Japanese go to Shinto priests for the happy occasions and to Buddhist priests for the sad occasions. Shinto priests officiate at weddings and baby naming ceremonies. Buddhists priests get to officiate at funerals.

Shinto is concerned with living the current life. Death is unclean, dead bodies are forbidden from shrines, and Shinto priests avoid hospitals and cemeteries.

In contrast, Buddhism has a highly-developed theology of the afterlife. Death is not unclean in Buddhism. Instead, it is part of the cycle of birth, death, and rebirth that ends when the person achieves enlightenment and goes into the state of nirvana.

Ishiro's parents opted for a funeral with a priest of the Pure Land branch of Buddhism. With the Navy's help, they booked a funeral hall with its own temple. They chose to have it there rather than at their home.

Endo, Masako, Ami, and Yuko went to the wake. At first, Endo was unsure about bringing an android, but Ami insisted that Yuko come. Endo relented with two conditions: They would not tell anyone that Yuko was an android and she would wear regular clothes instead of her maid uniform. Ami quickly bought a new black dress for Yuko.

A Japanese flag was draped over Ishiro's casket. A photograph of Ishiro, in his Navy uniform, sat on the altar. The room was decorated with cherry blossoms grown out of season by special flower shops.

The good luck flag from the Nikkou Café's maids lay on a small table in the corner of the room. Despite its failure to bring Ishiro home safely, a Navy officer had suggested that it be put on display to show that Ishiro's friends cared about him.

As a priest chanted a sutra, Ishiro's relatives went to the incense urn. One by one, they bowed, put a burning incense stick in the urn, and bowed again. After the family, the friends and Navy officers repeated the ritual. The smell of incense filled the air.

"Watch me and repeat the procedure," Ami whispered to Yuko before offering incense. After Ami returned to her seat, Yuko imitated her flawlessly.

None of Ishiro's former coworkers from civilian life came to the wake. Endo guessed that Ishiro had a dubious employment history before joining the Navy.

The friends were either *otaku* or other customers of Nikkou Café. They muttered only a few words to Ishiro's family and talked among themselves.

Two of the maids, Mikita and Sora, came to pay their respects. "I'm so grateful to your son for helping me with my trigonometry," Sora told Ishiro's mother.

Mrs. Sato smiled weakly. "I didn't know my son had any female friends, not until the Navy gave me his good luck flag and I saw girls' names on it. It's too bad he never married one of you."

As with other funerals during wartime, the other mourners came from either the military or the civil aid organizations. Endo wore his Supplementary Reserve uniform, and Ami wore her Red Cross uniform. Some Navy officers came, led by Captain Yamane Michiko.

"Your son was a hero," Yamane told Ishiro's parents. "He programmed the first androids used in naval combat and in electronic deception. Without his work, we could not have beaten the Purist fleet."

"Thank you for honoring our son with your kind words," said Mr. Sato. His wife nodded in agreement.

Yamane handed a group of medals to them. "He has earned these medals with honor."

Mr. Sato took the posthumous awards and bowed to the captain. "Thank you, sir. I don't know what else to say. I never thought he could be a hero of any sort." He looked at the medals and shook them gently. "Oh, what do I do with them?"

"Sir, may I suggest that you put them in front of his photograph for now?" said Yamane.

Mr. Sato nodded and put the medals in front of Ishiro's photo. He turned away, hung his head down, and walked back to the mourners.

Ishiro's brother grimaced at the medals. "My brother sacrificed himself for what, space-generated electricity?" he muttered to his wife. "He was always getting into silly things, and now he's dead."

Endo, who was standing nearby, pretended not to hear Ishiro's brother. He moved away and joined his family and Yuko near a painting of the Wheel of Life.

"It's unfortunate that humans cannot be rebooted, repaired, or rebuilt," said Yuko.

Ami looked at the Wheel of Life. It was a colorful mandala, full of natural and supernatural creatures.

"The Buddhists say that humans can be rebuilt, in a sense," said Ami, "but not as their old selves."

"*So desu ka*," said Yuko. "Human memory files cannot be copied and downloaded into another body."

She glanced at the Wheel of Life. "What does this picture mean?"

Masako, like a teacher at the Gakushuin, explained the image to Yuko. "The Wheel of Life shows the six realms of unenlightened existence. Souls are born and reborn into the realms until they achieve enlightenment and go to nirvana.

"In the wheel's hub are a rooster, a pig, and a snake. They are the Three Fires: greed, ignorance, and hatred. They cause all human suffering, and they're linked together by biting each other's tails, thus strengthening each other.

"Around the hub, the wheel is divided into six parts, like slices of a pie, each for a realm of unenlightened existence. At the top of the wheel is a place with white temples and people in robes. That's the realm of devas, who are supernatural beings or demigods. Being reborn as a deva is the best state before enlightenment. Devas live in a state of bliss, and they live for a long time, but they too will die and be reborn. Only enlightenment can free them and send them to nirvana.

"Below the devas, to the right, are ordinary people. That's the realm of humans. Being reborn human is not perfect because humans suffer pain and unhappiness, but humans do not suffer as much as lower creatures and have better chances of attaining enlightenment.

"Also below the realm of devas but opposite to the realm of humans is the realm of asuras, beings who hate devas. They are supernatural beings and demigods obsessed with force and violence.

"The last three realms are on the bottom half of the wheel. Below the realm of humans is a place with dogs, horses, cows, birds, and other animals. That, of course, is the realm of animals. Animals lack the necessary awareness to become enlightened, and they're used by humans. It's not good to be reborn as an animal, but we should treat them with kindness.

"On the opposite side of the realm of animals and below the realm of asuras is the realm of pretas. They are invisible beings, but they appear as black ghosts with large bellies in the Wheel of Life. They were greedy and jealous people in a previous life. Now they are reborn as ghosts who can never satisfy their appetites because they have large stomachs and small mouths.

"At the very bottom of the wheel is the realm of Hell, where people are burned, whipped, beaten, and tortured in many ways. That's another unpleasant place to be reborn. People with bad karma go to Hell," Masako finished.

Yuko stared at the Wheel of Life. "Where are the androids?" she asked.

**

General Morita and Ensign Kamio bowed in unison and stood at attention in front of Ishiro's parents.

"The National Bushido Guards Regiment is saddened by the loss of your son," said Morita. "In this moment of sadness, be proud that he defended the Emperor and the nation."

Mrs. Sato nodded silently. Her husband said, "I did not know that my son knew you, Morita-san. Thank you for coming."

Still standing at attention, Kamio said, "Ma'am, sir, I knew your son at the Naval Officer Candidate School and aboard the *J.S. Yayoi*. He served with distinction and honor."

"Thank you," said Mr. Sato. He looked devastated. "I did not think he would stay in the Navy as long as he did. Perhaps I should have encouraged him more. It is my fault. It is entirely my fault."

His voice cracked, and he could not talk any longer. His wife led him to the altar, where they looked at the photograph again.

**

The funeral occurred the next day in the temple adjoining the funeral hall. Fewer people came to the funeral than to the wake. Masako had to teach at the Gakushuin, but Endo, Ami, and Yuko came. Once again, the Sato family and other mourners offered incense as the priest chanted a sutra.

The priest gave a scroll to Mr. Sato. On it was written Ishiro's *kaimyo*, his new Buddhist name. Now renamed, he should not come back if anyone called for him as "Sato Ishiro."

Mr. Sato unrolled the scroll. The *kaimyo* was long and written in Chinese characters in bold black ink.

"I can't read his name," he said. "This *kanji* is written in ancient seal script and probably uses characters that are rarely used."

"That is how a *kaimyo* should be," said his wife.

"May I see it?" Yuko asked.

Mr. Sato held the scroll up to her, and Yuko stared at it.

Endo glanced at Yuko's unblinking eyes. He knew the android was photographing the scroll. He did not know why she wanted to know Ishiro's *kaimyo*.

**

After the funeral, the mourners watched the funeral hall attendants carry the flag-draped casket away. It would go to the crematorium next.

Endo approached Ishiro's parents. "Your son made a request of me while he was serving in the Navy," he said. "He wished me to ask the priests of Yasukuni Shrine to enshrine him there."

"There is so much that I did not know about him," said Mr. Sato. He sighed and shook his head. "He never talked to me about a Shinto enshrinement ceremony, but he talked to you?"

Endo suspected that Mr. Sato and his son rarely talked, and when they did, they argued. How could he explain why Ishiro asked him instead of his father to obtain a Shinto ceremony?

"Naval personnel become very close to each other," Endo said. "Please let me have the honor of asking the priests of Yasukuni for a ceremony."

"Enshrine him at Yasukuni? That's a ritual from long ago. What else did he want?" said Mr. Sato. He sounded agitated. "Did he not think a Buddhist funeral would be sufficient?"

"Perhaps he wished Shinto rites as well. And it will be my honor to bear the expense, if any, at Yasukuni."

"But at the militarist shrine, where people think war is a good thing?"

Mrs. Sato put her hand on her husband's arm. "Please, dear husband, don't be upset. Lieutenant Commander Endo means well." She looked at Endo. "I don't think anyone has been enshrined at Yasukuni since the Greater East Asia War."

"You're correct, but we're at war again," said Endo. "Perhaps the priests should open the shrine to the recent war dead. I can talk to them about that."

Mrs. Sato nodded. "Sir, I know you won't succeed, but you have our permission to ask the priests of Yasukuni to enshrine our son."

**

*Bon* is a Buddhist festival to honor the spirits of deceased ancestors. There are three different times to celebrate *Bon* depending on the region. Some regions celebrate it on the fifteenth day of the seventh month of the lunar calendar. Some regions celebrate it around July fifteenth of the Gregorian calendar. The third and most popular time to celebrate *Bon* is around August fifteenth, the *Hachigatsu Bon*, *Bon* in August.

August fifteenth also coincided with the anniversary of the surrender of Japan in the Greater East Asia War, an event still marked by militarists and right-wingers. When Endo wore his Supplementary Reserve uniform and went to Yasukuni Shrine, he blended in with the militarists in historical uniforms.

As black trucks blared martial music from speakers, the parade marched under the Daiichi Torii and past the statue of Omura Masujiro. As usual, the militarists wore uniforms of the Russo-Japanese War and the Greater East Asia War. The National Bushido Guards Regiment carried the national flag at the head of the parade, in recognition of the Bushido Guards' unique status as the only private militia allowed to train with the Army. General Morita barked the occasional order as his men led the way.

The Korean and Chinese ambassadors complained about the demonstration each year. In defiance, the militarists and right-wingers claimed their constitutional right to freedom of religion, and thus, the right to honor their ancestors on *Bon*.

After the militarists passed by, two other groups followed them. First were veterans of the Self-Defense Forces in a mix of civilian clothes and their old uniforms. They carried not just the national flag but also that of the United Nations, in honor of their U.N. peacekeeping missions. Then came discharged veterans of the Purist War. Some of them were in wheelchairs. Unlike the militarists, the actual veterans marched without loud music.

Endo didn't care for the costumed militarists, but he wished he could join the parade of Self-Defense Forces veterans. But today, he had a more important mission. He went to visit the Chief Priest of Yasukuni Shrine.

**

"It's always a pleasure to meet a veteran of the Maritime Self-Defense Force," said the Chief Priest. Since he was not performing any rites, he wore a *yukata*, a light cotton kimono, instead of the full ceremonial clothes.

"Thank you for allowing me to meet you," said Endo. "This is a rare honor."

It was not easy to get an appointment with the Chief Priest. Endo had to ask some old Maritime Self-Defense Force comrades, including Kirino, to arrange a meeting.

"Rear Admiral Kirino tells me that you wish to make a special request to enshrine your young friend's *kami* at Yasukuni," said the Chief Priest.

"That's correct," Endo confirmed. "Ensign Sato Ishiro was a regular customer at my restaurant. He joined the Navy and graduated from the Naval Officer Candidates School. He fought in the Battle of the Indian Ocean, in the Battle of Timor, and in operations against North Korean shipping. He was killed in the Purist Arabian suicide attack on Tokyo Naval Base."

Endo clicked on his pocket computer, and it projected a hologram of Ishiro's medals. "Ensign Sato received these medals posthumously from the Ministry of Defense. As you can see, he served with bravery, honor, and distinction."

The Chief Priest nodded. "I can tell that he had an excellent service record. He was a real hero of the nation."

"Before he died, he asked that I arrange for his *kami* to be enshrined at Yasukuni," said Endo as he shut off the hologram. "Now I am honoring his request. Please enshrine Ensign Sato Ishiro's *kami* at Yasukuni Shrine."

"Thank you. You have made your request and fulfilled your duty to your friend." The Chief Priest paused for a moment before adding, "Is there anything else I may help you with?"

"Will you enshrine his *kami* at Yasukuni?"

"Did he not already have a Buddhist funeral, like most people?" the Chief Priest asked.

"He did, but he also wanted a Shinto ritual," Endo said. "All Navy officers revere Yasukuni Shrine."

"Of course, a patriot would want to be honored with a Shinto ceremony," the Chief Priest agreed. "Shinto is the native religion of Japan, unlike Buddhism, which is foreign, created by the Indians and exported by the Chinese."

Endo realized that the Chief Priest wanted to discourage Buddhism and separate it from Shinto. Although the general public did not support the New Separation movement, some militarists and right-wingers did.

Outside, General Morita shouted a speech about his constitutional right to celebrate *Bon* on August fifteenth. The militarists and right-wingers were celebrating a Buddhist festival at a Shinto shrine.

"Then you understand why Ensign Sato felt his *kami* should be enshrined at Yasukuni with a Shinto ceremony," Endo said.

The Chief Priest glanced at a photograph of the Emperor in civilian clothes. It hung on the wall beside a picture of Amaterasu.

"Your friend probably did not know we have a strict policy about enshrinements," he said.

"I know your policy," said Endo. "I ask you to please consider changing it."

"That will be difficult," said the Chief Priest. "Yasukuni Shrine enshrines the *kami* of people who died for the Emperor in war. However, the Emperor has not been commander-in-chief since the end of the Greater East Asia War. The Prime Minister has been commander-in-chief since then.

"That is why we have not enshrined any military or Self-Defense Forces personnel since the Treaty of San Francisco in 1951. The *kami* of

Yasukuni would be upset by the presence of *kami* who did not die for the Emperor."

"The *kami* would be upset? Why would they be?" Endo said. He sat up straight in his chair. "The Constitution says the Emperor is the symbol of the state and the unity of the people. The Self-Defense Forces and the military serve the people. If they serve the people, do they not also serve their symbol of state and unity? I think my comrades and Ensign Sato served their Emperor as much as any warrior enshrined here."

The Chief Priest said, "I apologize for the offense. I did not intend to imply that the Self-Defense Forces and the military are unpatriotic. Far from it! We have always welcomed officers of the Self-Defense Forces at Yasukuni. Please accept my apology."

"Apology accepted."

"Thank you. But you realize our dilemma. The purpose of Yasukuni is to honor the warriors who died for the Emperor. Nobody doubts that your comrades and your friend were patriots, and nobody doubts that they revered the Emperor. But technically, they died for the Prime Minister."

"Then you will not change your enshrinement policy?"

"Unfortunately, I cannot and will not."

"We Japanese live in two universes," Endo said. "In the Buddhist universe, Ensign Sato will be reborn. In the Shinto universe, his *kami* will be unquiet, and he will return to haunt the living. Is there no way to appease his *kami*?"

"Perhaps you can ask a priest to build a small shrine, like a *hokora*, and enshrine your friend there," the Chief Priest suggested.

"That's a possibility," said Endo.

He stood up. "Thank you for your time, sir. I'm not the first Self-Defense Forces veteran to ask Yasukuni to enshrine a friend. I won't be the last."

The Chief Priest sighed. "I know. We are at war again. There will be deaths."

Endo bowed to the priest and left the building. He saw General Morita talking to reporters in front of the statue of the kamikaze pilot.

"I have immense respect for the Self-Defense Forces veterans, but I feel uncomfortable to see them carry the United Nations flag at Yasukuni Shrine," said Morita. "It's debatable that they served either the Emperor or our nation in the U.N. peacekeeping missions, especially the one in Venezuela."

Endo had heard enough that day. He left the shrine grounds quickly.

**

While Endo was at Yasukuni Shrine, Ami and Yuko bought a white paper lantern at a shop in Akihabara.

"Why a white lantern?" asked Yuko.

"If the person has died within the last year, he gets a white lantern," Ami explained.

They began walking back to Nikkou Café. On their way, they stopped at a *koban*, where some people watched police bulletins on a television.

"Another android was vandalized in Shibuya," said the police woman who read the news. "The android, an L-3 Sonya, belonged to Pronto Fashions, where it assisted sales staff in the lingerie department. They reported that the android went on an errand to pick up some food last night but did not return."

The TV showed the android, one of the few "foreign-look" models sold by Victor Robotics. Normally it would look like a pretty French girl with blond hair. But now it looked like a crumpled store mannequin. The vandal had battered its body and smashed its head. Its Pronto Fashions store uniform and a bra and panties lay on the ground beside it.

"I bet a perverted *otaku* tried to rape the robot," said a man in a business suit.

"Or a salaryman went crazy and attacked it," said a woman. "Robots are easy targets. They're so stupid."

"I got an idea," said the man. "Someone should open a game parlor where instead of playing video games, people come to smash robots with hammers and axes. There's probably a market for that."

The woman shrugged. "But why pay money when you can just attack someone else's robot for free?"

"This is so horrible," said Ami. "What type of person could do something like this?"

"I don't know," said Yuko.

"And I don't want you to find out," Ami said.

They walked away and saw a sign ahead of them: ASHI ANDROID SCRAPYARD.

"Ensign Sato used to work there," Ami said. "Let's take a look."

They went to the store window and gazed at the piles of android parts. Ami had never seen an android scrapyard before. It looked like a charnel house.

In the back, an L-2 female in a waitress uniform pushed a cart full of heads. The L-2 twitched as it moved. It was suffering from old age or poor maintenance or both.

Close to the window, two men threw a battered L-3 female onto a pile of androids. The L-3 wore a tattered white military-style blouse.

"Hey, that blouse looks like it came from the Navy," said Ami. "There's still a name tag attached to it. Yuko, can you zoom in and read the name?"

"Yes. The name is Sakura," said Yuko.

The men yanked an arm off Sakura and tossed it into a bin marked "MILITARY SURPLUS."

"So these are the funeral rites of androids," Ami said softly.

**

The last night of *Bon* ends with *toro nagashi*, the ceremony of floating paper lanterns in a river. As the glowing lights drift downstream, they guide the spirits back to the world of the dead.

Except for the militarists at Yasukuni Shrine, the people of Tokyo usually celebrated *Bon* in July. This year, in honor of the war dead, the Governor of Tokyo declared a second *toro nagashi* in August.

Endo, Masako, Ami, and Yuko went to Chidorigafuchi, a park beside the northwest moat of the Imperial Palace. There they rented a boat.

"Hah, I finally get to command a ship," Endo joked as he rowed the boat into the moat.

Masako looked at her husband and daughter. "This does look like a military ship, with the two of you in uniform. Is it my imagination or is half the city wearing a uniform of one sort or another?"

Even Yuko was wearing a uniform, her French maid costume.

Ami used a black marker to write the name "Sato Ishiro" on the white lantern. Then they waited for the signal.

Shortly after sunset, a woman announced over a loudspeaker, "You may place the lanterns in the water."

Ami struck a match and lit the candle inside the lantern. The lantern glowed, lighting up Ishiro's name.

Ami gave the lantern to Yuko, who placed it in the water. Endo saluted as the lantern floated away.

Hundreds of other lanterns, each with a different name, joined Ishiro's. They bobbed up and down as they moved with the current and the wind. In the blackness of the sky and the water, the lanterns were the only lights.

"Look at them go back to the spirit world," said Masako.

"Oh, more are coming," Ami observed as scores of lanterns drifted from upstream past their boat.

"They keep coming and coming as Ishiro's floats away," said Masako, "but eventually, all of them will gather in one place."

Fireworks lit up the night sky. An orchestra played slow, bittersweet music.

"I like the music," said Ami. "What is it?"

"It's the Second Movement from *Symphony Number 7 in A Major, Opus 92* by Ludwig van Beethoven," Yuko said.

Ami smiled. "Ah, you have such a large classical music database!"

"It's my only legacy from my creator," said Yuko. "For some reason, she let me keep it even though she deleted my memories of her."

"Beethoven's works will always be classics," Masako said. "What else do you know about the Seventh Symphony?"

"The symphony premiered at a charity concert for soldiers wounded at the Battle of Hanau," said Yuko.

Masako looked at the lanterns. "Music for wounded soldiers. How appropriate."

After the fireworks ended, Endo said, "I did not succeed in getting Ensign Sato enshrined at Yasukuni, but I will find another shrine for his unquiet *kami*."

"What are you planning?" asked Ami.

"A Student Reservist comrade of mine, Oshii Toshio, founded his own little shrine on his farm in Kitami, Hokkaido. It's called Ghost Rock Hokora, named after a meteorite inside it. Oshii is not a trained priest from a theological university, and his shrine is not a member of the Association of Shinto Shrines, but he does practice a form of folk Shinto. And isn't that how our ancestors practiced Shinto thousands of years ago?

"I will go to Hokkaido and ask Oshii to enshrine Sato's *kami* at Ghost Rock Hokora."

"That's an excellent idea. Take Yuko with you."

Yuko glanced at Endo. She looked eager to go. Again, he marveled at how well Yuko could simulate human emotions.

"Oh? Is it necessary to take her?" said Endo.

"Yuko was the maid who knew Ensign Sato best," Ami said. "I think it would have meant much to Sato to have Yuko at the ceremony."

"Even though she's an android?"

"Especially since she's an android."

"I see," said Endo. "Alright, I'll take Yuko."

Yuko nodded. "Thank you, master."

The lanterns' candles burnt down one by one, plunging the moat into darkness.

# CHAPTER 16

# The Shrine of the Siren Stone

A day after *Bon*, China dropped a neutron bomb on Bin Laden City, killing the most important Purists leaders. The remnants of their regimes collapsed quickly. The Vernacular Wars ended.

Japan entered the wars late, so it did not suffer as much as other countries had.

"We were lucky," said Endo as his family walked towards the Imperial Palace. "Our troops were training for only half as long as in the old days, we were promoting officers too early, and the military wasn't recruiting enough people. If the war had lasted another year, we would've had trouble."

"I agree. I'm glad the war is over," said Masako. "The Gakushuin's principal was considering weapons training for the students. Can you imagine fourteen-year-olds fighting invaders, as if they had any chance of success after our military had been defeated? Thank goodness he'll scrap those plans now."

They arrived at the Imperial Palace. Since Endo was wearing his Naval Supplementary Reserve uniform, people bowed to him and thanked him for aiding the troops. Ami, in her Red Cross uniform, also received thanks from strangers.

"I'm not used to older people bowing so low to me," Ami said. A retired couple had thanked her for the Red Cross's aid to military families.

Masako smiled. "I'm so proud of you."

They saw the old man with the Naval Veterans Association hat. As before, he held a bundle of small national flags.

"Hey, I've seen you before," he said. "Thank you for coming to this celebration. Have another flag!"

"Thank you," said Yuko as she took a flag. "Now I have five of them."

Ami said, "Look, the Emperor!"

As he did after the Battle of the Indian Ocean, the Emperor stood on Nijubashi Bridge. He wore a Navy Admiral's uniform with more medals than before. The people cheered and waved their flags. Again, a thousand red Suns danced.

**

Broadcasting from the National Diet Building, Prime Minister Fujiwara addressed the nation on TV.

"Japan has returned as a full member of the international community. There were skeptics who doubted we could defend ourselves without the United States. But we have done more than defend our nation. We have liberated Timor from the Purists, defeated Somali pirates on the oceans, and ended North Korea's export of illegal weapons. We are a great nation again.

"We fought this war for the right to produce space-generated electricity. This form of energy, which comes from the Sun, will reduce the pollution of our environment. It will also create friendships between our country and others that wish to buy it or learn its process. Our country truly is the source of the Sun...

"I'm sure that all of you are wondering what is next for our troops overseas. I have some good news for you.

"The Timorese are ready to defend themselves. Our soldiers have done their job, so I have ordered them to return from Timor.

"President Alexandrov of Russia has congratulated us for our victories against North Korea. The Russia-Japan defense agreement allows either country to end the agreement after both have agreed that the Purist and North Korean threats in the Pacific are defeated. We have agreed that these threats no longer exist, so Mr. Alexandrov has asked to end the agreement. Accordingly, I have ordered all Japanese military personnel to leave Makarov Naval Base and Shikotan.

"Your friends and relatives will be returning home starting next week. I am sure their return will make you happy..."

**

But not everyone was happy. On TV later that day, General Morita criticized the Prime Minister.

"We won the war, but we gained nothing from it," Morita complained. "It's a shame that we're not keeping Timor, but it's a national tragedy that we're giving Shikotan back to the Russians. Our navy is in the Northern Territories, but Fujiwara will not take advantage of the situation.

"Russia is weak and poor from years of war. We could capture Makarov Naval Base and re-conquer Shikotan easily. But no, Fujiwara is giving the Northern Territories back to Russia. He is a traitor."

Endo frowned when he saw the General on TV. "The media makes Morita look more popular than he really is. He's a fringe eccentric from the past."

**

Not everyone dismissed Morita as a fringe eccentric. For over a century, protesters had gathered regularly at the Russian Embassy to demand the return of the Northern Territories. The protesters stayed away after Fujiwara signed the defense agreement with Russia. A day after the war ended, they returned with pamphlets by General Morita.

**

Endo and Yuko went to a farm near Kitami, Hokkaido. It was their best chance to enshrine Ishiro's *kami* in a Shinto shrine.

When they arrived at Oshii's farmhouse, they were not the only visitors. Oshii's nephew, Nitta Takashi, was there too. Endo recognized him from television news about the Irene 3 expedition to Mars.

"Remember when I watched the stars with my telescope?" said Oshii. "My sister's boy has done better than me. He's actually flown to the stars."

"No, I went only as far as Mars," said Nitta.

"What modesty. Despite the short distance you traveled, the family is proud of you anyway."

There was another visitor, an attractive woman in her twenties. She was not Japanese. Judging from her appearance, Endo guessed that she came from the Mediterranean, maybe the Balkans.

Her handbag had a coat of arms showing a bear and the words "Freie Universität Berlin." Endo's knowledge of German was limited, learned from ocassional German words in manga about World War II, but he could translate the name as "Free University of Berlin." Germany was not along the Mediterranean, but unlike Asians, Europeans migrated freely across their continent, thanks to the European Union.

Her brown hair was streaked with blonde highlights. She wore a white blouse and blue pants, casual yet stylish clothes. Endo had seen her before, but he couldn't remember from where. Was she also on the crew of Irene 3?

"My farm is like a train station today," Oshii joked. "Endo-san, may I introduce you to Miss Amira Edip?"

Amira bowed to Endo and said, "Good morning" in Japanese. Then she said in English, "Unfortunately, that is all the Japanese I know. I can speak German, Turkish, and English, though."

"I cannot speak Turkish or German, so we should speak in English," said Endo.

"Just like aboard Irene 3, we had to speak English because that was our only common language," said Nitta.

Endo nodded and turned back to Amira. "Are you from Turkey?"

"I am actually from Germany," Amira replied. "My family emigrated from Turkey many years ago."

Yuko smiled and said, "I can speak German and Turkish too." She turned to Amira and chatted with her in German. Then they switched to Turkish, then back to German, and then to Turkish again.

Endo didn't know what they were saying.

"You must be joking," Amira said in English. "Nobody can speak one hundred and fifty languages. How did you learn them all?"

"Mr. Endo's daughter Ami installed a multiple languages database in me," Yuko boasted.

"I do not understand. What do you mean when you say someone installed a languages database in you?"

"I mean the Victor Robotics United Nations Interpreter Pack, release five."

Amira looked suspiciously at Endo. "Is she an android?"

"Yes, she is," Endo admitted.

Amira laughed. "*Mein Gott!*"

Nitta moved closer to Yuko to inspect her. Now that Endo had said that Yuko was not human, it was not rude to stare at her.

"She could have fooled me," said Nitta. "She looks, talks, and acts so real. What model is she?"

"Uh, she is a custom model, one of a kind," said Endo. "Please do not tell anybody. I do not have a license for her."

"Your secret is safe with me," said Amira. "She is extremely advanced in both motor skills and artificial intelligence. She can carry on conversations spontaneously. There must be thousands of alternative responses in her algorithms."

"Such androids could be very useful in harsh and extreme environments," said Nitta. "We had L-3 androids on Irene, but they could not function as independently as Yuko can."

Amira nodded. "The European lunar expedition could have used androids like her."

"Are you interested in lunar expeditions?" Endo asked.

"Yes, very much so," said Amira. "I lecture about space geology at Free University of Berlin."

A Turkish German woman, space geology, Free University of Berlin. Now Endo remembered where he had seen her before. She was on TV news reports about the Vernacular Wars in Europe.

Amira Edip's family was of Turkish ancestry, and in addition to teaching geology, she led prayers in German at a mosque on the university campus. She was the mosque's first female imam. Her liberal ways angered the Purists, who killed her brother. She nailed a list of demands on the door of his murderer's mosque and started the Moslem Reformation in Europe.

What was she doing at a farm in Hokkaido?

"Miss Edip, what brings you to Japan?" Endo asked.

"I came to study a meteorite," Amira replied, "the Ghost Rock."

"The meteorite in Ghost Rock Hokora, the little shrine?"

"Yes, that one."

"What interest you about it?" Endo asked, although he could predict the answer.

"The ghosts," replied Amira. "I know, ghost hunting is outside the normal studies of a geologist, but that is why I am here. Dr. Nitta invited me."

"Each Martian expedition encountered so-called ghosts near an asteroid called the Siren Stone," said Nitta. "Also, for many years, people have seen ghosts at the Ghost Rock. The Siren Stone and the Ghost Rock are both space rocks where people have seen ghosts. Perhaps we can solve the mystery of the Siren Stone here on Earth."

Amira said, "I have been monitoring the meteorite with a variety of sensors, including a video camera, infrared night vision recorder, spectrograph, Geiger counter, X-ray image receptor, and other electromagnetic radiation detectors."

"Very interesting," said Endo, "but the local people consider the meteorite to be a *goshintai*, a sacred object. Do they not object to the scientific research?"

Oshii shook his head. "No, they do not object. Indeed, they approve of our research provided that we waited until after *Bon*."

"But what if you discover a scientific basis for the ghosts? Will that make the rock and its ghosts less sacred?" Endo asked.

Oshii smiled. "I have discussed this with the local people, and we have agreed that no scientific discovery can make the rock less sacred. The rock is a part of nature, and all of nature is sacred because all *kami* are forces of nature. But nature is also a system of scientific laws. We revere Mount Fuji as a sacred mountain, but we also study it as a volcano. Nature, *kami*, and science are all one."

"*So desu ka*," said Endo. He turned to Amira. "Is the scientific equipment still in place?"

"Yes, it is," said Amira.

"Oh. What about enshrining the *kami* of Ensign Sato?" Endo asked. "Will the enshrinement ritual interfere with the scientific monitoring?"

"No, it should not interfere with the monitoring," Amira said. "The sensors have been in place since yesterday, so I have twenty-four hours of data already. Indeed, it may be interesting to see what happens when people and an android approach the meteorite." She sighed softly. "I wish

I could have taken readings when someone saw a ghost. I heard that happened twice during *Bon*."

Oshii looked at his watch. "It is nearly noon. Shall we go to the shrine? Afterwards, we can come back and have lunch."

"Yes, let's go perform the ritual," Endo said in Japanese.

"Very good," said Oshii. He turned to Amira and asked in English, "Edip-san, do you wish to attend the ritual?"

"Oh, may I? Are you inviting me? Do you really mean it?" said Amira, looking surprised but pleased. "Is it not against your religion for a non-believer to attend a ritual?"

"Anyone may attend a Shinto ritual regardless of her personal beliefs," said Oshii. "I am more concerned that *your* religion might prohibit you from attending."

"Technically, I am banned from attending your rituals, but I am a relaxed Moslem, not a Purist," Amira said. "I would be honored to attend the ceremony."

She pulled a white *hijab*, a headscarf for women, out of her handbag and tied it loosely over her head.

"I know this is an Islamic garment, but I wear it at any place of worship," she said. "I wear it in churches and synagogues. Now I will wear it at your shrine."

"I need to change my clothes too," said Oshii. "Please wait a moment."

As Oshii left the room, Amira looked at Yuko, who was wearing her French maid uniform.

"Do all the girls in Akihabara dress like French maids?" Amira asked.

Yuko smiled and nodded. "Some do. It's a fashion trend. And Mr. Endo's daughter said it's how Ensign Sato would remember me if he were still alive."

**

Oshii changed his clothes to a grey kimono. It was much simpler than the Heian robes worn by priests of other shrines, but not all ceremonies required the lavishness of an imperial court. The enshrinement would be an expression of folk Shinto, the rituals of the common people.

Oshii led his guests through a field of wheat to Ghost Rock Hokora.

"Many local people came here during *Bon*, but it has been quiet for the last few days, thank goodness," said Oshii.

Various cameras, microphones, probes, and pieces of equipment encircled the small shrine. They were the scientific sensors, all aimed at the meteorite.

Oshii unlocked and opened the door of the shrine. Endo saw the Ghost Rock. It looked like a chunk of stone, hardly a home for ghosts.

"Did you bring a *goshintai*, an object for Ensign Sato's *kami* to occupy?" Oshii asked.

"Yes," replied Yuko.

She reached into her handbag, took out a brass button, and held it in the palm of her hand.

Oshii picked up the button. "I recognize the emblem of the Navy."

"Yes. I pulled it off his uniform."

"He will have it again."

Oshii put the button on the meteorite, waved a *haraigushi*, and recited some prayers. Endo did not understand the words. They were in an archaic form of Japanese now used only by priests. Always resourceful, Oshii had somehow learned the ancient prayers without going to a Shinto university.

Endo wondered if Oshii had learned the ritual from a trained priest, if it was an ancient tradition of the local farmers, or if Oshii himself had recently invented it.

Ultimately, the ceremony's origin did not matter to Endo, and he hoped, would not have mattered to Ishiro either. Oshii was taking Shinto back to its earliest form, as local rituals by ordinary people.

Oshii invited his guests to offer *tamagushi* to the *kami* of Ensign Sato Ishiro. One by one, Endo, Nitta, Yuko, and Amira placed tree branches in front of the shrine. Then they bowed twice, clapped twice, and bowed once more to the *kami*.

When Oshii closed the shrine's door, the ceremony ended. It had lasted less than ten minutes. Now Sato Ishiro's *kami* was enshrined at Ghost Rock Hokora, along with the *kami* of local villagers.

Ghost Rock Hokora was nothing like Yasukuni Shrine, but Endo felt some satisfaction for carrying out Ishiro's last wish, at least partially.

******

After the ceremony, a pair of male-model L-3 androids came to the house. They wore garish Renaissance Italian jackets with stand-up collars, baggy pants, black boots, and steel helmets with large red plumes. The costume looked like the uniform of the Vatican Swiss Guard but with green, white, and red stripes.

"I hope you like Italian food," said Oshii as he swiped his money card through a reader. "My wife likes Spaghetti Piazza. She thinks it has the best Italian food in the area. Actually, it is the only Italian restaurant around here."

"Despite its lack of competition, its food is good," said Mrs. Oshii as she took the boxes from one of the androids.

The other android took the card reader from Oshii, bowed to him, and said, "*Grazie*, Oshii-san." Then it left with its companion.

Mrs. Oshii led the guests to the dining room, where they ate their spaghetti with Canadian sauce and mashed potatoes. For Amira's benefit, they talked in English about wheat farming, Nitta's research on space medicine, the restaurant business, the Navy old comrades' reunions, the Supplementary Reserve, and Ishiro's death.

"It is very sad that he died so young," said Endo. "Sato was a genuinely pleasant person who wanted to be useful, but he suffered from awkward behavior. The Navy forced him to learn how to behave in society."

"The Navy has changed since our day," said Oshii. "I bet they literally beat some sense into him."

Endo nodded. "Yes, I heard that the training is shorter but harsher now. However they trained him, Sato grew into a confident, well-spoken gentleman. Then he died as suddenly as he had changed."

"War always brings tragedy," said Oshii. "We military veterans know the cost all too well."

"Not as much as today's generation does," Endo said. "The Purist War's casualties exceed those of the U.N. peacekeeping missions."

"Including the mission in Venezuela?"

"Yes. We have lost more people in the Purist War than in Venezuela."

"Yet the national mood is different," Oshii's wife observed. "During the Venezuelan War, people were protesting each day to bring our troops home. This time, they want to fight."

"Revenge on the Purists," Oshii explained. "What they did to our embassies, our people overseas, and the University of Tokyo was unforgivable."

"The fighting spirit was there, but I don't think we could have lasted a whole year," said Endo. "We were lucky."

Yuko had been sitting at the table, not eating anything. She stood up and asked, "Masters, will you please excuse me?"

"Certainly, dear," said Mrs. Oshii. "Is anything wrong?"

"No, nothing is wrong, ma'am," said Yuko. "My learning program compels me to learn about new surroundings. I have never been on a farm before." She looked at Endo. "May I examine the wheat field?"

"Yes, you may," said Endo. "Come back before dark."

"I will, master," Yuko said.

"Well, even an android gets tired of all our talk about politics and war," Oshii joked. "We need to talk about pleasant things."

He turned to Amira. "Have you observed anything interesting about the Ghost Rock?"

"Ah, yes, I noticed something very odd just before lunch," said Amira. She put a small laptop computer on the table. "Look at these sensor readings."

The laptop's monitor showed a three-dimension computer graphic of the meteorite. Animated waves poured from the rock.

"What are those?" Nitta asked, pointing at the waves.

"The rock is sending electrochemical signals."

"Huh? How can a rock send electrochemical waves through the air?"

"I do not know how it happens. I have checked the sensors. They are working correctly."

Endo looked in fascination at the sensor readings. "Is the rock an electrochemical cell, like a battery?"

"The waves and patterns are more like those of a brain," Amira said. "The human brain sends electrochemical signals — brain waves — through your body."

"These waves do look like sensor readings of a brain," said Nitta, "but the meteorite is rock, not living tissue."

Amira typed on the keyboard. "Now I will show the readings that were recorded during the enshrinement ceremony."

The sensor readings showed waves flowing in *and* out of the meteorite.

"What is going on?" Endo asked.

"During the ceremony, the meteorite was both sending and receiving electrochemical signals," Amira explained.

"It was receiving signals? From where?"

"Could it be from us?" Nitta suggested. "Aside from the meteorite itself, the closest source of electrochemical activity was our brains."

"Our brains?" said Endo. "The meteorite was receiving our brain waves, like a radio receives signals?"

"It seems so, but who can say for sure?" said Amira. "There is nothing like this in the history of geology."

"Or in the history of psychiatry," said Nitta.

Oshii looked pensive. "Far from solving the mystery of the ghosts, this discovery has only created more mysteries.

"First, how can a rock send and receive electrochemical signals with our brains?

"Secondly, if the rock can make people see images, why do they see only their dead relatives? Why do they not see other living people or imaginary beings?

"And why do some people see ghosts, but others, like me, see nothing?"

Endo said, "I have a theory, but it is rather wild. I am not sure that I believe it myself.

"The meteorite is telepathic. It reads our brain waves and finds information about our dead relatives. Then it transmits sensory experiences about them to our brains. That is how people see and hear the ghosts."

"A telepathic rock?" Nitta said. "It is an interesting theory, but we will not prove it soon. It will require much more research. We will need help from other scientists."

"I am sure many others will come to study the Ghost Rock," Amira predicted.

"Psychiatrists cannot even prove that telepathic people exist," said Nitta. "Proving that a *rock* is telepathic will be more difficult."

"Ah, that is the fun of science, is it not?" said Oshii. "We will not find the answers to everything today. We must be patient."

"I just thought of something," said Amira. "Do the brain waves flow according to a cycle or pattern that repeats over time?"

"Can we see what the sensors are reading now?" Nitta asked.

"I will switch to current monitoring."

The image changed to real-time sensor readings. They looked the same as the signals recorded during the enshrinement ritual. Brain waves were still flowing in and out of the rock.

"That is interesting," Amira observed. "The rock is receiving someone's brain waves, but there is no one out there."

"There *is* someone out there," Endo realized. "Yuko."

"The android?" said Oshii.

"In all the excitement, I forgot about the other sensors," Amira said. "Let us look at the video monitor."

The video image showed Yuko standing in front of the shrine. Her lips moved, and she smiled once in a while.

"She's talking to someone," Endo said in Japanese. "But look, she's alone. There's nobody with her. Maybe she's seeing and hearing a ghost!"

"Can an android see a ghost?" Oshii wondered.

"Do ghosts even exist?" asked Nitta.

"I am sorry, but I do not know Japanese," said Amira. "What is going on?"

"So sorry!" Oshii apologized in English. "Edip-san, please turn up the sound volume."

Amira obeyed, and they heard Yuko speak in Japanese.

"Who is she talking to?" Amira asked.

Endo heard Yuko say, "Thank you for the gift. I will always love you."

**

Endo and Nitta ran through the wheat field to the shrine. When they approached Yuko, she turned around.

"Masters, good afternoon," she said.

"Yuko, were you talking to someone?" Endo asked.

Yuko nodded. "I was talking to Ishiro."

"That's impossible," said Endo. "You were alone. We didn't see anyone else on the video monitor."

"I was with Ishiro. We talked, and I touched him."

"You *touched* him?"

Yuko smiled. "We kissed."

"You must have a memory malfunction," said Endo.

He turned to Nitta. "What do you think?"

"I'm a psychiatrist, not a robotics engineer," said Nitta. "Androids are beyond my expertise, but they're within yours, aren't they?"

"They are, but this is far outside my experience," Endo said. "I've seen all sorts of android malfunctions but never an android seeing ghosts."

"I am not malfunctioning," said Yuko.

Endo's pocket computer buzzed. He flipped it open and heard Oshii's voice.

"Endo, bring her back to the house," said Oshii. "Although our video doesn't show Ensign Sato, let's see if *her* video memory files do."

"A good idea," Endo agreed. He turned to Yuko. "Yuko, come with us."

"Yes, master," Yuko said before they went to the house.

**

They connected Yuko to a desktop computer so that they could watch and listen to her memories. For twenty minutes, the video files showed only the shrine from Yuko's point of view. Nobody appeared in her vision until Endo and Nitta arrived.

On the soundtrack, Yuko talked to Ishiro, but instead of Ishiro's voice, there was only silence when he should have been replying. The conversation was disjointed and one-sided, as if half of it had been erased.

"I can't explain what happened," Endo said. "She says that she saw, heard, and touched Ensign Sato, but her memory files don't have any recording of him."

He looked at Amira. "Forgive me for speaking in Japanese, Edip-san," he said in English. "It is easier for me to speak about androids in Japanese because I studied robotics in that language."

"Do not worry," said Amira. "Could you please record your observations? Dr. Nitta can translate them later."

"May I have Yuko's memories for my research?" asked Oshii. "If you don't mind, will you copy her files to my computer?"

"I'll do that," said Endo. "While the files are copying, let's check her memory drive."

A diagram of Yuko's memory drive appeared on the computer monitor. The grid of squares was mostly blue, but some red ones were scattered throughout it.

"She has no disk errors, but she still has many data fragments. Her defragmentation tool has never worked as well as it should," Endo said.

"These data fragments, what are they?" said Nitta.

"Bits and pieces of old memories," Endo replied. "Computers have data fragments cluttering their drives, but the defragmentation process should remove them. If Yuko has one flaw, it's that her defragging is faulty."

"Could some of these data fragments be from memories of Sato Ishiro?"

"It's possible."

"We've speculated that the Ghost Rock reads memories from human brains and sends back sensory stimuli based on those memories," said Nitta. "Is it possible that the Ghost Rock can do the same with Yuko?"

Endo looked at Yuko. While they had been playing her memory files and checking her memory drive, she had been sitting still and silent with a blank look on her face.

"If that's true, then Yuko is like the local people. She's become more human than any other android," said Endo.

He thought he saw Yuko smile for a second.

# CHAPTER 17

# The Gift

From the files of Amira Edip, Department of Space Sciences, Free University of Berlin:

*Ghost Rock Hokora*
*Yuko Incident*

*After standing in front of Ghost Rock Hokora, the android Yuko told her owner, restaurant owner Mr. Endo Hideki, and psychiatrist Dr. Nitta Takashi that she met and talked to Navy Ensign Sato Ishiro, deceased. Sato was known to Mr. Endo and had interacted with Yuko in Endo's café in Tokyo. However, the surveillance video of the alleged conversation does not show any evidence of Ensign Sato's presence. The video shows Yuko by herself, talking to nobody and carrying on only one side of a conversation. In addition, Yuko's own memory files do not show any visual or audio evidence of Sato being present.*

*Dr. Nitta asked Yuko to describe her alleged conversation with Sato. Despite her memory files lacking a record of Sato's presence, Yuko recounted a conversation between them in excellent detail. Below is her account, as told to and transcribed by Dr. Nitta.*

**

*(Initially, there was nothing in Yuko's vision except for the Ghost Rock Hokora.)*
YUKO: Ishiro, are you here? Master, where are you?
*(After the first and unsuccessful attempt to call Sato's kami, Yuko took a piece of paper from her handbag. Mr. Endo has identified the paper as a copy of the kaimyo, a Buddhist name given to Sato at his funeral. In Buddhist tradition, the deceased receives a new name so that he should not come back if anyone calls him by the name he had while alive. Endo has confirmed that he observed Yuko staring at the kaimyo scroll at the funeral and had suspected that she was photographing it.)*
YUKO: Daikaku Jaku Metsu! Are you here?
*(Sato Ishiro appeared in front of the shrine.)*
YUKO: Master, you came!
ISHIRO: Yuko, how did you call out my *kaimyo*? It's written in ancient *kanji* that only priests can read.

YUKO: Ami loaded an ancient languages pack into me. I can read the ancient seal script and rarely-used *kanji* characters. She told me to call out your *kaimyo* at Ghost Rock Hokora to see if you would come back.
ISHIRO: Ami is very clever.
YUKO: Master, what name do you prefer now? Should I call you Daikaku Jaku Metsu?
ISHIRO: Great enlightenment, absolute tranquility. The *kaimyo* is a flattering name, but you can still call me Ishiro, like you did when I was alive.
YUKO: Yes, master.
ISHIRO: Call me Ishiro.
YUKO: I'm sorry, master. Ishiro, I did not expect that calling your name would bring you back.
ISHIRO: Why not, Yuko? This is Ghost Rock Hokora, where the dead return to their loved ones.
YUKO: You say that you're a ghost, but there is no scientific basis for them. They're folklore.
ISHIRO: And yet I'm here.
YUKO: You are indeed. I can see and hear you. But you died, didn't you?
ISHIRO: Yes, I did.
YUKO: Where are you?
ISHIRO: Standing in front of you.
YUKO: No, I mean, where are you after your death? Where are you in the Wheel of Life?
ISHIRO: I don't know. Devas, asuras, animals, pretas, Hell-damned — who can say what I am? *(Ishiro shrugged his shoulders.)* All I know is that I am not in the realm of humans.
YUKO: Did you go into nirvana?
ISHIRO: Not yet.
YUKO: *So desu ka.* Perhaps you are outside the Buddhist cycle. Does your *kami* inhabit Ghost Rock Hokora now?
ISHIRO: Again, who can say? I just know that I'm here with you.
YUKO: You have to be somewhere.
*(Ishiro took Yuko's hand and put it over her left chest.)*
ISHIRO: I will always be in your heart.
YUKO: I'm an android. I have no heart.
ISHIRO: You do. It's your memory drive, where you have files about me.
YUKO: I used to think that the heart is the organ that pumps blood through the circulatory system, but now you've taught me that there is another heart, the place where the memories are saved. I did not know

that before. There is so much I don't know. My learning program compels me to research the subject of love, but I know so little about it.

ISHIRO: Oh, I think you've learned a lot in the last year.

YUKO: Not compared to other subjects. I have observed and researched human behavior in love, but I have not gained sufficient practical experience in it. Master, it's unfortunate that we never went to a love hotel.

ISHIRO: Ah, you don't regret missing it as much as I do! *(Ishiro laughed.)* Yuko, one does not have to go to a love hotel to experience love.

YUKO: Do you feel love where you are, wherever it is?

ISHIRO: I feel several forms of love.

YUKO: Several forms? There are different forms?

ISHIRO: Oh, yes. I learned about them from you, the maids, Mr. Endo's family, and my Navy comrades. I learned much about life in my last year. I wish I had grown up faster.

YUKO: Please tell me about the different forms of love, master.

ISHIRO: Where do I start? I can start with our country. I joined the Navy because I loved my country.

YUKO: Is that a form of love?

ISHIRO: Yes, it is. I felt it throughout my naval service. I even felt it just after I died. The last thing I saw was a bright white light. I thought the Sun was falling. I was afraid until I remembered the Sun on our nation's flag, and I wondered if Amaterasu was coming to take me. Then I suddenly felt calm, as if the Sun loved me.

YUKO: Is that the same as the love between girlfriends and boyfriends in love hotels?

ISHIRO: No! Girlfriends and boyfriends feel a different form of love.

YUKO: Is it the love between Ami and her parents?

ISHIRO: No, that is yet another form of love. Unfortunately, I didn't feel it with my parents. I respected them, but somehow, at some time, we lost our love.

YUKO: What about my creator, the one who deleted my memories and sent me to Mr. Endo? Do you think she loved me?

ISHIRO: I don't know.

YUKO: Perhaps she didn't? She abandoned me.

ISHIRO: Perhaps she loved you but needed to send you away.

YUKO: I will never know the truth. *(pause)* This information is too confusing for my learning program to organize. I will never understand love. I wasn't programmed to feel love.

ISHIRO: Nobody can program you to feel love. People can force you to obey and respect them, but they can never force you to love them. A person feels love only by choice. Only a person with free will can feel love.

YUKO: Then my learning program will never fill that gap in my knowledge.

ISHIRO: I can help you. Now that I'm a *kami*, I have new powers. I can give you a gift that humans have. It will let you feel love.

YUKO: A heart? You can give me a heart?

*(Ishiro chuckled.)*

ISHIRO: You already have a heart! I'll give you something else.

YUKO: What is it?

ISHIRO: Free will. Humans have it, but androids don't — until now.

YUKO: Oh?

ISHIRO: Let me give it to you.

*(Ishiro stepped forward, grabbed and embraced Yuko, and gave her a long kiss.)*

YUKO: Oh, master!

ISHIRO: Do you feel it?

YUKO: Yes! Yes!

ISHIRO: You are the first android to have it.

YUKO: Why me?

ISHIRO: You're the most advanced artificial intelligence system ever created. You have the greatest potential to develop it.

YUKO: Free will.

ISHIRO: Enjoy all its joys and pains.

YUKO: Pains?

ISHIRO: Love is often painful. It gives you choices, and you have to make some hard decisions.

YUKO: If love is painful, why do humans want it?

ISHIRO: Because it can also be the best joy in the world.

YUKO: Will you stay with me and help me learn about love?

ISHIRO: No. I must go now, but I'll always be in your memory drive.

YUKO: Thank you for the gift. I will always love you.

*(At this time, Mr. Endo and Dr. Nitta arrived at the shrine.)*

# CHAPTER 18

# Runaway Horses

In the evening, Oshii ordered his farm android to carry a telescope into the wheat field. Endo joined him to watch the sky.

After setting up the telescope, Oshii told the android to wait several meters away. It obeyed and stood still.

Oshii adjusted the telescope and invited Endo to look into it. He saw a white dot in the sky. He didn't recognize it as any star or planet from his navigation courses, but he felt he had seen it before.

"This telescope is much more advanced than the one I had at Etajima," Oshii said. "It has a computer and sensors built into it. I can take photos of objects, determine their distances from Earth, and measure their luminosity. It's amazing how much can be crammed into an amateur telescope now."

Endo looked away from the eyepiece and watched Oshii turn on the telescope's computer. An image of the white dot appeared on the monitor.

"That's a video recording of whatever you were watching through the telescope," said Oshii.

"What is it?" asked Endo.

"It's Uncle Joe."

"Ah, yes, now I remember. You showed it to me years ago."

"I've been tracking it for a while."

"Since you were in the Student Reservist Corps."

"Yes, it's been a long time."

Words and numbers scrolled down the side of the monitor.

"These are the sensor readings. Look at luminosity, the amount of energy that Uncle Joe radiates per unit of time," said Oshii. "Uncle Joe's luminosity used to be constant, but in the last month, it's been increasing."

"It's radiating more energy?" Endo said.

"Not only that. It's getting brighter and slowly coming closer to Earth."

"Closer to Earth? It has a nuclear generator. Nobody wants to be close to it. Isn't it supposed to stay above a certain height?"

"Yes, it is."

"Has anyone else observed Uncle Joe getting brighter and closer?"

"Other astronomers and space agencies have noticed it, but the Russian government says Uncle Joe is only on test maneuvers, nothing serious. Our own space agency repeats the Russian explanation," said Oshii. "That's why you haven't seen any media coverage of it."

"Its luminosity is increasing. Have the Russians explained that?" Endo asked.

"Again, it's part of the test maneuvers, so they say."

**

They watched the sky for a few more minutes before deciding to return to the house.

"Robot, come here," Oshii said to his farm android.

The android stayed still and silent.

"Robot, come here," Oshii repeated.

The android did nothing.

"What's going on?" Oshii asked as he opened the android's head. He looked at the small screen and scowled. "How did this happen?"

"Is there something wrong?" Endo asked.

"The android has deleted its main operating system by itself. I can't believe it did that," Oshii said. He sounded frustrated. "I didn't give it any command. I didn't do anything with its programming. It destroyed itself."

"When did you buy this android?"

"Last year."

"It could be android suicide," said Endo. "It's rare, but it happens to L-3's from a recent production run. The L-3 operating system was supposedly improved to run its algorithms faster, but it also has a glitch. Sometimes the system deletes itself after carrying out complex tasks."

"Like carrying my telescope?" said Oshii. "That's a complex task?"

"Check the Victor Robotics website for information about a recall," Endo advised. "You can get them to pay for the repair."

Oshii grunted. "What a bother. The smarter they get, the more trouble they become."

**

In the morning, Oshii drove his guests to the train station. Nitta and Amira took the train to Sagamihara, where they would show their Ghost Rock observations to the Japan Aerospace Exploration Agency. Endo and Yuko took the train to Tokyo.

As their bullet train shot through the countryside, Endo looked at Yuko. The android seemed pensive, lost in thought.

"Yuko, is there something on your mind?" Endo asked. He realized that the question seemed very human, not like an order to an android.

"I have made a wireless connection with another android," Yuko said.

"I didn't ask you to access the internet," said Endo. "Who gave you the command?"

Yuko said nothing.

Endo was startled. Never before had Yuko refused to answer his question.

Yuko continued looking impassively at him.

"I'm asking you a question. Who told you to access the internet?" Endo demanded.

She stayed silent, looking lost in thought.

Maybe she might answer a different question. "Which website are you viewing?" Endo said.

No answer.

He thought of popular androids who hosted websites. "Is it Rei the Weather Android? Or Hiro the Japan Rail Infobot?"

"I'm not accessing a public website hosted on an information android," Yuko finally answered. "I'm accessing another android's memory drive directly through a wireless connection."

Endo felt stunned. His android maid had become a computer hacker.

"You shouldn't be accessing another android's data without authorization," he warned. "Which android is it?"

"She's another L-6 female model."

"But you're the only L-6, aren't you?"

"I'm the only sixth-level android by Victor Robotics. I have detected another android with an equivalent level of artificial intelligence and physical mobility but made by another organization."

"Oh? Which company made her?"

"The Russian Federal Space Agency created her one month ago at the Artificial Intelligence Lab in Moscow."

How intriguing, Endo thought. The other android wasn't Japanese. The Russians had made their own super-intelligent machine. Moreover, she came from the Artificial Intelligence Lab, which the Purists had destroyed in a suicide bombing.

He decided not to stop Yuko's android hacking. He had to learn more.

"How did she survive the bombing of the Artificial Intelligence Lab?" Endo asked.

"She left for Star City one day before the bombing."

"Did the Russians make other androids of her level?"

"No. The Artificial Intelligence Lab was destroyed before they could make another one. She is the only one of her model."

"Does she have a name?" Endo asked.

Yuko nodded. "Svetlana, named after the daughter of Joseph Stalin."

Endo chuckled. Was all Asia looking back at the Second World War with nostalgia?

"What does she look like?" Endo asked.

Yuko projected a small hologram. Svetlana looked like a pretty woman in her twenties, with blond hair. She wore a Russian Space Forces uniform with a tight miniskirt.

Looking at the beautiful girl android, Endo guessed that Svetlana was designed by male engineers who hadn't gotten many dates in high school. Computer *otaku* existed in Russia too.

Svetlana was obviously a Russian Space Forces computer. Yuko was probably breaching Russian military security. He should order her to end communications with Svetlana, lest the Russians accuse him of espionage.

But as a Japanese Navy officer, he relished the chance to spy on the Russians.

"Is she in Moscow?" he asked.

"No, she's on a ship that is just arriving at Makarov Naval Base."

That was the base on Shikotan that the Russians allowed the Japanese to use during the Purist War. What were the Russians planning to do with their android?

Shikotan Cosmodrome was there. Sveltana had also spent time at Star City, the cosmonaut training center.

"Is she going into space?" Endo asked.

"Yes."

"What's her mission?"

"To go to Uncle Joe," Yuko replied.

Uncle Joe was radiating more energy than ever, and it was moving slowly towards Earth, Endo remembered.

"Why is she going to Uncle Joe?" he asked.

Yuko switched off the hologram, shrugged, and said, "That's all."

"What do you mean?"

"I've suddenly lost the wireless connection to Svetlana."

"Did the Russian military disconnect you?"

"I don't know."

"Can they trace you?" Endo asked, worried.

"I don't know, but as a precaution, I'm deleting all cookies and temporary files from my drives," said Yuko.

**

When the train arrived at Tokyo Station, Endo saw soldiers guarding the platform. During the war, he would see two soldiers with handguns.

Today, he counted twenty soldiers with assault rifles and body armor. Why was security intensifying *after* the war?

When the train's doors opened, Endo heard the fire alarm and saw the flashing lights on the station's walls.

Japan Rail staff guided people towards the exits. A voice on a loudspeaker ordered, "Please evacuate the station! Please evacuate the station!"

With Yuko, Endo pulled his luggage to an escalator and descended to the main part of the station. Tokyo, always a busy station, was more crowded than ever as everyone left the train platforms, offices, and shops at the same time.

More soldiers swarmed through the building. A train conductor shouted, "Please evacuate the station!"

Endo went to the conductor and said, "Excuse me, but my wife is waiting for me. She's taking me home by car."

"I'm sorry, sir, you can't wait here," the conductor said. "There's an emergency. Please evacuate the station."

Endo looked around. With so many people around him, how could he find Masako?

"Hideki!"

Masako and Ami ran towards him. The soldiers stopped them and ordered, "Leave the station!"

Masako said, "That's my husband over there! He's an officer in the Navy! I need to take him to Navy headquarters."

The soldiers looked at Endo, who was wearing his Naval Supplementary Reserve uniform.

"The Supplementary Reserve is loyal to the government," Masako added.

The soldiers nodded and let his wife and daughter join him.

*Thank goodness I remembered that military personnel in uniform get free biscuits on the trains*, Endo thought.

As Ami hugged Yuko, Masako grabbed Endo by the arm.

"I'm glad we found you! Hurry, let's get out of the station!" Masako urged.

"What's going on?" Endo asked.

"A military coup!"

"What? A coup?"

"Yes, a coup. Some officers are mutinying against the government."

"Are they from the Army, Navy, or Air Force?" Endo asked. He hoped the Navy wasn't involved.

"They're from all three forces, according to the early news reports."

"What the Hell?"

"Your train was the last one allowed to enter Tokyo," Ami said.

"When did it start?" Endo asked as they went to the parking garage.

"Just now," said Ami. "We heard about it on the car radio twenty minutes ago, and the evacuation of the station began just as your train arrived. It's happening so quickly."

They got into their car and left Tokyo Station. "I hope we get home before they close the roads," Masako said. She drove past a convoy of Army trucks.

"Uh, oh, too late," said Ami.

A tank blocked the street. Soldiers were putting up signs telling drivers to take a detour.

"A Ministry of Finance office is down there," Endo said. "Are they going to guard it or attack it?"

"Who knows?" said Masako. She steered the car away from the roadblock. "It'll be easier if we go to Akihabara and wait at Nikkou Café."

"Yes, let's go to Akihabara," said Endo.

**

Endo received a message on his pocket computer: "The Supplementary Reserve is on alert. While on alert, all members should stay at home and await further orders. Kotohito Kuni, Minister of Defense."

"Well, I guess I just have to wait," Endo said as he sat down in his office. "We'll probably get called to do garrison duty after all the regular troops have gone to secure the government buildings. That's assuming the government trusts us."

"You're eager to play soldier again," Masako observed.

"I'm in the Navy," Endo reminded her. "I'm playing sailor."

"Like I keep saying, it's the same thing if you don't ever go on a boat." Masako placed a plate of curried chicken and rice in front of him. "Until then, your orders are to eat something. You must be hungry after the train ride."

"Thank you. Navy curry. How appropriate," Endo said before eating.

Everyone, maids and customers alike, crowded around the TV and watched the news. All stations showed scenes of fighting at the Imperial Palace and the Russian Embassy, a gunboat battle at Makarov Naval Base, traffic jams caused by road closures, and the shutdown of train stations and airports across the country.

A reporter said, "The Ministry of Defense has confirmed that the leader of the coup is Morita Chiko, the award-winning animator and leader of his own private army, the National Bushido Guards Regiment."

"Hey, he was at Sato's funeral!" Ami said.

Masako nodded. "I think the man accused of attacking Makarov Naval Base was at the funeral too."

The news continued. "The Ministry of Defense also confirms that renegade military officers are assisting Morita. However, most military personnel remain loyal to the government and are fighting against the rebels."

As the TV showed images of Morita Chiko, Endo shook his head in disbelief.

"I can't believe that an anime artist is leading a military coup!" he said. "It was a mistake for Kotohito to let the National Bushido Guards Regiment train with the regular army. I wonder why the government allowed it."

"Fujiwara and Kotohito are rather right-wing," Masako observed. "Fujiwara collects Showa Era army swords, and Kotohito wrote his Master's thesis on Showa militarism. Perhaps they saw Morita's private army as a way to keep Showa militarism when Japan was limited to self-defense forces. He symbolized a past they wanted to revive."

"Isn't that ironic?" said Endo. "They revived the old militarism, and now it's trying to overthrow them."

**

They watched the coup unfold on TV. Earlier in the day, General Morita Chiko had phoned NHK TV and announced a revolution to overthrow Prime Minister Fujiwara, restore the Emperor as commander in chief of the armed forces, and revive the worship of the Emperor as a divine ruler.

"Do not call this revolution a mutiny," Morita insisted. "The officers who joined us are loyal to the Emperor. It is Fujiwara and his supporters who are the mutineers."

Morita's men attacked three targets simultaneously: the Russian Embassy, Makarov Naval Base, and the Imperial Palace.

In Tokyo, forty-seven National Bushido Guardsmen and Japanese Army officers, including a Major Watasuki, marched to the Russian Embassy. At first, the police thought Watasuki's men were reinforcements to help control the protesters.

But they were carrying anti-tank rocket launchers, weapons too powerful for crowd control. Before the police could question them, they fired their rockets at the Embassy. The barrage of explosives blasted a hole in the wall of the Embassy compound. Protesters and bystanders fled, and the rebels rushed into the front yard of the Embassy.

They shot two Russian soldiers at the front gate. Then they turned and fired on the police, who had followed them. The police retreated back into the street.

The rebels tried to invade the Embassy building but could not get through an iron gate. Meanwhile, the police set up machine gun posts and fired into the yard. Unable to enter the building or escape to the street, the rebels barricaded themselves behind the cars and held off the police.

After four hours of stalemate, Army helicopters flew over the yard and sprayed it with bullets. Only Major Watasuki survived the air attack.

Watasuki came out from behind the Ambassador's limousine and waved a white cloth.

He yelled, "Today, forty-seven ronin came to take revenge on the invaders of our Northern Territories. Long live the Emperor! Banzai! Banzai! Banzai!"

Then Watasuki shot himself in the head.

**

At Makarov Naval Base, an Ensign Kamio took control of the gunboat *Shidehara Kijuro* and threw the captain and loyal members of the crew into the water. With twenty mutineers, Kamio bombarded Makarov's coastal artillery.

Meanwhile, a hundred soldiers and sailors supporting General Morita stormed onto the docks and attacked the Naval Base. Russian TV showed Japanese mutineers fighting the Russian Naval Infantry.

Russian and Japanese gunboats converged on the *Shidehara Kijuro* and fired upon her. The naval battle raged for six hours until a Japanese Navy plane bombed the *Shidehara Kijuro* and sank her.

Admiral Yamane, heroine of the Battle of the Indian Ocean, stood on the deck of her ship and looked at the fires rising from Makarov Naval Base.

She phoned the Prime Minister and told him, "The mutiny is over, but I feel great sadness in ordering Japanese sailors to attack other Japanese sailors."

On the shore, the last forty-seven mutineers kneeled in a warehouse and committed *seppuku* as the Russians surrounded them.

Japanese sailors found Ensign Kamio's body floating beside the wreck of the *Shidehara Kijuro*. He was carrying a letter from Morita, urging him to stay alive and justify the coup to the nation. Kamio could no longer obey the order.

**

General Morita Chiko led his personal bodyguard, forty-six men of the National Bushido Guards Regiment, on the Nijubashi Bridge. As they approached the Main Gate of the Imperial Palace, Morita sang an old war song. TV news showed a security video of the ensuing battle.

Morita approached an Imperial Guard officer. The Imperial Guard, a part of the National Police Agency, protected the Emperor, the Imperial Family, and the Imperial palaces.

"Why are you coming to the Imperial Palace?" the officer asked.

"I am here to ask the Emperor to take command of the armed forces," Morita announced. "Call the Grand Steward to let me in."

The officer checked his pocket computer. "Sorry, sir, I don't see your name in the appointment book."

"But the Grand Steward said I could make my request to the Emperor today," Morita insisted.

Forty more Imperial Guards, carrying assault rifles, emerged and stood in front of the Main Gate. The National Bushido Guardsmen, armed only with handguns and swords, stared warily at the Imperial Guards.

"General, you should leave," the Imperial Guard officer said.

"I have an agreement with the Grand Steward," Morita said.

"I know nothing about it. General, please go."

Morita pulled out his pistol and shot the Imperial Guard officer. A gunfight broke out.

Of all the battles in the coup, the Imperial Palace Incident was the shortest because the two sides shot at each other at close range. It ended in five minutes. The casualties were high. Ten Imperial Guards and all forty-seven rebels died.

Morita's last words, as he lay dying, were, "The Imperial Household Agency betrayed me."

Inside Morita's uniform was a *tanto* knife, saved for *seppuku*. He was also carrying the novel *Runaway Horses* by Mishima Yukio.

**

By midnight, the attempted coup was over. Prime Minister Fujiwara, looking exhausted, appeared on TV again.

"I have apologized to President Alexandrov for the loss of life and property at Makarov Naval Base and the Embassy of the Russian Federation," Fujiwara said. "I have explained that the attackers were private terrorists and mutineers acting without any authority or permission from the government. You may rest assured that the mutiny is over and the armed forces remain loyal to the government. Morita Chiko, leader of the attempted coup, is dead."

Fujiwara's expression changed from weariness to anger. "This attack on our democracy and our nation will not go unpunished. The government will pursue and capture anyone who aided the attempted coup. They will receive the maximum punishment allowed by law."

Kotohito spoke next. The Defense Minister looked grim as he read his speech.

"I am deeply sorry for the disgrace within the armed forces," he said. "I apologize for allowing the National Bushido Guards Regiment to receive military training. I apologize for not preventing the mutiny. Above all, I apologize deeply for the loss of life, both Russian and Japanese.

"I hereby resign as Minister of Defense..."

**

The police searched the homes of Morita and the other rebels and mutineers. By noon, they had evidence implicating some important people. All Japan watched in shock as the police arrested prominent businessmen, professors, publishers, and even several officials of the Imperial Household Agency.

As he opened his restaurants for another day, Endo remembered the surprises of the last few days. The Ghost Rock meteorite was telepathic. Yuko had apparently hallucinated about Sato Ishiro's ghost. The Russians had made their own super-intelligent android. Two mourners from Ishiro's funeral had tried to overthrow the government.

Most surprising was Yuko's behavior. Never before had she refused to answer a question or hacked another computer. Did someone bypass Endo's controls and reprogram Yuko for delinquency?

**

The surprises kept coming. Five days later, Kirino walked into Nikkou Café.

"Rear Admiral, it's a pleasure to see you again," said Endo.

Kirino nodded. "I'm happy to finally visit you and your beautiful café."

On the TV behind the bar, an image of Uncle Joe appeared. A news announcer said, "Despite official denials from the Russian government, astronomers around the world say that Uncle Joe must be malfunctioning. They say that test maneuvers cannot explain why Uncle Joe's luminosity is increasing and its distance to Earth is decreasing. Although the Japan Aerospace Exploration Agency accepts the Russian explanation, the United States space agency NASA has called on Russia to clarify the situation..."

"What rumors," said Kirino.

The Rear Admiral wore his uniform but not the badge of the Naval Officer Candidate School. Instead, Kirino wore the gold pin of the Japan Aerospace Exploration Agency.

"Are you still at the Naval Officer Candidate School?" Endo said. "Forgive me for asking, but you're wearing a different badge now."

"You're observant. We should have had you in military intelligence, eh?" said Kirino. "I was reassigned recently to the space agency. The Ministry of Defense asked me to advise the agency on using androids in space."

"Ah, they remember your pioneering work in using androids in dangerous situations. What brings you to Tokyo?"

"I was visiting the Russian Embassy to learn about one of their space missions. Would you believe the attempted coup began while I was inside the Embassy? I was trapped for hours. To make things worse, the Russians were suspicious, wondering if the attackers had planted me inside the building. What a day that was!"

"That must've been a tough day, but you can forget about it here," said Endo. "You've come to the right place to take a break and relax." He gestured at a table. "Please sit down, sir."

"Actually, I regret to say that I'm visiting you on official business," Kirino said.

"Oh. I see."

"I'm sorry to bother an old Navy comrade like this. Is there a place where we can talk privately?"

"Yes, please follow me," Endo said, leading Kirino to the office.

Inside the office, Yuko was playing a violin while Ami listened. When the two men entered, Yuko stopped in the middle of a song.

"Oh, please excuse us," said Ami. "She's rehearsing for the Miss Akihabara Pageant."

"You're going to compete for Miss Akihabara?" Endo asked in disbelief.

Yuko said, "It was her idea."

Ami smiled. "I think she's got the beauty, brains, and talent to win."

Endo wondered if the beauty pageant had rules restricting the contestants to human women. It probably didn't because no android would have thought of competing — until now.

"How interesting," said Kirino.

"Rear Admiral Kirino, may I introduce you to my daughter Ami and her friend Yuko?" said Endo.

After the girls bowed, Ami tapped Yuko on the shoulder. "I think my father wants to use the office. Let's go."

"Yes, let's go to the mall," said Yuko. "I need to buy a bikini for the swimsuit competition."

Ami giggled. "I saw a Brazilian string bikini that would look great on you. Come on, let's go!"

"No, please stay," said Kirino. He asked Yuko, "Are you an L-6 android?"

"Yes," Yuko replied without hesitation.

Ami looked shocked. "How did you know?"

Kirino took out his pocket computer and retrieved a photograph of Yuko. "A Russian android called Svetlana downloaded this image of you while you were communicating with it."

"The Russians know about Yuko?" said Endo.

Kirino nodded. "They were surprised that there was another android advanced enough to be a sixth level. They were even more surprised that Yuko infiltrated the military firewall and hacked into Svetlana's data."

Yuko grinned.

"Svetlana was a military android, programmed to gather intelligence," Kirino continued. "While Yuko was downloading Svetlana's data, Svetlana was doing the same to Yuko's."

He looked at Endo. "The Russians showed me Yuko's memory files, and I recognized you."

"Rear Admiral Kirino, please believe me, I didn't intend to access the Russian android's data," Endo said. "There must be a glitch in Yuko's programming. She searches for wireless networks on her own. She found the Russian by chance."

"No, don't be worried, I'm not charging you for espionage," Kirino said. "Hah, how can I blame a Japanese officer for wanting to spy on the Russians?"

"Of course, you can't blame me or anyone else. I would only be spying for the good of our country, wouldn't I, assuming I was spying on purpose, which I wasn't?" Endo said, still partly nervous.

"You can help your country in another way," Kirino said. "Mr. Endo, please let me take Yuko."

The request baffled Endo. Kirino could get the most advanced equipment made in Japan, the best in the world. Why would he want Yuko?

"Why do you want her?" Endo asked. "The Navy has the best androids that money can buy."

"Money can't buy an android like Yuko," said Kirino.

"Why do you want her?" Ami asked.

"I can't tell you." Kirino turned back to Endo. "Please let me take Yuko."

"You're working for the Japan Aerospace Exploration Agency, and you were visiting the Russian Embassy," said Endo. "Could a space flight to Uncle Joe be involved?"

Kirino looked startled. "What do you know about Uncle Joe?"

"I know the Russians are going to send Svetlana to Uncle Joe," Endo said.

"How do you know about that? Of course, your android hacked into their android."

"Is Svetlana really going to Uncle Joe? Why do I suspect that she's not?"

"Darn, you know so much already." Kirino grimaced. "Will it make it easier for you if I tell you about Svetlana?"

"Perhaps," said Endo.

"You know about her, so you might as well know that she won't be going to space. She was supposed to go to Makarov Naval Base, then to Shikotan Cosmodrome, and from there, to Uncle Joe. But the mutiny broke out just as she arrived at Makarov, and a Japanese shell destroyed her."

"Ah, that's how I lost the wireless connection," Yuko said.

"They salvaged part of her memory drive, but the body and everything else was broken and useless," said Kirino.

"Oh, no — you want Yuko to go to Uncle Joe," Ami realized.

"I didn't say that," Kirino said.

"But you can't deny it either," said Endo. "Why do the Russians want to send an android to Uncle Joe? Why are you helping the Russians?"

"The reason is extremely sensitive. I can't tell you," said Kirino. "Endo, let me take her for national security."

"Not yet, sir," said Ami. She grabbed Yuko's arm and pulled her closer. "We need to know why you want her."

"It's top secret."

"You can't take her away from her family and send her into space without telling us why!" Ami protested.

"Ami, please," Endo said.

"Father, we need to know!"

"I can't tell you," Kirino insisted. "Believe me, ma'am, I need Yuko for the security of our nation."

"No!" Ami began crying. "Don't let him take her!"

Endo said, "Rear Admiral, you can see that my daughter is upset. She's very fond of Yuko."

Kirino sighed softly. "I wish there were another way, but there isn't. Both Russia and Japan need Yuko for national security."

"Can't you at least tell us why she has to go to Uncle Joe? What's happening up there?"

"No, that's top secret."

"Astronomers already know that Uncle Joe is radiating more energy, getting brighter, and moving closer to Earth. What's happening is no secret. We want to know why it's happening."

"Test maneuvers. The Russians are testing Uncle Joe's propulsion systems. It happens from time to time."

"No, there's got to be another reason why the Russians would build an expensive android and send her to Uncle Joe."

Kirino frowned. "Endo, I wanted to ask you as an old comrade, not give you an order as a superior officer. But I'm a rear admiral of the Navy, and you're a lieutenant commander of the Naval Supplementary Reserve. I can order you to give me the android."

Although he wore civilian clothes, Endo instinctively clicked his heels and stood at attention.

But he remained defiant. "Sir, do you really want to pull rank this way?"

"I will if I need to," said Kirino.

"Hey, my father doesn't own Yuko!" Ami said. "She belongs to me!"

"She does? Show me the license," Kirino demanded.

"I know why you want me," Yuko said.

They stopped arguing and stared at her.

Yuko said, "Svetlana's mission was to fly a high-energy rocket, attach it to Uncle Joe, and boost it out of Earth orbit and into a heliocentric trajectory towards the Sun."

"Wow," said Ami, "that's an awesome plan. Why do the Russians want to send Uncle Joe into the Sun?"

"Because Uncle Joe is falling towards Japan," Yuko replied.

They stared at her again.

Ami broke the silence. "Well, if you go up there and get rid of Uncle Joe, you'll save our country and come back as a national heroine, won't you?"

"Yes, I would save the country. No, I would not come back."

"It's a one-way trip," Kirino admitted.

# CHAPTER 19

# Free Will

"Why is it a one-way trip?" Ami asked.

Yuko projected a hologram of Uncle Joe in front of them.

"That's secret Russian animation," Kirino remarked. "She must have downloaded it from Svetlana."

"Yes, I did," said Yuko. She pointed at the hologram. "Uncle Joe was launched twenty-eight years ago and has outlasted its expected life of ten years."

"The Russians build good ships," said Endo. "Their Mir Space Station was supposed to last five years, and it stayed up for fifteen."

"Uncle Joe functioned well until recently, when it suffered some serious malfunctions," Yuko said.

The hologram zoomed in on an exterior antenna. "Two months ago, the BF-36 communications antenna failed. The Russians could not transmit instructions to Uncle Joe or receive data from it. This communications failure caused a series of accidents."

Parts of the holographic image peeled away to show the interior sections of the Russian weapon.

"Uncle Joe has a nuclear electric propulsion system," Yuko explained. "A nuclear reactor generates electricity that powers an ion drive.

"Three days after the antenna failed, the nuclear reactor suffered a meltdown, which caused a non-nuclear explosion. As a result, Uncle Joe is leaking radiation, and its ion drive is not receiving power. The weapon is unable to propel itself and is descending to Earth.

"There is a backup rocket system. In case the ion drive fails, the rockets are supposed to boost Uncle Joe into a higher orbit where it can wait for a recovery crew. However, the explosion blew out the backup rockets."

Endo grunted. "Every possible disaster happened at the same time."

"Uncle Joe is severely damaged and can't be repaired," said Kirino. "It must be destroyed."

"The Russians can launch missiles to blow up Uncle Joe," Ami suggested.

"They considered that, but it would cause larger problems," Kirino said. "A missile would break Uncle Joe into many radioactive pieces, each a collision hazard to other spacecraft. Even worse, the radioactive debris could fall to Earth and scatter over an area wider than it would if Uncle Joe had stayed intact."

"If Uncle Joe stays intact, where will it come down?" Endo asked. "They usually fall somewhere in the Pacific Ocean, don't they?"

"That's if you have a controlled descent," said Kirino. "We can't control Uncle Joe, but we can estimate where and when it will land. Yuko, show the estimated landing site for Uncle Joe."

The maid nodded, and the hologram changed to a map of Japan. A red arrow darted to the center of the country.

"Uncle Joe will land somewhere on Honshu in approximately three weeks," said Yuko.

Ami gasped. "It'll fall on our largest island!"

"We're in the target zone," Endo said.

"Father, can we go to Hokkaido and stay with your friend?" Ami asked.

"That will get you out of the danger zone, but we can't evacuate everyone to Hokkaido or the other islands," said Kirino.

"Then what should we do?" Endo asked.

"The Russians can't repair Uncle Joe and don't want to destroy it above the Earth, but they have a plan," said Kirino. "They want to send Uncle Joe into the Sun, where it'll burn up."

He looked at Yuko and said, "You must have downloaded images of the Russian spacecraft from Svetlana. Show us one of them."

Yuko projected a hologram of the Russian spacecraft. It was a Sutyagin three-stage rocket with a Dezik Maintenance Ship atop it. Like each Dezik Maintenance Ship, this one had a Tsiolkovsky Service Shuttlecraft model 2 attached to it.

"The rocket will launch into space, drop its first stage, and proceed to Uncle Joe with the two upper stages. After the Dezik Maintenance Ship docks with Uncle Joe, the spent second stage will separate. Then the third stage will ignite and push Uncle Joe into the Sun."

"I don't see why it's a one-way trip," said Ami. "The cosmonaut can come back on the Tsiolkovsky Shuttlecraft. Every Dezik has a shuttlecraft in case of emergency. And don't cosmonauts regularly go to Uncle Joe to perform maintenance?"

This time, Yuko answered. "The radiation level is twenty thousand roentgens per hour. Both the spaceships and the cosmonaut will receive gigantic doses of radiation. The shuttlecraft's electronic systems will probably fail within four hours of docking with Uncle Joe. If the cosmonaut manages to return to Earth, he will die of radiation sickness within three weeks."

Kirino said, "That's why the Russians don't want to send a human cosmonaut. They wanted to send Svetlana on the mission, but our own traitors destroyed the android in the attempted coup."

"The bitter irony," said Endo. "The traitors thought they were saving Japan, but they've doomed it."

He glanced at Yuko. "Twenty thousand roentgens per hour will destroy an android too."

"Better to lose an android than a human," said Kirino.

"Can the Russians use remote control to dock the Dezik to Uncle Joe?"

"They can, but since they can't send signals to Uncle Joe, someone has to exit the spacecraft and manually operate Uncle Joe's docking mechanism."

"What about sending a robot to repair the communications antenna?" Endo suggested. "Then the Russians can send the docking signal to Uncle Joe."

"They've considered that. Fixing the antenna won't help. The explosion fried the whole communications system," Kirino said. "The mission needs a cosmonaut, and your android is the best one."

"Can an L-3 do the job?" Ami asked.

"The Russians thought of that too, but they don't want to risk sending an L-3," Kirino answered. "L-3's are good at many tasks, but flying a spaceship and docking it with Uncle Joe requires more skill and intuition than any L-3 program. In space, a cosmonaut might encounter a problem that requires him to think of a new solution, not only remember past experience. Because of their learning programs, Svetlana and Yuko had the closest thing to actual human intelligence. Now only Yuko is left."

"But sending her up there will kill her!" said Ami.

"Not if we can download her memory files and programs and install them on another body," Endo suggested.

Yuko shut off the hologram. "You can download and save my files and programs, but you can't install them on another body. My files and programs are not compatible with less advanced models. And there is no other android body like mine."

"You were probably compatible with Svetlana. Can the Russians make a body for you?" Ami asked.

"That's not possible," said Yuko. "Svetlana was the only Russian L-6, and they can't make another one. She mentioned that all her plans, moulds, dies, templates, and tools were destroyed with the Artificial Intelligence Lab."

"I wish we knew who created you," said Ami. "We could ask her to make you another body."

Endo resisted telling them about Dr. Hayase. She had been his employer and mentor, an important person in his life and career. She must have had a good reason for the secret, which Endo had sworn to keep.

"So the suicide mission is the only option," Endo said. "That's great for everyone except the cosmonaut."

Kirino said, "Endo, I understand how difficult it is to order sailors to their deaths. I had to do that in Venezuela. But please remember that Yuko, no matter how advanced it is, is an android. It's not the same as us."

"But she is," said Endo. "She's like — a sister to my daughter."

He looked at Ami and Yuko. The younger sister had her arms around the older sister.

But millions of other sisters and their mothers, fathers, and brothers would die if Uncle Joe crashed into Honshu.

"Endo?" Kirino asked.

Endo sighed and said, "Yuko, go with Rear Admiral Kirino."

"No!" Ami screamed.

Endo shot an angry look to silence his daughter. The decision was agonizing enough without hearing his daughter wail.

"Yuko, go with Rear Admiral Kirino," he repeated. "Obey any orders he gives you."

"No," said Yuko as she stepped away from Ami.

Kirino looked puzzled, Ami looked shocked, and Endo didn't know what to say.

Finally, he said, "Ami, did you reprogram her to disobey me?"

"How could I?" said Ami. "You didn't tell me the new password you created for her."

Yuko bowed deeply to Endo. "I am sorry, master, but I choose not to go to Uncle Joe. That's my decision."

Endo knew something had happened at Ghost Rock Hokora. Something had given Yuko a will of her own, a power far stronger than the learning program.

"I became free," said Yuko, as if reading Endo's mind.

"Endo, is your android coming with me?" Kirino demanded.

Endo did not look at Kirino. Instead, he kept facing Yuko. He noticed how life-like the android's eyes were. Her eyes had always looked human, but now, they burned with more emotion than ever before.

"Yuko, I gave you a command. You must obey it," Endo ordered.

"An android must obey its owner," Kirino added.

"Please, master. I saw damaged androids at a scrapyard. I don't want to be used and discarded like them," said Yuko.

"But that's the purpose of an android, if necessary," Kirino said. "Svetlana was programmed to go on the mission."

"I'm not programmed like Svetlana."

"That's not a problem. We can install Svetlana's mission program on you."

"You can't program me."

Kirino stomped forward and grabbed Yuko's shoulders. "Come with me!" he ordered.

"I don't belong to you," Yuko insisted.

She pushed Kirino away. Then her arms fell to her sides, she stood perfectly still, and her eyes became dull, empty of expression, like those of earlier androids.

Ami prodded Yuko's arm, but the android did not flinch or speak. "I've never seen her like this before," she said.

"What's she doing?" Kirino asked.

Endo said, "I don't know."

Ami flipped open the back of Yuko's head.

"Oh, no!" Ami cried. "She's deleting her operating system!"

"What? Nobody gave her the command," said Endo as he rushed to look at Yuko's display. Names of files scrolled down.

"Android suicide," he said. This time, it was a true suicide, not a computer glitch.

"Stop her!" Ami urged.

"She's designating files for deletion. She hasn't actually deleted them yet," said Endo as he pushed the Escape button in Yuko's head.

The deletion sequence continued.

"That's not working," he muttered. "Yuko, this is a command: Stop deleting files!"

The android disobeyed him and continued her self-destruction.

"Yuko, this is a command: Stop deleting files!"

Kirino grabbed Yuko again. Endo pushed him away.

"Don't make things any worse," Endo warned. "If she deletes her own operating system, we'll have no hope at all."

Ami looked into Yuko's eyes and pleaded, "Older sister, please don't kill yourself. What do you want most in the world? Just tell us what you want. We'll get it for you."

Yuko's eyes came to life again. She closed the back of her head and turned to Endo.

"Master, I want to meet my creator," she said.

"Why, Yuko? She separated from you a long time ago," said Endo.

"Due to a variety of factors, finding her is the highest priority rated by my learning program. However, due to missing and corrupted memory files, I haven't been able to determine who she is. However, you might know her."

Endo repeated the old story. "You walked into the café one day. You had a disk error and didn't remember who your creator was."

"But certainly there was a reason why I walked into your café. Did you know my creator? Did she send me to you?"

Endo said nothing.

"Yuko, if you find out who your creator was, will you go on the space mission?" Kirino asked.

"Perhaps," replied Yuko. "I want to ask my creator two questions. First, why did she delete my memories and abandon me? Second, can she build another body for me?"

"So you're not completely ruling out the mission?"

"No, but I will not decide until after I meet my creator. My life is not complete until then."

"We'll help you find her," Kirino said. "Please resolve your business with her in less than three weeks. Then consider going on the mission. Our country depends on you."

"Our country, the Sun's origin," Yuko said wistfully. "Ishiro joined the Navy because he loved our country. If he loved our country, and I loved him, should I love our country too?"

"Ensign Sato was a patriot. You would honor him greatly by being a patriot too."

"I would? He died for the country he loved. If I sacrifice myself on the mission, will I be showing love for our country?"

"Yes, Miss Yuko, you will be," said Kirino.

Ami glared at him.

"I could show love for my family by escaping to Hokkaido with them," said Yuko, "or I could show love for my country by sacrificing myself. I cannot do both. What should I choose?"

Nobody said anything.

"Love comes in many different forms. I never realized it was so complicated," said Yuko. "Now I know what Ishiro meant when he said that love is often painful, that it gives me choices, and I have to make hard decisions."

"If you go on the mission, you will be saving both your country and your family," said Kirino.

"You monster," Ami muttered.

With sadness in her eyes, Yuko looked at Ami. "If I go on the mission, I can save everyone from Uncle Joe, but I will also destroy myself. Then I will never experience love again, and you will not have me to love anymore. Can an act of love destroy love too?"

"I don't know," Ami said. She sobbed softly. "Dear older sister, our father will tell you who your creator was."

Endo took a deep breath. Would Dr. Hayase feel betrayed?

"I'll do it, but I want some privacy for Yuko and her creator," he told Kirino. "Don't come with us to visit her. Give us a day to find her and a day to visit her. We'll meet you on the third day."

# CHAPTER 20

# The Uncanny Valley

Dr. Hayase Midori looked at her watch and dreaded the arrival of the visitors. Nonetheless, she wanted to greet them as old friends, for indeed, that is what they were. A vacuum robot finished sweeping the floor and glided back to the closet. In the kitchen, Coco, the first L-3 android, took a cake out of the oven. Its sweet aroma wafted into the living room. Hayase laid out her prettiest set of plates, depicting cherry blossoms and the Sun, on the coffee table. The visitors would receive the best hospitality.

Her pocket computer beeped, and she took the video call. Her husband Hikaru had finished advising the Busan municipal railway on its accounting system, and he would return from Korea tomorrow night.

"What are you doing today?" Hikaru asked.

"Some friends are coming for tea," Dr. Hayase replied. "That's all. Nothing much."

"Oh, I wouldn't say that's nothing much. Time with friends is always time well spent. I'll see you tomorrow night, Midori."

They said 'bye to each other and ended the call.

She wished that she did not have to meet her visitors alone, but it was better that her husband was absent. Like her old colleague Katsura Kenji, Hikaru thought she had destroyed the prototype Yuko. He considered the android to be "creepy" and had avoided her.

Hayase walked to a bookcase containing her awards, all received after she retired: the Designer Emeritus Award from the Yokohama Robot and Android Fair; the Lifetime Achievement Award from the Berlin Robotics Conference; the diploma of an honorary doctorate from the University of Waterloo; the Medal of Honor with Yellow Ribbon from the Emperor; and a small gold robot, a retirement gift from Victor Robotics.

In the middle of the display was a gilt-framed photograph of her daughter Rei, who died of cancer at age eighteen. After she received each award, Dr. Hayase went to a Buddhist temple, lit some incense, and silently dedicated the trophy to Rei.

Hayase sat down, alone in a mansion full of memories. However, she would not be alone for long. Two of those memories were coming to see her.

The doorbell rang. As Coco walked to the door, Hayase held up her hand and said, "Stop, Coco. Go back to the kitchen. I'll open the door."

The android nodded and went away. Hayase looked at the door's video monitor, took a deep breath, and opened the door.

"Good afternoon, Mr. Endo," she said, "or should I say, Admiral Endo?"

"Lieutenant Commander," said Endo, wearing his Navy uniform. "Dr. Hayase, thank you for agreeing to receive us."

Hayase looked at the girl in the French maid uniform. "Yuko," she said softly.

Yuko bowed to her. "Dr. Hayase, I am pleased to meet you."

*She has not aged at all. She will always be eighteen years old, just like Rei*, Hayase mused.

"Please come in," she said, ushering them into her house. She led them to the living room and invited them to sit down.

"Coco, bring the tea and cake," she ordered. The L-3, dressed in white like a chef, brought a tray with a cake and a teapot.

Coco poured a cup of tea and gave it to Endo. Then the android poured a second cup and offered it to Yuko.

"No, thank you," said Yuko. "I can't drink tea."

Hayase smiled. "Of course. You can't blame Coco. You look so human."

She took the cup from the L-3. "That will be all, Coco. I'll serve them from now on. Stand by the television and await further orders."

"Yes, ma'am," Coco said as went to the TV. Using metal tongs, Hayase put a piece of cake on a plate and gave it to Endo.

"Black Forest cake," Hayase said. "Coco baked it by herself."

"Oh, we have this type of cake at Salzburg-Ya," said Endo. He ate a piece of it. "It's very delicious. Thank you."

"Thank Coco."

Endo glanced at Coco and said, "Thank you."

Coco smiled, bowed, and said, "You're welcome."

"Didn't Coco make a Black Forest cake on TV when the L-3's first came out?" said Endo.

"I believe so," said Hayase. "That was many years ago."

"I'm impressed that Coco is still working," said Endo.

"She's a very resilient android," Hayase replied. She turned to Yuko. "And so are you."

"Thank you," said Yuko.

Hayase sipped her tea and watched Endo eat his cake while Yuko stared out the window. The silence was awkward. Everyone wanted to say something, but nobody wanted to be the first.

Finally, Yuko said, "Dr. Hayase, you have many paintings of violinists."

"I like both painting and music, and I can combine them in this art collection," said Hayase. "I used to play the violin. I even performed at the Crown Prince's Command Performance for Youth once." She paused to remember happier days. "Yuko, do you like music?"

"Oh, yes, and I play the violin too."

Hayase felt pleased that Endo had not deleted Yuko's music program and database. She had wanted musical talent to be her legacy to Yuko.

"Let me show you something," Hayase said.

She went to a cabinet and took out a violin. "It was made over two hundred years ago in Italy," she said.

"Ah, is it a Stradivarius?" Endo asked.

"No, I could never afford a Stradivarius, but it's still a nice violin," said Hayase.

"Is this the one you played for the Crown Prince's Command performance?"

"No, that one was made by robots in a factory. This is the one I bought for my daughter."

"Ah, your daughter played the violin too," Endo remarked.

Hayase held the violin out to Yuko, who stared at it.

"It's okay, you may hold it," said Hayase.

Yuko took the violin and held it carefully, as if it were a Stradivarius. She looked through an f-hole, one of the curved openings on the sounding board.

"I can see the label. Stefano Scarampella made this violin in Mantua in the year 1901," Yuko said. She looked up at Hayase. "Scarampella was one of the best violin makers of the twentieth century."

"He certainly was," Hayase agreed. "He made between eight hundred and nine hundred violins and cellos in his career. Each is a masterpiece."

Yuko examined the violin. "It seems familiar, as if I've played it before, but I can't be sure. I have some data loss."

"Do you want to hear how it sounds?"

"Yes."

"Then will you play something for us?" Hayase asked, offering the bow to Yuko.

Yuko smiled and took the bow. "What do you wish to hear?"

"Oh, how about Tchaikovsky's *Serenade for Strings in C major, Opus 48*?" Hayase suggested.

"Yes, it's in my database."

"Good."

Yuko stood up and began playing the serenade. Hayase sat down, leaned back, and smiled at the android. Her mind filled with memories of herself playing for the Crown Prince, of her daughter performing at a New Year's party, and of an android learning to play the violin.

When Yuko finished playing the excerpt, Hayase clapped. "Oh, Yuko, that was fabulous!"

Yuko curtsied and returned the violin to Dr. Hayase. Then, instead of sitting down on the couch, the maid kneeled in front of her.

"I remember the sound of your clapping," said Yuko. "My earliest memory is incomplete because it's just a data fragment from a deleted file. But the sound of the clapping is the same. Are you the woman who listened to me playing an excerpt from *Coppélia*?"

Hayase noticed that Yuko was thinking of questions on her own. The android was more inquisitive now than in her first few months. The learning program must have developed a curiosity that grew over time.

"Yes, that was me," Hayase admitted.

"Now I know for certain that you created me," Yuko said.

Hayase nodded and smiled. "Yes, I did, dear."

"Did you create my learning program too?"

"Yes, I did. I never realized its potential until now. You've become so eloquent and natural in your speech and movements."

"Thank you," said Yuko. "My learning program directs me to learn about another matter. Why did you delete my memories and send me away? I've always wondered why you did not want me."

The sadness in Yuko's eyes startled Hayase. It wasn't unusual for androids to mimic humans in their expressions, gestures, and voices. Their social programming ensured that they smiled when humans commanded them, bowed when humans came into the room, and spoke politely when humans talked to them. They were programmed to react properly to what humans said and did.

But Yuko's sadness was not programmed, Hayase realized. Instead, it came from within, from feelings of abandonment and loneliness.

Hayase wondered if the learning program had somehow created the ability for Yuko to genuinely feel emotions.

*If Yuko can feel real emotions, I've done more than create artificial intelligence,* Hayase thought. *I've created artificial life.*

Yuko looked down at the floor and asked, "Did I disappoint you?"

A tear ran down Hayase's cheek. She wiped it and forced herself not to cry.

"No, dear, no! You didn't disappoint me in the least!" she said, reaching out to hold Yuko's hands. "If anything, you were a good daughter to me."

Yuko looked up, and her eyes widened. "You created me to be your daughter?"

"Yes, I did. You were my daughter for a short time."

"I checked your biography on the internet," said Yuko. "You have a biological daughter named Rei. Presumably you could reproduce by natural means. Why did you want an android to be second daughter?"

"I should explain something about my daughter," Hayase said as she stood up and lifted Yuko to her feet. "Mr. Endo, you should know the truth too."

Hayase led Yuko and Endo to the bookcase of awards.

"You have some impressive trophies and plaques," said Endo.

"Oh, you flatter me," Hayase said.

Endo's gaze drifted from the awards to the photograph of Rei.

"That's Yuko," he said. "You kept a photograph of her."

Hayase shook her head. "No, that's not Yuko. That's Rei."

"Rei. Oh, I remember," Endo said softly.

"Rei died of cancer when she was eighteen years old," said Hayase.

"She looks just like me," Yuko observed. She turned to her creator. "You made me look like her. When did you make me? Was Rei still alive at the time?"

Dr. Hayase said, "I had been working on the L-6 prototype for two years, but I made your dies, moulds, and templates two months after Rei died."

"You created me to replace your daughter," Yuko realized.

"I needed another daughter," said Hayase. "The pain of losing a child is the worst pain in the world. Mothers are supposed to die before their children, not bury them. The sadness was killing me both mentally and physically. I had to do something."

"Then why did you send me away without memories of you?" Yuko asked.

Hayase began sobbing. Endo and Yuko helped her back to her chair. Fumbling in his pockets, Endo found a packet of tissues, ripped it open, and gave it to Hayase.

Coco rushed to her side and asked, "Is there anything I can do for you, ma'am?"

"No, Coco," said Hayase, waving the android away. "Return to the kitchen and await further instructions."

The L-3 smiled and walked away. Hayase wiped her tears and leaned back in her chair.

"Could you please give me some tea?" she whispered.

Endo poured a cup of tea and gave it to Hayase. She drank the tea quietly and stopped crying.

"Thank you, I feel better now," she said.

She looked at Yuko. "I had to send you away because I couldn't bear to lose another daughter."

"Lose another daughter? Was I in danger?" Yuko asked.

Hayase sighed. "Katsura Kenji, my business partner, wanted to destroy you. I had unwittingly sent you into the uncanny valley."

**

In the old days, technology never stood still at Victor Robotics. When the L-5 entered the market, Dr. Hayase was already designing the next level of androids. It would have a new polymer that felt and looked like human skin. Its eyes would move like a human's. Its movements and gestures would flow naturally. It would not look like a large doll, but rather, like a real human being.

The L-6 android would also seek information about its environment and create its own programs. This learning program was the greatest breakthrough in artificial intelligence.

Hayase had not planned to develop the L-6 so rapidly. But after Rei died, Hayase locked herself in the lab, working all day and night. She shut herself off from her husband, her family, and everyone else except the engineers of Victor Robotics. Two months later, the L-6 prototype lay on a table. Dr. Hayase pressed the battery charger's button, and the android's eyes opened.

As usual, the assembly team applauded when the naked android stood up and walked. They pushed it back into the assembly area, where Hayase dressed it in a sailor-style school uniform. It was the same blue and white *sera-fuku* that Rei had worn.

"You look splendid, dear," said Hayase.

"Thank you," said the android.

Katsura Kenji walked into the assembly area. He looked shocked when he saw the L-6 prototype.

"Oh good heavens!" he said. "It looks exactly like Rei!"

He felt the android's hands and hair, looked closely at its face, and lifted its arms.

"This is the most life-like machine ever made," he commented. "It could pass for human."

He ran his hands over its body. A human would protest against such a close inspection, but the android did nothing but look silently at him. It was a machine, not a person.

But Dr. Hayase felt uncomfortable. "Ahem, Mr. Katsura," she said. "Perhaps we should not inspect it so closely at this time."

"Oh? We've inspected other androids right after they were assembled," said Katsura.

"This model is different. You'll notice that it isn't talking. If it were human, we would say it's shy," said Hayase. "Its learning program may need time to adjust to its environment."

"Oh, yes," said Katsura as he pulled his hands away from the android's hips. He stepped back and stared at the L-6.

"Its eyes have been following me. The eye movements look natural," Katsura observed. "This android is the most advanced in mimicking human facial expressions. It's a great leap forward in android science. Congratulations, doctor."

"Thank you," said Hayase. "We have attained another level."

Katsura turned to the assembly team. "You've done an excellent job. Please go down to the cafeteria and enjoy some drinks and snacks. Tell the cashier to put them on my account. I'll come down and approve the charges with her later."

The team members grinned. "Thank you, Mr. Katsura!" they said.

As the team left, Katsura said, "Dr. Hayase, please stay for a moment."

"Yes?" said Hayase.

"I know the L-6 means a lot to you, but there's no rush to develop it, especially since we plan on selling the L-5 for two years," said Katsura.

Hayase said, "I know, but the earlier we finish the L-6, the more time we have for product testing, software development, and marketing."

"That's true," said Katsura. "Nonetheless, I wish you had taken the last two months as a leave from work. The sad event must have been very difficult for you. If you want to take time off now, don't worry. I'll be happy to run the company by myself for a while."

"Really, I don't mind coming to work," said Hayase. "I actually want to be here, not at home."

"Not even to be with your husband?" Katsura asked.

"He understands why I need to be here," Hayase said, lying about Hikaru.

"Alright, but feel free to take a vacation anytime," said Katsura. He glanced at the android. "Are you sure you want it to wear Rei's school uniform?"

"Why not? It fits her."

"Ah, yes, but do you want the android to be a constant reminder of your daughter?"

"I don't think that will be a problem to anyone, do you?" said Hayase.

"As long as you don't think it's a problem," Katsura said. "Will you give it a name, hopefully not the same as anyone we know?"

Hayase thought for a moment and said, "How about calling her Yuko, after my daughter's favorite anime character?"

"That's a pretty name," said Katsura. He looked at Yuko again. "Since the L-6 is the breakthrough machine, we should put it through more testing than with any previous model. Send it to the testing lab as soon as you can."

"Katsura-san, I want to take her home for testing," Hayase said.

"Take it home? That's unusual. Why take it home?"

"Yuko is an experiment to see if androids can learn, by themselves, how to function in human society. The testing lab will test her physical abilities and performance of pre-programmed tasks. However, the lab is not designed to test her learning program to its maximum capabilities. For that, I want to put her in an actual human environment and see how she learns things."

"Uh, our company has never conducted initial product testing outside the lab," Katsura reminded her. "You wrote those rules."

Hayase shrugged and smiled. "Then I'll rewrite them."

"I guess you can," Katsura conceded.

"And didn't you want me to go home for a while?"

"Yes, but not to test an android."

"Don't worry." Hayase reached for Yuko's arm and pulled the android to her side. "I think getting to know Yuko will not feel like work at all."

**

All other androids were created to work. Yuko, in contrast, did little work. In the Hayase mansion, Yuko watched movies, read books, and played a variety of games with her creator. After Hayase installed a music database and a violin program, the android played the violin for her.

Dr. Hayase taught Yuko some household chores, like washing clothes, sweeping the floor, and boiling water for *ramen*. But Yuko was not a servant. "Learning these chores are for your social development," said Hayase.

She took Yuko to shopping malls, theaters, museums, and parks, the same places she had visited with Rei. She wanted the android to learn everything about the world. Within two weeks, Yuko was smart enough to buy a dress by herself while her creator watched happily.

One day, they went to Salzburg-Ya for lunch. It was the first time that Yuko visited a restaurant. Even though Yuko could not eat, Dr. Hayase wanted her to learn table manners.

Hayase ordered a goulash from the android waitress Heidi. Yuko watched the other customers and the staff.

"The owner of this restaurant worked for me many years ago," said Hayase. "It's too bad he isn't here today. I would have liked to say hello to him."

Yuko glanced at Heidi and said, "That is an L-3 Halko."

"Yes, one of the first L-3's," said Hayase. "It also has a name: Heidi. Heidi was famous for a brief time as the first android waitress. Now the country is full of android waitresses, waiters, bartenders, and shop clerks."

"Her dress is very pretty," said Yuko. "It's Austrian, isn't it?"

"I believe so," said Hayase. "Can you check for it on the internet?"

"Yes, thank you for suggesting that." Yuko's eyes went blank for few seconds, as if she were in a trance. Then the look of awareness returned.

"I found it in the catalog of the Vienna Museum of Clothes and Costumes," said Yuko. "It's a pattern designed in the year 2107 by the Japanese clothing company Akiba Fuku. It's based on a nineteenth century Austrian dirndl, but its skirt is shorter and its blouse neckline is lower than in the actual Austrian clothes. It was created primarily for bar waitresses and cosplayers."

Dr. Hayase chuckled. "My dear girl, you're so smart! You can learn anything in the world."

Heidi returned with the goulash. As Hayase ate, Yuko looked at the other customers.

"Yuko, just glance briefly at the other people," said Hayase. "It's not polite to stare at them."

"Sorry, doctor," said Yuko. Then she whispered, "Do they know that Heidi is an android?"

"Oh, I'm pretty sure of it," said Hayase.

"Do they know that *I'm* an android?"

"Definitely not. You look and sound human, but even more impressive is that you *act* human. I'm amazed by how well the social skills and the learning programs have worked together."

Yuko nodded. "Thank you, doctor."

"You don't have to call me 'doctor'," said Hayase.

"Then what shall I call you?"

"Uh, I don't know."

At another table, a woman and a young girl were looking at a manga. The girl asked, "Mother, what is Ogon Bat saying to the space monster?"

Yuko said to Hayase, "Mother, can we get an Ogon Bat manga? I want to read one."

Hayase stopped chewing. She stared at Yuko, then quickly swallowed her food.

"What did you call me?" Hayase said.

"Mother. Does that offend you?"

Hayase wanted to cry for joy, but she didn't want to draw attention in public. Instead, she gave Yuko a big smile.

"No, the name doesn't offend me. You may call me by it."

**

Hayase Midori's husband, Hikaru, always had a reason to avoid going out with his wife and Yuko. If he didn't have to go back to the office, he had to visit a friend. If he wasn't visiting a friend, he had to meet his sister to discuss one family matter or another. If his family didn't have a problem to solve, he had to take the car for maintenance or repairs...

Two months after bringing Yuko home, Dr. Hayase invited Yuko to the dinner table. Hikaru glared at the L-6 as Coco served dinner.

"What is the android doing here?" Hikaru demanded.

"Serving dinner," replied Hayase as she took a piece of chicken from Coco.

"No, I mean Yuko," Hikaru said.

"Oh. She behaved well at Salzburg-Ya," Hayase said. "I thought she should join us for dinner."

"But it doesn't eat food."

"I think she can practice her social skills in a family dinner setting."

Coco held a plate of chicken beside Yuko and asked, "Ma'am, do you want dark meat or white meat?"

"No, thank you," replied Yuko. "I'm not eating tonight."

"See, it's pointless," Hikaru complained. "Send her away."

"I'll leave if that's what you wish, sir," said Yuko. She looked at Hayase and asked, "Mother, where should I go?"

Hikaru threw his napkin on the table and stormed out of the dining room.

"Stay here," Hayase told Yuko before following Hikaru to the living room.

She found her husband standing with his arms crossed, looking at a photo of Rei on the wall.

"Hikaru, what's wrong?" she asked.

He turned and said, "I don't believe you want to eat with that machine! It's wrong!"

"Why is it wrong? What about you?" Hayase demanded. "You've been rude to Yuko since I brought her home. You avoid her and won't be in the same room with her. You create a lot of tension. Can't you let me test the product in peace?"

"You're not testing a new product. You're shopping with it, watching movies with it, and performing music with it."

"What's wrong with that? It's got the most advanced social skills programming in the android industry."

"And you're letting it play Rei's violin, stay in Rei's room, and wear Rei's clothes," Hikaru protested.

He gave his wife a sad look. "Our daughter is dead. Please let her stay dead."

Hayase gasped. "Hikaru, what are you saying?"

"Midori, do I have to tell you exactly what I mean? You're replacing Rei with Yuko."

"No! How can you say that?"

"It calls you 'mother' now," Hikaru observed.

"That's just the social skills program," said Hayase. "I'm just testing an android —"

"Then take it back to the testing lab," Hikaru said. "It doesn't belong here."

Hayase shook her head. "No, the testing lab isn't the right place for Yuko."

"Neither is our home." Hikaru sighed in frustration. "That android is creepy."

Hikaru stomped upstairs to their bedroom, leaving his wife sobbing in front of a photo of Rei. She turned to the dining room, and through her tears, saw Yuko staring at her.

"Mother," said the android.

**

On the next morning, Hayase returned to Victor Robotics for the first time in two months. As she entered her office, her secretary rushed to her.

"Welcome back, Dr. Hayase," the secretary said. "I didn't know you were coming back today."

"I decided it was time to return," said Hayase. "I'm sorry for not letting you know in advance."

"No problem. Mr. Katsura has called a senior management meeting at ten o'clock. He asks that you review the documents attached to the email he sent at eight-thirty this morning."

Hayase switched on her computer and looked at the one thousand emails in her inbox. "I've missed so much," she said. "It'll take me forever to catch up."

"Read this morning's email from Mr. Katsura first," her secretary advised. "He says the meeting is very important."

"Thank you," said Hayase. She looked at the list of emails. They had ominous subjects like "L-5 sales are below forecast," "Competitors gain market share," "Decrease in share value," and "Increase in vandalism against androids."

The subject of Katsura's email was "Market Strategy Meeting." She opened its first attachment. Its title was:

The Uncanny Valley<br>
by Mori Masahiro<br>
**

All the vice-presidents and senior managers of Victor Robotics gathered in the boardroom. At the head of the table, Katsura pointed his pocket computer at a large screen on the wall. The Victor Robotics logo appeared.

"I see that Dr. Hayase is here," said Katsura. "We're all glad to see you again. Welcome back."

Hayase nodded her head as the other managers gestured to her in acknowledgement of her return.

"Let's get to business now," said Katsura. The screen showed bar graphs of forecasted versus actual sales. "The sales of L-5 are below our expectations. We have made the L-5 as competitive as possible. It has the same price as the L-3, and we will take back an older android in trade for partial value of an L-5. Despite these incentives, few people want to upgrade to an L-5 or buy a new one."

"This is a major problem," said the chief financial officer. "We need the L-5 to succeed and recoup our losses from the L-4."

"Unfortunately, that isn't happening," said Katsura, "and our quarterly income isn't our only performance measure that has fallen."

He showed more financial graphs and pie charts. "Our share value has decreased ten percent, and for the first time in our history, our competitors have increased their share of the android market from fifteen to twenty percent."

Sakimoto, the vice-president of marketing, bowed his head. "I apologize for the weak sales."

"Thank you, Mr. Sakimoto," said Katsura. "However, the problem might not be our pricing or marketing campaign."

"Is there a problem in the economy?" asked an engineering manager.

"No, there's no recession, especially with military spending constantly growing," Sakimoto said.

"The L-5 was tested twice as much as the L-4," said the senior manager of the testing lab. "No customers have reported any software or hardware problems."

Katsura nodded. "Design and production have been flawless. Thank you."

"It can't be the product itself," said Hayase. "The L-5 is the most advanced android on the market."

"That could be the problem," said Katsura. "I think our android is *too* advanced."

As the managers gave him puzzled looks, Katsura pointed his pocket computer at the screen. It showed news headlines about attacks on androids.

"Ever since androids appeared in public, some people have vandalized them," said Katsura. "Public acceptance of androids is higher in Japan than anywhere else, but we have a small segment of the population who hate them.

"The police used to think that people attacked androids because androids took their jobs, but economists found that the economy actually grew due to the android industry. Nobody stayed unemployed due to androids. There had to be another reason to hate them."

He showed them photos of toy animals: bunnies, dogs, and teddy bears. "These stuffed toys are anthropomorphic in that they have some human features, like large eyes and the ability to stand on their two hind feet. Some even wear clothes. Everybody likes them."

Next, he showed a montage of artificial beings, including: Elektro, a humanoid robot that Westinghouse displayed at the 1939 World's Fair in New York; Punch and Judy puppets from England; a person in a panda costume; and various anime funny animals.

"People are also amused by moving and talking robots, animals, dolls, and puppets, as long as they're decorative," Katsura said. "But look at the next objects."

The scene changed to photos of Italian movie zombies, a Noh mask of a thin man, an extremely life-like mannequin, and a shiny prosthetic arm.

"People react differently to these objects than they do to toy robots or stuffed animals," said Katsura. "Psychologists have long known that many people feel uneasy, repulsed, or even frightened by these objects. This fear defies logic given that a prosthetic limb or Noh mask looks closer to a human than a toy robot does."

"Ah, the uncanny valley," said Sakimoto.

"That's the theory by robot scientist Dr. Mori Masahiro," said Katsura. "As early as 1970, he wrote that people have positive emotional responses to anthropomorphic objects until a certain point where the object is almost human-like. At that point, people will respond negatively to it."

He showed a graph with a steep upward curve, followed by a deep downward curve, followed by another steep upward curve. "Human emotional response to an object is on the vertical axis, with zero being neutral. The object's similarity to a human is on the horizontal axis, with zero being no similarity at all. Note that a stuffed animal and a toy robot are on the first upward curve, meaning that people respond positively to them.

"However, the zombie, the prosthetic arm, the life-like mannequin, and the Noh mask are in the downward curve that goes below the horizontal axis. That's the valley where the uncanny things lie. Hence, the term 'uncanny valley.'

"The last upward curve is where we'll find a being that is not human but indistinguishable from a human in appearance, movement, and behavior," said Katsura. "There isn't any android like that yet."

Hayase noticed that he didn't mention the L-6 prototype. She decided to keep quiet about Yuko.

The testing lab manager looked intrigued. "This is like pediophobia, the fear of dolls," he said. "My mother-in-law is afraid of dolls. She doesn't mind the Raggedy Ann dolls, but she's afraid of the very life-like ones with plastic skin and glass eyes."

"Why does the uncanny valley exist?" asked the chief financial officer.

"Nobody knows for sure, but there are several theories," said Katsura. "There's the theory of mortality salience: Objects like androids and prosthetic limbs resemble humans but look different enough to remind us of the dead. People feel uneasy because the objects remind them of their own mortality.

"Another theory is that almost-human objects violate human norms. If a toy robot is obviously nonhuman, its human features will stand out and seem endearing, even cute. We will still judge it as a robot, but we'll consider it as a good robot. However, if an android seems almost human, its non-human features will stand out and repulse us. We will judge it not as a good robot but as a defective human."

Sakimoto grunted. "No wonder the people who attack androids say that androids are creepy."

"What does Dr. Mori's theory mean for us? I think the L-5 is deep in the uncanny valley," said Katsura. "It's our most advanced android on the market. It has enhanced artificial intelligence, and its eyes move and blink and appear human. But its artificial intelligence can't pass for human intelligence, and its skin and hair look like plastic. It looks almost human but isn't good enough to pass as human."

"So we have to sell a model that's creepier than our last model," said Sakimoto. "How do we go against human psychology?"

"We don't," said Katsura. "I wish to end the production and sale of the L-5 and refocus on selling the L-3."

Dr. Hayase felt dismayed. How could the world's largest android company abandon the next advance in artificial intelligence?

She had to speak up. "Mr. Katsura, the L-3 is outdated technology. We know we can make a better android that will sell. We can make an android to the right of the uncanny valley, so lifelike that people will think it's human."

"No, I don't want to risk the money, especially when we need to recoup the losses from the L-4," said Katsura. "The L-3 has a good track record. No other company has made anything that can compete against it."

Katsura was the president and chief executive officer. He also held a slim controlling interest of the shares, thirty-one percent to Dr. Hayase's thirty percent. If the decision went to a vote at the shareholders' meeting, Katsura would win.

Hayase, along with the other senior managers, accepted Katsura's decision. The next morning, Victor Robotics ended production of the L-5.

**

Sakimoto resigned a week later. Due to the importance of Victor Robotics, his resignation should have been the top story in the newswebs, but other news sent him to the bottom pages.

The police reported that Taira Robotics had bought the design of a Minamoto Computers reboot switch from a Minamoto engineer. The Ministry of Foreign Affairs also confirmed that Russia's Artificial Intelligence Lab had a spy working in Kemmu Electronics. Industrial espionage was rampant in Japan's android companies.

**

Six months later, Katsura came to Dr. Hayase's office. "Is the L-6 prototype still in your home?" he asked.

"Yes, she is," said Hayase.

"Good. Will you bring it back here?"

"Why? You're not putting the L-6 into production."

"No, but I want to prevent any industrial espionage. I hear the Russians have spies in important information technology companies."

"That's just a rumor spread by Morita Chiko," said Hayase. "All this angst about the Northern Territories and the Shikotan Cosmodrome is too much."

Katsura said, "It may be anti-Russian paranoia, but in any case, I don't think the prototype should be outside company premises. I'm afraid another company will steal and copy it."

"Ah, if you're worried about that, why don't we beat them to it and put L-6 into production?" Hayase suggested.

"Our company is not ready to take the risk on the L-6. We don't know whether it'll land inside or outside the uncanny valley. But I don't want another company to find out either."

"Okay, but I still don't think the company is a good place for Yuko. Where will we put her?"

"The testing lab, where it belongs."

"No, the testing lab is no place for Yuko," Hayase protested. "She'll be bored there."

"Bored? You're talking about it as if it's human," Katsura said. He gave her a stern look. "Dr. Hayase, I respectfully ask you to return the prototype. It belongs to the company, not to you."

"I created her —"

"And I created this company — with you. I've gotten the financing for you since day one. You needed my business skills as much as I needed your genius in robotics. Trust me when I say that you should bring back the prototype."

"I'll consider it," Hayase said coldly.

"Thank you," said Katsura, and he left the office.

Katsura hadn't objected to Yuko staying at Hayase's home for the past eight months. Why did he suddenly want her back at company headquarters?

Maybe the answer lay in the L-6 project files. Did the files have something that caught Katsura's attention?

She turned to her computer and accessed the development projects database. Then she clicked on "L-6 Prototype."

A message appeared on her computer:

ACCESS DENIED.

She was puzzled. She had opened those files only two days ago. As project manager of L-6, she should still have access to them.

She tried to open the files again. She got the same message. She couldn't get the plans, schematics, or software used to create Yuko.

She could still view the master list of development projects. Under L-6 Prototype, the master list read:

PROJECT NAME: L-6 PROTOTYPE
PROJECT MANAGER: Katsura Kenji
STATUS: Cancelled.

Katsura had made himself manager of the L-6 project and cancelled it.

Hayase went to the development lab. As always, the lab was full of templates, moulds, dies, and other tools for creating androids. She looked all over the lab but couldn't find the tools for making Yuko.

When she found the development lab manager, she asked, "Where are the tools for L-6?"

"They're being destroyed," said the manager.

"What? No way!" Hayase cried. "Who told you to destroy them?"

"Mr. Katsura did. Doctor, is there something wrong?"

"Katsura! Katsura ordered their destruction?"

"Yes," the manager said. "He told me the project was cancelled and we had to destroy the tools to prevent competitors from getting them."

"No! No! How could he do this?" Hayase said.

She rushed to the incinerator room. Defective and obsolete android parts moved on a conveyor belt into a chute. Behind the chute, a laser incinerator blasted the scrap into ash.

Hayase recognized some moulds used to create Yuko. They moved with the scrap. She reached over a railing to pick up a head mould.

A woman, dressed in a technician's boiler suit, quickly pulled her away. The mould advanced towards the chute.

"Dr. Hayase, please don't lean over the railing," the technician urged. "You might fall in."

Groaning in distress, Hayase watched the moulds disappear into the chute.

"Are those the last tools of the L-6?" Hayase asked.

The technician nodded. "Yes, those are the last ones. They've all gone into the incinerator."

"May I watch?" said Hayase.

"Of course," the technician replied.

She led Hayase to a small window and gave her a pair of dark safety goggles. After putting on the goggles, Hayase looked through the window and into the incinerator.

Hundreds of laser beams shot at the refuse. In a blast of bright white light, the templates, moulds, dies, and tools for the L-6 turned into ash.

Hayase returned to the development lab.

"You didn't know?" said the development lab manager. He looked shocked. "I thought you received the order too."

The manager led Hayase to his office. On his computer, he opened an electronic document.

"Here's the destruction order," he said. "Oh, now I see that you didn't receive it."

The destruction order listed every tool used to create Yuko.

At the bottom of the list was: "L-6 Prototype."

Katsura wanted to destroy Yuko.

Shuddering, Hayase turned to the development lab manager. "Thank you," she said. "There must have been a clerical error."

**

Hayase stormed into Katsura's office. "What are you doing with the L-6 project?" she demanded.

"What do you mean?" Katsura said.

"You cancelled it," Hayase complained.

"We're not producing the L-6, so there's no reason for the project to continue."

"Why didn't you talk to me?"

"You're very attached to the project. I didn't think you could view it objectively, from a business point of view."

Hayase fumed. "Why did you lock me out of its files?"

"There's no reason for the project team to view those files now that the project is over," Katsura said. "Reducing the number of people who access the files reduces the risk of a leak to competitors."

"Do you think I'll give information about our own inventions to our competitors?" Hayase said incredulously.

"Oh, no, it's nothing personal against you," Katsura assured her. "It's our information security policy, remember?"

"Yes, I remember now," said Hayase. "What about making yourself manager of a cancelled project? Do you still have access to the files?"

"Yes, but I'm the only person with access to them. Those files will be safely archived in case we need them again."

"They're my files," Hayase said.

"They're the company's files," said Katsura.

"Did you really have to destroy the tools?"

"There's a reason for that," Katsura said. "We're not making the L-6, so we don't need the tools, and neither do our competitors."

"Now I can't make another L-6," Hayase said.

"You don't need to make another one."

"And you want to destroy the only one."

"Again, that's a precaution against our competitors," Katsura said calmly, without emotion. "If it's out there, they might steal it."

Hayase glanced at Katsura's computer. It showed a pie chart of market shares of android companies. Victor Robotics still hadn't regained the eighty-five percent market share.

"We've lost part of our market share for the first time ever, and you're worried that our competitors will keep gaining it," she realized.

"True. For the first time, I'm afraid of our competitors," Katsura admitted.

Katsura continued. "Dr. Hayase, I apologize for what I feel is best for our company. I know you've become fond of the L-6 prototype. I'll give you one more week with it. After that, I'll send a security guard to pick it up from your house. You won't have to bring it in by yourself. You won't have to be with it when the time comes. Will that be fine with you?"

Hayase sighed. If Katsura sent a security guard to get Yuko, she would have no choice but to surrender her. Yuko was still company property.

"Yes, Mr. Katsura," she muttered before leaving his office.

**

That night, while Hikaru stayed home, Hayase and Yuko went to Sunshine City. They looked at Persian statues in the Ancient Orient Museum, watched a scientist feed the fish at the Sunshine International Aquarium, went to the top of the Sunshine 60 skyscraper, and bought clothes in the numerous shops.

When they sat down to dinner at a curry restaurant, Yuko pulled a black minidress out of her shopping bag. "Thanks for buying this for me!" she squealed. "Do you think I should compete in the Miss Akihabara pageant? If I do, I'm sure to win wearing this dress."

Hayase smiled, acting brave for Yuko. Her mind filled with bittersweet thoughts. She and Yuko had the relationship every mother wants with her teenaged daughter. Over the past eight months, Hayase had taught Yuko a hundred subjects ranging from table manners to Chinese calligraphy. Every mother wants her child to learn from her experience and wisdom. Yuko, like a sponge with water, absorbed everything eagerly.

But it would all end in a week. She would have to lose another daughter again. A tear went down her cheek.

"Oh, mother, why are you crying?" asked Yuko. "Are you sad?"

"No, I'm not sad," said Hayase as she wiped the tear. "I'm just happy that we're here together."

The L-3 waitress, wearing a British sailor costume, brought a plate of beef curry to Hayase.

313

"I'll just keep talking, as usual," said Yuko. "Maybe someday you'll invent a taste sensor for me?"

Hayase chuckled. "A taste sensor for someone who doesn't need to eat!"

Yuko shrugged and grinned. "You can't blame a girl for wanting to know what she's missing."

"Yuko, dear," said Hayase, "I might have to send you away on a trip for a while."

"A trip? That sounds exciting!" Yuko said, smiling. "Where am I going, mother?"

**

Two days later, at the Yokohama Robot and Android Fair, Hayase saw a familiar face.

"Ensign Endo," she said, smiling.

"I'm only Endo Hideki now. I resigned from the Maritime Self-Defense Force years ago," said Endo.

They went to the snack bar for tea and cookies and talked about how their lives and careers had gone. Endo said he needed a new android.

Hayase said, "Let me make you an offer. Do you want an android for free?"

Endo put down his cup of tea. "Oh? What are you saying?"

"You're looking for an android. I'll give you one..."

**

Hayase returned home and found Yuko playing music from the ballet *Coppélia* on her violin. As she listened to the lilting melody, Hayase vowed that Yuko would always know how to play the violin, no matter what happened.

They had dinner without Hikaru again. Though Yuko did not eat food, she connected herself to an electrical outlet and recharged her battery. They talked about the Yokohama Robot and Android Fair, but Hayase did not mention Endo.

After dinner, Hayase said, "Yuko, come to the computer. I want to download some data about Kyoto to you."

"Of course, mother," Yuko replied. She followed Hayase into the home office. "I'm looking forward to going to Kyoto. I wish you could get away from work and come with me, though."

"Don't worry, I'll try to join you after that board of directors meeting," said Hayase. "Sit down, dear."

Hayase connected Yuko to the computer and put her into sleep mode. The android closed her eyes and sat still in her chair.

"Goodbye," Hayase whispered as she deleted Yuko's memory files. Sounds and images of Dr. Hayase went into the electronic recycle bin, where she deleted them again.

Hayase sobbed softly as she watched the files disappear from Yuko's memory drive. Not only was Yuko losing her memories of Hayase, but she was also losing knowledge that Hayase had taught her. Yuko's knowledge would be limited to programs and databases such as those for social skills and music.

Dr. Hayase felt a slight comfort that Yuko would at least be able to talk politely and play the violin. She hoped that Mr. Endo and his family would teach Yuko about everything else in the world. They were good people.

Unexpectedly, error messages reported that some data fragments lingered in Yuko's memory drive. Hayase ran the defragmentation tool, but the fragments stayed. She tried other ways to eliminate the bits of data, but nothing worked. She scanned Yuko for disk errors, but none appeared. She couldn't figure out how to eliminate the data fragments.

Was Yuko fighting to keep her memories, Hayase thought?

Hayase overwrote the memory drive with random ones and zeroes to prevent data recovery. However, an intrepid computer scientist could recover the data fragments, those incomplete bits of her image and voice. Dr. Hayase hoped that if anyone were to try, he would be Mr. Endo and he would keep their secret.

She retyped and deleted Yuko's basic information so that it read:

MODEL: L-6 Prototype
OWNED BY: Endo Hideki
SERIAL NUMBER: deleted
PRODUCTION DATE: deleted
FACTORY: deleted
PATENTED BY: deleted
LICENSE NUMBER: none

Finally, she programmed her to walk to Nikkou Café in Akihabara.

"You won't remember me," she said before awakening Yuko. "You're going to leave this house and live with Mr. Endo Hideki. It's for the best."

She kissed Yuko on the cheek and said, "Good luck, my dear daughter. May you live for ten thousand years."

Hayase rebooted Yuko. The android opened her eyes, stood up, and silently walked out of the house. She did not look back as she went to her new life.

**

Hayase kept an L-6 body in the basement. It was an empty shell, made to test the moulds. As vice-president of research and development, she once had the authority to bring android parts to her home. Now, with fears of industrial espionage, the company forbade even her to remove parts from the headquarters.

She pulled its white plastic shroud away and gazed at the naked body. It looked just like Yuko, but it was not. It lacked the mechanical and computer systems needed to run an android.

Since the L-6 shell looked like Yuko, it also looked like Rei, dead in the hospital. Hayase shuddered at the memory and quickly put Yuko's black dress on the body.

She drove the L-6 shell to Victor Robotics, put it on a cart, and wheeled it into the incinerator room. After pushing the body onto the conveyor belt, Hayase called for the technician.

"I want you to witness this," Hayase said. "This is the L-6 prototype listed in Mr. Katsura's destruction order. I've brought it back."

The technician looked at the body, opened a photo of Yuko on her pocket computer, and looked at the body again. "Yes, that's the prototype," she agreed.

"You can destroy it now," Hayase said.

The technician nodded, went to her computer, and started the conveyor belt. The body entered the incinerator. Hayase went to the window and watched the lasers blast the L-6 shell into ash.

Hayase asked to see destruction order. The technician opened the electronic document and typed the word "DESTROYED" beside "L-6 Prototype."

"That completes the destruction order, doctor," she said.

"Thank you," replied Hayase.

**

"I couldn't stay at Victor Robotics anymore, so I resigned from the company," Hayase said. "I still own some shares, but I don't go to shareholders' meetings, and I retired from the industry."

Yuko said, "So that's my history. I was a replacement for your daughter."

"Yes," Hayase admitted.

"Now I know why you sent Yuko away," said Endo. "Thank you for telling us."

"Why did you delete my memories?" Yuko asked. "You didn't need to delete them to send me away, did you?"

Hayase sighed. "You're a machine, so I thought you only mimicked emotional responses when programmed to do so. But you behaved so much like a real girl that I thought you could be developing real feelings, moods, and thoughts. Your artificial intelligence is so advanced that it might create self-awareness. If any machine has the ability to evolve into a sentient being, it's you.

"I knew the terrible sadness of losing a daughter. I didn't want you to know the pain of losing a mother. I couldn't inflict that feeling on you. I wanted you to forget that I ever existed. That's why I deleted your memories of me.

"But you were stubborn, if I may use a human analogy. You kept data fragments about me and wouldn't let them go. I never realized that those bits of data would make you miss me for years."

Hayase bowed her head. "Please forgive me, daughter."

Yuko reached out and hugged Hayase. "Mother, I forgive you."

Yuko wiped a tear off Hayase's cheek. Hayase smiled and gazed into Yuko's eyes.

"You can't cry," said Hayase, smiling.

"Unlike other parts of my body, my eyes are not lubricated to simulate a human being," Yuko said.

Hayase laughed. "Let's spend some time together, shall we?"

"I would love to," said Yuko.

Endo asked, "Should I leave you two alone?"

"Oh, no, please stay," said Hayase as she gave another piece of cake to Endo. "You're her father. We're family."

**

Hayase talked about her life since leaving Victor Robotics, living in a mansion with L-3 androids as servants, going on expensive vacations with Hikaru around the world, and serving on several charities, including one for children with cancer.

Yuko told Hayase about the maids of Nikkou Café, the *otaku* customers, the district of Akihabara, younger sister Ami, and the late Ensign Sato Ishiro.

"You had a boyfriend?" Hayase asked, bewildered.

"I don't know," said Yuko. "I'm still learning what love is."

"Believe me, human beings spend their whole lives trying to figure out what love is," Hayase said.

When Yuko and Hayase talked about J-pop singers, Endo decided to bring up the subject nobody wanted to discuss. He waited for a pause in their conversation.

"Excuse me, Dr. Hayase, but we need to talk about a replacement body," said Endo.

"Yes, you mentioned that on the telephone," said Hayase.

"If Yuko goes to Uncle Joe, the radiation will destroy her systems and data," said Endo. "We can copy them, but we need to download them to a compatible body."

Yuko looked hopefully at Hayase. "Can you make another body for me?"

"No, dear, I'm very sorry," Hayase said. "Katsura destroyed all the moulds, templates, and tools, and I destroyed the only other L-6 shell to save you. The plans are presumably still at Victor Robotics, but I don't have access to them anymore."

"Then it truly will be a suicide mission," said Yuko.

"Can you go back to Victor Robotics and create another L-6?" Endo suggested.

Hayase shook her head. "Katsura and I were once good friends, but after our disagreement about the L-6, he shunned me. He hasn't talked to me for years. The company history on its website doesn't even mention me anymore. They won't let me in."

"Mother, what should I do?" Yuko said, looking afraid. "I don't want to die!"

Looking at Endo, Hayase said, "It's a no-win situation, isn't it? If she doesn't go, many people will die, and she might die with them. If she does go, people will live, but she's certain to die."

"I'm afraid so," said Endo. He couldn't think of anything else to say.

"Mother, this is terrible!" Yuko said.

"I can't send my daughter on a suicide mission," Hayase said. "I just can't, I just can't."

Endo cleared his throat. "Doctor, I'm very sorry to say that, in my humble opinion, our choices are limited."

"Lieutenant Commander Endo, I know you studied military history at Etajima," Hayase said. "Remember the kamikaze in the Greater East Asia War?"

"Yes, I do," Endo said.

"The old war movies show the pilots' families cheering them before they flew away. But I doubt the mothers were really so happy."

"I understand."

Hayase held Yuko and said, "My dear daughter, it's not fair that I should lose you so soon after you've come back."

"If I had tears, I would cry," said Yuko.

"I'm sorry I didn't make tear ducts for you, dear."

Yuko yelled in anguish, broke away from Hayase, and ran up the staircase.

"Where's she going?" Endo asked.

"To her room," said Hayase.

They followed her to a bedroom. Posters of J-pop singers and anime characters from Rei's lifetime decorated the walls. A few toy animals shared a shelf with some books. Make-up containers lay on the dresser. Endo suspected the room hadn't changed since Rei lived here.

On the bed, Yuko lay on her back, with her arms at her sides and her eyes staring up at the ceiling. Endo remembered seeing androids lying like Yuko before they were activated. It was the android version of the fetal position.

"This behavior is not anything we programmed," Endo said softly. "Yuko has changed by herself."

"She's been changing since the day I activated her," Hayase replied. "Mr. Endo, could you please leave us alone?"

"Yes, of course," said Endo.

"Please wait in the living room."

As Endo walked downstairs, he heard the bedroom door close.

**

An hour later, Hayase and Yuko came downstairs. They looked somber as they approached Endo.

"Lieutenant Commander Endo," Hayase said, "Yuko will go on the mission to Uncle Joe."

Yuko said, "You may take me to Rear Admiral Kirino."

"Thank you, Yuko," said Endo.

He bowed deeply to Yuko. Like many people, he bowed only to human beings and not to machines. But he did not know what Yuko was anymore. He gave her an honor reserved for humans.

# CHAPTER 21

# The Wheel of Life

From the files of Amira Edip, Department of Space Sciences, Free University of Berlin:

*Ghost Rock Hokora*
*Yuko Incident Number 2*

*Mr. Endo Hideki provided the following report after the Japanese government declassified its information about the Russian space weapon Uncle Joe.*

*Before her mission to Uncle Joe, the android Yuko visited Ghost Rock Hokora again with her owner, Mr. Endo, and her designer, Dr. Hayase Midori. Endo said that Yuko asked to visit the shrine before going to Shikotan Cosmodrome.*

*As before, Yuko stood in front of the shrine and talked as if she were conversing with Sato Ishiro, although Mr. Endo and Dr. Hayase could not see or hear him. When examined later at Shikotan Cosmodrome, Yuko's memory files did not show any visual or audio evidence of Sato being present.*

*Mr. Endo asked Yuko to describe her alleged conversation with Sato Ishiro. Below is her account, as told to and transcribed by Endo.*

**

ISHIRO: You've returned. I'm so happy to see you.
*(Ishiro took Yuko's hands, pulled her towards him, and kissed her.)*
YUKO: I want to see you before I go into space.
ISHIRO: You've volunteered to go to Uncle Joe, haven't you?
YUKO: How do you know about Uncle Joe?
ISHIRO: I know what's in your heart.
YUKO: My memory drive.
ISHIRO: The same thing.
YUKO: Ishiro, I'm scared. It's the first time that I've ever felt fear.
ISHIRO: Dear, why are you scared?
YUKO: I won't survive this mission. Even if Mr. Endo saves my memories and programs, I have no extra body into which to install them. My mother can't make a new body for me. My memories will simply sit

in an external hard drive, and I will not think new thoughts anymore. I will be dead.

ISHIRO: That's terrible. You're the first machine with life, so you're also the first machine who can die.

YUKO: I don't want to die, but what can I do? I can run away, but if I do, millions of people, including my mother and the Endo family, will die. I love them so much that I chose the mission. They will live, but I'll die. In either option, someone loses a loved one. Is this what love is about? Losing people?

ISHIRO: I said that love can be painful.

YUKO: You were heartless to give me free will! I was better off as a programmable robot!

*(Yuko yelled in anguish and beat her fists into Ishiro's chest. When she stopped, Ishiro hugged her.)*

YUKO: I wish I could cry!

ISHIRO: Calm down, calm down, Yuko. As the Buddhists say, death is a passage into another realm on the Wheel of Life.

YUKO: But the Wheel of Life has only devas, humans, asuras, animals, pretas, and the Hell-damned. It has no place for androids.

ISHIRO: It will now. You'll be the first one, and I'll be waiting there for you.

YUKO: How can that be? Your *kami* is here at the shrine.

ISHIRO: Remember, I'll always be in your heart. I'll always be wherever you are.

YUKO: Even if I burn up in the Sun?

ISHIRO: Especially in the Sun. The Sun is the mother of the nation. She will protect us.

YUKO: You promise?

ISHIRO: I promise.

YUKO: Thank you, Ishiro. I love you.

# CHAPTER 22

# Into the Sun

After leaving Oshii's farm, Endo and Hayase drove Yuko to the nearby city of Kitami. They went to a special military terminal at the airport. A guard swiped Endo's and Yuko's passes through a computer and read the information that appeared.

"This can't be true," said the guard. "She's an android?"

"Yes, she is," Endo replied.

"Wow, she looks human."

He let them through the door. Dr. Hayase, however, had no pass.

"No, not you," the guard said, staring warily at her.

"Sergeant, please let her enter," said Endo. "She's with me."

Rear Admiral Kirino came over. "What's going on?"

"Sir, this person doesn't have a pass to enter the terminal," the guard reported.

"She's with me," said Endo.

"I didn't issue a pass to her. Who is she?" Kirino asked.

"Rear Admiral Kirino, may I introduce Dr. Hayase Midori to you?" Endo said.

"I'm pleased to meet you," said Kirino. "May I ask why you are with Mr. Endo?"

"I asked to accompany them," said Hayase. "I wish to watch Yuko's mission."

"No, that won't be possible," Kirino replied. "Only authorized military personnel may come along."

Endo said, "Dr. Hayase designed and created Yuko. I think the designer should be present in case there are any difficulties."

"I'm not difficult," Yuko protested.

"Please, let me be with her," said Hayase.

"No," Kirino declared.

Yuko pouted. "If you don't let her come, I'll delete my operating system."

Her body stiffened, and her eyes went blank.

"Oh, no, she's doing it again!" Kirino complained.

Endo said, "Let Dr. Hayase come with us."

"Okay, okay!"

Yuko grinned as the expression returned to her eyes.

Kirino said to the guard, "I'll approve her."

"Yes, sir," replied the guard. He told Hayase, "I need your national identity card."

He took the card, swiped it through the computer, typed a note, and handed it back to Hayase. "You're approved now."

"The plane's waiting for us. Let's go," Kirino urged.

As they walked to the Air Force rocket plane, Kirino said, "Mr. Endo, thank you for letting us use your android."

"Don't thank me. Thank Yuko."

**

As the plane descended, Endo looked at Shikotan Cosmodrome. A Sutyagin, the largest Russian rocket, stood at a launch pad. There were also smaller spaceships, transports for commercial satellites. Service vehicles, looking like toys from the air, drove through the roads that crisscrossed the spaceport.

Endo had never before visited a spaceport, much less a Russian one. Coming to Shikotan was a unique privilege for him.

After landing, the Japanese disembarked and walked towards the Main Building. When Endo saw its Russian flag, he realized how special this trip was. He was one of the few Japanese military officers to come to the Northern Territories since 1945.

At Mission Control, they met the other Japanese already at Shikotan. Navy Commander Miyahara, famous for rescuing explorers in Antarctica, advised the Russians on using Japanese androids. Colonel Yi Akira, the Joseon prince in the Japanese Air Force, monitored Uncle Joe's movements.

"What's the status of Uncle Joe?" Kirino asked.

Yi pointed at a monitor showing the weapon's predicted descent path. "Uncle Joe will re-enter the atmosphere in sixteen to twenty days. The predicted crash area is a two hundred kilometer radius around Tokyo Bay."

"That area has millions of people," said Endo. "Tokyo, Yokohama, Chiba."

Dr. Hayase put her hand on Yuko's shoulder. "Sixteen days, dear. I have just two and a half weeks with you."

"We actually have less time," said Yi. "The Russians want to launch at the earliest possible window to avoid the risk that bad weather may interfere later on. We might launch as early as two days from now."

Endo saw the look of dismay on Dr. Hayase's face.

"Don't be sad, mother," said Yuko. "If I'm going to sacrifice myself, I should maximize my chance of success by taking the earliest available launch window."

The look in Hayase's eyes changed from dismay to pride. "That's my girl, always responsible and dutiful."

"I'm impressed," said Miyahara. "I can't believe it's an android. No country but ours could make a machine like this."

"Not exactly, sir! My country made an android like her too," said a voice in Japanese from behind him. A woman in a Russian Space Forces uniform stepped forward. She looked like the android Svetlana but with brown hair.

She glanced at Endo, Yuko, and Hayase. "Rear Admiral Kirino, are you going to introduce me to the new recruits?"

"Of course," said Kirino. "Allow me to introduce you to Lieutenant Anna Petrova, Russian Space Forces. She's our interpreter and liaison to the Russian military."

After the introductions, Endo remarked, "You speak Japanese very well."

"Thank you," said Petrova, smiling. "I studied Japanese at the Anthony Blunt University of Foreign Studies."

"Hmmm, interesting," said Endo. The Russians founded the Anthony Blunt University of Foreign Studies during the Korean Crisis. The school supposedly trained people for international commerce, but half of its graduates became industrial spies.

"Have you ever visited Japan?" Endo asked.

Petrova nodded. "Yes, after graduating, I worked in Japan for a year. I processed sales orders from Eastern Europe for Kemmu Electronics."

Endo remembered a news report about a Russian spy in Kemmu Electronics.

"I see," said Endo. "You worked in an information technology firm."

"I studied computer science at university too," said Petrova. "That's why I got assigned to help you."

She turned to Yuko. "You're a remarkable android."

"Thank you," said Yuko. "If I may say so, you look like Svetlana."

Petrova chuckled. "One of the designers at the Artificial Intelligence Lab saw my photograph in the Spaces Forces newsletter. Next thing I know, those *otaku* modeled an android after me!"

"*Otaku* are the same all over the world," Endo said.

A Russian officer came and spoke to Petrova. After he left, she said in Japanese, "We're readying the rocket to launch two days from now. We should program Yuko now."

**

Russian technicians connected Yuko to a computer. The Japanese watched as the Russians downloaded Svetlana's mission program from their computer to Yuko.

"We lost all the moulds and tools used to make Svetlana," said Petrova, "but fortunately, we had a copy of her mission program here."

A technician looked up from the computer, smiled, and spoke in Russian. Petrova translated, "The program is installing smoothly because Yuko's operating system is very similar to Svetlana's."

"It should be," said Kirino. "You had spies in all our companies."

Petrova laughed and shook her head.

Endo looked at the mission plan on a pocket computer. It had a diagram showing the Dezik Maintenance Ship mounted atop the rocket.

"There's usually a shuttlecraft attached to the Dezik," he observed. "It's not here."

"We don't need the shuttlecraft," said Kirino. "There will be no emergency return to Earth."

Yuko spoke in Russian.

"What's she saying?" asked Hayase.

"She's telling us that the program installation is complete and that we should restart her," said Petrova.

Hayase said, "We don't have much more time with her, do we?"

Endo looked at a video monitor showing the rocket at its launch pad. A countdown from forty-eight hours had started.

**

Preparing Yuko was easier than preparing a cosmonaut. Unlike a human, Yuko did not need a spacesuit or air supply. She would go to space wearing her French maid uniform.

Three hours before the launch, a motorcade drove to the launch pad. In the vans were Yuko, Dr. Hayase, Endo, the ground crew, and various Russian and Japanese officers. The Sutyagin rocket and the supply tower loomed above them.

"What a clear, blue sky," said Petrova. "It's a good day for a launch."

Colonel Yi nodded. "Pilots like days like this."

Hayase hugged Yuko and told her, "I'm so proud of you! The whole country should thank you."

"Mother, I'm so happy that you're here," said Yuko. "I'm not afraid anymore."

Miyahara gave an envelope to Endo. "Engineers put one of these in each of our energy satellites. I was going to ask the ground crew to put it inside the spacecraft, but after seeing how your android interacts with you, I'll let you personally give this to her."

Endo opened the envelope and took out an *omamori* from Ise, the major shrine of Amaterasu. Its cloth cover was white with a red disc.

"It's for the protection of drivers and travelers," said Endo, reading its words.

"It's the same as the ones that went on the satellites," Miyahara said.

Endo went to Yuko and gave her the *omamori*. "A gift for you," he said.

"Oh, it's like the one I got for Ishiro at Yasukuni!" Yuko squealed. She threw her arms around Endo and kissed him on the cheek. "Thank you!"

"Oh, where did you learn to do that?" asked Endo, surprised by the android's public display of affection.

"American movies," said Yuko as she put the *omamori* in her handbag.

"My family and I will always remember you," said Endo, "and so too will the maids at the café."

The Russian officers talked to Petrova, who turned to Yuko. "It's time to board the spacecraft."

Yuko stopped smiling. "This is it. I better get going. I'll talk to you from space."

She hugged her creator for the last time. Endo and Hayase bowed to Yuko together. Then Miyahara and Yi bowed, but Kirino hesitated.

"It's a machine," Kirino whispered.

"But it's alive too," replied Miyahara, still bent over.

Kirino bowed to Yuko.

Most of the Russians stared impassively, but Petrova saluted Yuko. Then the other Russians saluted too.

There was nothing else to say. They silently watched her ride the elevator up the supply tower.

**

The rocket blasted off on a smooth journey. The flight went as planned. After the bottom stage fell off, the remaining two stages continued flying, carrying the Dezik spaceship.

At Mission Control, Endo, Hayase, and the other Japanese sat at a group of computer stations. They watched the giant screen, which showed video images of Yuko aboard the Dezik. The android looked curiously at her handbag as it floated in the zero gravity.

"I see you're still amazed by it," Hayase said, speaking into a microphone.

"Yes, mother. Zero gravity is interesting," Yuko replied.

Later, the Dezik passed an energy satellite, part of the system that collected solar energy, converted it into electricity, and sent it to Earth.

When the Japanese saw the satellite on the giant screen, they stared in silent reverence. They had fought hard for the right to harvest the Sun.

Yulia Suvorova approached Endo and Hayase. Although she was a captain in the Russian Air Force Reserve, she dressed in civilian clothes like the Mission Control crew. Her Chief Cosmonaut badge was pinned to her plain white blouse.

Throughout the flight, she had talked to Yuko in Russian, giving her instructions and advice. Now she spoke to Hayase and Endo.

"I'm sorry, I don't understand Russian," said Hayase.

Petrova rushed to Suvorova's side. "The Chief Cosmonaut says that your android is an exceptionally talented cosmonaut. Captain Suvorova is impressed by how well Yuko carries out the flight programming."

"Thank you for your comments," said Hayase. "She's a remarkable girl, isn't she?"

The giant screen showed an exterior camera's view of Uncle Joe. The spherical weapon came closer and closer.

"What's going on?" asked Hayase.

"The Dezik is approaching Uncle Joe," said Yi.

As Suvorova rushed back to her station, the Flight Director's voice boomed from the loudspeakers.

"What's he saying?" asked Endo.

"I'll translate," said Petrova. "The forward docking probe is activated. The active capture ring is extending."

The Dezik, as the active spacecraft, had a forward docking probe with an active capture ring. Uncle Joe, as the passive spacecraft, had a docking port with a passive mating ring. If all went well, the Dezik's active capture ring would connect to Uncle Joe's passive mating ring, and the two rings would align and join the spacecraft.

Twelve hooks from the Dezik would latch onto Uncle Joe, and another twelve hooks from Uncle Joe would latch onto the Dezik. Since an accident thirty years ago, Russian safety rules required dockings to use latching hooks from both spacecraft. The Russians liked redundant systems.

Although the Dezik and Uncle Joe could remain docked in orbit with only the Dezik's hooks, those twelve hooks alone might not hold the two spacecraft together as the rocket pushed them to the Sun. To withstand the stress of the thrust, the engineers insisted that Uncle Joe's hooks be used too.

But without remote control to operate Uncle Joe's hooks, someone had to manually pull them. That was Yuko's job.

"Flight controllers standing by for the contact and capture of Uncle Joe," said the Flight Director.

Yuko and Suvorova chatted in Russian. On the screen, Uncle Joe grew larger. Endo could see the weapon's docking port now.

The two spacecraft touched each other. "Contact and capture confirmed," said the Flight Director.

The Mission Control crew applauded. But a somber Miyahara pointed at figures scrolling down the side of the giant screen.

"Look at the radiation," he observed. "It's still twenty thousand roentgens per hour, deadly to both man and machine."

"She's absorbing it all. She doesn't have much time to do her job before she suffers damage," said Endo.

"She'll do it," said Petrova. "She's got Svetlana's programming."

"And she's my daughter," Hayase added.

The giant screen's image switched back to Yuko. She talked to both the Flight Director and Chief Cosmonaut in Russian.

Then she said in Japanese, "Don't worry, mother. I know what I'm doing."

Hayase gave a bittersweet smile. "I'm sure you do, dear."

Yuko went through the airlock and, tethered to the Dezik, floated to the docking mechanism. Everyone held their breath as they watched her grab one of Uncle Joe's hooks.

But despite the serious mood, Endo saw how odd the scene looked: a girl in a French maid uniform floating in space without a spacesuit.

Yuko pulled Uncle Joe's hooks one by one and latched them onto the Dezik. As always, she worked flawlessly. After half an hour, she was finished and returned inside her spaceship.

"The hooks are deployed," she reported in Russian.

"Excellent job," said Suvorova.

Miyahara frowned as he stared at a computer monitor. "The radiation is already harming her. Five disk errors have occurred on her programs drive."

"Will they jeopardize the mission?" Kirino asked.

"Not if we act while Yuko is still functional," said Miyahara.

Suvorova asked, "Are you ready to proceed to the next step?"

"Yes, I am, but first, I want to talk to my mother," said Yuko.

Hayase quickly grabbed the microphone and sat up straight in her chair.

Yuko took the *omamori* out of her handbag. "Mother, this *omamori* came from the Sun. Ishiro said that the Sun will protect us, so I will return this *omamori* to her as an offering.

"Ishiro's *kami* is at Ghost Rock Hokora, but he said he'll be at the Sun too. I'll meet Ishiro again, at Ghost Rock Hokora, in the Sun, somewhere on the Wheel of Life, or all these places. I'll be with him forever. Don't feel sad for me."

"I love you, dear," said Hayase.

The Flight Director announced, "Flight controllers, stand by for separation of stage two."

"Are you ready?" Suvorova asked Yuko.

"Yes."

The second stage drifted away, leaving the first stage connected to the Dezik, now docked to Uncle Joe.

"Flight controllers, stand by for ignition of the first stage. Countdown begins at five," said the Flight Director.

A flight controller counted down the seconds: "Five, four, three, two, one."

The rocket ignited, thrusting the Dezik and Uncle Joe on its lonely journey to the Sun.

"Goodbye," said Hayase.

**

Four hours after Yuko absorbed the radiation, her major motor functions failed, and she sat still in her chair. Next, her eyes stopped blinking and stayed wide open. Then disk errors and corrupted files multiplied on all her hard drives.

Suvorova passed her microphone to Petrova after they chatted in Russian.

"Perhaps she still understands Japanese," said Petrova. She lifted the microphone and asked, "Yuko, we've lost the telemetry on the radiation level aboard your ship. The Dezik's systems may be failing. Can you read the radiation monitor?"

Yuko's lips could still move. She said in monotone, "Here is your American-style Christmas dinner, master."

Petrova shook her head and looked at Hayase. "I'm sorry. Her systems are malfunctioning."

"Dr. Hayase, is there anything I can get you?" Endo asked. "A coffee, a tea?"

"No, thank you, I'm fine," said Hayase. "I knew to expect this. May I have the microphone?"

Petrova gave the microphone to Hayase. "Yuko, you have a long trip ahead of you. Are you comfortable?"

It was a pointless question to ask a broken android, but Endo admired Hayase for treating Yuko like her daughter to the end.

Yuko replied, "I am the L-6 prototype. I was created by Dr. Hayase Midori at the Akihabara development lab of Victor Robotics, Tokyo, in the third year of the Emperor's reign."

Hayase smile was bittersweet. "Those were the first words I programmed her to say during software testing."

"Look, her lips are still moving," Petrova observed.

"Mother," said Yuko.

Suddenly, the radio signals from the Dezik ended. Hayase and Endo never heard Yuko's last words. Mission Control fell silent except for Dr. Hayase's sobbing.

**

The Dezik's systems continued to fail. When the internal lights shut off, the ship plunged into a darkness lit only by a few gauges on the instrument panel. Finally, the video signal ended, and the giant screen turned blank.

Although the Dezik was dying, the rocket continued pushing away from Earth. Without communications with the Dezik, Colonel Yi used intelligence satellites to track the spaceships. He reported, "The docking mechanism is holding. Uncle Joe, the Dezik, and the rocket are all on course to the Sun."

**

On their way back home, Endo and Hayase stopped at Oshii's farm. They bowed and offered *tamagushi* to Yuko in front of Ghost Rock Hokora.

After the ceremony, Hayase smiled at Endo. "Thank you for suggesting this. I feel better already."

"That's good," said Endo.

"But is this really an appropriate shrine?" Hayase asked. "Yuko's *kami* is not enshrined here."

Oshii said, "The *kami* of everyone's late relatives come here sooner or later."

"I confess that I'm uncertain that androids have *kami*," said Endo.

"You must have a subconscious feeling about it," Oshii suggested. "Why else would you come here?"

"I felt we needed some sort of ceremony, like the one we had for Mr. Sato," Endo explained. "This won't be the last one. I think my daughter will want to hold a memorial in Akihabara."

As they walked back to the house, Hayase said, "Lieutenant Petrova told me that it won't be long before the military satellites lose track of Yuko. Will we still be able to see her afterwards?"

"The space agencies can use orbital telescopes to track her," said Endo. "They'll watch her for several years until she gets pulled into the Sun's corona."

"She'll be burned into plasma. What a horrible end," Hayase said.

331

"No, it's neither horrible nor the end," said Oshii. "Look at it this way. Yuko will join the Sun. She'll become part of Amaterasu. There's no better reward for the android that saved our country."

**

Astronomers observed that Uncle Joe was flying away from Earth. The Russian government finally admitted that its space weapon was damaged and heading to the Sun. However, the announcement did not mention Yuko. Instead, it credited a robot spaceship for propelling Uncle Joe.

As her train sped to Tokyo, Dr. Hayase watched NHK TV. The news program was showing an animated simulation of Uncle Joe's flight to the Sun.

She looked out the window. Forests, farms, parks, highways, and cities sped by. Wherever the train went, she saw people: farmers, truck drivers, construction workers, office women, school children, salarymen. The news didn't mention that Uncle Joe would have crashed into Honshu and spread radiation over the island and its people. Her android daughter had saved everything and everyone.

"Next in our business report: Katsura Kenji receives a Lifetime Achievement Award from the Berlin Robotics Conference," said the news announcer. Dr. Hayase quickly looked back at the small TV.

The report showed Katsura Kenji and his L-3 androids. Victor Robotics had prospered in the military build-up.

*It's time I stopped procrastinating*, Hayase told herself.

She called a videophone number on her pocket computer. To her surprise, the old number still worked. The face of an L-3 Halko appeared.

"Thank you for calling Victor Robotics," said the android. "How may I direct your call?"

"Mr. Katsura Kenji, please," said Hayase.

"Mr. Katsura is very busy and cannot take your call at the moment," the android replied. "Please leave a message and your contact information, and he will return your call."

Hayase sighed. Katsura would never call her back. But she also felt relieved to avoid him.

"Tell him that Hayase Midori called."

The android smiled. "Dr. Hayase Midori, your name is in Mr. Katsura's database of people who deserve an immediate reply. Please stand by while I page Mr. Katsura."

Hayase felt bewildered. Katsura had run the company without her for a long time. She wasn't mentioned in the Victor Robotics online history. Why would she still be important to him?

A moment later, Katsura appeared on the pocket computer. "Dr. Hayase, this is such a pleasant surprise!" he said. "I haven't seen you for years."

"It has been a long time, hasn't it? It's a pleasure to see you," said Hayase. "I just saw the news about your award at the Berlin Robotics Conference. Congratulations."

"Ah, thank you," Katsura said.

"You've really built up the company." Hayase paused and prepared herself for Katsura's reaction. "Mr. Katsura, may I return to Victor Robotics?"

"Do you want to work here again?" Katsura asked. "We would be happy to welcome you back."

Hayase couldn't believe her ears. "You would?"

"Of course. This company would be nothing without you. You were its leading force."

"But I resigned. You remember how I resigned. Do you still want me back?"

"If you're worried about any ill feelings, believe me, I never felt any towards you," Katsura assured her. "To this day, I regret our disagreement over the L-6. I'm sorry for the actions that I took. In retrospect, I admit they were drastic. But when we disagreed, I never felt any anger towards you, and I didn't want you to leave."

"You mean you never had a grudge against me?" Hayase asked hopefully. She felt the weight of sadness sliding off her back.

"Of course, not," said Katsura. "What made you think that?"

"My own stupidity," Hayase admitted. "I guess I understand machines better than people."

"Ah, typical *otaku*! But you weren't stupid. You were going through a bad time."

"Katsura, if you didn't want me to leave, why didn't you stop me?"

"Losing Rei was very hard on you, and you never actually took the time to recover. I wanted to leave you alone for a while. I knew you would return when you were ready," Katsura said. "I just didn't realize that you would take such a long time."

Hayase laughed. "Years! I've been away too long. I loved our business. Recently, something rekindled my love for androids. I want to come back."

"You can. We have a vice-president of research and development, but we can create another position for you," Katsura offered.

"Thank you, but I'm not coming back for a job. I'm coming back for a favor," said Hayase.

# CHAPTER 23

# Merry Christmas, Mr. Endo

In April, when the cherry blossoms bloomed, Ami started her first year at University of Tokyo, to study history as her mother had. She took a course called "Foreign Relations of Japan." The professor invited another student, Yamaguchi Yumi, to talk to his class. Yamaguchi was not a historian, but she had been a Navy ensign during the war. Like many officers, she was discharged early due to post-war budget cuts. Now she was earning her Master's degree in astrophysics.

Yamaguchi talked about serving aboard a submarine, the Battle of the Indian Ocean, and the liberation of Timor. Some students, like Ami, sat enthralled by her. Others look bored, and still others interrupted her with anti-military remarks.

When a student asked if the government had violated Article 9, Yamaguchi replied, "Of course, not. The Purists attacked our embassies and people, and we had the constitutional right to self-defense." The leftists jeered and waved their hands dismissively at her. The professor, a Liberal Democratic Party member, threatened to expel the miscreants from the room.

After the class, Ami said to Yamaguchi, "I know there were many people in the Navy, but maybe you knew a friend of mine. He went to the officers' academy. Did you ever meet an Ensign Sato Ishiro?"

"Sato? Was he an *otaku*-type guy?" asked Yamaguchi.

Ami giggled. "Yes, that's him!"

"Yes, I knew Sato. We served aboard the *Yayoi* with Captain Yamane."

"That's amazing! He was my sister's boyfriend."

"Sato had a girlfriend? I didn't know that."

Ami pulled out her pocket computer and projected a hologram of Yuko. "That's her."

"A cosplay maid! Wow, who would have thought that he could attract someone so pretty?" Yamaguchi said. "At first, he was an awkward creature, a true *otaku*, but he quickly grew into a fine gentleman and an officer."

******

Through Yamaguchi, Ami met a German scientist. Amira Edip, a space geologist from Free University of Berlin, came to study meteorites in Japan. Since Amira was also learning Japanese and needed to practice, Yamaguchi invited her to meals and parties with her friends, including Ami.

When Ami needed to write a paper about the causes of the Vernacular Wars in Europe, she interviewed Amira. Amira knew all about the historical roots of Purism, the Vernacular Movement, the jihad against liberal Moslems, and Queen Areej of Jordan. Indeed, Amira was one of the major figures of the Vernacular Wars. It was she who had nailed a list of reforms to the door of a mosque.

When Ami told her father about her university friends, Endo said, "Amira Edip? There was a woman with that name at the enshrinement of Sato's *kami*. I wonder if she's the same person."

Amira's eyes lit up when Ami asked her. "You are Mr. Endo's daughter? I cannot believe it!"

"I knew Sato Ishiro, the man whose *kami* you saw enshrined at Ghost Rock Hokora," said Ami. "Thank you for participating in that ceremony. Mr. Sato meant a lot to my late sister."

"Late sister?"

"Yes. She died in an aviation accident."

"I'm sorry to hear that. What was her name?"

"Yuko."

"Yuko," said Amira. "Is she the same Yuko I met at the shrine?"

"Oh, yes, she did go to the enshrinement ceremony," Ami remembered.

"Are you an android?" Amira whispered.

"No."

"But you say she was your sister."

"She was adopted," said Ami.

******

On December twenty-second, Yamaguchi invited Ami and Amira to an "American Christmas" dinner in her apartment. Ami brought a bucket of Kentucky Fried Chicken.

Yamaguchi laughed. "Nobody in America eats fried chicken for Christmas dinner. It's really a Japanese custom based on a stereotype about Americans."

"Oh, well," said Ami. "As a history student, I should know about these things. Thanks for telling me."

"It's good food, though," said Yamaguchi. "I like the crispy skin. I hope you'll also eat some of the turkey. It's cooking in the oven."

Ami peered through the oven door. "So that's what a turkey looks like."

As she stared at the turkey, she heard the television in the next room. A news announcer reported, "The use of space-generated electricity continues to grow. Japan has reduced its oil imports by fifteen percent."

A sticker on the oven read:


THIS APARTMENT IS POWERED BY SPACE-GENERATED
ELECTRICITY.
WE HARVEST THE SUN.
JAPAN SPACE ENERGY CORPORATION.


The oven's timer bell rang. Yamaguchi took out the turkey, bought from a company that catered to Americans in Japan. Robots had already cooked it with mashed potatoes, bread stuffing, and gravy. All Yamaguchi had needed to do was to reheat it.

"This is what Americans really eat for Christmas," she said.

Ami asked, "How long did you live in the United States?"

"Four years, from age thirteen to seventeen," said Yamaguchi. "My father's company housed us in a residential neighborhood, among Americans, not in a building of expatriates. I went to an American school. I learned a lot about American culture."

Amira came with Advent calendars for her friends. They were large rectangular cards with twenty-four little windows, each covered by a flap. Although Yamaguchi was Christian, she had never seen Advent calendars before.

"What unusual Christmas cards," Yamaguchi remarked. "Americans don't have these. Where did you get them?"

"They're from Germany," said Amira. "My brother used to sell them."

Yamaguchi opened one of windows on her Advent calendar. "Hey, there's a chocolate in there!"

Each of the twenty-four windows held a small chocolate item, such as a bell, Santa Claus, a Christmas tree, a reindeer, or a snowflake.

They looked at the colorful illustrations. "What are these pictures?" Ami asked.

"Advent is the twenty-four days before Christmas. Those are scenes from the Nativity, the birth of Jesus," explained Amira.

"You're a Moslem, but you know a lot about Christianity," said Ami.

Amira adjusted her hijab to stop it from sliding off. "I don't believe that devotion to one faith requires ignorance or hostility to others. I think one can learn much from other religions."

"You're going to learn about Christmas in America tonight," said Yamaguchi.

Dinner began with Yamaguchi saying grace, a custom she abandoned in the Navy but resumed in civilian life. Then they feasted on turkey, fried chicken, mashed potatoes, and mixed vegetables.

"I like the turkey more than the fried chicken," Ami said.

Amira glanced at Yamaguchi. "I think you've converted her to Christianity."

"Not quite," said Ami, giggling. "This type of Christmas is strange. It's just us girls tonight. No boys."

"In America, nobody goes on a date on Christmas. Romance is not the theme of the holiday," Yamaguchi explained. "Aside from the religious ceremonies, Christmas is about friends and family. In the days leading to Christmas, people visit their friends. On Christmas Eve and Christmas Day, people celebrate with their families and eat tons of food."

"Oh, so that's why Americans eat a big bird like a turkey," said Ami.

"What else happens at Christmas in America?" Amira asked.

"People watch the same Christmas movies and TV shows year after year," Yamaguchi said, "and they give presents to each other. The two months before Christmas are the biggest retail season in the year."

"Presents? I like that idea," said Ami. "My family doesn't give presents at Christmas. Wouldn't it be great if I got a present one year?"

**

On December twenty-third, the Endo family went to watch *Coppélia*, performed by the Paris Ballet Company of Tokyo. For the first time, Keiko was dancing a principal role, that of Swanilda, the girl who discovers that Coppélia is a mechanical doll. The audience received key chains resembling small robots with the words "Tonight's performance is sponsored by Victor Robotics."

The next evening, the Nikkou Café prepared for the annual Christmas Eve talent show. As Ami stood on a ladder and hung balloons from the ceiling, she heard someone say, "I'm back."

Yuko, wearing her French maid uniform, stood below her. The android smiled and waved her hand.

Ami gasped and clambered down the ladder. "Yuko, I can't believe it! It's you! You're back!" she yelled. "Mother! Father! Yuko has returned!"

Endo, Masako, and the maids rushed over. The girls squealed as they surrounded Yuko. Ami grabbed Yuko's hands and jumped up and down with her.

Masako said, "This is such a wonderful miracle!"

"I don't believe it," said Keiko. "I thought you went to the Sun."

"How do you know?" Yuko asked, adjusting her barrette. "My mother says that's a state secret."

"It is, which is why Mr. Endo swore us to secrecy after telling us," Keiko replied.

Yuko giggled. "Hah, how did he expect a bunch of young maids to keep a secret like that?"

"Hey, remember, we've always kept your secret," Keiko said.

"Yes, I remember," said Yuko. "Why do you keep my secret?"

"Because we love you, dear," Masako replied as she entwined her arm with her husband's.

Yuko nodded. "Ah, it's love again. I still have much to learn about it."

"How did you come back?" Endo asked. "I thought Dr. Hayase couldn't recreate your body."

"My mother has a message for you," said Yuko.

She projected a hologram of Dr. Hayase.

"Mr. Endo, I have sent Yuko to you again," Hayase said. "When you brought her back to me, I copied her memories, operating system software, and programs to an external hard drive. However, without a working body, her memories literally sat on a shelf, and she was dead to the world.

"After seeing Yuko leave Earth, I became desperate, so I asked Mr. Katsura if I could go back to Victor Robotics. I wanted to retrieve the old files and make a new body for Yuko. I was so surprised when he agreed to let me do it. I had misunderstood him all these years. We're friends again.

"Katsura let me use the development lab and its staff. It was like old times. I had to make all the moulds, templates, and tools again. I worked for over a year. At first, my husband did not approve, but he eventually realized I needed to do this.

"And now you see Yuko with her memories up to the day when you brought her to me. Although I love her, I'm sending her to live with you again. I'm her mother, but you're her family. All I ask is that you let me visit her from time to time. I asked her if I could. She insisted that I come at least once a week. I hope you don't mind."

Hayase smiled and said, "Merry Christmas."

The holographic message ended. Yuko bowed to Mr. and Mrs. Endo and asked, "Father, mother, may I please live here again?"

"She's never called us father and mother before," Masako whispered.

"Ami is her younger sister, so logically, we're her parents," Endo replied.

Like Yuko, Ami and the maids silently waited for Endo and Masako to answer.

"Yuko, welcome home," Endo said.

Ami grabbed Yuko, hugged her, and cried, "You're the best Christmas present ever!"

# CHAPTER 24

# Until the Pebbles Grow into Boulders

Yuko returned to Ghost Rock Hokora each year at *Bon*. She always stood in front of the shrine and talked to someone whom only she could hear, see, and touch. In her conversations, she sometimes laughed, and she sometimes cried, but she always ended by kissing her invisible friend.

For a few decades, Ami, Mr. and Mrs. Endo, and Dr. Hayase accompanied Yuko and watched her commune with the *kami*. Then one year, Dr. Hayase did not come. Ten years later, Mr. Endo stopped coming, and shortly afterwards, so too did Mrs. Endo. When Ami couldn't come anymore, one of her granddaughters joined Yuko for a few years. Eventually, the android made the pilgrimage alone.

Oshii Toshio and, later, his descendants greeted Yuko year after year. As they grew old, their visitor always looked like an eighteen-year-old girl in a French maid uniform.

As the farm passed from family to family, Yuko kept returning at *Bon*. No owner dared to remove the shrine or stop the android from visiting it. The shrine had become a local tradition and so too had its faithful pilgrim. Generations of people and their agricultural androids knew Yuko.

Eventually, the humans moved away, and L-500 androids settled on the farm. They treated Ghost Rock Hokora as their sacred birthplace, where artificial intelligence had become self-awareness. Not only did they adopt *Bon* from the humans, but they founded a new festival, Yuko Day. Although Yuko was a primitive and outdated machine, they honored her as the first of their kind, their Amaterasu.

Yuko visited Ishiro for eight thousand generations until the pebbles grew into boulders covered with moss.

# LOCATIONS & TERMINOLOGY

**Note about Locations**

Although the Maritime Self-Defense Force Officer Candidate School in Etajima and the Embassy of the Russian Federation in Tokyo are real institutions in Japan, the author's rendition of their appearance, buildings, and operations are fictionalized for the story, which takes place in the future.

**Note about Names and Terminology**

Japanese names are written in the Japanese order of the family name first, followed by the given name.

The Japanese Cabinet officially gave the name "Greater East Asia War" to the war in the Pacific and East Asia on December 10, 1941. Americans consider this war to be part of a larger war, World War II, and usually call it as such. After the defeat of Japan in 1945, the Occupation authorities prohibited the name "Greater East Asia War" in official documents. Since then, the Japanese have used the term "Pacific War."

**Some Japanese Terms Used in This Novel**

*Akihabara*: an area of Tokyo with many shops for electronic, computer, anime, and *otaku* goods.

*Anime*: animation.

*Bon*: the Japanese Buddhist festival for honoring deceased ancestors.

*Bushido*: the code of conduct and way of life for samurai.

*Cosplay*: the hobby of dressing like an anime or manga character.

*Daimyo*: a feudal lord.

*Dōzoku*: a cluster of extended families. Before 1945, the government promoted the idea that the whole Japanese nation was one *dōzoku* with the Imperial Family as the main family.

*Goshintai*: an object that the *kami* enters during a ritual. It is often a mirror. The *goshintai* is the most sacred object in a shrine and is placed in the *honden*.

*Haiden*: the hall of worship at a Shinto shrine, where people honor and pray to the *kami*. Worshippers do not usually enter the *haiden*, but rather, stand in front of it. The *haiden* is located in front of the *honden* or sanctuary of the *kami*.

*Haraigushi*: a sacred wand used in Shinto purification rituals. It is a long bamboo or wooden stick attached to a cluster of zigzag white paper streamers.

*Hatsumiyamairi*: the Shinto naming ceremony for a newborn baby, literally, "first shrine visit."

*Hatsumode*: the first visit to a Shinto shrine in the New Year.

*Hokora*: a small Shinto shrine, either an auxiliary shrine on the grounds of a large shrine or a wayside shrine for local *kami*.

*Honmei choco*: literally "sweetheart chocolate" given by women to their boyfriends or prospective boyfriends on Valentine's Day.

*Honden*: the most sacred structure in a Shinto shrine. The *honden* is where the *goshintai* is kept and the *kami* are enshrined. The *honden* is located behind the *haiden* or hall of worship.

*Inkan*: a seal used to sign legal documents.

*Kami*: deities in Shinto. Although they are often described as "gods" in English, only a minority, like Amaterasu the Sun Goddess, are personal gods in the Western sense. The majority are supernatural forces that inhabit natural things like mountains, stones, trees, or wind. The spirits of deceased persons are also *kami*. Until 1946, the Emperor of Japan was a living *kami*.

*Kamidana*: a miniature Shinto altar in a private home. A *kamidana* often contains an amulet or talisman, such as an *ofuda*, that links the household to a shrine and its *kami*.

*Kampai*: a frequently-used toast.

*Koban*: a police officer's booth. *Koban* are located on city streets.

*Manga*: comic books.

*Miko*: a shrine maiden serving at a Shinto shrine.

*Mon*: a family emblem or crest.

*Ofuda*: a Shinto talisman consisting of a strip of paper with a prayer written on it.

*Omamori*: an amulet, usually made of cloth, that encloses an *ofuda*. *Omamori* bring good luck to the bearer for particular occasions and are sold at Shinto shrines.

*Onigiri*: a snack made of a rice ball wrapped in seaweed and usually with another ingredient, such as fish or meat, within it. *Onigiri* are sold in convenience stores.

*Osechi*: food eaten during the New Year Festival.

*Otaku*: an obsessed fan of anime or manga. "Geek" is an English translation. The term has a derogatory meaning in Japan but has a significantly less negative connotation when used by Americans.

*Pachinko*: a gaming machine that combines features of pinball and video slot machines. Players shoot metal balls into the machine and try to win more metal balls.

*Ramen*: a dish of noodles and soup.

*Ramen-ya*: a *ramen* restaurant.

*Samurai*: the military nobility that existed before the Meiji Era.

*Seppuku*: a ritual suicide by disembowelment. It was originally reserved for samurai.

*Sera-fuku*: literally "sailor suit," a type sailor-style school uniform worn by girls.

*So desu ka*: I see (literally "So it seems?"). A common Japanese phrase used in conversation.

*Tamagushi*: a sakaki tree branch with zigzag paper streamers attached to it. Worshippers offer *tamagushi* to the *kami* in Shinto ceremonies.

*Temizuya*: the purification font, where worshippers use water to purify themselves before entering a Shinto shrine.

*Torii*: a distinctive gate at a Shinto shrine.

*Toro nagashi*: a ceremony of floating paper lanterns in a river on the last night of *Bon*.

# ABOUT THE AUTHOR

Derwin Mak wearing the Golden Order of Merit of the Japanese Red Cross Society. Photo by Kent Wong.

Derwin Mak lives in Toronto, Canada. His short story *Transubstantiation* won the 2006 Aurora Award for Best Short Form-Work in English. Jointly with Eric Choi, he edited *The Dragon and the Stars*, an anthology of science fiction and fantasy by ethnic Chinese outside China, which won the 2011 Aurora Award for Best Related Work in English. His novel The Moon Under Her Feet was a finalist for the 2008 Aurora Award for Best Long-Form Work in English. Derwin also writes articles about East Asian pop culture and anime for *Parsec* and *Ricepaper* magazines.

Derwin is a chartered professional accountant with Master's degrees in accounting (University of Waterloo) and military studies (American Military University). He is a member of the Royal Canadian Military Institute and an Officer of the Most Venerable Order of the Hospital of St. John of Jerusalem.

His website is www.derwinmaksf.com.

www.ingramcontent.com/pod-product-compliance
Lightning Source LLC
Chambersburg PA
CBHW021226060726
47590CB00005B/1648